THE CURSE OF THE LOST WHITE CITY

THE CURSE OF THE LOST WHITE CITY

JAMES GRAY

IGUANA

Published by Iguana Books
720 Bathurst Street, Suite 303
Toronto, Ontario, Canada
M5V 2R4

Many thanks to Erica Pomerance, Shea Lowry, Eddy Malenfant, the Chief, Brian Hatlelid, Valérie Lavoie, Louise Allard, and Ronnie Epperson for their encouragement and collaboration during the writing of this book.

Publisher: Greg Ioannou
Editor: Rodney Boyd
Front cover image: James Gray
Front cover design: Fernande Forest, Graff-x Communication Inc.
Book layout design: Fernande Forest

Library and Archives Canada Cataloguing in Publication.

Gray, James, 1950-
[Lost white city]
The curse of the lost white city / James Gray.

Previously published under title: The lost white city.
Issued in print and electronic formats.
ISBN 978-1-77180-113-3 (pbk.).--ISBN 978-1-77180-114-0 (epub).--
ISBN 978-1-77180-115-7 (kindle).--ISBN 978-1-77180-116-4 (pdf)

I. Title.

PS8613.R3878L67 2015 C813'.6 C2015-902165-0
C2015-902166-9

This is an original print edition of *The Curse of the Lost White City*.

For Némo and Félix

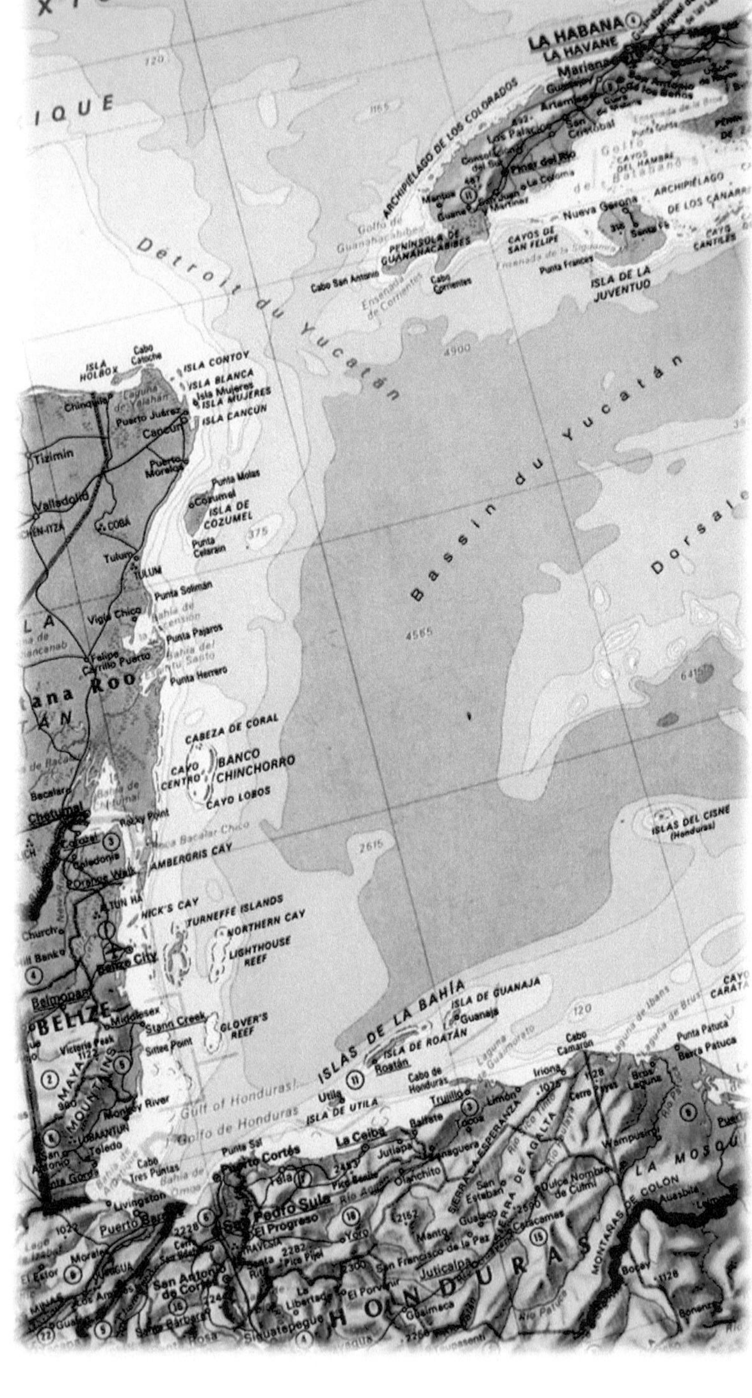

LA HABANA
LA HAVANE
ARCHIPIÉLAGO DE LOS COLORADOS
Pinar del Río
Nueva Gerona
ISLA DE LA JUVENTUD
PENÍNSULA DE GUANAHACABIBES
Cabo San Antonio
Cabo Corrientes
Détroit du Yucatán
Bassin du Yucatán
Dorsale
ISLA HOLBOX
Cabo Catoche
ISLA CONTOY
ISLA BLANCA
Isla Mujeres
ISLA MUJERES
ISLA CANCÚN
Cancún
Puerto Juárez
Puerto Morelos
Tizimín
Valladolid
Cozumel
ISLA DE COZUMEL
Punta Molas
Punta Celarain
COBÁ
Tulum
TULUM
Punta Soliman
Vigía Chico
Punta Pájaros
Felipe Carrillo Puerto
Punta Herrero
Quintana Roo
CABEZA DE CORAL
BANCO CHINCHORRO
CAYO CENTRO
CAYO LOBOS
Bacalar
Chetumal
Rocky Point
Corozal
Caledonia
Orange Walk
AMBERGRIS CAY
ALTUN HA
NICK'S CAY
TURNEFFE ISLANDS
NORTHERN CAY
LIGHTHOUSE REEF
Belize City
Belmopan
BELIZE
Middlesex
Stann Creek
Sittee Point
GLOVER'S REEF
Victoria Peak
MAYA MOUNTAINS
Monkey River
LUBAANTUN
Toledo
San Antonio
Punta Gorda
Cabo Tres Puntas
ISLAS DEL CISNE
(Honduras)
ISLAS DE LA BAHÍA
ISLA DE GUANAJA
Guanaja
ISLA DE ROATÁN
Roatán
Utila
ISLA DE UTILA
Gulf of Honduras
Golfo de Honduras
Cabo Camarón
Punta Patuca
Iriona
Trujillo
Cabo de Honduras
La Ceiba
Puerto Cortés
Tela
Livingston
Puerto Barrios
San Pedro Sula
El Progreso
Yoro
San Antonio de Cortés
Santa Bárbara
Juticalpa
Dulce Nombre de Culmí
MONTAÑAS DE COLÓN
LA MOSQUITIA
HONDURAS

Introduction

It was in 1519 when the Spanish explorer Hernán Cortés first heard reports of a great and glorious city hidden in the remote mountainous rain forest of La Mosquitia, an obscure region found near the northeastern coast of Honduras. La Ciudad Blanca, otherwise known as the Lost White City, was rumored to contain immeasurable amounts of gold and riches ripe for the picking. But the thick jungle proved to be an impossible obstacle for Cortés, and after many attempts to find the mythical ruins, he was forced to give up. Since then, stories of these limitless treasures have fuelled the embers of countless expeditions, but to this day, real proof of the city's existence has yet to be found. The following is a recipe of adventure, treachery and vengeance, proving that most of the time it's better to let sleeping dogs lie.

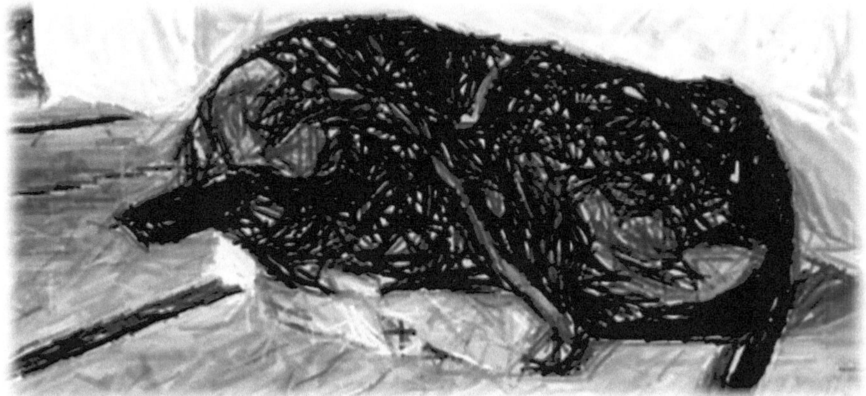

Sometimes, when I start to think about the way things happen, it drives me crazy. There are just too many possibilities, too many formulas and maybe too many timely coincidences.

It all makes me wonder who is really in charge.

PART ONE

Being out in the middle of nowhere may seem like a strange place to start a story, but it has to start somewhere. It's all a question of choice.

Alone and sailing on the tail of an early December cold front that had come down hard and fast from the Gulf of Mexico a few days before, I was feeling tired and abused after being slammed around by a confused sea that refused to settle down. Like it or not, that strong northern breeze was essential to push my boat south, and as any serious sailor will tell you, the art of navigation is about being in the right place at the right time. Yeah, I guess that was part of it.

However, after being out there in the right place at the right time for that long, the legendary magic and raw beauty of a passage at sea was starting to wear thin. As those steep, dark mountains of water rushed by, I kept asking myself why anyone would even think about heading out into such a formidable place. Nevertheless, just because I was living a moment of doubt didn't mean that things were not working out. On the contrary, ever since I had pulled the pin and headed out on a sailboat to re-discover myself, it was clear in my head that I would never turn back.

In the beginning, living the dream had seemed to be a pretty exciting plan. It was like getting a second chance. But after a few years of vagabonding around the Caribbean, the novelty of this personal renaissance of mine had started to erode. Worse than that, the stash of screw-you money that I had saved up was in a final phase of meltdown. However, I still had a few cards up my sleeve. I liked writing, and after digging up an old friend in France who had connections in the magazine business, I began to pen a series of articles for a glossy French monthly called *Aventura*. It was stimulating work, and I could write at my own speed on any subject I wanted, as long as it had a Caribbean theme running through the story. For a while I wrote about places and people; then as the work became regular, I became a little bolder.

It was in my nature. My first mistake was to have chosen a topic that had turned out to be hotter than a Havana heat wave. It was a piece about the Russian mafia's foothold on the Cuban drug trade, and I don't mean pharmaceuticals. Trafficking narcotics in Cuba is a complex subject, and the deeper I dug, the smellier it became. It was perfect for the magazine but not too good for the writer. My other mistake was a classic result of inexperience; once the article was finished I should have left Cuba, but I didn't. And it almost cost me.

•••

One evening, I was leaning up against a crowded mahogany counter knocking back a few mojitos in my favorite bar at Rio Baracoa, just west of Havana. On stage, there was a local band dishing out that fine Cuban Cumbia beat that makes everybody want to get up and move. The place was grooving, the booze was cheap, and I was starting to feel more and more like part of that hot Latino scene. At that moment, the woman I was waiting for walked in through the front door, weaved her curves through the dancing throng, and made a beeline for my perch at the bar. Alicia was as light and lovely as a tropical breeze and always had a fresh smile on her face. What's more, she had some excellent contacts with the Cuban underground, some of whom had supplied me valuable information for the magazine piece that I had just published for *Aventura*. My relationship with this woman had gone well, in fact, really well, and that evening we had made plans to celebrate.

When Alicia finally reached my side of the room, she stopped and kissed me on the lips. For the last few months, that had become her way of saying hello. She was a pure Cubana, and could be so very sensuous when she wanted to be. But there was something missing that night; it was the smile. I saw it right away. There was something wrong. Then, to my surprise, she whispered into my ear very clearly that I was about to have a visit from some heavyweights with Russian accents who didn't like my writing, and if I stuck around any longer, my life wouldn't be worth much more than the plastic-tipped butt of that cheap Muriel Cigar wasting away in the ashtray next to my glass. Sure, the news shook me up and down like the maracas player going at it on stage. But when I think about it now, I really had it coming. From then on, my only choice was to get the hell out of that homey bar, and fast. I looked my precious Alicia in the eyes, hugged her dearly, then headed to the men's baño, and slipped through the open window into the night.

I was out of breath from the run and the music had long gone by the time I reached the dinghy dock. As I shortcut my way through a ragged patch of sea oats that grew near the water, I saw a dark pickup splash through a muddy puddle of rain water and skid to a stop beside the thatched roof shelter where the fishermen kept their equipment. Diving onto the sand, I held my breath as three oversized gorillas jumped out and grabbed the poor old watchman who only seconds before had been calmly sitting under a small awning minding his own business. I could clearly see the old fellow shake his head and point a finger to the place out in the lagoon where my sailboat was moored. Then he shrugged and made a rapid gesture toward a small rubber dinghy tied to a post at the end of the wharf. The thugs went over and looked down at the little inflatable. Then the big guy with the baseball bat jumped down into the boat and started to whack at the small outboard engine that hung off the stern. It wasn't long before the plastic cover went flying, and shortly after, it was the carburetor's turn. They all laughed and rambled on in Russian about something I couldn't understand, except that it was obvious that they were going to wait for the dinghy's owner to show up and the owner was me. But I had other plans.

The water was cold, and it was a long swim out to *Numada*. That's the name of my schooner. With some difficulty, I finally reached the boat, climbed the stern ladder, flopped down on the deck, and lay there shaking. Was it hypothermia, or was I just plain scared? Whatever it was, this wasn't the time to lie around because sooner or later the guys on the dock would put two and two together, and find a way to come out and pound my head in with that Major League Louisville Slugger that they had brought along. So after taking a minute to analyze my situation, I snuck up to the bow, undid the mooring lines and slipped away. Looking across the water toward the dock, I could just barely see the Russians waiting for me under that faint pool of light. Well, they would have to hang around a long time. Pity, I did like Alicia; she was really my kind of woman. I guess I still owe her one.

With no more reason to stay put, I let the steady offshore breeze silently push the twenty-ton schooner across the bay and out into the Straits of Florida.

Once clear, I hoisted the sails and headed southwest into that murky night, thanking my lucky stars for the clean getaway. I had already decided that the Central American country of Honduras would eventually be my next stop. To be more precise, it was La Mosquitia that I had my eye on. It is an isolated and sparsely populated region of Honduras, way off the beaten trail and about five hundred miles to the south of my position at that moment. Spanish-speaking settlers, Garifuna people, and small pockets of indigenous tribes have been living there for centuries. But as is the case for similar outposts around the planet, this area was on the verge of some big changes. Vast deposits of oil and natural gas had been discovered offshore, and there was supposedly lots of gold in the mountains inland to the south just waiting for takers. A month earlier, while working on the famous piece about the Cuban drug trade, I had proposed to the editor at *Aventura Magazine* to write something about La Mosquitia and this upcoming industrial invasion. And bingo, he had jumped at the idea and even sent me a pretty good starting advance. It was a lucky thing too, because before sailing out to the perimeter, I planned to haul my boat out at the Puerto Cortés Naval Base shipyard on the northern coast of Honduras and make some overdue improvements. The poor old girl was beginning to look a little neglected. Spending time in a boatyard would be a radical change from my upbeat Cuban lifestyle. But all I had to do was get the job done and continue on my way to La Mosquitia and make sure not to get sidetracked by another romantic liaison or get mixed up in some other kind of unpredictable sticky situation. However, in Latin America, that was easier said than done.

As I sailed my boat into the pitch-black night, it didn't take long before I began to relax and let my adventurous life at Puerto Baracoa fade away. Besides, finding myself suddenly out at sea once again, I had other things to think about. For long dark hours, I sat at the helm and made sure that I wouldn't run into a Cuban fishing boat. They often trawled at night without navigation lights. But the lightning flashes coming out of the northern sky were my real concern. From the looks of things, it seemed as if that strong cold front from the north that people had been talking about, was about to move in, and that meant lots of wind. I tried to raise a marine forecast on the Single-Sideband (SSB) radio that I used for weather reports, but all I could pick up was a raving evangelist preacher with a Bible-Belt drawl, squawking about how to get a ticket straight to heaven. But at that moment, it wasn't really my problem. I kind of knew where I was headed; it was in the other direction.

When daylight finally came, the western point of the Cuban coast was just barely visible underneath a dark and heavy squall line to the south. I attached the tiller with a bungee cord and ducked inside and slapped together a gooey peanut butter and jelly sandwich and washed it down with a mug of lukewarm tea. That was breakfast, nothing extravagant, but it did the job. Once back outside in the cockpit, I noticed right away that the wind had changed its tune. There was a new deeper growling sound coming from the rigging so I reduced sail. Soon afterwards, it began to blow harder until it became obvious that my little jaunt south wasn't going to be exactly a pleasure cruise. The rest of the day was spent bucking against the turbulent crossed currents found in the Strait of Yucatán. Time and again, *Numada* would rise up a steep, foaming wave and fall over the top with a loud bang, causing the whole damn boat to shake and shudder like a voodoo child. Often, the bow would bury itself in a wave, sending salty brine exploding up and over the cabin roof and a shower of water raining down over me. I could only duck my head, curse and then maybe laugh at my own dismal situation. Above me, the sails were dripping wet and stretched to their limit, but there was no other solution. To make any headway at all, I had to push the boat and push myself as well. Out there on the edge, that was the way it worked.

Just before dark, I spotted a freighter not too far off to starboard so I decided to give it a call on the VHF marine radio. That's the one that I use for short-distance communication with other boats.

"Cargo ship, cargo ship, northbound cargo ship, this is the sailboat *Numada*."

I hadn't spoken to anyone for the last two days, and my own voice seemed like someone else's.

"Cargo ship, cargo ship, northbound cargo ship, this is the sailboat *Numada*."

No answer. I watched as the big ship's bow dipped and punched into the sea sending white water flying up into the air. Maybe they were busy, or seasick. Then, after a long silence, another voice crackled through the speaker.

"Sailing boat *Numada*, this is the *Bay Island Trader*. Come in."

"Yes, hello. How are you this evening, sir?"

"Not too bad, and you?"

"It's a little rough, but everything is holding up. Would you happen to have a weather update? I can't seem to pick up anything off my Single-Sideband radio."

"Standby, please," said the voice. He had a sense of humour.

There was a short pause.

"Yes, sir, for some reason the marine weather station in Miami is not broadcasting tonight. But according to today's noon weather fax, the northeast breeze will slacken off this evening and back around to the east, then build to twenty-five knots from the southeast late tomorrow afternoon."

"Copy that," I said.

It wasn't good news, but it wasn't all bad news either. The cold front was about to blow itself out, but the wind went too far to the southeast the next day. That meant fairly stable weather, but I'd be hard over and beating into a typical stiff trade wind. The voice on the radio came back again.

"*Numada* is the name of your boat?"

"Right, it is."

"That is a Garifuna word. It means 'friend.'"

"Yes, it does. Are you Garifuna?"

"I am, and captain of this ship. Do you speak Garifuna?"

"I just know that one word, *numada*."

"That's a good one to know."

There was another silence, so I picked up the conversation. "*Bay Island Trader*, where are you bound for?"

"Tampa, Florida. Yourself?" he said.

"Puerto Cortés, Honduras."

"Ah, we were there two days ago. I'm curious, is your boat a ketch?"

"No, it's a modern schooner, sir. The two masts are of equal height."

"And what's the length?"

"Fifty feet over all."

"Fiberglass?"

"No, steel."

"Nice. How many crew do you have?"

"Just me, myself, and I." Silence again. It was as if the Garifuna captain was trying to figure out if I was brave, stupid or both.

"A single hander. It must be tough sometimes."

"Yes and no. The boat is well set up, and the sails are small to handle. It's actually not too difficult, but I prefer a crew."

The voice crackled out over the failing signal, but I just caught the end.

"…and good luck to you too, friend *Numada*."

"Safe passage to you, *Bay Island Trader*."

As predicted, a few hours later the wind began to shift and die down, the sky cleared, then the stars appeared one by one. It was as immense and mysterious as always, and so completely impossible to comprehend. As I watched the show above, my mind wandered. I thought about my escape, about sweet Alicia, the girl I had to leave behind in Cuba. What a pitiful way to say goodbye. Then that little hamster running around in my head started to go at it, and I began to wonder about myself. Would I ever be able to stop being a nomad? Maybe never. I was born forever curious to find out what was around the next bend in the road. Then I thought about the crew on the freighter I crossed paths with earlier. What a life it must be, looking after that ship day in and day out, week after week, year after year. I had always admired those who spent their lives on cargo ships. They were real globetrotters, and their ships were their homes, their countries. I had also spent most of my life globetrotting. After studying communication arts at university, I began to make documentary films in Northern Canada. Later on, I became a full-time war correspondent for Radio Canada and the Canadian Broadcasting Corporation. I loved the action and was well-appreciated because I could work in both French and English on the same project. As the years went by, I began to travel to different war-torn countries. It was intense, exciting, and at times important because my work gave those back home a chance to see and understand what was going on in far-off places. But one day, while covering the first days of the bloody conflict in Kosovo, the car in which I was passenger ran over a land mine and boom – my world fell in on top of me. I was the only one of my film crew who survived. Six months later, I was an emotional wreck with too much spare time on my hands and not much going for me. So I pulled the plug, bought a secondhand sailboat, and headed south with one idea in my head: to discover the Caribbean.

The boat I chose was a heavy, oceangoing fifty-foot schooner with two oversized, identical masts. For harnessing the wind, as many as four sails could be used at once. Down in the engine room, there was an eighty horsepower auxiliary diesel, a necessary evil. The hull was made of quarter-inch plates of steel, built to travel a long way and to withstand most conditions the wind and the waves could offer. But to be honest, after three days alone at sea fighting with the elements, the boat wasn't the problem; I was. Perhaps I had become a little soft while hanging around the bar at Puerto Baracoa. Or maybe I was just getting older, because the strain and fatigue of sailing alone was beginning take its toll. I needed a break and I was almost out of food, so as the boat took care of itself, I went inside, made another tea and studied the chart to look for shelter. A little further down the Yucatán Coast was a wide pass through a reef that led into Bahía de la Ascensión, a wide deep-water bay that seemed well-protected. Once inside, I figured that I could rest up a little, pick up some supplies, then continue on southward toward Honduras. I punched in a new waypoint on the GPS and eased off. Ten long hours later, *Numada* motored into the calm waters of the turquoise lagoon just in front of the village of Punta Allen. However, just before I let the anchor go, the engine suddenly quit. The temperature gauge was up in the red indicating that the machine had overheated. To try and restart it was out of the question, so I dropped the eighty-pound hook with a splash, and as the chain rattled out, the boat slowly turned windward.

In the fading dusk, I could see a half a dozen small fishing boats hauled up on the beach beside some drying nets. Tucked in behind a cluster of swaying palm trees sat a row of small houses. It all seemed calm and peaceful, a good place to spend the night and maybe even longer, but I had other plans. After more rattling, I locked off the windlass and a hundred feet of chain links went tight. The anchor was stuck fast to the bottom. With a sigh, I cracked open a beer, sat on the cabin roof and listened to the sounds of the small waves breaking on the beach a few hundred yards away, but soon my thoughts brought me back to reality.

After finishing off my brew, I lifted up the engine cover, grabbed a flashlight and started probing around. Right away I saw the problem, well, one of the problems. A section of the engine cooler had split open, and seawater was siphoning out, a major issue because with the cooler gone, the engine would always overheat and shut down. Then I spotted some more trouble; the head gasket was leaking oil. As my eyes followed the trail of dark lube that dripped down toward one of the engine mountings, the old French axiom *Jamais deux sans trois* (Bad things happen in threes) came to mind. I could clearly see that one of the fixtures holding the engine to its base had broken off. The big block was now attached by three suspension mountings instead of four. It became clear at that moment that the rest of the trip down to Puerto Cortés would have to be done completely under sail. But that was okay, as sailing was the boat's primary function. However, sometimes the engine came in handy when times were tough, or for docking, or going against a strong current. For my adventure out to the Mosquito Coast, these things would certainly have to be fixed, and that would mean more delays and, of course, more expenses at the shipyard in Puerto Cortés. At that moment, the image of a friend of mine came to mind.

His name was Chief, or the Chief, depending on the situation. The Chief had spent a good part of his life looking after the great engines that ran ships like the *Bay Island Trader*. I had first met him years ago just after I had bought my boat. *Numada* had been dockside, stuck in a small fishing port on the Saint Lawrence River, and, you guessed it, it had engine problems and I felt kind of useless.

"Looks like you have a little problem there. Maybe I can help," said a voice from somewhere above. I had been sitting on deck with a cracked engine manifold in my hands trying to figure out what to do next. When I looked up, there he was, standing there on the dock in a halo of sunlight like some kind of celestial vision right out of a Hollywood film. Two days later, he had gone through the entire engine, and it was running like a new sewing machine. Since then, the Chief always kept track of where I was because on top of being an engine doctor, he was an addict for adventure. Working on board my schooner was his way of forgetting the intense engine-room rumble that came from the belly of the ten thousand–ton buckets of rust that he was married to for eight months a year.

The next morning, I unfolded the spare dinghy and rowed over to the small hotel on the beach, found a phone, and called my engineer friend who was somewhere between Newfoundland and Québec City.

"Chief, it's me. Jacques."

"Jacques Legris, hey, I was thinking about you the other day. Where the hell are you anyway?"

"On the Yucatán Coast. Where are you?"

"On a cargo ship somewhere in the Gulf of Saint Lawrence. Where else? Hey, what about Cuba? Have they put you in prison yet?"

"Not quite. Had to leave kind of suddenly. It's a long story. I'm on my way to Puerto Cortés with the boat."

"Cortés. Was there years ago. There used to be a shipyard…"

"Yeah, there still is. I'm going to haul out there in a few days."

"And I bet that you need some help, right?" said my friend.

"How did you guess? Are you available for a little dirty work?"

There was a short dramatic pause at the other end, and I could almost hear the Chief's brain beginning to grind.

"Perfect timing. I'm finishing a six-week run tomorrow and ready for something new. I like Puerto Cortés; it's a lot warmer than anywhere in this country. I'll book a flight and be down there as soon as I can. Meet you at the shipyard."

"You bet, Chief. See ya there." It was as simple as that.

Feeling boosted from my telephone conversion, I picked up a few supplies, rowed back out to the boat and prepared for the next leg of the trip. Not long after dark, I hit the sack. However, later on that night, the sound of something bumping up against the hull took me out of my sweet dreams. It sounded like trouble. Rolling out of my bunk, I instinctively grabbed the can of pepper spray that I kept close to the main cabin entrance. Carefully removing the safety latch and putting on my swimming goggles, I slipped the nozzle through the open companionway that led into the cockpit. *Numada* was anchored facing into the wind, a good thing for me because if I had to pull the trigger, the wind would distribute the spray toward the stern, the same direction as the noise. Suddenly, two invaders came up the transom ladder and stepped on deck. They were young, dressed in the classic shorts and faded T-shirts, and each was armed with a machete. I waited until they got closer then gave them a good long blast. When the stuff hit their eyes, they both dropped to their knees and began to howl. I really don't think that they knew what had hit them. Over the noise of the wind and their groaning, I heard a third guy shout something up to his buddies. A few seconds later, he climbed up on deck. This time, I slid open the hatch and sent another shot of spray in his direction, but missed. He was too far away. In a flash, he dove straight overboard and that was it. Great, except I was stuck with a couple of skinny, half-blinded Mexican kids wailing like sick puppies. I pitched their machetes over the side then gave each of them a towel and waited until they calmed down. Maybe it was because of the goggles that I was still wearing, but they looked frightened.

"You guys are lucky I didn't shoot you with a gun 'cause you'd be dead! Now scram! *Vamos, pronto!*"

My visitors jumped over the side and swam to shore. That was it for my little rest stop. There was no way that I was going to go back to sleep and wait for those freaked-out kids to return with weapons a little more serious than a few rusted machetes. Sure, one could say that I was looking for trouble anchoring in a place like that. Perhaps, but sooner or later you have to put the hook down somewhere. In that part of the world, marinas are few and far between. So what else is there to do? The trick is to expect visitors at all hours, both good and bad.

I sat on deck and stayed awake most of the night, reaching the conclusion that at least I wouldn't die from boredom. That would be my karma for the time being. When the sky finally began to lighten, I brewed some coffee and cooked a few hardboiled eggs. An hour later, as a yellow sun rose up over the horizon, I was back out at sea heading south toward Honduras. As the morning came alive, the wind picked up, the boat gained speed and I began to savor every mile that slipped underneath the hull. Twenty-four hours later, *Numada* passed into the sheltered side of the long barrier reef that runs just off the coast of Belize. It felt wonderful to be gliding over this turquoise, tropical sea. For a rare moment in my life, I felt a wave of perfect harmony run through my body and it lasted for hours. This was real sailing; it couldn't get much better. Funny thing, when I'm offshore, I have a sense of freedom and belonging even when conditions are tough. It's on land where things get complicated.

Two days later, I breezed into the Bay of Puerto Cortés and, as they say, "hoped for the best and expected the worst." Because the bay was so big and fairly well-protected from the trade winds, over the years Puerto Cortés had developed into one of the biggest deep-water seaports in the Caribbean. I sailed in through a dozen anchored ships waiting for a space at the large commercial dock. Once through the maze, I approached the big cement pier in front of the naval base. That's when I noticed the familiar figure standing on the end; it was none other than my friend the Chief. In fact, I would have been surprised not to have seen him there. He waved and shouted out something, but I was still too far away to understand. I steered toward the dock and closer to the wind, slowing down the boat as much as I could. The Chief was dressed in his usual fighting gear: cut-off jeans, ragged short-sleeve, blue-collar shirt, little ugly black socks and scruffy leather shoes. I coasted *Numada* in gently alongside the dock and quickly dropped the sails. Immediately my friend grabbed the dock lines with his big hands and secured the boat. He looked as the Chief always looked, a little overweight, but still packing that devilish smile of his. His hair was a mess, and he hadn't shaved for at least a few days.

"That was a pretty slick docking, Mister Captain, under sail too. I guess that your engine is still a running kind of cockeyed. Right or wrong?"

"Forget the engine. Chief, I'm so happy to see that face of yours that I could almost kiss you."

He replied in typical Chief style. "Yuck, don't even think about it. Hey, by the way, I thought you'd never make it here. I've been waiting since yesterday."

Then the Chief jumped on board. The last time I'd seen him was up in the Bahamas about two years before. Back then, my schooner was in top shape, but in the heat of the tropics, it didn't take long before things began to slip into disrepair. The Chief was always quick to get to the point, and after looking up and down the deck, he had his own way telling me.

"It seems that there's been a certain kind of slackness around here, don't you think? It looks like your dreamboat needs some love."

"Yeah, I know. But I've been busy putting my love somewhere else."

"Oh, another woman I suppose," he replied a little sarcastically. The Chief loved to be sarcastic. It was part of his thing.

"But alas, it's over and done with. I had to leave her in Cuba."

"I guess that you're close to being a real sailor now, with a woman in every port. But, you know, women can be a big responsibility." He also edged at times on misogyny.

"No, not really, Chief, it's just a question of priorities. You must know all about them."

"No sir, I leave that to the experts," he shot back.

"Well said, Chief, but tell me, my good friend, where have you been for the last seven hundred days?"

"Six hundred and eighty-seven to be exact, Mr. Legris. I've been extremely busy, working on slightly bigger models of vehicles — real ships with real engines — and I've also been depositing real paychecks in my bank account. Real priorities, don't you think?" he said, looking at the condition of *Numada*'s deck. The Chief knelt down and ran a hand over a rusty chain plate.

"Looks like paint is on back order. What's the problem?"

"Well, to tell you the truth, there isn't any paint to be found in Cuba."

"Another excuse, I suppose," said the Chief, shaking his head.

"Don't worry, that rust is just cosmetic. You know what they say down here in the Caribbean — a little putty and a little paint, make de old gal look like what she ain't."

"They say that in Québec as well, but I have a feeling de old gal of yours is going to need more than a little makeup."

I was starting to feel guilty. "Chief, I know that I've neglected more than a few things lately, but the boat got me here and that's what counts. Right?"

He flashed his famous grin. "Right, and she'll take you away too. I just have to get you started."

That's what the Chief liked to do the most, make order out of chaos. It made him feel wanted. After I checked in with the base commander, the crane came over to the slip and started to prepare its straps for the big lift. Within an hour, the schooner was propped high and dry amidst a banged-up collection of military patrol boats and private yachts all in for repairs that would probably never happen. There wasn't a puff of wind anywhere, just a burning hot ball of fire above. It was going to take me some time to adapt. But my real worry wasn't the weather; it was my friend the Chief. He had only ten days before his next run on a cargo ship bound for Newfoundland. As he wrote down a list of things to repair, it was becoming more obvious by the minute that the refit was going to take a lot more than a few weeks. I looked around and suddenly the place seemed more like a ship's cemetery than a shipyard. I could already smell trouble brewing.

•••

The Central American country of Honduras is the world's original banana republic. Today it exports hundreds of millions of dollars' worth of the fruit to North America and Europe. The problem is that this money does not return to the good people of Honduras. A banana picker still works for less than ten dollars a day, and that's good news for Chiquita and Dole. I wasn't in the banana business, nor a multimillionaire, but I could pay a guy a little more that Mr. Dole and company. One thing for sure, to get the job done in a hurry, I was going to need to find a lot more cash and some serious help. But as they say in French, *Il y a toujours un bon dieu pour les innocents.* (There's always a good God for the unwary.)

Ronnie Rackman

When Ronnie Rackman got up early that morning and stepped out onto the balcony of his small bungalow on the hill, he saw sails on the horizon. They were heading in the right direction: Puerto Cortés. Ronnie, who was skinny, not too tall and pushing fifty, went back inside, filled a cup with black coffee and returned to watch as the schooner sailed into the bay. Unshaven and a little hungover, Rackman got dressed and then escaped from the house before his wife and three young children awoke. That boat out there in the bay was heading toward the naval base. It could mean new business, which was exactly what he needed. Although the boatyard was a military operation, Ronnie had managed to corner the market for repairing yachts. He could speak both Spanish and English, and he knew how to work with fiberglass and where to get the materials for most of the small jobs that came in. He would subcontract the bigger jobs to the locals, skim 50 percent off the top and then kick back some of it to the base commander.

He entered the cantina and came out with a stuffed tortilla in one hand and a Coke in the other, then sat in the shade near the dock and watched as the new arrival finally docked near the two-hundred-ton travel lift.

He stood up for a better look. "That one will be here for a while," he thought. "Nice."

The naval base tolerated Ronnie Rackman because the base commander told his subordinates to leave him alone. Ronnie knew that, at this rate, he would be on easy street in a year or two. His hired hands did the work for fifteen dollars a day, and he charged the clients five times that rate. Ronnie also ran a modest drug and prostitution business — tailored to frustrated, landlocked sailors waiting for their boats to be repaired. After the new arrival had gotten settled, Ronnie would go over and offer some friendly free advice.

DOUG BARKER

Doug Barker wore a nasty scar above his upper lip that his moustache couldn't hide. Despite a slight limp and graying hair, he was in fairly good health for a man pushing sixty, but he looked like a has-been rock star. When he wasn't sporting a ponytail, he wore a bandana around his head to keep his hair from falling in his face. His cut-off T-shirt and long baggy cargo pants were his boatyard clothes.

He scratched his ass and walked up to the foredeck of the big dry-docked yacht that he had been living on for the past year. He was curious about the new arrival. Barker had managed to stay alive in Honduras for more than a decade, ducking bullets, dodging corruption, and profiting from other people's naïveté. That was not unusual in these parts. It appeared to be the favorite pastime of many in the southern latitudes. But lately, this small-time hustler felt that he was the one being hustled. He had become one of Ronnie's main clients. Ronnie had hired him and a crew of five full-time laborers to renovate *Esmeralda*, a big, green motor sailor that he was in charge of. Barker wasn't the one footing the bill. He was just managing renovations for the yacht's real owner — Igor Zarkin, an aging, self-proclaimed philanthropist, who was busy making deals in Tegucigalpa.

Things weren't all that bad. Both booze and cocaine were cheap, and as for women, Ronnie had been keeping Barker well supplied. That was a good thing because it kept his mind off Valeska, his ex-girlfriend. Valeska De Sela was his associate's niece and one of the most fascinating creatures he had ever known. They had been lovers on and off for a while, but she had dumped him for good after she had discovered that he was a regular at the local bordello. After the breakup, Barker felt a new sense of freedom because he could get laid anytime he wanted and without all the hassle of dealing with that untameable alpha female. However, after a while he realized that despite Valeska's complicated personality, he actually missed her. She had the kind of energy he liked in a woman, and deep down, he'd do anything to have her back even if she did drive him crazy sometimes.

Barker leaned up against the yacht's tall mainmast and watched as the frame of the gigantic blue travel lift wheeled slowly across the shipyard. It was carrying the new arrival in its straps. Judging by its looks, that two-masted schooner would be in the boatyard for some time. As the crane turned, Barker noticed the small Québecois flag that hung limply off the stern. He scowled. He disliked French Canadians. He had been born in Alberta and was brought up believing that the Québecois were troublemakers. In fact, he didn't like English Canadians, either. They always acted as if they were squeaky-clean. "Those nice Canadians, aren't they friendly!" people would exclaim. That made him sick, because they were as bad as the Yanks and even more hypocritical. One thing was certain: He would never go back to the Land of the Maple Leaf and the Beaver, not on his life. Not as long as there was that arrest warrant for tax evasion hanging over his head. Screw that. He was much better off in Honduras, where he was anonymous and free.

He took another puff of his cigar and went below deck. A dark-skinned Garifuna girl from the other end of town was trying as best she could to tidy up the yacht's chaotic main salon.

"*Chica*," he shouted over the intolerable whine coming from the Shop Vac that she was pushing around. "Come here, I'll show you a spot that you missed. It's in my cabin."

The girl switched off the vacuum cleaner and followed Barker along the narrow corridor to the master's suite. She knew exactly what spot he was referring to.

The Chief

"Hey, Chief, enough of this slavery for today. The heat is killing me."

The Chief was up in the forepeak trying to put some order to the mess of tools that lay on the cabin sole. It had been another long, hot afternoon and we were both thirsty. I went into the galley and fixed two glasses of rum loaded with lime juice and ice.

"Come on. Let's go sit up on deck and get some air. Viva Honduras," I said, and took a long drink of rum.

"Yeah," he said, lowering his glass, "that does the job." The Chief was no stranger to Flor de Caña.

We talked, catching up and telling stories while the shipyard grew quiet and the night crept in. Now and again, a couple of soldiers would walk by on patrol, each with an American-made combat rifle hanging by a strap over a shoulder. The shipyard or boatyard, depending on the size of the vessel in for repairs, was an essential part of the Honduran Navy and its responsibility to look after, even if half of the boats there were privately owned.

"You know, I was down here once on a freighter in the seventies," said the Chief out of the blue. "I had shipped out on a bucket from Halifax. We headed south and delivered half a load of asphalt to Tampico, Mexico, and then came down here to Puerto Cortés and emptied the rest. It was my first real voyage at sea. There wasn't much to do on board except bang off the old paint with a chipping hammer and cover up the rust with primer. That's all I did. Most of the guys in the crew would just dream of collecting enough cash to jump ship, but that wasn't my goal. I just wanted to travel, and was convinced that working on a ship was the best way to see the world. I can remember coming in to Puerto Cortés because I lost my virginity here. I must have been about eighteen and she must have been twice that." He swallowed more rum. "But after that, I really learned about the female species through trial and error."

"More errors than trial I bet," I said.

"Well, let's just say I made a lot of errors, believe me. Now I've found a magic formula. Handle with care and in small doses," he said, and smiled.

"Like between runs at sea?"

"Sure, because there aren't too many hanging out down in the engine room. That's one of the hard-core realities about working aboard a ship. Even so, I loved every minute of it back then, but after a while, it just turned into a job. You can get lonely."

"Yeah, I know what you're talking about."

"Maybe you do and maybe you don't," the Chief said. "But in this boatyard, you're going to face other problems that are a little more down to earth than feeling lonely. Like getting the job done as fast as you can. Don't get stuck in this place. It could bring you under."

"Here? I'll be out of here in a few months."

"I hope so. But if it starts to get complicated, put *Numada* back in the water and leave as fast as you can. If not, this whole scene will eat you alive."

We talked until evening and slowly ran out of rum and words. I don't know what time it was when I finally fell asleep, but for a while I kept thinking some more about how the lifestyle I had adopted was maybe more than I had bargained for.

•••

The gunshots began after midnight. Because of the distinct hollow echo they made, I thought they might be coming from the big hangar at the far end of the boatyard.

"I'm sure glad your boat is made out of steel. I'm going to lay low," the Chief whispered.

He disappeared through the hatch in typical Chief fashion and I sank back onto my own bunk, and the noise slowly faded away. Gazing up at the stars through the opening overhead, I began to meditate on the prospect that I could be stuck in that crazy boatyard for a while so I had just better make the best of it.

The next morning, a fellow came by. "Hey, *Numada*, you guys getting set up all right?" Uninvited, the stranger climbed up the long ladder and slipped under the shade of the tarp. "Ronnie Rackman the name," he said. "I repair boats."

"My name is Jacques Legris." We didn't shake hands.

"Jock?"

"Not Jock, Jacques. It's French for James."

"Nice to meet you, Jock. Are you in for a refit?"

"Yeah, I guess. I'm working on a list of things to do."

"I know what you mean. Might take a few pages. This boat of yours is sure gonna need a shitload of work. You try to do it with those toys you have as tools and you may be here a long time. I can promise you that. But I have five guys working and I can get more any time I want. And we are fully equipped for any kind of work you need." He was standing too close to me. "See that?" He pointed a stubby thumb at a dark green motor sailor just ahead. It must have been about eighty feet long. I tried not to look impressed.

"Big boat, big problems. But who does it belong to anyway?"

"A businessman in Tegucigalpa. He's almost never here, but his associate lives aboard full-time — sometimes alone, sometimes with a woman. You'll meet him one way or another, but it's better for you if he's sober."

"He sounds like a charming situation. I'll try to stay out of their way," I said.

"You can try, but nothing ever happens the way you want it to around here. You'll end up meeting them sooner or later." The guy was standing too close to me; his breath smelled like raw onions.

"What kind of work are you doing for them?" I asked.

"Renovation, and lots of it. We're installing a big watertight hatch on the foredeck. We also took out a few cabins and made a large cargo hold. More practical for hauling things."

"A small cargo ship with sails. Good idea. What do they plan to haul?"

The guy didn't answer. Just then the Chief came out on deck and rinsed himself off with the hose. "Jesus, it's hot down there in the hole. Jacques, my man, you have a few minor problems. The engine cooler's perforated big time; you'll need a new one."

"That's what I thought."

The mechanic wiped himself down with a dirty towel.

"You'll have fun finding that here," said Ronnie.

The Chief turned around.

"Chief, this is Ronnie. He fixes boats."

"What kind of engine are you working on?" asked Ronnie.

"A Perkins 436M," grunted the Chief.

Ronnie Rackman stole a look inside *Numada*'s main cabin. The floor had been lifted and the top of the engine removed. An impressive cluster of greasy tools, dirty rags and engine parts was scattered about. He whistled.

"Looks serious. If you want some free advice, I suggest you consult my diesel mechanic. He could give you guys a hand." That sounded kind of strange. After thirty years working as a full-time diesel mechanic, there wasn't an iron horse on the planet the Chief couldn't repair.

"No thanks, buddy, I'll figure it out sooner or later. Trial and error, you know."

"Sure, you're the boss," Ronnie said without looking at him. I changed the subject.

"You hear shooting last night?" I asked.

Ronnie smirked. "Sure did. Some of the boys were talking about it this morning. They caught two gay corporals going at it like hamsters behind the big hangar. Some guys started shooting over their heads for fun. It's just too bad they couldn't have wired them up to the grid. At the rate they were going at it, the electric company could've made some extra voltage." He laughed. "Down in this neck of the woods, if you're queer, you don't want to get caught out in the open with your pants down, especially on the naval base." He looked at us both. "You know what I mean?"

"Not a bit surprised, but don't worry. We'll be careful," the Chief said flippantly as he opened a bottle of water and swallowed half a liter before disappearing back inside.

Ronnie looked at his watch. "Gotta go, buddy, but by the way, if you ever require some weed or anything stronger, I'm not hard to find." He started down the ladder, then stopped. "And if you ever want to get laid, I can set you up, too. Women only, though."

From inside, the Chief muttered, "What a jerk." He came back on deck. "Is he really gone?"

"Yeah, it's clear."

"Good."

We sat down and began to size up the work to be done, but Ronnie Rackman was right about one thing: I was going to need a few pages because the list was long.

"First of all, you've got to pull the Perkins and take it over to the shop — where they can take a real look at it," the Chief told me.

"Pull the engine?" Shit.

"Sure, it will be much easier to work on. Besides, once it's out of there, you'll have a chance to paint the engine compartment and put in better sound insulation. By the way, you'll also need a new propeller shaft. This one is ready for the scrapyard."

"Ouch." It sounded painfully expensive.

"Yep, they're probably going to have to machine a new one and that will put you back at least a year's worth of rum."

"Are you serious? So at least a grand. Ok, what next?"

"The engine needs another head gasket and an engine support has broken off."

"Yeah, I saw that up north when I stopped in Punta Allen."

"There's plenty of rust underneath the floors as well. You'll have to do some cutting."

"It didn't look that bad the last time I checked."

"It's bad now, believe me. But this is as good a place as any to get it done. Hope you got some bucks stashed away in your mattress, though, because this is gonna take some."

"Yeah, right." I was trying to stay positive, but long streaks of rust stained the deck. The plastic port lights were fogged with age and needed replacing. The bow pulpit had been bent out of shape as a result of a collision with a dock in the Bahamas. Everywhere I looked, it was bad news. Ahead of me loomed weeks of grinding and scraping.

"Too bad I'll be leaving soon," said the Chief. "You'll be okay, there are lots of guys around here ready to work. You just have to find the right ones."

The Chief pointed at *Esmeralda* just ahead of us. Our new buddy Ronnie was on deck talking to someone who looked like the boss. He occasionally pointed over to *Numada*.

The Chief laughed. "You can always ask that guy."

"Don't worry," I said, "I'll find my own crew."

•••

It was already midmorning and the temperature was pushing the thirty-six-degree Celsius mark. The air was heavy and still. The only movement was the sea, gently swelling up against the big cement wall that protected the yard. Out in the bay, four huge cargo ships sat at anchor. They were waiting to load up with bananas. Over to the left, two rusted hulks lay half-submerged with only their deckhouses above the waterline. Perhaps they had been victims of a hurricane or had just been dumped there and forgotten.

As the sun rose, the yard came to life. As we removed the sails from the booms, several young soldiers beat their clothes on a stone and rinsed out the soap with cold water from a tap fixed to a cement sink. Between the abandoned US Navy gunboats, someone had rigged up a long clothesline, and rows of shirts and dark jeans hung drying in the sun. At least the military ships in dry dock had some practical function. The US Navy had built and used this base to train and equip local troops to go in and stop communists from taking over Central America. This was all during the Cold War, when the only good communist was a dead communist. After the deals had been made and the treaties signed, a few hundred thousand innocent victims lay in unmarked graves. As is usually the case when wars end, foreign influences departed, leaving the shell-shocked survivors to try to figure out what the fighting had been all about.

•••

The Chief's ten days of vacation seemed to evaporate like a puddle of rainwater after a tropical shower. On his last evening in Puerto Cortés, I decided to take him out for dinner in town. After washing up, we took a taxi to a small Chinese restaurant that the driver had recommended. Inside, the place was empty except for the owner's family, who ate quietly at the far end. Through a hole in the wall, we saw two guys working around a big iron stove that kept sending small explosions of orange flame up toward the ceiling. We sat down and tried to figure out the menu, but we needed help from the owner, who finally suggested that we try meal number six. Number six seemed to be like number four and number three and even number one. It took a long time to prepare, and twice the chefs almost set fire to the restaurant. We were glad to be sitting by the front door. The only things Chinese about the food were the chopsticks and the fortune cookies. There was even a typo on the Chief's fortune: It read, Your ability to juggle many tasks will take you far.

"Some kind of joke?" said the Chief, looking perplexed.

"Don't look at me. It's your cookie."

My fortune cookie read, Here and Now.

"Simple enough," I said, and I slipped the piece of paper into my pocket.

"Fortune cookies, come on. Let's get out of here," said the Chief.

•••

At around midnight, a gale barrelled in from the north. When the tarps we had strung up to shade *Numada* began flapping wildly, the only thing I could do was to dash out and cut them away. The boat shook a little, then a lot. My dry-docked schooner was braced by big timbers tied together by a network of heavy nylon rope. There wasn't much else to do but hang on and hope that the whole thing wouldn't topple over.

The Chief was up at first light. He packed his bag. He had a plane to catch and a ship waiting for him in Québec City. All he had to do when he got there was to climb on board, go down in the hole and take care of a couple of huge diesel engines for a few months. The freighter would be doing the milk run from Montreal to Newfoundland. Together we went out to the road and stood in the shelter beside the guardhouse.

"Well, Jacques Legris, I hate long goodbyes." At that moment a taxi appeared from around the bend and he flagged it down. "*Señor, aeropuerto por favor*," he told the driver. (To the airport please.) But just before climbing in, he turned and said, "Save a little work for me." He got into the front seat and slammed the door.

"Hey Chief, I owe you one, *amigo*."

"Don't mention it. And try to stay out of trouble."

The car sped away. I felt lonely watching that old, beaten-up taxi disappear around the bend in the road.

THE HUMAN ZOO

It rained heavily all that week, so I had to work inside. I got down into the cupboards under the sink in the galley and cleaned them out. Then I started to bang at some of the rust from the inside of the hull. It flaked off like shale. I cursed a little, then banged and pounded until the pots and pans fell off the shelf above. Cakes of rust fell out from everywhere. And it was just the beginning.

When the rain changed from a downpour to a drizzle, I wandered around the waterlogged boatyard. Scattered around the place were a few other people working diligently on their own problems. At the far end of the yard, there was a peculiar guy calmly sitting under a fair-sized fiberglass hull. I stepped out of the rain and joined him.

"Another day lost," he said to me as I waded through a puddle of muddy water. The man was in his mid-seventies. He was bald, wore frameless eyeglasses and had a Mahatma Gandhi look to him.

He stood up and shook my hand. "My name is Ben, I'm an Israeli."

"Jacques. I'm a Québecer," I said.

"Ah, so you are Jacques." At least he could pronounce it right. "I already know your name and what boat you arrived on. News travels fast here in the yard. But everything else is slow. The workers won't be here today, they weren't here yesterday, and they probably won't be here tomorrow." He took his glasses off and cleaned them with his clean white T-shirt. "You know, I'm a philosopher. We have always a different way of seeing things. I've been living here at the boatyard for two years now and I kind of like it. You know why? It's the perfect place to study the human animal. Sometimes, I feel like Charles Darwin. Why go any further to study human evolution? Here, we have it all. From the very primitive to the most advanced, but the latter is harder to find around in this place. Ha! It's a human zoo and I like zoo life, especially this kind." The man seemed mildly crazy, a kind of rare misfit, but interesting and intelligent at the same time — perhaps someone whom I could count on if things turned sour.

"It's all about choice," he continued. "Did you know that? Everything we do is about choice."

I nodded. “Sure, Ben, the thing is that you chose to stay here, but for me it’s more like necessity.”

“But why is it so necessary?”

“Because my boat needs a refit.”

“You neglected it a little?”

“Yes, more than a little.”

“That’s where you made your choice. You chose to neglect your boat. The rest is just the result of that choice.” He smiled. “A sequence of events that you generated by your own procrastination brought you here, so you see…”

I was trapped. After he talked for a long time, during which I politely listened, he finally said, “That schooner of yours will keep you busy for longer than you think. I hope that you have lots of patience because you are going to need all you have; you can bet on that.” His eyes were bright and almost laughing. “So don’t forget, my name is Ben and my boat’s name is Choice. Good name for a boat, right? You better go now and get back to work. The rain is letting up. Now is the time to choose work over discussion with a new neighbor, right, Jacques?”

I walked away.

Near Ben's boat, a man who introduced himself as "Joe" was measuring a piece of steel plate. His forty-five-foot cutter had been squeezed in between a forgotten wooden trawler and a smashed-in military gunboat. Joe was well over six feet tall, and wore a pair of trashed blue jeans and a long-sleeved white shirt stained with paint. He had a good smile and spoke slowly in a heavy German accent.

"He just doesn't know when to quit. Don't worry too much about him. I'm sure that I myself have wasted at least two months listening to him ramble on since I've been here. You have to choose your moments. Yes, it's all about choice."

He laughed and looked over to the corner of the boatyard where *Numada* was sitting. "You'll be here for a good while. You will just have to get used to Ben and everything else in this place." Joe had been at the naval base for over a year and still had lots to do before heading back out to sea. As the rain began to fall, we sat underneath the white hull of his boat and looked at *Numada*. "I bet you're trying to figure out where to start." Joe took a rag and wiped off a pool of rainwater that had collected on his workbench. He dried his hands with a towel hanging on the prop. Above on the transom, I noticed that the name *Libertade* had been painted in bold black letters and smiled to myself. "My friend, we are all in a permanent state of shock in this boatyard. Many of us could use psychiatric help." His thinning salt and pepper hair stood straight up in the wind. He looked like a mad scientist. "Sooner or later, everyone here goes crazy, you'll see. Have you met that guy living on the big motor sailor over there?"

"Nope, not yet."

"Well, you surely will. He's a real number. A Canadian, like you."

"Oh, yeah?" Lately, I rarely thought of myself as a Canadian. If anything, I am more of a Québecer at heart but I never talked about it that much. Nationalism is always a sticky subject, and after seeing what it had done around the world, I had become more of a pluralist; the world was my country.

Joe finished his cigarette and flicked it into a puddle.

"What does *Numada* mean, anyway?"

"Friend. It means friend in Garifuna."

"Well, I hope that your boat is still your friend when you are finished and ready to sail away."

"And I hope that your *Libertade* will still mean freedom to you when you take off." We both chuckled.

"We'll see soon enough. This place is full of surprises."

"Yeah, both good and bad. But I don't plan on sticking around for a long time."

Joe laughed. "Well, as Ben probably told you — it's all about choice."

After leaving *Libertade*, I strolled past some rusted hulks, a punched-out fiberglass trimaran and some other forgotten dreams. I couldn't stop thinking about my situation — my choice.

Behind a pile of marine junk close to the sea wall, there were two more plastic hulks that would probably never touch the sea again. One had a broken mast lying on its deck, the other had rainwater pissing out of a crack near the keel. I was just about to go back to *Numada* when a woman's voice cut through the dull thuds of breaking waves pounding up against the sea wall. "Patrick, Patrick, je ne trouve pas ton truc. Où est t-il!" (Patrick, Patrick, I can't find that thing. Where are you anyway?)

"*Merde! Merde! Armelle, ouvre tes yeux bordel!*" bellowed a voice from deep inside the rusted steel hull. (Shit, Armelle, just open your eyes for chrissake!)

"*Patrick, tu es nul, vraiment nul!*" (Patrick, you're absolutely useless!)

This yelling was coming from the deck of another derelict hull. I moved in for a closer look. Someone had dumped strips of teak planking in a haphazard pile. An old welding unit sat in the rain, a piece of plywood floated in a large puddle, and tools lay all over the place. Underneath the hull, bits of rusted metal were heaped beside two overflowing drums of garbage and cases of empty beer bottles. I crawled up the improvised ladder a see a woman, about twenty-five years old, dressed in loose-fitting rags. Her skin was tinted a rust color and her hands were filthy.

"*Bonjour,*" I said.

I thought she was going to fall off the deck. "*Vous m'avez fait peur.*" (You scared me.)

"*Excusez-moi,*" I replied. (Sorry.)

"*Vous parlez français*?" (You speak French?)

"*Oui, je m'appelle Jacques — Jacques Legris.*"

(Yes, my name is Jacques — Jacques Legris.)

I saw her face soften. "I'm on the steel schooner that came in a short while ago."

She nodded. "My name is Armelle." She reached over and firmly shook my hand then looked over at *Numada*. "You have a beautiful boat compared to ours. We have been trying to fix it for months, but there are many, many things to repair."

I looked up and down the flush deck of hers. It had just been plated with new steel but already rust had moved in.

She called out, still in French, "Patrick! The guy with the big gray-and-red sailboat is here. He's from Québec!"

A young man with dishevelled brown hair popped his head out of a hole in the deck. His bearded round face was smudged with brown gunk — part grease and part slime. He scratched his head. "So that thing belongs to you," he said, also in French. "Not bad, I like it," he laughed. "You have almost as much work to do as we do, no? I want a closer look."

"Yeah, sure. Anytime you want."

"Cool."

The brown-haired head disappeared back into the hole, and shortly afterwards, a chipping hammer began to pound away.

"I hate that noise, it drives me completely crazy," Armelle said. She was pretty. She leaned closer and in a softer tone whispered, "I'm going to start to hate him soon. He's turning into an extremist, *un vrai fanatique de bateau* (a real boat fanatic)." She sighed, put a hand on the ladder and proceeded to climb topside. "Now, I have to get back to work or he'll be pissed off at me. We'll talk later? It's impossible to say anything intelligent with that racket going on all the time."

I decided that Armelle was sexy. It seemed to me the guy inside with the dirty face and bad temper was lucky to have her around. "Ok, *à plus tard* (see you later)," I said, and climbed back down the ladder. Later, I sat in the cockpit and watched some soldiers playing soccer on a small muddy field over by the bunkhouse. Without a war or a major disaster on their hands, they had a pretty good life. Fed, sheltered and clothed by the government, they seemed well-off, like scouts at summer camp. Most of these young soldiers were under twenty and probably none of them would ever leave Honduras.

Cutting through a hole in a low bank of clouds, a bright ray of late afternoon sun bathed the yard with a sharp slash of light that contrasted with the thick bank of dark rain clouds that hung above the mountains. It was beautiful, but it only lasted for a minute before the red ball of fire dipped behind the distant mountain to the west. As the sky cleared and night moved in, the shipyard fell silent once again.

Later that evening, Patrick and Armelle climbed the ladder and joined me on deck for a beer. In the dim light of the oil lamp that hung off the boom above the cockpit, they told me their story in a mixture of English and French, with some Spanish thrown in for good measure. Living in a boatyard sometimes developed a special language between residents.

"We're Swiss, not French. We are ski instructors who work half the year in the Swiss Alps teaching rich tourists how to go down the mountain without breaking their legs. Two years ago, Armelle and I came to Honduras on vacation. Do you know where the Bay Islands are? We were hanging around the Island of Útila until one day we met a guy who had a sailboat. He invited us out for a sail. Before we knew it, we'd bought the damn boat. *Un coup de foudre!* (It was love at first sight!) It was a crazy thing to do but we're crazy people. Imagine — *nous sommes des skieurs professionnels* (we are professional skiers). Now we have a sailboat! *On est loco-malade d'avoir embarqué dans ce bordel de merde!* (We must be really loco-crazy to have gotten mixed up with this bullshit project)."

Patrick drank his beer as if he were trying to swallow the entire can at once. But halfway through, he stopped and let out a loud belch.

"But when we started out, it was fabulous," Armelle interjected. "The owner showed us how everything worked. Then, after we paid him, he disappeared without a trace. It was just before the rainy season. And as soon as it started to rain, we discovered that the deck above our heads leaked like a sieve."

Patrick finished off his beer with another long swig and then interrupted Armelle, "*C'était de la folie pure.*" (It was absolutely insane.)

"Every time it rained, the whole boat would get soaking wet, and things began turning green with fungus. The first time we sailed her on our own, two sails tore. Rotten right through! What a hopeless mess! Then we discovered that the hull was rusting out underneath the floor in the main cabin and that the engine needed to be replaced." He lit a cigarette and took a drag.

"We arrived here at the naval base ahead of a big hurricane," Armelle said. "The guys here didn't even want to take us out of the water because it was too dangerous for the travel lift. Big waves began to roll in and we were tied to the slip, going up and down like a yo-yo. Night was almost upon us and we were about to lose our boat. It was banging up against the cement walls of the jetty and began to take on water. Then, suddenly, the yard workers got the lift running and took us out of the water. We were saved by the skin of our teeth. After that, the hurricane hit. It rained here for two weeks solid." She took a breath. Then Patrick put an arm around his girlfriend and took up again where she left off.

"The boat kept filling up with water. We were bailing it out with our pots and pans because the bilge pump was finished. That's how much it was leaking through the deck. It felt like we were sinking, although we were sitting right here on the hard ground in this junkyard of a place. After the storm passed, the place was a real disaster zone, with no food in the stores and no electricity for thirty days. It was hell. When things went from bad to impossible, we left for Switzerland to work and make some money. Now, six months later, here we are again. We're broke. And then we met Dog Barker." Patrick pointed to the big, dark green motor sailor.

"Dog is the one who lives on board *Esmeralda*. You know him?"

"Dog Barker? Is that his name? I've heard about him."

"He's quite a number."

"What do you mean?"

"That depends."

They both laughed, looking only at each other. Then Patrick turned to me and lowered his voice. "When he arrived here, we worked for him on *Esmeralda* before Rackman and his gang of clowns moved in. Once Dog gets the boat back in the water, he wants us to work as full-time crew. He's even given us an advance to help us with our own repairs."

"By the way, he's looking for a skipper."

"A skipper? I have my hands full here for the moment."

"Too bad. The three of us would make a great team. Though I'm not too sure he's on the right side of the law."

"So what's his project?"

"He's working for a man in Tegucigalpa. In fact, they're partners."

"Señor Zarkin is the owner. They have some kind of deal, a project they want to develop on the Mosquito Coast. But it's not drugs. I don't think."

"Sounds mysterious."

"It is, but Señor Zarkin pays well," Patrick said.

"It would be fun to run that ship and forget *Honky Tonk* for a while," said Armelle.

"Forget who?" I said.

"*Honky Tonk*. It's the name of our boat. I guess we are stuck with it. It's supposed to bring bad luck if you change the name of your boat."

"So they say, but I changed *Numada*'s name and she's still floating."

Patrick shrugged. "When we arrived here, all we wanted to do was fix *Honky Tonk* and then make a little money chartering. Now, here we are, working like slaves — and worse, now we owe money to Dog Barker."

"*Ce n'est pas possible!*" Armelle said. (It's impossible.)

"Come on, Armelle, maybe we'll pay it back crewing for him."

"*Es-tu malade?* (Are you sick?) If we spend any more time with Monsieur Dog, he'll ruin us."

"Patrick, pass me another beer," I said.

He handed me a can from the half-empty case of Salva Vida, then took a long drink from his own. "This place is like a curse. You may feel positive now, but just wait. You'll understand what I am saying pretty soon."

Just then, there was a loud knocking on the underside of the hull, and someone began climbing up the ladder.

"*Merde!* (Shit!) It's him, Dog Barker," said Armelle. Whispering, she bent toward me with a little laugh, "Jacques Legris, you are in for a real experience."

In no time the man was standing on deck. His paint-covered shorts and torn T-shirt were the typical boatyard uniform, but the Rolex watch and the gold chain around his neck weren't, and neither was the fat Cuban cigar sticking out of his mouth. Supported by his rather large nose, was a pair of thick Coke-bottle glasses that magnified his eyes. He looked around, then at us.

"Hi, Patrick, I knew it was you. I thought I heard someone speaking Swiss or French or whatever the fuck it is that you guys talk."

Patrick winced.

Dog looked at me and grinned. "I'll be damned! You're not French too, are ya?"

"No, I'm Québecois. I'm from Québec. My name is Jacques Legris."

"Barker, Doug Barker's the name." When we shook hands, his grip felt moist and cool, almost reptilian. "But are you French or English?" he said.

"A little of both," I replied.

"I bet that you're more on the French side," he laughed. "Imagine that, a goddamn Québec separatist right here in Honduras."

I should have pushed the son of a bitch overboard. But the loud mouth sat down on the cabin roof and took a puff on the short stub of his cigar. He hawked and spat. I heard the gob hit the cement. He frowned, looking up and down *Numada*'s cluttered deck. "It looks like you got a bit of work to do, Mr. Frenchman from Québec." I caught his eyes examining Armelle's long brown legs. "Hey, I'm looking for that little yard rat, Ronnie Rackman. His coolies were supposed to close up that new cargo hatch they built on deck. It leaks like a sieve. I'll shoot every one of them before I clear out of here. I swear to God, you got to watch those bastards all the time. Rackman's guys are really a useless bunch of bums with very sticky fingers. Half my tools are gone. Lucky I got doubles. Shit, I'm supposed to be out of here by the fifteenth of December. The way it looks, it will be more like the fifteenth of December a year from now." He took another puff and flicked the burning butt over the side. "Don't worry, it won't blow up your ship, there's still lots of water down there." He was talking to me. "So if you see Rackman, make sure he knows that I'm looking for him. But for Christ's sake, don't tell him that I want his balls for bookends; he won't show if you do, and I need the fucker to come in and repair his latest mess tomorrow." He glanced at the *Honky Tonk*. "What's going on over there, anyway?"

"We're fed up, that's all."

"Fed up or not, we made a deal. If you're having trouble, just come and see me. Funny how you Frenchmen like steel boats. You know, they all end up looking like rust buckets sooner or later." The visitor turned around, climbed back down the ladder and faded away into the night.

"That was Monsieur Dog. He's not such a bad guy once you get to know him," Patrick said.

"Yeah, but I'm not too sure that I want develop our relationship any further."

"I need another beer," said Patrick. He popped it open with a screwdriver. Then it dawned on me.

"Hey, I get it. His real name is Doug Barker, but you pronounce Doug like Dog. Dog Barker is a perfect name for him."

"Whatever, Doug, Dung, or Doggie or just Dog, it's all the same to me," said Armelle.

"So what does the Dog do anyway?" I couldn't resist.

Armelle made a face. "He and the owner of the yacht—"

"—whose name is Señor Zarkin—"

"Yes, Zarkin and Dog are preparing a big archaeological project on the Mosquito Coast."

"Mosquito Coast, could be interesting, no?" I said, trying not to sound too curious.

"Could be. Zarkin has tons of money and is a part-time archaeologist who specializes in lost Mayan ruins."

"Fascinating."

"His goal is to preserve these kinds of sites throughout Honduras. But Dog Barker is also a prospector, and it seems that while he was prospecting for gold down on the Mosquito Coast, he stumbled upon some kind of lost Mayan city. According to him, there are artifacts there that are worth a fortune. Somehow, he teamed up with Zarkin, and they have been planning to exploit this site ever since."

"Smells funny to me," I said.

Armelle smiled. "But there is some truth to it."

At that moment the journalist in me suddenly woke up. I had to get to know this guy Dog Barker at all costs. This could develop into a great idea for *Aventura Magazine*.

After my friends left, I lay down on deck and listened to the surf breaking on the beach. I thought about the deal they had made with Señor Zarkin and the Dog. From where I lay, I could see a light on inside the main cabin of *Esmeralda*. I watched as Barker stepped out on deck and started to pace around, talking to himself. After a few minutes, he went inside, put on some country music, then turned up the volume. It was Marty Robbin's, and the song was El Paso, classic gunslinger stuff. I have to admit, it was kind of nostalgic.

My original plans were beginning to have some serious problems. *Numada* wouldn't be back in the water for a while, the article I was supposed to write was a long way from completion, and the magazine's advance I had been fronted was already half spent. For part of the night, I sat on deck staring at *Esmeralda* thinking about my new writing project, and the more I thought, the better it seemed. I would have to learn everything I could about Dog Barker, Zarkin and their claim to the lost Mayan ruins in La Mosquitia. I could easily skipper their yacht and prepare a series of articles for *Aventura* without anybody on board ever knowing. Once my new work was published, I would be long gone on my own boat. It sounded almost too good to be true.

The Inferno Bar Caper

The next day, it was back to the brutal reality of my own renovation project. I started to strip out part of *Numada*'s inside cabinetry. It was a depressing job that took the whole day. That evening I bumped into Patrick on one of the small muddy streets near the bridge. He had left Armelle back at the house.

"She's pissed off with me and doesn't want to work on the boat anymore. Worse than that, she won't let me touch her. *Ma vie sexuelle avec Armelle est terminée*," he said gloomily. (My sex life with Armelle is finished.)

"That doesn't sound good, Patrick."

"It's the shits. She doesn't trust me anymore."

She was probably right, I thought to myself, but it really wasn't my business.

We decided to go to one of the small bars off the main drag of Barrio el Porvenir. After knocking back a few beers, we staggered over to a restaurant, ordered up some fried chicken and joined the locals yelling at a soccer match on TV. But Patrick had more on his mind than chicken and soccer. "Hey, Jacques, it's Saturday night, why don't we go downtown to the Inferno Bar? There'll be lots of hot *chicas* (young women) there, and they like *gringos*. They think that we're all millionaires. Maybe we'll find some good shit there, too."

"What kind of good shit?"

He bent over from across the table and whispered, "I know a guy who sells the white stuff, *la grande dame blanca*, you know, cocaine. It's clean, fresh and just in from Colombia. Are you in?"

Cocaine meant nothing but trouble to me. I'd seen it up close, and this place was way too small for me to start mixing with coke dealers. "Don't you think it's a little dangerous, *mon ami*? We're living on a military base in a country that is as twisted as a bed spring."

"Don't worry, Jacques Legris, half the people on the naval base are on something illegal. It's no big deal. You can always bail out if you think it's too hot. I have a gut feeling that you're going to like the Inferno Bar. It's not like any place you've seen. I'm sure of it."

We grabbed a taxi and in five minutes were at the front door of the sleaziest bar in town. The red neon sign above the door seemed to say it all. Below, standing guard in a pool of red light, were two friendly guys armed with 9mm submachine guns. They frisked us before they let us in.

The inside was dark and smelled like crotch. A wall of Mega Bass speakers pounded my ears. I could make out various human forms scattered around in the shadows. Bathed by the blue light of a follow spot, a stripper was gyrating around a brass phallus. Her greased-up body spun nearly out of control until she sank onto a shaggy fake polar bear rug on the plywood stage. We moved in closer for a better look. In the thick smoke, I could see several dozen gawking sailors, and as my eyes got used to the dim light, I could make out more G-stringed women working the floor. Stationed at each end of the room stood a guy with a sawed-off shotgun. Behind the bar was a sweaty bartender with a handgun stuck in his belt. If this wasn't hell, it was right next door.

"How do you like it?"

"How do I like what?"

"The Inferno."

"Hot," I said. But I really felt like heading for the door. The place reeked of trouble.

We were shown to a table. Immediately, two girls came over and asked us to buy them drinks. The waitress was right behind them. Patrick ordered a pitcher of beer. Suddenly, my chair was tipped back and I was looking up at a pair of gargantuan, coffee-colored breasts. Their owner slowly tilted me all the way down onto the floor.

"An Inferno attack!" screamed Patrick.

The woman laughed, helped me up, then righted my chair. "That was..." was all I could say.

"You ain't seen nothing yet, my friend. The Inferno is out of this world!" He handed the girl a few bucks and she moved on. "Hey, Jacques, see that guy over there beside the bar? He's the one who sells *le coco* (cocaine)."

"Go for it, we've come this far."

Patrick got up and went over to the man. They exchanged hands signs and headed for the men's room.

While he was gone, another woman wearing a skin-tight black dress sat down beside me, unzipped my fly and started to rub my cock. "Mmmm, Mister. *¿Tu me gustas*." (I like your style.) She smelled like cheap hotel soap and mouthwash. I couldn't help wondering how many guys she'd done so far that evening.

"No, not tonight, *mi amore* (my love)."

She tried to keep on but I pulled her hand away.

Meanwhile Patrick arrived back at the table, and flashed a grin as soon as he caught on what the girl was up to.

"Hey, who's the breeze?"

"I don't know, just looking for business I guess."

"Well, are you going to give it to her?"

"No way. I've got other plans." The woman got up and disappeared into the crowd. After an hour, the freak show was beginning to get kind of boring.

"Hey, Pat, how long do you want to stick around?"

"The place starts to liven up around midnight."

Suddenly some loud shouting came from the other end of the bar. There were too many people in the way to see anything, but I heard glass breaking and a woman with a high voice yelling at a man to stop it. All of a sudden, the crowd parted for a group of bouncers who ejected an unidentifiable number of men from the building. The door closed. The bouncers disappeared. The crowd returned to its original shape as if nothing had even happened.

"See, Jacques, there's no fooling around here. It's probably as safe as any bar from where you come from. Come on, I'll treat you to a line of some of the best powder on the Spanish Main."

"Sure, let's do it," I said. We locked ourselves into one of the stinking bathroom stalls. Pat pulled a baggie out of his pocket.

"*Santé*," he said.

I took a snort. The stuff almost knocked me flying. "Jesus Christ, that's strong."

"Not like the shit we get at home. Here, have another toot."

I filled up the other nostril and my eyes started to water. Patrick followed suit. Then we wiped off our noses and left the washroom feeling no pain.

"Hey, wasn't that like a kick in the head? Maybe now you'll want to stick around."

I didn't. We were the only guys in the place who were not merchant marines. I was starting to feel like the whole bar was watching us. "No. Let's get out of here while we can."

Pat shook his head, grinned and pointed to one of the girls.

"I've got plans. That little mama over there in the black dress is pretty hot." I thought about Patrick's girlfriend. If she only knew, but maybe she did.

"Yeah, looks like she's got your number. But I'm hitting the road. Good luck. Thanks for the blow." I wasn't sure I'd ever see Patrick again. Out on the street, there were no taxis in sight, but the air was good and the streets were full of people, so I walked.

Though it was midnight, people were still out enjoying the night air. I passed a pool hall with its garish green florescent lights and the sound of pool balls knocking together, a sure sign of intense action around the table. Pausing briefly, I watched the game of pool through the open window. In a hole-in-the-wall snack bar next door, a few families sat on white plastic chairs and watched a movie on TV. I was tempted to go in for a midnight snack, but it would have been like entering a private house. A large pig tethered to a pole was eating from a pile of garbage. Across the street, there was another bar — the music from this one was lonely and romantic.

A few minutes later as I was walking through the guardhouse gate at the naval base, a woman walking toward me brushed up against me and said, "*Hola*" in a soft voice. Her fragrance was sensuous.

My mind flashed back to Alicia, the woman I had known in Cuba. It had been so absolutely good that sweet souvenirs still lingered in the back of my mind. She was all a man could ever want, and she had an appetite for sex that would leave me gasping for breath. She had saved my life that night in the bar when she had whispered those few words in my ear about the Russian mafia. So far, I hadn't come across that sort of loyalty or tenderness in Puerto Cortés.

As I made my way into the boatyard, an unseen voice from above bellowed, "Hey, that you, Frenchman?" It was Barker.

"Yeah, it's me alright."

"Well then, come on up for a drink!"

I climbed the long aluminum ladder to topside and came face to face with the man that everybody in the boatyard loved to hate. He was wearing only a pair of boxer shorts.

"I just screwed a new whore. Was that ever fun! You must have seen her; she just left."

The image of the woman at the entrance popped into my head. It must have been her. "Yeah, we crossed paths at the entrance gate."

"Not bad, eh? Have a drink. There's plenty."

"Why not?"

"Right this way, the bar's in the main cabin."

I followed him inside the wheelhouse, down a series of mahogany steps, and into a sumptuous main salon. The room was cold and smelled of stale cigar smoke.

"Sorry for the mess, but it's always like this."

The main cabin had large windows. In the galley, there was a stainless steel stand-up refrigerator, a freezer, an electric stove and a dishwasher. With a drink in one hand, he led the way into the front section.

"There used to be four other guest cabins here, but we took them out to make room for the new cargo hold." The vast empty space was lined with panels of marine plywood. There was a wide, recently built cargo hatch above us. This was the famous cargo hold that Ronnie Rackman had talked about.

"We're slowly turning this thing into a mini-coastal freighter. But Rackman and his guys work so slow, sometimes I wonder if I'll ever be out of here."

"What kind of freight are you going to be trans—?"

"—all kinds of stuff." The Dog led me to the master's quarters. "Look at this, it's my own little playing field." The king-size bed hadn't been made in at least a week. "Now let me show you the engine room."

We went down a few stairs into another cabin, where a washer and dryer combo sat covered with a pile of dirty clothes. "This is where we keep the tools. But here, this way…" He led me into the engine room. There were two big yellow Caterpillar diesels. For an instant I thought about my friend the Chief. He really hated Caterpillar diesels. "They are a curse," he used to say. But Barker didn't seem to mind.

"We cruise at twelve knots. And the two generators over there are big enough to run a goddamn shoe factory. I got everything double on board, backups to backups. Nothing goes wrong on this ship that can't be repaired."

The engine room was dirty and smelled of lube oil. There was a pile of mover's blankets in one corner, some caked with mud. Nearby, there was a heap of dirty rags.

"Don't worry about the mess, once the new cargo bin is completed, this area will be as clean as a Dutch whore."

I followed the Dog back to the main salon.

“And I have more guns than the Honduran Navy — all of them licensed and loaded. The poor bastard who tries anything funny with me is in for a surprise. Oh shit, I forgot, what are ya drinkin’, Frenchman?” Dog opened the bar and took out two crystal glasses.

“Got any scotch?”

“Will this stuff do?” I was surprised. Lagavulin was one of the best, and hard to find in most big cities, let alone in Honduras. He poured a generous shot and slid the glass in my direction. “There’s plenty more where that came from.”

Barker swallowed a double shot, poured himself another one, and landed in an overstuffed chair. He began to talk in a phony Southern drawl. “I’ve been here for ten years, moved down from Alberta. I used to work as a bush pilot and a gold prospector. But now you can’t do a goddamn thing without running into some kind of inspector, tree hugger or tax collector. So I moved down here and started my own business. To hell with them — shit!” He’d spilled his drink on his shorts. “Since I’ve been here, it’s been good. I’ve staked three mining claims for gold, and there’s lots of it.” He leaned toward me and lowered his voice. “Made some good money too, and you can be sure it’s all tax-free. Ha! Screw them bastards. I’ll never, never pay taxes again to those money-sucking vampires. Down here in Honduras, I’m a free man. Hey, by the way, want to invest in an opal mine? I got one. Look.”

The Dog stood up unsteadily and grabbed a big pickle jar that was wedged on a small shelf among the liquor bottles. He unscrewed the lid, which was covered with dust. About twenty small greenish-blue stones rolled out onto the table. “Just this here will be worth about ten grand when it’s all polished up. Zarkin and I are working on a project together. This is his boat, you know. I’m just fixing it.”

“What kind of a project? Tell me more.” I wanted him to put it in his own words.

“Archaeology. You know anything about archaeology?”

“Not much.”

“Well, we have a dig planned in La Mosquitia.”

“That’s a pretty remote place,” I said.

“It sure is. I’ve been all through that area, prospecting for gold.”

“There’s gold down there?”

“There’s gold, there’s oil, and there are large sites of Mayan ruins.”

“You’ve seen some?”

"Man, have I ever. Hey, do you smoke? I got some Cohibas in that box over there, compliments of my boss, Señor Zarkin."

I went over to the cabinet and chose a cigar out of the box. Barker struck a match and fired it up for me. He was close, and as I puffed to get the thin going, his face, which was lit by the match that he was holding, seemed to change. It was as if he was somewhere else.

"Yep, I've seen lots of ruins but nothing like these ones. It's a city, a forgotten city, an enormous find, and waiting for takers."

"What about the government? There must be some kind of law protecting a place like that."

"No way, my friend. In La Mosquitia, the rules are a little different; you just go in and help yourself."

Out of the Frying Pan

At least the bottle of Aspirin was in its proper place. As for my aching head, that was a different story. It was afflicted with flashes of the previous night: eating at the greasy spoon with Patrick, the Inferno Bar caper, the sweet-smelling woman at the guardhouse gate, and late night session with my neighbor, the Dog. As the night sky faded away into morning, I lay on the bunk listening to the low moaning coming from the rigging. The sound was different when it blew out at sea, signifying that the wind was pushing me on to some new destination. With the boat stuck in dry dock, it just implied I was going nowhere fast.

I arose reluctantly, though I could have stayed in my bunk for a few more hours. *Numada*'s interior resembled a war zone. The chart table was covered with tools and torn, oily rags. In place of a floor, two narrow planks partially covered a big hole; at the bottom was an empty cavern, the place where the engine sat. In the head, instead of a functioning toilet, there was a plastic bucket. My new reality started to sink in. I had become a victim of my own folly. I took a long swig of water from a plastic bottle and looked through the companionway. Strong gusts of wind were coming in straight off the bay and dark foaming waves were breaking over the wall just behind *Numada*, sending spray high into the air. Just another day in paradise.

On the street outside the naval base, a few locals were busy preparing their street stands for business. A dilapidated dump truck thundered through a large puddle, sending a shower of brown water all over the sidewalk. The sea had been rough during the last few days and there was not much to be had at the fish market. Some tired-looking fishermen worked without talking, unloading crates of freshly caught fish. A little further along, I stopped and watched as two men standing in a cayuka heaved a five-foot-long shark onto the dock. The big fish landed at my feet with a thud, still twitching.

It started to rain, so I sought shelter under the tin roof of the cantina and asked the woman behind the counter for two eggs, black beans and coffee — the standard local antidote for a hangover. I sat staring at the shark lying alone and forgotten on the dock, its power and beauty slowly draining away thanks to a bad move it had made out at the reef. The rain pounded harder and time stood still. Then the woman shuffled over with my food and a bottle of hot sauce.

"*Buen provecho*." She smiled. (Enjoy.)

As I ate, I couldn't take my eyes off the shark waiting to be cut up and sold by the pound. Then, with the quick flick of its tail, it disappeared over the side and into the water. I guess that it got tired of waiting.

Through the downpour, the women carried their shoes in one hand and rolled-up newspapers full of fish in the other. A small group of passengers waited patiently in front of the fruit stand for a battered yellow bus to take them to work in the center of town. These people worked six days a week, for ten hours a day, in the cramped sweatshops of *zona libre* (the zone for foreign-owned clothing manufacturers) — making jeans, blouses or hi-tech running shoes for the North American middle class. A rusted dump truck careened around the corner on its way to a banana plantation. In the box, corded shoulder to corded shoulder, crouched hungry-looking men with machetes.

Finally, the rain stopped. On my way back to the base, I saw two guys beating someone up. I ran to the group and saw that the someone was Patrick. I grabbed one guy from behind and threw him to the ground. The other guy yelled something and fled, and the guy I'd thrown followed.

Patrick lay on the ground, curled up. He groaned.

"Pat, it's me, Jacques. Can you move?"

He sat up, rubbing his head. His knees were covered with dirt and his right arm was badly scraped. His eyes were bloodshot. "*Merde, ils m'ont volé.*" (I got ripped off.)

"Forget the money, you're lucky to be alive."

"Jacques, what are you doing here?"

"Who were those goons?"

"No clue. They rushed me from behind. I didn't see a thing. Man, I feel like shit. Armelle's going to kill me."

"You haven't been home yet?"

"No. I was on the way."

"Yeah, she's going to kill you alright."

I helped him to his feet and brushed him off. "Come on, I'll walk you back to your place."

"No, I'll be okay. I have to leave this fucking country. It's really insane." He turned away and began to limp down the lane that led to his house.

I returned to *Numada* and began my day of work, but while I tried to figure out where to start, I couldn't help thinking that the list of misfits who had entered my life in Puerto Cortés was growing by the day, and Patrick was now definitely part of the list along with Dog Barker, Ronnie Rackman, German Joe and Ben the philosopher. I was no different. Could I really count on any of these people if I had to? My question came with a loud knocking on the hull.

"Hey, Captain! You up there?"

"Yeah, just a minute."

I climbed through the companionway and looked over the side to see German Joe with a Honduran *hombre*. "Jacques, this is Mario. He's a damn good welder, one of the best in Puerto Cortés, and he's looking for work. I have a feeling you're ready for some help."

I invited them on board for a guided tour.

Mario looked part Maya, part something else. He had a sympathetic air about him. According to Joe, Mario was an ex-navy welder and knew everyone on the base. Although he spoke poor English, he spoke it.

I explained that I was going to need a lot of work done on the hull. And when I finished, he grabbed a hammer and immediately started banging away on the interior of the hull.

"*No hay problema.*" Then he kneeled down and pointed with his chipping hammer. "Here, lots and lots of cutting. *Aqui también, aqui y aqui posiblemente.*" (Here, and here, and maybe here too.) He banged and prodded his way through the boat, testing the soundness of the metal. I could see he was serious. "Mario make everything *nickelo* (shine) again. Measuring tape, *por favor*?"

I dug out a tape and he measured and jotted notes on a piece of cardboard.

German Joe grinned at me. "I felt the same way. Don't worry. You'll love the experience. Besides, once you start working, a year goes by pretty fast in this place."

"A year? No way. I'll be out of here before that."

"That will depend on your luck and Mario's punctuality."

"Deck — what you want me to do on deck?"

We went topside and walked across the deck as a light rain began to fall. The pattering noise on the tarpaulin grew louder until it sounded like galloping hooves. We had to speak loudly just to be heard.

"Mario fix this. Mario replace that. *Fácile* (Easy)." Then my new employee, who was now soaked to the skin, went through the boat again, measuring and calculating how much steel and tubing he would need. "No worry," Mario smiled. "Mario fix good. You see." Mario's list had grown and spilled onto another page.

Joe sat on the deckhouse roof smiling while holding a piece of plywood over his head to protect himself from the rain. "While you guys do all that, I'll have time to finish my boat, sail around the world and come back for a visit," he said mockingly.

"Yeah, Joe, maybe you can, but a guy can dream."

When Mario finished taking notes, I finally asked the big question.

"How much, Mario? How much do you charge?" Without hesitating he answered.

"Me charge fifteen US dollars a day with welding equipment. You pay the welding rods, the gas and Coke."

For a moment, I thought that I was dreaming but then I thought of Mr. Dole and his banana pickers.

"No, Mario, I'll pay you twenty dollars a day." The welder looked at me as if I was a little crazy.

"Mario like this. Okay."

"It's a deal, Mario. You're my man."

We shook hands, and he left but not before promising to be on the job the following day.

Shortly after Mario and Joe left, Patrick and Armelle dropped by. "Hey, Patrick, you look a little better."

"*Ouais*, I slept a little, but I still feel like I got run over by a bulldozer."

"We came to a big decision this morning," Armelle said, looking at Patrick. "We're going back to Switzerland. No more boat, no more mud, no more rust or stinking engine to fix."

"And no more trouble like last night," Patrick said.

"This whole adventure has become a nightmare." Patrick reached for Armelle's hand and she squeezed his in return.

"What about Dog's job offer?" I said.

Patrick lowered his voice and moved closer. "Fuck Dog. He mustn't find out we are leaving, because he will want the money back that he lent us and with interest. Please don't say anything to him."

"What Patrick isn't saying is that he spent it all and can't pay it back," said Armelle, releasing Patrick's hand and crossing her arms.

"Ouch. I don't know Dog Barker very well, but I can bet he will be furious," I commented.

"Look, we're leaving him our boat and all our tools, which are worth more than a few thousand bucks."

"Does he really want your boat?"

"It doesn't matter if he wants it, or not. We're leaving, and Mr. Dog Barker can have our damn boat to do with as he pleases," said Pat.

"Well, it's your decision. I won't say anything."

"Jacques, maybe you would like to take over our house, no? It's a lot better than living here on the base while your boat is getting a makeover, and our rent is only a hundred bucks a month. We're going to pack our things tonight and leave in the morning. Come over this evening and see the place for yourself."

"Sounds good to me but keep it a secret for now. You wouldn't want Dog to know that I'm moving into your place. I'll tell him a little later."

Patrick patted the hull of my boat thoughtfully. "Funny, I'm going to miss you and this crazy place."

A few hours later, I walked to their house, the last one on the road. It was surrounded by mud and a few big trees, and there was a rushing creek in the backyard. A friendly-looking pig played in a pile of leaves in the yard next door. I passed through the front gate, hopped across puddles of muddy rain water and knocked on the screen door.

"*Entrez!*" Armelle called out.

Armelle and Patrick were packing. The kitchen sink was plugged and dirty dishes were piled up everywhere. Cockroaches and ants covered the countertop.

"Every time it rains, they cut off the water. It doesn't make sense," said Armelle.

"Nothing makes any sense around here," said Patrick.

They both looked like they had reached the end of their ropes. Life in the shipyard, their rusted-out sailboat, their chaotic house in the hills, and their crazy adventure had been too much. Now they were focused on returning home to the Alps in time for the ski season, where they claimed to make good money teaching people how to look good on the slopes. It would certainly be more fun than working on their doomed boat and waiting for Dog's footfalls.

"Et le ski est un sport sexy (And skiing is a sexy sport)," said Patrick, dragging a large sail bag into the living room.

"We'll soon forget about our *Honky Tonk* nightmare and the Dog. A few days ago, Dog offered to pay me to fuck him." She lit a cigarette and stuffed more clothes into a big canvas bag that was sitting on the kitchen table. "Never in a million years would I let that filthy man touch me."

The house was small, but it would do fine after a good scrubbing and fumigating. As I was leaving, I spotted an old motorcycle propped against the side of the house.

"That yours?"

"Yeah, it was on board *Honky Tonk*."

I looked it over. The tires were in good shape and it seemed to be in fair condition. "A Jawa, they are popular in Cuba."

"Well, it's yours if you want it. I'm sure as hell not going to take it back to Switzerland."

"Thanks," I said.

"Just keep watch out for the stray dogs. They have no manners and love to go for white *gringo* legs."

"I'll keep that in mind. What about the papers?"

"There are none, nobody gives a shit about papers around here. Just climb on, let her roll downhill and pop the clutch. She'll start, you'll see."

"Okay, I'll give it a try." After a short sprint, I jumped on board. I gave it a couple shots of gas and it took off, a cloud of bluish smoke spewing from the exhaust pipes. "I've got wheeeeels!" I yelled as loudly as I could.

I roared down the dirt trail toward the naval base though a refreshing shower of cool, light mist. There wasn't a soul anywhere, not even a stray mutt looking for a juicy *gringo* leg. After turning onto the main road that ran along the beach, I cranked it up to about sixty kilometers an hour. It was like flying. I felt like riding on forever. But before I ran out of gas, I turned around and cruised back to the boatyard, coasting through the narrow entrance gate. I zigzagged my way through the collection of dry-docked military boats over to where *Numada* sat high and dry on stilts. When I cut the engine, there was a deep silence, followed by the sound of waves crashing up against the decrepit sea wall.

By mid-afternoon the next day, a patch of sun began drying up the dank air. The yard was coming alive. Hired hands, full-time yard workers, my friends the misfits, and some new arrivals all emerged from their hiding places like cockroaches and resumed their work. Later on, as the temperature and humidity climbed, I heard grinding, hammering, sawing and swearing coming from the direction of the big green yacht. Things seemed to be back to normal, but Mario, the new welder, was nowhere in sight. What had happened to all his plans, his *no hay problema* bullshit? He had sounded so promising at our first meeting, but if he didn't show his grinning *no problema* face pretty soon, I would have to make some big decisions. I sat down on the deckhouse, trying to stay positive. There was nothing to do but be patient and prepare for the eventuality that the welder might not show up.

It was late afternoon when I finally got the soldiers to bring over the crane to lift the two masts off the deck. One by one, they were hoisted straight up and over, then laid onto blocks of wood near *Numada*. Then it was time for the engine to find its place beside the masts. My boat was just a hulk now. Its market value had just dropped by half, but I reasoned it would be worth it later, once everything was put back in place. In the lingering daylight, I left everything on deck and moseyed over to the liquor store. I bought two good cold beers and sat at the outside table beside the resident mangy, talking bird in the wire cage. Together, we watched the evening chase the afternoon away. Funny thing, the bird did most of the talking.

THE MOVE

For the next week or so, I drifted in and out of moods, encounters and expenses. Lots of expenses. But I was well-settled in my new house now. Armelle and Patrick had left discreetly for Europe. By the time the Dog had learned about their departure, they were gone.

"Ronnie just informed me that those pathetic little dreamers took off for Switzerland and won't be coming back."

"You're kidding!"

"They owe me money."

"Oh yeah? What about their boat?" I asked.

"What about it? It's just good for the scrap yard."

For the next couple of weeks, I only saw the Dog on a few brief occasions. He was often away in Tegucigalpa, but Ronnie and his boys worked steadily on his boat.

During that time I slowly moved a few of my possessions to the house on the hill. And no one seemed to care, certainly not Barker. For a hundred bucks a month, I had a sagging spring mattress bed, cold running water, a blocked sink and a lethal-looking gas stove that hissed and popped every time I'd start it. I spent long hours washing the floors, sweeping and trying to put some order to a joint that had been neglected for so many months by the former tenants. I brought up some bed sheets, a few pots and pans, and the coffee maker from the boat. I figured that it would do justice to that great Honduran coffee that I was starting to enjoy. Within a week, I had accepted the insects and began to feel right at home.

Back at the boatyard, things were looking up. Mario finally showed up for work with a helper. My job was to provide them with the materials they needed. One morning, they requested a new tank of acetylene and additional welding rods. While we sat under the hull making plans and figuring out how to arrange transportation for the material, Dog sauntered over.

"Hey, Frenchman, I'm going into town to pick up stuff. Wanna come?"

I went over to Mario, who was about to weld a piece of steel plate into place. "Mario, do we need anything in town?"

Mario lifted up his facemask. He was dripping with sweat. "We need more welding rods, zinc primer paint, sanding discs and a big cold bottle of *refresco* (soda)."

I yelled over to Barker, "Okay, count me in." Within minutes I was sitting beside the Dog in the cab of his pickup truck. In the center of town, Barker swung onto a dingy street that was empty except for a few men stretched out in the shade and sleeping off the previous night's bad rum. I wasn't exactly surprised when the Dog wheeled the truck close to the curb and stopped in front of the Manila Bar, the second sleaziest bar in town.

"It's never too early for a beer and a good lay. Maybe Sylvita's there. She's something else, man. I'd crawl a mile over broken glass just to get into her pants. Come on, it'll be worth the visit."

Once my eyes had adjusted to the darkness, I saw half-awake prostitutes half-ready for business. In one corner of the room stood a goon with a semi-automatic handgun tucked into his belt. The walls were dark red and covered with garish artwork, mirrors and sundry objects left behind by countless wharf rats and homesick sailors. Dog ordered and the waitress drowsily served us two bottles of Salva Vida. She was pretty, and she had a devil with a nasty-looking pitchfork tattooed on her right breast. If only tattoos could talk.

An elderly man in a suit was sitting over in a dark corner at the far end of the bar. He looked like an insurance salesman gone walkabout. Beside him, a tall black girl slowly gyrated on a small wooden box. Her pelvis was about two inches from his nose.

Just as we were finishing our first beers, two girls appeared from a back room and nudged up beside us. “Look, Frenchman,” Dog said, “the one on the right is Sylvita. She’s mine. I don’t know about the other one, but hey, it’s my dime. Go for it.”

The two women wore almost identical dresses with easy access to the interior. One of them came right up to me, dropped down on her knees and unzipped my jeans. “*Hey mi amor. Me provokas*,” she said. (Hey, my love, you provoke me.)

The Dog laughed and grabbed his nuts. “Shit, Frenchman, lucky you. You’re an instantaneous hit. I’m going to be entertained by Sylvita for a while. See ya later.” With that, he disappeared into the back room and I was left alone with the other woman.

“*Ven, ven conmigo, por favor*,” she said, pulling me behind the bar. (Come with me please.) A few minutes later, we were upstairs in a small, dimly lit room. Another lovely was sitting on a chair beside the bed wearing only a black bra and panties.

“For you, two for one, okay.”

As I stood, they stripped me naked, then led me into the bathroom and turned on the shower. The water was warm; in fact it was the first hot shower that I had taken in months. The girls took their clothes off and joined me. Delightful was the only word I could think of. After the hot water ran out, we dried off. They massaged my body from head to toe with fragrant oil. I fell into another world.

The three of us ended up in bed. I watched the two girls as they caressed each other. They were good at what they did; in fact, they even gave me a few new ideas. After a while, I stopped watching and joined the party, and I helped them out as much as I could. There was a lot of laughing, and the big bed in the center of the room turned into a tangled mixture of bodies, sheets and pillows. Overheated and spent, we returned to the shower for a final scrub down in the cold water. Feeling rejuvenated, I returned downstairs to the bar where the Dog was waiting for me.

"What do you think?"

"Not bad, not bad at all."

"Did you get fucked good?"

"What happens upstairs stays upstairs."

"Ah, you must have got the two-for-one special. A guy can't go wrong here. It's the best place in town. I should know. I've been to every one." He smiled and slapped me on the back. "Now, let's go pick up those supplies that you need." I was starting to appreciate the better side of this guy.

The rest of that week there wasn't much to do except work, eat and sleep. Happily, I could see that, every day, I was getting closer to getting my boat back in the water. Despite the oppressive heat, Mario and his gang always worked, and when darkness fell we would string up lights for the night crew. The welder would call the shots, and, with his helper, cut and place pieces using a chain hoist. Once the sparks began to fly, I would leave them to their own devices, because after a twelve-hour shift, I was ready for a break.

One evening, just after the welders had started, I heard a voice shouting from the deck of the big green motor sailor.

"Hey, Frenchman, come on over. You're working too hard."

"Señor Dog." Mario pointed at *Esmeralda*. "*Hombre loco*." (A crazy man.)

The Dog was standing on the foredeck dressed in his classic cut-offs, glass in hand and hair untied. He looked very drunk.

"Come on up and have a snort of whisky."

Mario looked at me. "No problem."

It had been a long day. I was pretty tired and a good shot of whisky wouldn't do any harm, so I washed myself down with the hose and climbed onto the deck of *Esmeralda*.

"Fix yourself a glass," the Dog said as I stepped into the salon. He was stretched out on a sofa beside a twenty-six-ounce bottle of rum. "The icemaker is beside the freezer. Jesus, it was hot today. What the fuck are you doing to that boat of yours anyway, cutting it up for scrap?"

"Cheap shot. My boat's going to make you jealous someday," I replied.

"Jealous of that? Man, you gotta be kidding."

I didn't answer.

"Boats are more trouble than they're worth. I can't wait till they finish working on this one and leave me alone. Rackman's gang of clowns are driving me nuts. So far, they have done every job at least twice."

"So I noticed."

"Ah, you have? I didn't think you cared." He chuckled.

We started drinking and talking loudly. Soon we were like old sailing buddies. I poured myself another shot. As it grew later, the scotch in the bottle dwindled. We told each other stories, impossible stories, half true and half bullshit. It was like some kind of contest.

"Look, the guy shot me here." Dog pulled up his dirty shirt and showed me a good-sized scar just above his beer gut.

"No way."

"But the bullet hit my rib and then bounced off. Was I lucky! But he wasn't. I had just enough time to grab my piece and shoot the bastard in the head and I'll show ya what with." Dog went over to the kitchen and pulled out a semi-automatic 9mm pistol from a drawer under the counter. “It was his last robbery. Here, have a look.” He shoved the gun into my hand. It felt solid and cold. “Watch out where you point that thing, Frenchman; it’s loaded! After I capped that son of a bitch, I had to clean my wound with gasoline, because that’s all I had. I rode out of that hellhole on horseback. It took me two fucking days to find a doctor. Man, was I fucked up!” The Dog seemed proud of himself. He showed me the rest of his arsenal that he kept in the stern cabin. “I got more guns on board than the whole Honduran Navy. Look, my Uzi here. In the case there is a new 9mm Beretta, and this here is one of my favorites, a good old AK-47, loaded up and ready for action. I call them my enforcers. They come in real handy for some of the work I do. Know what I mean?”

I did.

We returned to the main salon. At that moment, a young, well-molded woman walked through the hall door that led to the front end of the yacht. “This is Valeska De Sela. Valeska, meet the Frenchman. Shit, what’s your real name, again?”

She was barefoot and wearing only a long white sleeveless shirt. She was in her early thirties, had short jet-black hair and dark piercing eyes. Her *café-crème* skin seemed to glow. When she looked at me, I swear I felt a current of electricity run through my body.

"My name is Jacques, Jacques Legris."

"Oh yeah, but I like Frenchman better," said Barker.

"I've heard a few things about you," said the woman.

"Good or bad?"

"A little of both, I'm afraid."

"Well, don't believe a word you hear. They're all just rumors."

Valeska approached and we shook hands.

"*Mucho gusto*," I said. (Pleased to meet you.)

"*Igual*," she replied and lowered her eyes. (Same here.) Valeska had a special kind of beauty, but she was not traditionally beautiful. She was the result of some kind of *métisage* (mix) for sure. She walked gracefully into the main salon, poured herself a glass of cold water, squeezed some lemon into it and turned. "I'd join you for a drink, but it's been a long day and I am tired." She disappeared into the front section of the yacht. I heard the cabin door close and then lock with a soft click.

"Valeska is my partner's niece. She's here on business."

"She seems to be quite special."

"She is," said Barker and looked away. "How do you like living up in the hills?"

"It's okay, but far from the base."

"I don't know where your house is, but you gotta be careful going up there at night. There's lots of *banditos* (bandits) around here and it's open season on us *gringos*." The Dog went into the galley and returned with a bundle wrapped in cloth. "Here, stick this in your pocket. You never know." He handed me a Saturday night special with a pearl handle. "It's loaded. Here's a box of spare ammo, and remember, an unloaded gun ain't worth shit. You've got two bullets in the barrel, not six. That's why it's so small. You can hide it anywhere, but if you put it in your pants, be careful not to blow your nuts off. If you get into any trouble, just shoot the fucker, make sure he's dead, then lose yourself for a few days. That's the way it works around here. That fool Patrick should've had a piece on him. He could have saved himself all that hassle." He poured himself one more scotch and carelessly spilled some on the table.

“You know,” he slurred, “I didn’t appreciate those two Swiss shits running out on me like that. They were going to work for us as crew. They would have made good money.” Dog stood up and peered out the big cabin port light toward *Numada*. “All that work must be costing you a fortune. How do you manage?”

“I’m beginning to ask myself that very question.”

“Maybe I can help. You’re a good sailor, aren’t you? I watched you come in last month. It was real slick, and you were alone too. My associate in Tegucigalpa told me to look for a skipper, one who knows how to sail. The job pays well. You wouldn’t be looking for a little extra work, by any chance?”

“Give me some time to think about it. The extra money could come in handy.” I looked at my watch. “Hey, it’s getting late. I’ve got to go.”

He accompanied me up on deck. “Well, Frenchman, it’s been a pleasure. Come over anytime. But don’t forget, if ya have to use that gun, shoot low, ’cause they’re goin’ to be riding Shetlands! Get it?” He laughed out loud. Then he started to cough, I thought he was going to puke everything up over the side. He disappeared inside the cabin as I climbed back down to reality. I left the base and rode my Jawa up the dark trail to my shack.

The Saturday Night Special

How bizarre to be packing a pistol. I don't know why I took the gun. Maybe it was just a macho thing. But homicide in Honduras is almost a national pastime.

That night, I sat outside on my small balcony sipping rum and lime while weighing the pros and cons of Barker's proposition. But more pleasant than the rum I was savoring was my recent encounter with the enchanting Valeska De Sela. She radiated something that I had never felt from a woman. Was it the way she looked at me? The touch of her hand, her intense gaze? One thing for sure, she managed to kindle a fire in a barren place inside my soul. Was she the elusive partner that I had been looking for all these years?

As I pulled into the boatyard on my sputtering Jawa early the next morning, I spotted Valeska on the deck lowering a heavy box to the ground with a rope and tackle. The line had gotten caught up in the scaffolding that had been erected close to the hull of the *Esmeralda,* so I went over to help. Then I watched as she came down the ladder. She looked so sexy. And she knew it.

"Thanks. I was afraid that the whole thing would flip upside down."

I lifted the heavy box and loaded it into the big SUV that she was driving. "Hey, you wouldn't be going to San Pedro, by any chance?" I asked.

"*Si, ahora.*" (Yes, right now.)

"Would you mind if I come along? I have to pick up some material for my boat."

She bent over and slipped on her sandals, then looked at me. When our eyes met, something intense passed between us. "I'll just let Dog know." She went back over to the big yacht, climbed halfway up the ladder and yelled, "Dog! Your Canadian neighbor needs a ride to San Pedro." In her Spanish accent, she also pronounced his name Dog instead of Doug.

"What neighbor?" he called from the deck.

"Jack, Jack Legris," she called. She Anglicized my name, which I found charming.

The Dog was too engrossed yelling instructions to his workers to reply. Valeska led me over over to a shiny black SUV and took off her sunglasses, revealing intense dark brown eyes. "He's in a foul mood this morning because of a hangover. He drinks too much. Let's go." She climbed in behind the wheel.

I hopped in on the passenger side and caught Valeska's eyes as she briefly checked herself in the mirror. Then she turned the key, put her sunglasses back on, and off we went. In a few minutes we reached the road that snaked through the rolling foothills between Puerto Cortés and San Pedro Sula. The terrain was covered with pine trees and rock formations. As we climbed higher, the air grew fresher and the breeze felt good. Valeska drove at least thirty kilometers per hour over the speed limit, passing everything in sight.

"What do you have to do in San Pedro?" I asked.

"Boring things, like return a burned-out fuel pump to the supplier and pick up some hoses for one of the engines."

"I need a piece of exhaust hose myself, so we'll shop at the same place."

"That makes things simpler."

Valeska stepped on the gas and flew past a bus that was spewing black exhaust. After that the road was clear, so she kept the needle stuck at 130 km/h.

"You work with Barker?" I ventured.

"My uncle, Igor Zarkin, and Dog are associates on a specific project."

It was the perfect moment to get her version. "What type of project?"

"We want to develop an ancient Maya city in La Mosquitia and eventually turn the site into an archaeological center. There are considerable Maya ruins in the area, and my uncle wants to conserve them before someone goes in and cleans the place out. Barker was the one who first discovered the location. According to an old law that's still enforced, the site is registered in his name because it was his discovery. People have been searching for it for years, but they must have been looking in the wrong place. He met my uncle, sold him the idea, and together they flew in and spent a few days scouting out the area. That's when my uncle decided to invest. He's become completely obsessed with the ruins he saw. It seems that it is even larger in area than Copan, and contains thousands of artifacts, huge carvings and an incredible amount of stone structures. It's the last Mayan stronghold and has been lying there undiscovered for centuries. It's an amazing opportunity for me to be involved in something like this. Except that these days, Dog and my uncle don't really see eye to eye. In fact, they don't get along at all, anymore. But they've gone too far to back down now. My uncle has the money, brains and connections. Dog has the drive and the guts to run the operation in the field. And Dog owns the property. But neither one trusts the other."

"What's your role?"

"Well first of all, I am the only bona fide archaeologist on this team. I studied at the University of Honduras in Tegucigalpa. I'll be working in the field. When it's set up, I'll be working with the crews and selecting the most valuable artifacts, making sure that they are brought out in one piece. I'll be responsible for classifying and conserving them in our warehouse until the archaeological museum in Tegucigalpa is built."

"Big job."

"Yes, but I love that kind of work. I also love the adventure. The idea of uncovering a lost Maya city is totally amazing."

"You're right about that. Valeska, can I ask you something personal?"

"Sure, go ahead."

"What's your unprofessional relationship with Barker?"

"Ooh, I think that's what you wanted to know ever since you met me."

"Perhaps."

"Well, let's say that the energy between Dog and me has always been rather ambiguous. But these days it's more business than anything else."

"How so?"

"It's a complicated story. My uncle introduced us a few years ago — before this project got underway. We became lovers. He's so self-confident and ready to take risks. And he is very charming even though he's rough around the edges. For a while it worked out perfectly. The work, and the, uh how can I say, the pleasure, as well. He was different from any man I had ever known, and I, of course, was somewhat younger. It lasted for about a year, but it was a stormy year."

"So what happened?"

"I found out that he liked screwing young *chicas* when I wasn't around. And there's another thing: he's become addicted to power. My uncle doesn't really trust him anymore. Hey, I have already told you way too much. We just met and look at me."

"Yes, but there's a beginning to everything."

"That's what worries me."

She became silent, lost in thought. As she drove on, I watched her out of the corner of my eye.

After a few more miles, I said, "So it's not easy for you."

"What do you mean?"

"I mean that you are stuck mediating between your uncle the dreamer and the Dog who is in it for keeps."

She laughed. "I'm doing it for my uncle. He's like a father to me. If not for him, I would change jobs."

I could picture her trying to separate the two quarrelling men. Igor Zarkin, whom I imagined to be a cultivated, sensitive and very wealthy philanthropist, would be the perfect mark for Barker, who could be both intimidating and a salesman.

"And now you come along just to make it even more complicated."

I looked over and she turned her head. Our eyes met.

"What do YOU mean?" I said.

"You'll see." She smiled coyly. She slowed down and gave room as we passed a broken-down bus on the road. A few dozen forlorn-looking passengers watched as two men changed a back tire.

"Zarkin is not your typical Spanish name."

"Not at all. My great-grandfather was born near Saint Petersburg, in Russia. He was only about twenty-five years old when he came here. He had a degree as a mining engineer packed in his suitcase — along with a few connections. It was just after the revolution of 1917. He did very well in this country, much better than if he had stayed in Russia. Later, he married into a well-established Honduran family. I am part Maya, part Spanish and part Russian."

Her face had a certain strength, a special kind of beauty. But despite her appearance of candour, I had the feeling she was mixed up in something a lot bigger than she let on. I lowered my window even further and a warm blast of air filled the interior.

"What part of Canada are you from?" she asked.

"Québec."

"What brought you down here in the first place?"

"I was looking for something different."

"You don't work?"

"I work on my boat full-time."

"I mean a real paying job."

"I used to work for a television network."

"Doing what?"

"I was a war correspondent."

"That sounds interesting."

"It really was, but it became too intense and I decided to take a leave of absence."

"What do you mean?"

"A leave of absence is when you temporarily leave your job. I wanted a change, a new lifestyle."

"Like...?"

"Like move onto a sailboat and to start off, visit the Caribbean. It's an old dream that I've had since my teens."

"But what do you do for money?"

"I have a small apartment building in Québec City. I live off the rent, but after I pay the expenses, it's only just enough to get by. During the last few years, I've written articles for a magazine published in France. With that, I can make out okay. And I like the freedom it gives me."

"Freedom? It's never free," Valeska mused. "So tell me: What kind of freedom are you talking about?"

"Personal freedom. Up until a few years ago I was heavily involved in a career and it almost killed me. I'm not just talking about the dangers of war zones. I'm talking about the pace and the pressure. I left all that behind when I decided to come down here."

"But you live alone."

"Yeah, I just haven't found the right woman."

"I know what you mean. I have a hard time settling down myself."

There was a short silence. "Writing interests me. What do you write about here in the Caribbean?"

"I like to write about things most people can't even imagine exist. For instance, I spent some time in Cuba just before coming to Honduras. I wrote a series of articles about the Russian mafia and how they control the illegal drug trade."

"Sounds exciting. I'd like to read your articles."

"Sure, anytime."

She stepped on the gas and passed another bus.

"What about you, Valeska? Where are you from?"

"Not too far from here." She flashed me a smile. I placed myself on hold for a while, slipped down in my seat, put my knees on the dash and watched the countryside zip by. Soon we approached the San Pedro Sula city limits. Piles of garbage and abandoned and stripped car carcasses littered the roadside. As she drove, Valeska discreetly removed her rings and watch and slipped them under the seat. She downshifted to third gear and used compression to slow us in time to stop for the upcoming red light.

The road after the intersection was lined with ragged, tumbled-down shacks constructed from rusted tin sheets, rotted plywood and fringed plastic tarps. People were gaunt, hardly noticing the passing traffic. A little further into the city center, we passed a Wendy's restaurant, a GMC dealer and a Sears clearly in business for the ten percent of the population who controlled ninety percent of the country's wealth.

Valeska turned the pickup onto a narrow street and began to fill me in on the protocol. "This is one of the most dangerous cities in Central America.

Just go about your affairs and try not to look too much like a lost tourist. I'm going to put this thing in a guarded parking lot." She turned suddenly at a side street, turned again and hit the brakes in front of a razor-wire gate. An armed guard put down his newspaper, slowly got up from a wooden bench and slid open a big chain-link gate on wheels. Valeska flashed a smile then drove into the compound. "This is a safe enough parking place, but only if you have the guard on your side."

"How do you do that?"

Valeska pulled out a hundred-*lempira* bill (about ten US dollars) from her pocket and handed it to the guard. "You pay him extra," she said once we were out of earshot.

We walked to the crowded sidewalks of Third Avenida, weaving our way through the throngs of people to the marketplace. My intriguing companion took my arm as we ducked inside the maze of canvas-covered stalls where sidewalk venders sold outdated collections of cheap shoes, counterfeit watches, umbrellas, sunglasses and whatever else would satisfy a local looking for a deal. While we weaved through the narrow lanes of outdoor kiosks, I sensed that wide eyes followed our every step. But this didn't seem to bother Valeska as she led the way while reviewing the long shopping list that Barker had given her. I guessed that she had been here dozens of times before. When I mentioned a few things that I needed, she pointed to a store on the corner.

"*Muy fácil.*" (That's easy.)

Suddenly, there were two gunshots behind us, and screaming and shouting. Two men hurried past us, shoving people out of the way. Police officers with guns drawn pursued the two men. Valeska and I hid in a doorway. Her warm perspiring body pressed against mine for a few precious seconds. We heard three more gunshots. People in the crowd threw themselves to the ground, screaming. At that moment it seemed only natural to wrap my arms around Valeska. When things settled down, our eyes met and I almost thanked those bandits out loud for their perfect timing.

Late that afternoon, we finished our shopping. But Valeska gave me the impression that there was something else on her list. About fifteen miles from the town, she turned the truck onto a dirt road, put it in park and looked at me, her dark eyes shining. "I'm going to take you somewhere." She drove us along a dirt road. The truck kicked up a long cloud of dust. She carefully navigated a trail that ended under a cluster of tall pine trees.

She turned off the ignition. The only sound was the wind blowing through the branches. A stream gushed out of a rocky crag, cascading into a small, clear pond just below us. “This was once part of my father’s property. I used to come and swim here all the time when I was a kid.” She led me down the narrow trail to the water’s edge, stripped off her clothes and dove in. From the water, she called, “What are you waiting for, sailor? Are you afraid of water?”

I wasn’t. I dove in with her. She disappeared underwater and came up in front of me and, wrapping her legs around my waist, gave me a long kiss. “*Peligroso, Jack Legris, peligroso* (Danger, Jack Legris, danger),” she said. “I’ve been wanting to do that all day with you.” Before I could respond, she let go, swam over to the falls, hoisted herself up onto a flat rock and let the water shower over her body. “Come on, there’s room for two.”

So I went over, hauled myself out of the water, and we sat behind the waterfall. I wrapped my legs around her, pressed up against her back and slipped my hands down over her breasts.

Afterwards, we slipped back down into the water, swam over to the quiet end of the pool and lay together on a rock. I dropped my gaze, rolled over on my back and said, “It’s the here and now that really counts, don’t you think?”

It wasn’t long before I could feel her fingers on me, then her lips.

As we made love, I wondered if this was just a sexual encounter between two strangers. She teased me, caressed me. I did the same. Just as I thought that I was going to explode, she said, "Take me from behind this time, Jack."

•••

The sun was a lot lower on the horizon when Valeska finally wheeled the truck back onto the main road. She drove hard and didn't say a word. Soon she broke the silence. "You and I could go far together."

I looked at her.

"You'd be the perfect skipper for *Esmeralda*."

"Sure, but I don't think that we'd do much sailing." I rolled up the window a little. Valeska wasn't really listening. She took her watch from under her seat and slipped it back on her wrist, then slipped her two rings back on. "Oh shit, it's late. I was supposed to be back by 5:00. Look what you made me do!"

"No, look what you made *me* do."

She laughed and looked nervously in the mirror as she smeared on some fresh lipstick, a little risky at 100 km/h. I offered to drive, but she just shook her head as we passed a slow-moving truck. For a while, we didn't speak. I thought she was trying to decide what to tell Dog. She brought the truck around a curve and slowed a little. Something was going on up ahead. A group of men were staring at a shirtless body lying motionless by the side of the road. They waved frantically for us to stop. Instead, she floored it. "That's an old trick. That man is fine, and if we stopped, those people would have attacked us."

Just before the next village, we blew by a schoolyard. A black and white football bounced out onto the highway. It sounded like a bomb going off when it burst. "Bad luck for those kids," I said. She was silent.

It was after sundown when we arrived back at the base. The black SUV, which was spotless when we left that morning, was now filthy. Valeska parked beside *Esmeralda*. Within seconds, she was climbing the ladder to *Esmeralda*. Halfway up she turned and put a finger to her lips.

I grabbed my supplies and walked toward *Numada*, but before I had walked twenty steps, Rackman popped out from behind the motor sailor's long keel. "Hey buddy. Have a good time in San Pedro? The boss is sort of pissed off. He really doesn't like guys fooling around with his woman."

"And I don't like guys who don't mind their own business."

Later that evening, I heard Barker and Valeska arguing on the deck of the big yacht. The next morning, I saw her drive away.

A few days later, the Dog invited me over to his yacht for a drink. When I arrived, he was already pretty far gone. "What took you so long? I almost finished the bottle by myself." He got up, grunted, poured himself a double shot and spun around, looking me in the eyes. "I'll get straight to the point if you don't mind, Frenchman. Valeska and I had a little… She went back to Tegucigalpa."

He took a Colt .45 from a drawer. He opened and closed the barrel. "Nice piece, eh?" He gave me a strange look and pointed the thing at me.

"You know, it's no fun working for Mr. Z. He thinks he owns me. Now he's got Valeska busting my balls. And you? I don't know where you stand. I think that that bitch is going to use you to get to me. That's the way she works." It was as if a breaker had flipped inside his head. He staggered around the room, waving the revolver and babbling.

"Hey, Barker, chill out. Put the damn gun away."

"Why, you afraid I might kill you? I could. I already killed one poor son of a bitch."

"Yeah. You said that already."

"That shithead was dead standing up. I've got you all pegged, the whole damn bunch of you. Frenchman, just watch yourself."

I got up and walked out. As I climbed down the ladder, Barker came on deck and fired his pistol in the air. "I'm the boss around here, understand! Just call me God! Just call me God!"

Back on my boat I sat on deck and continued to watch the show on board *Esmeralda*. Barker pranced around for a few more minutes shooting his gun off at the sky. Then he went inside and put on some music. It was Marty Robbin's singing his famous El Paso song again. But this time, the volume was turned up loud and the same tune played on and on and on and for a while, the Dog was singing along.

THE REAL STORY

The following week, I sent a query to *Aventura* to tell them that I had started to prepare a series of articles about a lost Maya city that had been discovered in La Mosquitia. But this time, oddly enough, I heard nothing from *Aventura*. I called their office in Paris. They told me that the magazine had been sold and that the submissions editor with whom I had been working was no longer with the magazine. Worse than that, their protocol had changed; they were no longer giving advances. I sent my queries to other publications, but with no luck. I was out of work.

One evening, after a long day of boring work at the yard, I got home later than usual. The wind had picked up again, and drops of rain began to fall just as I pushed open the rusted gate and rolled my born-again Jawa into the courtyard. The metallic squeak of the gate as it closed triggered a chain reaction. From somewhere, a dog barked, somebody shouted and a downpour followed. It lasted two full days.

During those days of heavy rain, Honduras gave me the impression of a country someone had stuck on the map with some sort of cheap glue. With the incessant downpour, the whole place felt as if it was slowly peeling off the face of the earth. My shoes had turned greenish and were starting to disintegrate. On the kitchen floor, something crunched under my bare feet. In the dim light, I saw thousands of ants. It was a little too much. Rather than fighting this army of creepy crawlies, I went back to the naval base.

When I got there I saw that there was a truck parked beside *Esmeralda*. Valeska, Barker and a big Garifuna guy got out, but they didn't see me where I stood half hidden behind a big brass propeller of a military boat. I watched as the Garifuna went back and lowered the tailgate and lifted the door. Meanwhile, a crew of a fishing boat secured their vessel to the dock. Valeska talked to various men as they appeared out of the shadows.

She was wearing skin-tight jeans, black boots and a molded black T-shirt. The peak of her ball cap cast a shadow on her face.

Barker supervised the men while they unloaded material onto the dock from the truck. I could see compressors, a few generators, digging gear and dozens of boxes. Valeska stayed by the dock crane and said something to the operator. Immediately a motor started, and the lift swung over and, one by one, loaded the crates onto the fishing boat. When one landed a little heavy with a thud, I heard Valeska's voice: "Hey, Carlos, *quidado por favor*!" (Please be careful!)

After about half an hour, the transfer was completed. While Barker counted the crates that had been placed on board the boat, Valeska handed a small bag to a bearded guy on deck and another one to a neat-looking man dressed in a military uniform. Then Barker went over to Valeska and touched her on the shoulder. She pushed his hand away and said something. They exchanged a few heated words before she spun around and climbed into the passenger side of the five-ton. It took off immediately.

I didn't hear the guard sneak up from behind, but I felt the business end of his rifle press into my back. "Hey, *¿que buscado*?" (What are you looking for?)

"*Nada* (nothing)," was all I could muster, but I guess that wasn't the right answer. He pushed me and I fell to the ground with a thump. Then he kicked me in the ribs with one of his boots, then put a knee on my back. I felt a sharp pain.

"Okay, okay, take it easy," I said. For a moment, I could hardly breathe.

The overgrown gorilla lifted himself off, and slowly, I got to my feet, and then, with the nose of his rifle stuck into my back, the guard took me over to the big hangar that housed the travel lift. Once inside, I saw Barker sitting on an overturned plastic bucket with one of his eternal fat cigars hanging out of his mouth.

"Frenchman, what a pleasant surprise to see you here. I hope that you didn't get roughed up too much, but the guard didn't know who you were. Just following orders, that's all."

He paused as one of the men from the fishing boat walked up to us. "*Listo Señor Barker*." (Ready, Mr. Barker.)

"Okay, Ramón, don't forget our deal. We'll be in touch."

The man nodded and left.

"Have a seat," he pointed to a wooden crate placed in front of him.

"No, I prefer to stand."

"Suit yourself."

He stood up and stretched.

"You know, Frenchman, you don't seem like such a bad guy. You and I need to have a little talk." A funny smile formed on his lips and he looked away. For the sake of my health, I didn't ask for further explanations. Barker wiped his brow with his T-shirt. "Damn hot night. We'll be more comfortable on *Esmeralda*. Come on."

In a few minutes, I was standing face to face with Barker in the yacht's main saloon.

"First of all, imagine this, Mr. Z wants to meet you in Roatán during Christmas break. It's official."

"Maybe it is for you guys, but I want to know more before I decide to get involved."

"Fine. I got nothing against that."

He went over to the liquor cabinet.

"You want a shot?"

"No."

He poured one for himself and began to explain.

"Rumor has it there's a lot of gold in the mountains just a few days upriver from Mosquito Coast. So a few years back, I rounded up a small crew and went east into La Mosquitia. One night, we camped on a large sandbar near a waterfall. The next day, I looked for streams where I might pan for gold. So there I was, in the middle of nowhere, wading up this shallow stream that was clear as crystal, and I began to come across some large stone ruins. Everything was covered with trees and roots, but underneath there were lots of strange sculptures of white stone.

"Then, a little bit further along, we found a huge goddamn white pyramid that was also partly grown over. There was an opening and of course we went inside. Man, the cavern was huge, no — massive. It went on forever. My Indian guide was sure this was the very center of the Ciudad Blanca. It was a real jackpot. Within a week, we realized that we had discovered the mother lode of priceless Mayan artifacts. Much better than gold!" He leaned closer. His breath smelled like a bar during closing time. "I staked out a claim as soon as I could, in sections, the way it's done. That took two weeks. Hell, it almost killed me. It's rough living in that jungle." He took a puff on his cigar and without thinking blew the smoke in my face. For a second, I felt like puking. "And all that shit up at Ciudad Blanca is sitting on a mineral claim that is registered in my name at the government mineral claim office in Tegucigalpa. In a way, a property like that is worth more than gold or drugs, not half as much trouble and nobody interferes. We've already begun bringing stuff out. You may have noticed I've got the naval base here on my side too. The commander understands the situation perfectly."

"You paid him off."

"Of course, that's the way it works. Once all that equipment reaches the location next week, my handpicked crew will be setting up camp. There are buyers all over the world. Christ sake, it's just like printing money." He crossed the cabin and grabbed a small jade statuette off a shelf. "See this? There are hundreds like this one up at the site. I can sell each one for over $5,000 a pop. The stone carvings can be easily sold for over fifty grand. I've been up there a half a dozen times and once even brought back some gold plates. Imagine what they're worth! We want to clean out this place as fast as possible, before the archaeologists find out."

"So you, Valeska and her uncle are all involved?"

"Yes, in a way. And all this came from a lucky discovery that I made while looking for gold. Valeska's uncle is financing everything and is quite happy with his share of the profits from anything I take out. He's the guy with the connections. He thinks there will be a part two: a first-class archaeological site in the middle of nowhere. But giving guided archaeological tours is not really my thing."

As the Dog continued explaining the setup, I just kept wondering why he was sharing secrets — and with so much detail. I could see he was attracted prestige, wealth and power. By sharing his secret, he had opened a door. Perhaps he wanted me to be his backup. Why else would he be telling me this? The more that I heard, the farther I wanted to go. All I had to do was to play it cool and when I knew more, start writing the articles for *Aventura*. If things got a little too hot to handle, I could always jump ship, disappear over the horizon and write the story up somewhere safe. Perhaps, sooner or later, I would find out the exact location of Ciudad Blanca, go there and see it with my own eyes. But one thing for sure, if the Dog got wind of my writing project, my life wouldn't be worth more than the price of a bullet. I stood up and touched the ribs where the soldier had kicked me. I still felt queasy.

"So where the hell is this place?"

"In the heart of La Mosquitia, not far from the Mosquito Coast. It's some of the roughest country in Honduras. Everything that scratches, bites or stings, crawls or slithers lives there. And the natives, they're superstitious as hell. They think that the Gods of the Great Winds curse the place. I don't know what they're smoking, but whenever I've gone up there, it's been real quiet, no wind at all.

"There was a guy named Theodore Morde, back in 1939, claimed he had found some incredible ruins he was certain were Ciudad Blanca. He'd even written something and filmed the Ciudad Blanca with a movie camera. So Morde went to see people in London who were willing to invest in a major expedition. Some people say that he committed suicide, others say that the poor guy was run over by a car." The Dog took a deep breath, emptied his drink and banged the glass on the table. "But whatever the hell happened, the knowledge of the exact location of the place died with him." He bent over the wrinkled map on the table and studied it for a few seconds. His eyeglasses made his eyes appear to bulge out. "If you play your cards right, well…" He laughed again, but his wild laughter quickly became a hysterical wheeze and then a heavy cough. "Where the fuck did I put those pills?" The Dog searched through his pockets and found what he was looking for. "These damn things are going to kill me if the booze don't first." After he managed to calm down, he continued, "Shit, what I've taken out so far is only a drop in the bucket. When *Esmeralda* is ready, she'll be all geared up to transport goods by the ton and we'll set up camp in Roatán. And no one will be the wiser because we still look like a charter boat."

I still had one question. It was a little crazy, considering, but oh well. "What about Valeska?"

"Valeska?" He looked a little confused. "Uh, right now Miss V. should be on her way back to Tegucigalpa. Sooner or later, she'll take over from him because he can't live forever." He laughed sardonically. "Then it will be just the two of us running the show."

That week, the Dog and Ronnie flew to Miami to pick up some electronics.

Then I got a surprise visit from guess who.

"Hey, Jack, can I come up?"

Before I could answer, Valeska was already halfway up the ladder. She was wearing tight shorts and a Miami Dolphins T-shirt. Her head was covered by a green ball cap with Bad Hair Day written just above the peak. I put down my tools and helped her on board.

"I like the hat. What's the reason for your visit?"

"Another gofer job. I had to pick up another piece for one of the engines. It arrived at the airport in San Pedro this morning," she said and gave me a warm kiss. "I missed you, Jack."

"How long will you be around this time?"

"Until the day after tomorrow — before Dog and Ronnie come back."

"Yeah, I noticed that they weren't around. It's been kind of quiet here lately."

"Good, no prying eyes." She smiled and kissed me again.

"Valeska..."

"Don't let him spoil anything. I'm doing my best just to keep things going smoothly between us. That's it."

"What about your uncle?"

"He really wants to get rid of him, but without Barker, there's no access to La Ciudad Blanca."

"So your uncle should give him something else to do, something that will keep him out of the way," I said.

Valeska hesitated. "Yeah, something that would make him disappear."

"Like?"

"Like buying him off."

She paused, then her eyes lit up. "Jack, I have an idea. It's Sunday and nobody's around. Let's go to the beach. There's a beautiful stretch out past the Garifuna village, on the other side of Puerto Cortés."

The idea sounded good, but I could hear the Chief's voice in the back of my mind the time he advised me to stay out of trouble. "Sorry, Valeska, I have a ton of things to do today."

"My ass you do, Jack Legris. You're just chicken to ride on that bike of yours with a crazy girl on the seat behind you." She moved in close and placed her hands behind my waist, pulling me toward her. "I'll make it worth the trip."

Twenty minutes later, we were speeding down the road on the Jawa. Valeska was pressed up against my back with her arms wrapped around me. Each time we passed a house, we could smell the farm animals or cooking fires. It took a while to navigate through the deep puddles of water that had been left over from the rain the day before.

Gradually, the muddy road turned into a narrow sandy trail, then to a hard-packed beach. We passed a cluster of tin-roofed shanties and fishing nets. This was the beginning of the Garifuna village. It was obvious that the Garifuna weren't used to visitors. The kids stared; the adults smiled, but with unsure expressions.

A little further on, the sand became too deep to ride on, so we parked the bike, kicked off our shoes and walked along a wide stretch of golden sand. There were no people on the beach, only the occasional mangy dog or stray horse. Our hands brushed together as we explored the overturned hull of an abandoned fishing dory.

We walked against the trade wind, only stopping from time to time to drink water out of the bottle that Valeska had brought along. A few miles or so from the village, we stripped off our clothes, ran into the breaking waves and dove in. After exhausting ourselves in the water, we returned to shore, lay down on the hot sand and just listened to the surf.

"Valeska, you never did tell me your real story."

"Maybe I don't have a real story."

"Where were you born? Who are your parents? Where did you grow up?"

"I was born in San Pedro Sula and brought up on my father's banana plantation. That was the place I took you to."

"I remember."

"I was an only child. I don't remember much except that life was peaceful until the situation in Nicaragua — between the Contras and the Sandinistas. Despite his relative wealth, my father was a socialist and always paid his workers well. He was also speaking out against the big American companies for buying up the best farmland in Honduras and exploiting the workers. A couple of henchmen from a big multinational came to see him one day, but he refused to sell. One night, during a plantation worker's rally, some vigilantes hired by that same fucking company came in and shot into the crowd creating chaos, then they shot my dad. After that, we lost our land. They bought it for peanuts. That's when my mother and I moved in with my uncle. I guess that was in the mid-eighties."

"Where is your mother now?"

"She's being looked after in Tegucigalpa. She has Alzheimer's disease."

"That's rough."

"Yes, but she is well taken care of. My uncle makes sure of it. I go to see her when I can, but I'm not sure that she knows who I am. That makes me sad but sometimes when she smiles, I have a feeling that forgetting about the past is a good thing."

"Perhaps it is. What about this uncle of yours?"

"Igor Zarkin is a good man. He brought me up, and I've been working for him ever since I graduated from university. He paid for everything. Now we're working on the project in La Mosquitia. Developing a project is exactly what I would like to do, and the La Mosquitia region has always attracted me. My uncle eventually wants to incorporate it into the master plan for a national park that the government of Honduras has started in that area."

"In La Mosquitia?"

"Sure, the Río Plátano Biosphere Reserve is in La Mosquitia. It's the only one in Honduras and it's a very big deal. Haven't you heard of it?"

"No, nothing about a biosphere project, but I've heard lots about the Mosquito Coast. Have you ever been there?"

"Just once. I flew in on a chartered plane with Dog and my uncle. Dog's a good pilot; he landed that plane right on the river near the ruins. We explored there for days."

"So what's it like?"

"It's one of the few remaining areas of virgin tropical rain forest in Central America and covers about two thousand square miles. And there are prehistoric Mayan artifacts. There is plenty of pine, cedar, ceiba and mahogany. You can also see rosewood, sapodilla and all kinds of orchids. You don't see that in many places north of Panama."

"A kind of Amazonia of Central America."

"Exactly, and it's only a few hundred miles that way." She pointed toward the long stretch of empty beach.

"If we continue our walk along the beach, we could be there in about a week. Shall we try?"

"No, no, *calmos chica calmos* (calm down), I don't want to be eaten alive by sand flies."

I said, "I'd rather sail out there."

Her eyes lit up. "On *Esmeralda*?"

"It could happen."

"I knew you would like the idea. I told you already that I'd talked to my uncle about you. We need a guy who we can trust to skipper the boat.

Think about it. It would be good money and we could work together. Would you do it?"

"Maybe." I thought of old Ben back at the boatyard and his theory about choice.

"Look, Jack, I'm sure he will make it worth your while. He'll pay you well, don't worry."

"No, I'm not worried about that. I just wonder how much work we could really get done. When you're around, I have a hard time concentrating, and I think that being so close to Barker there would a problem sooner or later."

"My uncle will handle Dog. Besides, I think that Dog cares more about making money, than what's going on between you and me. Besides, if he ever becomes impossible, it would be the perfect excuse to dump him." As she laughed, I thought of Chaucer who once wrote: Very often I have heard a truth said in jest.

"That's the second time that you have said something like that," I said.

"So?"

"Humm, sounds dangerous, like a Cold War about to turn hot."

She shrugged. "Sometimes conditions make associates into enemies. My uncle should know. Russian blood runs thick in our family, and my uncle is used to dealing with guys like Dog." She smiled and let herself relax as I began to massage her back. For a while we didn't speak. The sound of crashing surf filled the void.

"Yes, right there, feels so good," she finally said. "I think I'll hire you as my private masseur instead of a boat skipper."

"Okay, and then what?"

She propped her chin up with her hands and looked out to sea. I continued, working down to her lower spine, then slowly went down to her beautiful butt, and worked it for long minutes before slipping my hand between her legs.

"Do you know you're turning me on?"

"And you've been turning me on ever since I saw you this morning," I answered.

We kissed.

After we made love, we both lay there for a moment, holding each other. But Valeska rolled onto her back, shading her eyes from the sun with one arm. I sat up and ran my eyes over her sand-sprinkled body.

Suddenly she jumped up and ran into the surf. I followed her. We swam past the sandbar toward the turquoise rolling seas.

Back on the beach once more, we lay on the sand and let the warm trade wind dry us off. Our conversation drifted back to La Mosquitia.

"Tell me more about the people who live there."

"Poor, very poor. There are three peoples — the Miskito, the Pech and the Tawahka. They've inhabited La Mosquitia for perhaps thousands of years. The problem is that big logging companies are after the pine and mahogany. Clear-cutting and erosion are killing the rain forest, and if ever there's a major hurricane, the flooding could be catastrophic."

"What is the Honduran government doing?"

"The government? It's a sick joke; corruption is everywhere. Ecology means nothing when your family has only rice and beans to eat."

I changed the subject. "Valeska, I saw you and Dog at the yard the other night when that boat came in."

She grimaced. "I know you did. But it's no big deal. We're covered. We have the contacts at the base. We do what we want. Dog's got a bunch of ex-soldiers lined up who aren't afraid of anybody."

"Yeah, I know. One of them gave me a very sore rib."

"I know that, too. I'm sorry, it was bad timing." She looked uneasy.

"Where should I have been?"

"Not spying on us. That's what it looked like to the guy who bumped into you on the dock."

"Perhaps, but Barker seemed kind of upset about the way I was handled. He even invited me back to *Esmeralda* to talk about the project."

"I know that, too. The story got back to my uncle and he told me everything. I think that they both have become aware of your potential value as part of the team."

"And what about you? What do you think?"

She rolled over, sat up and took a deep breath.

"Jack, I think that we're in trouble big time. I'm very attracted to you and it's scary."

Ciudad Blanca was one thing, but Valeska was another. Her special kind of beauty, her intelligence and the way she came on to me — now this. All the alarms were going off, but I had to keep going. I was exactly where I wanted to be.

•••

It was late afternoon when Valeska and I finally pulled into the boatyard and almost crashed the bike up against some empty forty-five gallon drums that the yard workers had dumped near my boat. We laughed ourselves silly but quieted abruptly when we spotted Rackman and a few of his guys underneath *Esmeralda*. They were adjusting one of the big propellers.

"Shit, what's going on? They're not supposed to be here," said Valeska, as she descended from the Jawa. Rackman came over to greet us.

"Sorry to break up your fun but we got back early. I hope it didn't upset any of your plans." He stared at Valeska.

Valeska climbed the big ladder that was leaning up against the *Esmeralda*.

Rackman looked over at me with a grin. "If you want my free advice, you better kept it in your pants. Barker has jealous streak and can get rather nasty."

"If you want some of my free advice, Rackman, keep your nose out of my business."

•••

Early the next morning, I met Valeska in the yard behind the big hangar. I immediately noticed a dark bruise on one arm.

"What happened?"

"It's Dog. Last night he got drunk, broke into my cabin and tried to rape me. If that pig ever tries to touch me again, I'll shoot him with his own fucking gun."

She sounded convincing, There was no doubt, but her loathing was spreading. She read me perfectly.

"Jack, don't get involved. I'm returning to Tegucigalpa this morning. This is my problem and I need to solve it, myself." Then she spun around and walked away, but not without turning back one more time. As our eyes met, I knew right then and there that perhaps some day, if things worked out, we would sail away together.

The Island of Roatán

By mid-December, the naval base was on the verge of closing down for Christmas. I hadn't even submitted a proposal for an article to *Aventura* and the work on *Numada* wasn't even half-completed. And even worse, the little money I had in my emergency fund had set off the low-level alarm. Then, the mechanic at the diesel shop broke it to me that my engine block was cracked and that would mean more big bucks down the drain. There was only one way out, and it came faster than I had expected.

While working on a small welding job with Mario one day, I heard the Dog shout out. He was standing with Rackman up on the deck of *Esmeralda*, with a telephone in his hand.

"Hey, Frenchman, Señor Zarkin wants his boat down in Roatán. If you want the job, you better decide now 'cause we're goin' to leave in four days. He'll pay you two thousand on arrival. US dollars, cold cash."

Good timing, I thought. But it took me a few long seconds to give my answer. "Okay, I'm in."

For the next few days, Mario and I worked together, usually wearing soot-colored welding masks, thick leather aprons and fireproof gloves. I began to appreciate how hard he worked. We worked mostly during the cooler hours of the night under dozens of glaring light bulbs strung up like pears. It was tough going, but as we hammered and bent the steel plates into place, we communicated in our own strangely functional language — a pidgin consisting of Spanish, French and English. One by one, we cut and shaped the new pieces of metal for my schooner, while the hissing sound of acetylene gas took over from the pounding. It was as if we were between heaven and hell, living in our own world of flying sparks, molten metal and white flame. We had become sculptors caught up in the task of fusing steel together into a form that would carry me out of that place and over the blue waters of the Caribbean Sea.

•••

The sun was high over the hills when I arrived at the yard. As I parked the Jawa, I noticed that a new girl had arrived on board *Esmeralda.* She was about twenty years old, tall, athletic-looking. She was up on deck cleaning what had already been cleaned while the Dog sat there on a deck chair talking on the phone.

"Hey, Frenchman," he called over to me. "Come up, we've gotta discuss a few things."

He showed me where his charts were and explained the electronics. It all seemed straightforward. He introduced me to the new girl on board. "Shirley's from the Bay Islands and will be doing the cooking, the cleaning and any other odd job that I ask her to. They're putting us in the water tomorrow afternoon and then, around 2200 hours tomorrow night, it's off to Roatán." He slapped the side of the wheelhouse with his hand. "A little over twenty-four hours and I'll be out of this hole, and it's about fuckin' time." Dog swaggered down the deck toward the bow. "Look, everything is clean and put away, like a real efficient yacht should be."

I peered down into the cavernous empty cargo hold lined with heavy-duty panels of new marine plywood.

"There's lots of room down there, that's for sure," I said.

"Yeah, and we're going to need all of it."

For a moment, I studied the new lifting equipment between the wheelhouse and the foremast. The big new electric winches and the block and tackle system could easily handle heavy, heavy loads.

"What about the sails?" I said, looking up at the rig.

"They're all new, so is the roller furling system. You've probably noticed that the mainsail is inside the mast. You push a button and out she comes. No fuss, no bother." He put a foot on top of the huge windlass up at the bow as if he was claiming a new territory.

"That's good, because I think that we're a little shorthanded for such a big boat," I said.

"Rackman will come along, too, and he'll give us a hand. He's fished all over the Bay Islands and knows Roatán fairly well. He's also navigated up and down the coast a few times. Besides, if any of the work he did fails, he'll be there to fix it."

Shirley appeared from inside the cabin, carrying a tray with two full glasses of ice, some lime and a bottle of rum.

"Join me for a quick one — ha, ha!" Just then his cell phone rang, and I could tell by the way he answered that he was expecting the call. "Yes, exactly, bring it all down to the point with the *lancha* (a motor-powered launch) and we'll transfer it as planned. Sure it's a safe place, the best. No one will bother us there, don't worry." There was a short pause. "I'll tell you when we get to Roatán." The Dog hung up, smiling.

"It's in the bag."

After a shot of Flor de Caña, I went back to my boat and told Mario, who was working overtime, that I was going to take *Esmeralda* over to the Bay Islands.

He didn't like the idea at all. "Señor Jacques, I think Dog is a fucked-up, dangerous man. My family and I want you to spend Christmas day at home with us. It will be an honor for us. My wife will make us a wonderful dinner. *Fiesta grande, si.* (A big party.) You will be happy, eat lots of good food, drink *mucho cerveza* (lots of beer) and relax."

It was obvious that Mario's invitation was genuine. But at that moment, my mind was made up. I was itching to get away from dusty, dirty Puerto Cortés for a few days. And, of course, Valeska would be out there too; another incentive and maybe the most important.

"Perhaps you're right, Mario, but my mind is made up."

I gave him the rest of the day off, then went back to my place up in the hills and spent a quiet evening looking over the paper charts that I had of the region. It was a pretty straightforward sail, and with any luck, we'd be there in less than twenty-four hours.

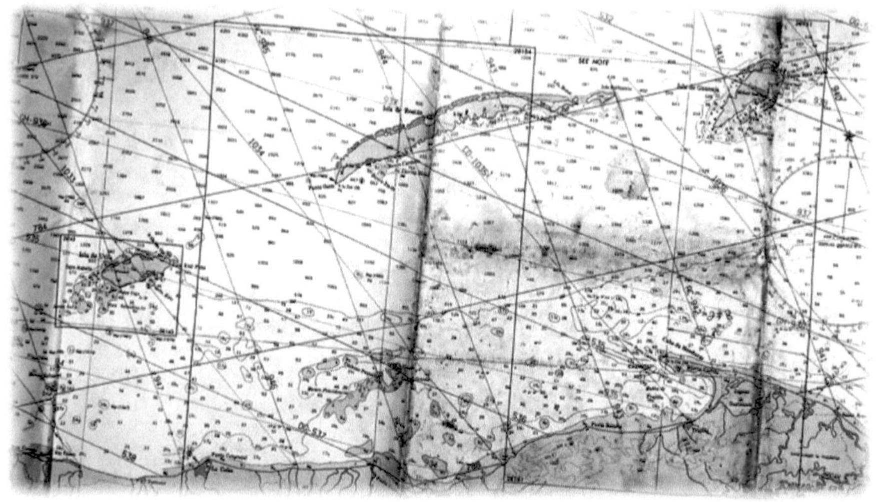

I spent the first part of the following day relaxing. I slept, packed a small bag for the trip, and rested. The plan was to leave that night when the wind died down.

Beep, beep, beep. The alarm on my watch brought me out of a deep sleep. It was 3:00 p.m. on land or 1500 hours on board *Esmeralda.* Ship time always meant adapting to the twenty-four hour system. But whatever system it was, it was time to get moving. I felt a little nervous as I grabbed my sea bag and headed down the dusty little trail on my Jawa toward the base. It was the first time that I would find myself a skipper of somebody else's yacht. I'd have to wing it.

When I arrived at the yard, the huge 200-ton sling was already in position to lift *Esmeralda* off its cradle and carry it over the slip. The Dog was up on deck shouting down at the soldiers who were preparing the move. "Don't let those straps scratch the hull of my boat! Hey, Rackman! Watch those morons! Tell them to be careful."

Ronnie Rackman was supposed to be in charge of the operation on ground level, but the soldiers would only listen to Barker and he wouldn't listen to anybody.

I climbed up on the deck just before they took the long ladder away, and came face to face with Barker. "Look how these guys work. They're going to destroy the boat before it hits the water. They don't even know how to run their own travel lift. Can you believe this?" He shouted down again at

Rackman, "Find some pieces of carpet to put in between the straps and the hull, Ronnie. I don't want any scratches."

"Pieces of carpet? In Honduras? You gotta be joking," Rackman shot back.

"Well, think of something, wise ass. If the paint gets damaged, it's coming out of your pay check."

Finally, after a lot of shouting, hand signals, and cursing, the thick black keel dipped ever so slowly into the water, like a woman dipping her toe in first. She found it nice and warm, so the rest of her 80 tons followed. The job took close to four hours of hysteria, but after a lot of unnecessary grief, *Esmeralda* was at dockside. Now all we had to do was prepare the boat for sailing. I spent another three hours tightening up the stays and shrouds. Finally, at 9 p.m., Shirley plunked a fat, greasy chicken on the cockpit table where the Dog was already seated. That's when Valeska showed up.

"I didn't know that you would sail with us."

"Yes, there have been some last-minute changes."

Barker put a hand on her shoulder. "Shit, I forgot to tell him, Valeska. Just too busy here."

She pulled away from him and turned around. "Sorry, Jack, he should have let you know, but the main thing is that I made it. What a long drive. I'm exhausted, I can hardly see straight. I'm going to my cabin to rest up a little." She stepped inside and continued down into the main saloon.

"Bitch." Barker took his eyes off the spot Valeska had occupied seconds before. "Let's look at the charts," he said coldly. I followed him to the wheelhouse.

"Frenchman, take a look at this. Here's the chart plotter. I guess you can figure it out yourself. I could never understand the damn thing. Once we're out of the bay, all you have to do is set the course and make sure that the autopilot is turned on."

"It's not that easy," I said.

Valeska reappeared. "Jack, whose watch am I on?" she asked.

"Mine, I guess. Ronnie and Mr. Barker here will be together for the other one. Four hours on, four hours off. I'll wake you when it's time," I said.

She nodded and went back inside. She seemed awkward, like she was playing a new role and just couldn't get used to the part.

Shirley shuffled up from the galley with a pot of coffee and poured us each a cup, managing to spill a few drops on the chart table.

"Go get a rag and wipe that stuff up before it ruins the varnish," said Barker without looking at her. "Frenchman, it's time to leave this hellhole. You're the captain from now on, so don't screw up."

Within an hour, *Esmeralda* was on its way out to sea. Behind it, the Bay of Puerto Cortés was a mirror sparkling under an intense full moon. It would be clear sailing all night. The Dog was at the controls, happy as hell to be underway, puffing on another one of his fat, juicy cigars. At that moment, despite everything that had transpired between Dog and me, I was glad to have made the decision to leave. The fresh sea breeze, and a ship moving underneath my feet again, made it all worthwhile. There was only one thing to do: get the boat to Roatán.

For some reason, I thought about my philosopher friend Ben back at the yard. One of his favorite sayings was, Everything had its price. I wondered how much this trip would cost me.

Half an hour later, *Esmeralda* passed the last channel marker, turned northeast and left the shelter of the immense bay. Suddenly, the heavy yacht started to buck up against the steep, short waves. A surprisingly strong breeze was blowing. I increased speed slightly and the bow plunged into each short wall of water, sending spray flying high up over the deck and all the way back to the bridge. The Dog seemed a little taken aback.

"Shit, we got it right on the kisser. We'll have to push this thing if we want to get to our meeting point on time. I'll tell you our plans. Some guys are waiting for us at a small lagoon at the end of Punta Sal. It's a well-protected hole-in-the-wall about forty miles down the coast. They have some shit to transfer on board."

"What kind of shit?"

"A few cases of equipment for the guys who are setting up at the Ciudad Blanca."

It was strange to be picking up cases of equipment at Punta Sal; that was a remote spot on the chart and known as a hideout for coastal pirates.

"Why Punta Sal? What's the catch? You said this was supposed to be a straight trip over to Roatán."

"Hell, Frenchman, there are some things I don't even know myself. Madame is calling the shots, not me. In other words, she's the boss."

Barker shifted off the seat, and standing up, he put his back to the wind.

"Don't worry, man, nobody's going to see anything. Punta Sal is so remote it's off the chart. Once the transfer's done, we'll head out, probably just before sunrise, and continue on as if nothing ever happened. When we reach Roatán, we'll offload onto a barge we have at a place called Port Royal. It's one of the best natural harbors in the entire Caribbean. The kind of place where everybody minds their own business. By the way, to be honest with you, we're picking up a load of guns that will be sent to our crew on the Mosquito Coast."

"Guns? Nobody said anything about guns."

"Yeah, I wonder why. It's a hot subject, and the less said, the better. But these guns are strictly for self-defense 'cause things can get a little hairy in La Mosquitia. Once the transfer takes place, we'll head back to French Harbour where you'll meet the man."

"The man?"

"Yeah, Zarkin. Who else?"

The Northeast Coast

The wind had started blowing even harder, and the big yacht was slamming into steep head seas. Our speed was down to about ten knots (18 km/h).

Dog was on watch up on the flybridge. He yelled down, "Hey, Frenchman, I'm nodding off. You gotta take over. By the way, you're doing great. Keep it up!"

Was that actually a compliment coming from the Dog's mouth?

I went up and took his place. The next few hours were easygoing, so I let Valeska sleep. I was alone on deck, just punching the boat the best I could into the wind. Five hours at the helm passed quickly; the auto pilot did most of the work. Nevertheless, I was glad when the Dog and Ronnie showed up on deck.

"This is our heading. It's my turn for a nap."

I went inside and collapsed on a bunk in my cabin. The sheets were clean, and the monotone rumbling of the two powerful engines soon sent me into a deep sleep.

It must have been about an hour later when I heard a loud knock on my door.

"Wake up, Frenchman, we need you on deck."

When I got out on deck, the first thing I realized was the boat was rolling uncomfortably from side to side and the only way to stop that would be to put up the main sail. Navigating that tub with some canvas up would make the ride a lot more comfortable. I shook the cobwebs out of my head and climbed onto the bridge above the wheelhouse. It was still pitch black and blowing strong.

"Barker, it's time to put the mainsail up."

"Okay," Barker said, "this is how it's done on board this ship—" and before I could say anything, he pushed a button, an electric motor whined and the big mainsail started to unfurl its way out of the mast. "It's a great invention, don't you think?"

"Yeah, but you're forcing it too much. It would be better to slow down and point up into the wind."

"Uh, oh, yeah. That's why you're here. But it's unfurling. Look at that." For a second, Barker seemed almost like a kid with a new toy. Then the thing jammed. "Shit, something's wrong. It ain't working the way it should!"

He pushed the "roll in" button, trying to pick up the slack as the sail flogged violently in the head wind.

"God damn! It's jammed up tight. Rackman, go check it out."

Ronnie didn't look very eager to go out on that pitching deck. In fact, he looked rather green. So I went onto the foredeck to check things out. When I got to the mainmast, I had to hang on and wait for a lull, the boat was rolling so badly.

"Point into the wind," I yelled to Barker. When the boat settled, I climbed onto the boom to try to figure out what was wrong. The only option was to roll up the gigantic mainsail and start again, but it was obvious that all the tugging in the world wouldn't free it up. I made my way back over the wet teak planks to the stern and climbed up to the bridge. The Dog was pissed.

"It's jammed solid," I told him. "So we'll have to live with it like that until we reach Roatán. There's nothing I can do out here."

"Will it break the sail?" asked Barker.

"No, there's not enough sail out. We'll just keep it filled with wind and it'll stop flapping. Watch."

I took the helm and eased off a little. "It will keep the boat from rolling so much. Feel the difference? The boat is being stabilized by the sail."

For a moment, Barker looked ahead in an attempt to comprehend what I had told him. "Ronnie is fucking seasick," he said. "He'll be worthless until it calms down."

"Yeah, okay, I think Valeska's in the same condition. I feel good, though, so go get some rest if you want."

Barker grunted and went inside.

I peered into the darkness as we plodded in choppy seas. There was nothing on the horizon. No lights, just a lonely, empty, dark sea and a big full moon in partly cloudy skies. Whenever the moon shone fully, the water came alive and sparkled. Whitecaps were everywhere; at times, the big yacht would shudder as it banged into the head sea, which slowed it down a few knots. Other than that, we were making pretty good progress, heading straight for our rendezvous at a place that, on the chart, seemed no more than a narrow hole in a cliff.

I went below, double-checked the GPS and marked a new position on the paper chart. Sure enough, we were right on the button. I felt a soft hand caress the back of my neck.

"Jack, how's it going?"

"Good, I guess. How are you doing? You've been hiding ever since we left."

"I wasn't feeling good, so I took some Gravol and finally dozed off." She lowered her voice. "When I was lying in bed, I could hear Ronnie and Dog talking. They were in the cargo hold, and I could hear their voices coming from the new ventilation ducts that run right through my cabin. I think they're up to no good."

"What kind of no good?"

"I don't know, I couldn't hear everything they said, but there's going to be trouble. I can feel it. Sometimes I would like to dump them both over the side."

Valeska looked in my eyes. "Dog told me that he gave you the .38 a while ago. Do you still have it?"

"It's in the drawer under the chart table. I'm not going to carry that thing around on me anymore. It's bad energy."

"Yes, but it could save your life, maybe mine too."

I pulled the drawer open and showed her the piece.

"Good, keep it there. It could come in handy someday."

"Valeska, sometimes you scare me."

I went outside and climbed up to the small flybridge above the wheelhouse for a breather. Up there, the fresh breeze hit me head-on and gave me a rude awakening. It was blowing about thirty knots.

Shortly after that, Valeska came up and sat with me, turning her back to the wind, but didn't say a word. After a long time, she got up and went inside. I was almost glad when the Dog and Ronnie finally came out on deck. After we chatted for a while, I relaxed. Maybe these two guys weren't as bad as Valeska told me they were. When I thought about it, perhaps she was the one who was causing all the trouble. There were just too many unanswered questions. Maybe she just needed someone on her side, and I happened to be there at the right time. Then I began to doubt everything I had done to get myself in the position I was in. The whole thing began to feel like a setup. Damn, how blind I had been ever since that woman had crossed my path! I decided that, once in Roatán, I would find a way to disappear.

A few hours later, the sky began to clear off to the southeast, and all of us on *Esmeralda* could see the silhouette of the rocky shoreline of Punta Sal.

"Perfect," said Rackman. "Puerto Escondido is right over there. See where the waves are breaking on the rocks? We'll go in just to the left of where the surf is breaking."

"You've been here before?" I asked.

"Sure, but not with this boat. Remember, just keep in the center of the entrance or else we'll need a new keel."

I sped up the engines. Gradually, *Esmeralda* picked up speed and slipped inside the narrow entrance on the back of a wave. Inside the lagoon, all was calm. The bay was like a lake, surrounded by palm trees and a sandy beach.

"Look, there they are," said Valeska.

Off to the left, close to shore, sat a big black *lancha* with three 150hp outboards hooked onto the stern. The thing was built for speed. It came over and tied up alongside us. There were four Latinos on board. They were well armed and nervous.

Valeska went down on deck to greet the guys. "*¿Todo bien?*" (All good?) She pointed to the crates. "Before they come on board, I want to see inside."

She climbed onto the *lancha* and inspected the merchandise. I was standing on deck beside Barker when I caught a glimpse of what was inside the crates. Maybe a dozen AK-47's, with plenty of boxes of ammunition, all neatly packed and ready to go. Barker said without looking at me, "The guys working at the site in La Mosquitia will be a lot safer with some hardware. We had to load this shit up here — it's not the kind of thing that you do at a military naval base."

Valeska finished her inspection. It was time to test the new hoisting equipment. "Okay, Dog, load it on board," she said, harshly. In a few minutes, six wooden crates had been hoisted on board *Esmeralda.* The operation was short and sweet. Once the crates had been stowed below in the new cargo hold, Valeska locked the hatch and put the key in her pocket. Then she handed a waterproof bag to one of the guys on the *lancha,* who immediately opened it up and briefly inspected its contents. Then he nodded to the guy at the wheel and they were gone. The Dog and Ronnie watched, surprised at her initiative.

Valeska came up and joined me on deck. "It's done, Jack; we have everything we need. Now let's get over to Roatán as fast as we can and unload this stuff." She saw that the guys had gone below and whispered, "Remember what I said about the guys? I wasn't thinking straight. They'll be alright." She kissed me softly on the lips.

"Forget it, Valeska. We'll work it out later. I've got to set a new course."

Still a little confused about her change of attitude, I went inside the pilothouse and put in a new waypoint on the GPS. With a push of a button, the autopilot took over. From then on, we were back on cruise control.

Esmeralda headed east toward Roatán as the four of us stood together on the bridge making small talk and watching the sunrise. Everyone knew that we had enough weapons to start a small war.

"I'm hungry. Ronnie," Barker said, suddenly, "go wake up Shirley. She'll fix us all some breakfast. That's what she's here for."

"Relax, Ronnie, I'll check in on her. She was in pretty bad shape last night," said Valeska and disappeared below. Barker snorted and spit over the side, then took a seat beside me and heaved a sigh of relief.

"Frenchman, so far so good. You're probably a little surprised about Valeska. Sometimes she likes to play the role of a real little general, but she'll be okay in a while. Right, Ronnie?" They laughed between themselves.

The day progressed as we slowly moved off the coast. The Island of Roatán was about fifty miles to the east. Off to the port side, there was the tiny Island of Útila, hardly visible in the haze. It was the most westerly of the Bay Islands. We were making good time.

Around 1400 hours, Dog and Ronnie took over, but instead of going to my cabin, I stretched out in the cockpit and watched as a few gulls played in the wind turbulence created by the boat's passage. I tried to sleep, half-listening as Valeska talked on the satellite telephone in fluent Russian to her uncle.

As we approached the island, I could see several dozen luxurious homes that had been built among rolling hills and forests on the high cliffs; they had fine views of the turquoise sea below. These homes were in stark contrast to the poverty on the mainland. We followed the coastline, sailing past small private beaches and ample anchorage. It was late afternoon when Ronnie pointed toward the two poles that marked the cut in the reef. A short time later, *Esmeralda* slipped into a large lagoon where a smattering of expensive-looking houses lay hidden in the densely forested hillside.

"Well, we made it. Welcome to the pirate capital of the Caribbean, otherwise known as Port Royal," said Dog. "See the barge on that point over there at the far end? That's where we'll tie up and dump our little cargo."

There was a shed-like structure built further back, half hidden by trees, and behind that, an airstrip. We motored up alongside. Two islanders were waiting to take the dock lines. Near some large cargo containers that sat on the barge were tools scattered here and there. A stainless steel shotgun leaned up against one of the open container doors.

Valeska made the introductions. "*Amigos*, this is Jack Legris. He'll be working for us as skipper on *Esmeralda*." For some reason, the Dog seemed nervous. We shook hands, but the reception was cool. They quickly unloaded the merchandise and stashed it inside the waiting container.

"Dog," she said, "call my uncle and make sure that the chopper will arrive on time. I don't want any screw-ups." The Dog scowled. It was clear that Igor wanted his niece to run the show.

Later she took me aside. "How do you like it so far? Easy, isn't it? My uncle set it all up out here. Don't worry about the shore crew; they can be trusted."

"Yeah, but I bet that they were handpicked by Barker."

"Yes, but we're paying them."

"What about the police or the navy patrol?"

"It's simple: There aren't any out here."

"And the cargo? What's the exact destination?" I asked, hoping for a real answer.

"That's between my uncle and the pilot," said Valeska. "They will be delivered to the excavation crew in La Mosquitia. That's all that I can tell you. Jack, nobody knows more than is necessary. Tomorrow morning, we shall head over to French Harbour. That's where we'll meet up with my uncle."

"I'll be ready when you are."

"Great," she said. She got up and went over to speak with the shore crew who were clearing a small landing pad near the shed.

I napped on deck until Shirley woke me up to share a meal with Dog, Ronnie and Valeska. While we sat there devouring leftover chicken, I began to feel uneasy about Valeska. I decided to just do my job and forget about romance.

After the meal, while Valeska was inside the yacht's main cabin going over some details with Barker, Ronnie and I managed to fix the mainsail roller mechanism. At one point, I could hear Valeska's voice drifting out of an open deck hatch. She sounded angry. "My uncle knows what he's doing. He's handled this type of thing for years. So just follow the fucking game plan, Dog!"

Valeska was in control now. As she came up on deck, the breeze lifted her dark green linen skirt and I saw that she had a holster strapped around her thigh that held a jet-black 9mm pistol. I had to admit, she turned me on.

Later on, while I was going over the charts again in my cabin, there was a knock. I opened the door and the woman slipped inside. "You must think that I'm a tyrant. Don't be misled. I'm just trying to put Dog in his place. I'm sorry if I am being too direct with the orders, but for now, that's the way it has to be. I've got to make this work, so please, just play along like you're doing, and it will all make sense later. My uncle is counting on me, and I am counting on you."

"I'm doing my best to adapt, Valeska."

"Be patient, Jack. I promise, things will improve. I am just trying to stay on top of the situation. There are some changes about to be made, and after that, things will be much easier. I want to be close to you, Jack. I know that we can do great things together. Just give me a chance to prove it. Believe in me; all I ask is for some time." She left via the narrow corridor that led to her cabin and closed the door. I was left without a clue. I decided to bend with the wind and let things work out by themselves.

Around 2300 hours, deep thumping of helicopter propellers began to drown out the sound of distant surf. The dark-colored chopper landed on the dimly lit landing strip. In only ten minutes, the cases of weapons were all loaded inside. The helicopter took off and flew toward the Mosquito Coast.

•••

The next morning, we moved the boat out of Port Royal and headed to French Harbour, about ten miles to the west. The wind was blowing hard as I unrolled the sails and, after they'd been trimmed, *Esmeralda* took off. We were travelling an easy ten knots.

"This is the way it should be," Valeska said. "Jack, you've given life to this boat. It's wonderful!"

There was a gust of wind and the big yacht heeled over. The bow dipped into a wave sending a shower of spray up and over the deck.

"Yes! I love it!" she exclaimed.

Esmeralda was really cooking now, hard over and beating into a twenty-five knot breeze. "She sails pretty good for a cargo ship," I said and then looked at Barker sitting alone in the vast cockpit, seemingly lost in thought. I didn't care. The bow plunged again and the vibration made the ships bell ring loudly. Another gust of wind hit and *Esmeralda* heeled over until turquoise seawater spilled up over her leeward deck.

The Dog shouted over to me, "Jesus, Frenchman, you're going to tip the damn thing over."

"No way, man, this is a sailboat and it's got to react to the wind. That's the way it works." With another gust, the boat heeled over even more. The beer cooler slid across the deck and stopped at Barker's feet. A wall of salty spray flew up and over the entire yacht and completely soaked Ronnie, who was wedged in a seat up on the flying bridge.

"Hey, Frenchman, you're going to sink us!"

I eased off a little until the yacht straightened up. "Is that better?" I winked at Valeska. She was standing just beside me and feeling just as high as I was. "Here," I said to her, "take the wheel." I moved over.

"Are you sure?"

"Try it, just keep it straight. There's no danger."

She wrapped two hands on the big wheel and spread her feet. "Wow."

"Keep going. You're doing fine." I was right behind with my hands on her waist. "Don't worry, it's not going to capsize. Steady as she goes. That's it. You're a natural."

"Jack Legris, this is amazing and so are you."

"I'm not too sure about me being amazing, but at the moment this entire yacht is in your hands, so enjoy."

I looked over at Barker as he sat rigid on the cockpit seat. I thought that he would boil over. "How long are we going to continue on like this? We've got to get to French Harbour before dark," he said.

"We can't go any faster than this. We've reached hull speed; even those two big engines downstairs couldn't get us to move this fast. So relax."

Another curtain of spray flew up and doused the Dog. His Hawaiian shirt was soaked. "Ah, shit, Frenchman. She's driving this thing worse than you were."

Valeska and I laughed at the same time.

"You'll have to get used to this, Barker. It's what life on a sailboat is all about."

I went over to the winches and adjusted the sails while Valeska hung onto the wheel. By the contented look on her face, I knew that she had crossed over into a new territory. That was good, because despite everything, I was, for one more time, beginning to wish that we could escape together. But before that happened, I had work to do.

•••

The French Harbour entrance was easy despite the absence of channel markers. With the sails furled, I slowly motored *Esmeralda* deeper into the bay and through the narrow pass into a lagoon, where a small marina was located. The docks were completely protected from all weather, and there were armed guards at each end of the property. Once we were tied to the dock, Dog, looking perturbed, called for a taxi and left.

"He's gone to get the Jeep," said Valeska. "I'm going to meet Uncle Igor at the airport and take him to the hotel."

I was a little surprised. "He won't stay on the boat?"

"He prefers his privacy. You and Dog can meet us around 7:00 this evening at Rick's American Restaurant. He knows where it is." She left me at the dock and walked up the path to the yacht club, where another taxi was waiting.

While Shirley washed down the deck, I went for a walk to check the place out. There were a few other sailboats dockside, belonging mostly to retired Americans who'd settled in for the winter. It appeared to be a tame place, exactly the kind of setup I always tried to avoid while cruising on my own boat. I strolled up the hill and had a beer at the yacht club bar. The view was perfect.

I could see *Esmeralda* innocently tied up to the large visitor dock in the lagoon below. It was about three times the size of any other boat in the harbor. She looked like a rich man's toy. Another hidden detail: the boat was loaded to the gunnels with Barker's own private collection of assault weapons, enough to scare off anyone who got too close. There was absolutely nothing to draw suspicion. I took out my small camera and took a few photos. They would come in handy for my magazine article.

After a long walk down a narrow road that looped through some posh properties, I went back on board *Esmeralda* just before dark, only to come face to face with Barker. "You're supposed to stay on board. We keep watch 24–7 on this boat."

"Barker, my orders come from Valeska, not you."

The Dog backed off. "Suit yourself. Dinner with Zarkin is around 7:00."

"Yeah, I know. Valeska told me."

"Hmm, you two are becoming quite a team. I wonder how long it will last?"

Then the phone rang. Barker answered and went outside. "Know where I'll be. Don't fuck up," was the only thing I could make out. He came back inside, poured himself a stiff drink and disappeared into his cabin.

I had a shower, put on some clean clothes and joined Barker on deck, where he was talking with Shirley. When she saw me, she lowered her eyes and went inside without a word.

"Ready?" he said.

I nodded. "Where's Ronnie?"

"He's on his way. Let's go, the boss is waiting."

We left the marina in the Jeep, heading east along the island's main road past the small port town of Coxen Hole. The road narrowed, snaking toward the highlands that formed Roatán's center. As we bounced over pockmarked asphalt, the Dog shouted over the racket of our thick-treaded tires. "This road is hell, especially at night."

We passed a slow-moving pickup truck and barely missed an oncoming tourist bus. As we climbed into the hills, the air became cooler and drops of rain started to bounce off the windshield. We reached the highest point on the road, and then we started travelling downhill. The Jeep's tires hummed as our speed increased.

"When did you meet Zarkin?" I asked.

"About five years ago, on a plane coming back from Miami. I told him what I had discovered in the jungle and he decided to get involved. We've been working together on this thing ever since, and now it's finally starting to happen."

A couple of kilometers later, the Dog swung the Jeep down a narrow lane, through thick jungle foliage. He parked beside several expensive cars. On a hill sat a large white clapboard house with a screened-in balcony. Its wide veranda offered a magnificent view of the sea. Inside the restaurant, because that's what it was, a few gray-haired clients were seated at the bar, drinking beer and getting older by the minute. On a massive TV in the corner, the Giants were playing the Bears.

The bartender recognized the Dog and pointed us to a table on the outside deck, where a large man in a white suit was sitting with his back to us. His cigar sent up a veil of bluish smoke.

Valeska leaned against the railing, relaxed in a tight black dress and simple necklace of white pearls. She looked stunning. I caught a whiff of expensive Chanel as she kissed me on each cheek.

"Well, well, you're a little late, gentlemen." Zarkin stood up and we shook hands. His grip was firm, and when he pulled his hand away, I noticed the sparkle of a diamond ring. The man was certainly over eighty, older than I'd expected. Otherwise, he appeared exactly as I had imagined: aristocratic and very elegant. He had a pencil-line moustache and fine gold-rimmed glasses on his hooked nose.

Valeska smiled at me and put one hand on her uncle's shoulder.

"Please have a seat," he said. "I've heard good things about you, Monsieur Jacques. I'm glad you've decided to help us out." Though spiced with a Russian accent, Mr. Z's English was near perfect. The bartender brought over a bottle of ice-cold Veuve Clicquot and poured us each a glass.

"Nothing but the best," said Zarkin. He had overdosed on Azzaro cologne that blotted out Valeska's fine fragrance. Even the bougainvillea and orchids that grew nearby were having a hard time. "I understand that you are a Frenchman from Canada."

"Not exactly a Frenchman. I'm from Québec, a Québecois. There's a difference."

"All the same race of shit-disturbers," said Dog.

"Come on, Dog, you can do better than that," Valeska objected.

"I find Canadian politics most amusing," said Zarkin. "You live in the best country in the entire world yet some people want to separate. Those separatists should try living in Russia for a while and compare lifestyles. I wonder what they would think then."

"Yeah, it's a never-ending story and another reason why I left," I said.

A king-sized order of langoustine arrived at our table with a bottle of Chardonnay on ice. We ate slowly as we made each other's acquaintance. Seeing Zarkin and Dog together for the first time made their business partnership seem odd.

After a while, Zarkin said, "I raised Valeska after her father was murdered. Although our family had money, we were Sandinista supporters. We went through difficult times, misunderstood by both sides. It cost us dearly. Things are better now."

The Dog smiled a little foolishly and glanced at his watch.

"I propose a toast to our new skipper," said Zarkin,

The Dog shot me a cool glance from across the table. As the meal progressed and the wine flowed, he became bolder. He had a bone to pick with Zarkin — over money, naturally. Eventually, he stood up and left the table. He went to the bar.

"He's an impatient and dishonest man, and someday he'll pay for that," said Zarkin as he watched Barker disappear. He wiped his brow with the table napkin. "Jacques, I'm glad that you are going to be skipper of *Esmeralda*. Valeska felt you'd be the perfect man for the job and I trust her judgment. The timing is perfect. We need someone who knows what he is doing, a man we can rely on. I think a fellow like you will make the difference to our little organization." He looked at me square in the eyes.

"But there are a few things that I can't quite figure out," I said. "Do both you and Barker own rights to the land where the ruins are?"

"They are now in the company's name. We are co-owners. He found the place, but I am the financier. Without my money, there would be no project."

"And without his discovery, there would be no project?"

"Exactly, but things will be different soon. I'm going to buy him out, you know — as they say, make Barker an offer he can't refuse."

"But, Señor Zarkin, he's not going sell; he wants it all."

"Maybe so, but there are other ways that may help that scoundrel pack his bags. However, before it comes to that, I will take him to court. I have proof that Barker has been cheating us on the renovation costs. He's colluding with Rackman, and they've been skimming off the top for months. They both are a liability to the project. I need people that I can trust completely. I have a lawyer building a case that will prove that Barker is a fraud. In fact, I can have him arrested any time I want and he knows it. Barker will sell, I am sure of it."

Valeska looked at me, then at her uncle. "Uncle Igor, careful, he's coming back to the table."

Barker crossed the floor while he talked on his cell phone. There seemed to be a problem on board *Esmeralda*. "Okay, just shut down the main circuit breaker. I'll be there as soon as I can." He hung up. "Ronnie says there's a strange smell coming from one of the electric panels. Something is overheating. I have to go back and take a look. You'll have to find a taxi."

"I'll go with you," I said.

"No, no, don't bother. Stay here and enjoy yourself. I'll look after this with Ronnie." With that, Barker hurried out of the restaurant, but Zarkin didn't look worried. Valeska seemed strangely distant, or lost in thought.

Conversation turned to Zarkin's latest passion. "Jacques, this job could be a chance of a lifetime," he said. "Once we sell enough artifacts, I plan to make Ciudad Blanca into a world-class archaeological center. Something like the ruins of Copan here in Honduras or the pyramids at Chichen Itza up in Mexico. It will be a major attraction, an important addition to the tourist industry in this country. Valeska will be in charge." A waiter came over and refreshed our wine glasses. Zarkin stopped talking until the man had left. "Selling select pieces that we take out of there this year will allow us to turn the dream into a reality. There is an extensive worldwide market for these objects and the prices are skyrocketing."

"Don't worry, Jack, there are enough artifacts to make everyone happy," Valeska added, winking at her uncle.

"Soon you'll see the site with your own eyes. There is no other place like it in Central America, or in the world for that matter," said Zarkin. He smiled and shook his head. "I can read your thoughts. You want to know where the site is, don't you? But you'll have to wait a little while longer before I reveal its location, my friend. Up until now, it has been a guarded secret between Barker and myself. Even Valeska hasn't a clue, despite the fact she accompanied us once."

Valeska added, "When we flew out there, they wouldn't let me even look out of the plane's window until we landed on the river. I just know that it's somewhere in the mountains, south of the Mosquito Coast."

"You'll both learn its precise location soon enough. Now, Monsieur Legris, let me tell you more about your assignment. Twice a month, you will take *Esmeralda* from Roatán to a river entrance on the Mosquito Coast. You will pick up the artifacts then transport them to our depot in Port Royal, Roatán, where they will be cleaned and classified and safely packed in crates." He took another sip of wine. "All you have to do is sail the yacht and make sure it arrives safely and on time to each destination. The ground crew will do the heavy work. Valeska represents me. Until we finish up with Barker, I want her to keep stricter control over the financial transactions. The people who work for me are specialists in what they do. Out there on the Mosquito Coast, we need a good navigator. After each delivery, $4,000 is for you. US dollars. Cash. If something breaks, call me and I'll send somebody out to fix it. If you need anything or have a problem with anybody, let me know. I don't want any trouble. And I expect you to keep your mouth shut. Officially, *Esmeralda* is a charter boat that visits the Mosquito Coast."

I nodded in agreement, but what the hell was I getting myself into?

"And … I'm counting on you to keep an eye on Valeska. She's all I've got."

I looked over to Valeska, then back to old Uncle Igor. "Okay, sir, count me in."

"Here's to our new partnership." As our glasses clinked, I couldn't help wondering if I would ever be able to escape this arrangement in one piece.

As if to ease my qualms, Zarkin handed me an envelope. "This is for bringing my boat to Roatán. There's a little more than I promised. You've earned it. Welcome aboard."

So I had now joined one big, happy family: the beautiful, dynamic, sexy girl, her millionaire uncle, and a thriving business-in-the-making. I had just become my own victim, trapped in my own plan. I faked another smile, shook hands with Zarkin, kissed Valeska. It was getting late, so we finished our drinks and got in a waiting taxi.

The Bumpy Ride Back

Zarkin sat beside the driver, and Valeska and I sat in the back. By now, Zarkin was rambling. He had begun to repeat himself. Valeska put her hand on mine, then gently moved it over me. I closed my eyes, feeling a little high from all the wine. I leaned my head back and enjoyed.

"I'd rather spend the night with you," she whispered in my ear. "But I need to take care of my uncle while he's here. We'll be together on the boat. Jack, I'm really looking forward to that."

Suddenly, bright headlights came up from behind. A big, dark pickup truck pulled alongside us. Our driver swore. There was gunfire. The driver slumped. Our car swerved. I felt weightless as our vehicle lifted off the ground and began to roll.

"This must be it," I thought. I remember flying through the air, cartwheeling free in a slow-motion spin and then landing face down on a cool, wet muddy surface. I felt no pain. I heard no noise. All I could do was attempt to float back up to the surface again, back to the place I was before. But the space I had once known was gone, and the future was dark and empty. Was this death?

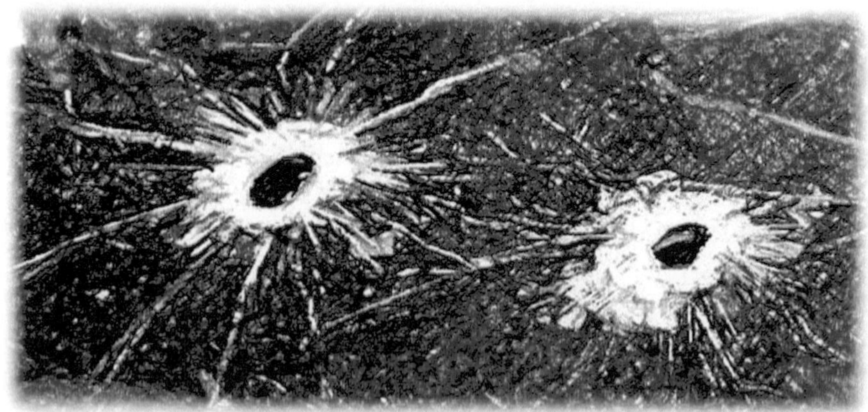

I vaguely remember beginning to focus on the shadows. On the ceiling above me, something small and dark crawled along slowly, stopping and then moving again. I closed my eyes.

A bird cawed outside a window. Thin rays of sunlight cut through the lowered shutters that separated the brightness outside from the dankness inside. A nurse appeared and calmly began cleaning the mud off my legs with a cool wet sponge. She didn't say a word, but I could feel the care through the slow movement of her hands. When the nurse left, her shoes made a clip-clop noise.

I awoke sometime later. There was a small brownish dog sniffing at a pile of muddy clothes in the corner. They were mine. I had an IV that was connected to a half-empty bag of fluid. The skin surrounding the IV port was blue and swollen. My head was bandaged. My chest hurt so much I could hardly breathe.

A doctor entered the open door and looked at me. He pulled a chair next to the bed and said quietly, "There's nothing I can do for you here. You have too many fractures in your right arm. You need surgery as soon as possible. We just aren't equipped for that at this hospital. You will have to be moved to a facility that can provide a higher level of services than we can." He left before I could really comprehend what he had said, or even ask for something to reduce the hammering ache in my skull.

I closed my eyes and tried to make sense of the words I had just heard. My entire body was throbbing with a deep, grinding pain that intensified as I lay there. Something was wrong with the right side of my head. It felt numb. I had serious injuries to my arm, my shoulder and my ribs.

A nurse materialized beside me and shook her head at the tubes in my arm. "That's not right, the needle isn't in the vein. That's why your arm is so swollen. This isn't good at all. Who did this?" She unstrapped the tube connecting the needle in my arm. "You're going to feel a pinch." She found a vein with the needle. "Don't worry, I've been a nurse for fifteen years. The swelling should go down now."

"What happened?" I didn't recognize my own voice.

"They found you at the bottom of a ravine. The driver is dead. Señor Zarkin is still unconscious. He received three bullets to his chest."

"And the woman?"

"Only scratches and a slight concussion."

I closed my eyes and tried to relax.

"You're lucky. At first, they thought you were dead. Do you remember anything?"

"Not much. Where are the others?"

"In a room at the end of the hall. You need to go to a real hospital; this is just a clinic. The woman who was in the accident with you has chartered a plane that should arrive this afternoon to take you to Tegucigalpa."

"I want to see her." For a second, I couldn't remember her name.

"She's with Señor Zarkin."

"Oh yes, Zarkin," the name was familiar.

With much effort, I sat up slowly and swung my legs over the side. I stood up. The nurse helped me get my balance. A dull, throbbing pain shot through my right shoulder down to my arm. Every joint in my body ached. I shuffled down the dank corridor, pushing the IV pole.

Zarkin was lying in a small, dark room that smelled of disinfectant and bug spray. His lips and eyes were swollen. His chest was wrapped in bloodstained white cotton. When Valeska saw me, she froze for a second.

"Jack." She looked frail. Her face was scratched and her fine black dress was covered with mud. She had an ice pack on one foot. Zarkin lay there, looking up at the ceiling, unable to speak. His skin had lost its color. I tried, but I couldn't say anything, and for a moment, the room started to spin. The nurse felt me go and held me up.

"They weren't ordinary bandits," Valeska said in a low voice. She was trembling and there was fear in her eyes.

"Barker?" I asked.

"Who else? We were set up, Jack. I should have seen it coming."

A few hours later, I was loaded into an ambulance. Zarkin was on the gurney next to me. Once it reached the airport, paramedics wheeled us toward a two-engine plane. Valeska was a blur. There were a few nurses and a doctor standing around Zarkin. It didn't look good. Everything seemed to be going too fast. I could feel Valeska's hand caressing my face. I remember a door closing and the roar of the engines as they turned over. Then nothing.

The next thing I knew I was a passenger riding in another kind of ambulance, racing at high speed through what seemed to be bumpy, narrow streets. I saw the world rushing by through the rear windows. Twisted electric wire attached to wooden poles, clouds of dust, street signs, beeping horns and billboards full of people with smiling white teeth and bottles of brown soda. This was Tegucigalpa, the heart of Honduras.

When we finally arrived at the hospital, the medics unloaded us in front of the emergency department. They rolled me past groups of tired, ill people. Some were standing, others were sitting hunched over, and a few were stretched out on the floor. There weren't enough plastic chairs to go around.

No one said a word. They just moved aside as if they'd seen this before: a *gringo* being escorted by two or three paramedics, while the local sick and injured had to wait in the corridor for days before getting treated. My stretcher had a high-pitched squeaking wheel. The corridor smelled strongly of formaldehyde and I felt very cold.

They placed my gurney in a tiny room and moved me carefully onto a narrow cot against the far wall. There were no windows. There was a single florescent light. It was a private room, albeit the size of a broom closet and located next to the morgue. In the corridor beyond the separation, I could make out people talking in low voices. After a while, a youthful nurse came and took blood, and soon after that, an orderly with a plastic pan asked me if I wanted to urinate.

"*Más tarde*," I said. (Later.) At that moment, I just couldn't handle having to pee in a bedpan.

A doctor came in and asked a few questions. Then a nurse injected me with a green painkiller. I passed out thinking about organ trafficking. Perhaps my body parts would pay the bill for the airlift to Tegucigalpa. The sound of the accordion door sliding open woke me up. It was another orderly with a plastic bottle of water and a small cup.

"*¿Un poco d'agua, señor.*" (Would you like a little water, sir?) He seemed more sympathetic than the previous one.

I drank straight from the bottle, my first drink since Roatán. Another doctor came in and pulled the door closed behind him. He wore a clean white coat and held a clipboard in one hand. He examined my arm and said, "Multiple fractures, but I can operate. It will be complicated, but I'm confident we can do a good job. This is the best hospital in the country." I could barely see his face in the dim light.

"You know best."

"But this surgery will cost you."

"How much?"

"About fifteen thousand US dollars."

That was like another kick in the ribs.

"No, *gracias*, Señor Doctor, I'm going back to Canada as soon as I can. I don't have to pay anything in Canada. It's free."

"Free? Canada is a socialist country?"

"Yes, we have free health insurance in Canada. It covers everything."

The doctor looked at me suspiciously. He must have taken me for an American *gringo*, but the idea of having to deal with a Canadian *gringo* with access to free health care took some wind out of his sails. He tried to negotiate, he lowered his price, but there was no way I was going to pay. Finally, he left.

For a few long moments, I lay there alone, thinking about my next move. There was really only one choice: return to Canada. But first, I had something more urgent to do. I managed to get up, wrapped myself in a sheet, stepped into the corridor and asked a nurse where the toilet was. She looked at me with an uncertain expression and pointed down the hall.

I must have looked like a zombie. No matter, I walked on, pushing my IV pole past dozens of people waiting on white plastic chairs. Some ate snacks out of crumpled tinfoil, a few talked together in low voices, while others just stared blankly. I finally found the bathroom. It contained a single toilet and no light. Used toilet paper had been tossed in a corner, the sink was blocked with crud and the walls were filthy. Beside the rust-stained toilet, a sour-smelling mop sat in a dirty plastic bucket. If this was the best damn hospital in the country, I wondered what the others looked like.

Later someone came into my room and gave me morphine. It felt good. When I awoke, I felt a little better and began thinking about how to get back to the coast, back to where I should have been before this mess got out of control. It wasn't going to be easy.

The door slid open and the orderly scurried into my room. "Señor Legris." I nodded. The door slid shut, followed by another long silence. A few minutes later, the doctor came in, followed by another man in a suit whom I'd never seen before. The doctor went through his routine and fed me another dose of pills. The other man seemed to be some sort of administrator.

"Where is Valeska?" I asked.

"*Calmos, calmos, Señor*," said the orderly. (Relax, sir.)

A sharp pain ripped through my chest and I started to cough up a little blood. The orderly grimaced, wiped off my face and changed the top sheet. After that, I must have nodded off. When I woke up, the small room was empty, and for a while I just lay still and listened to the faint shuffling sounds that came from the corridor. Just when I was beginning to feel as low as I could get, the door quietly slid open and someone walked in. In the dim light, I could make out the outline of a woman.

"Valeska?"

As she approached my cot, her eyes widened. "Jack, what have they done to you?"

"Luckily, not much. Do I really look that bad?"

She took a breath and I could see a tear run down her cheek.

"Hey, I am so glad to see you."

She sat down on the chair beside my cot and wiped her eyes with a towel. She looked as if she had been crying a lot.

"Your uncle?"

"He's gone. The funeral was this morning. I can't believe that this has happened."

"Valeska, I'm so sorry. This has turned into a real mess."

"And what about you? When are they going to fix your arm?"

"They're not. I have to go back to Canada."

"Canada? But are you strong enough to leave?"

"Strong enough or not, I've got to get out of here."

Valeska lowered her voice. "Listen, I contacted some people in Roatán yesterday. The wreck of that taxi has disappeared. There are no traces and the police aren't saying a word."

"It's Dog Barker; he set the whole thing up. That piece of shit."

"He organized everything right under our noses. We were completely taken in."

But despite the tears and reality check, Valeska seemed completely grounded. She looked at my bandaged arm. "What do you need?" she asked.

"A pair of shoes; mine were lost in the accident. And I haven't eaten since I got here. Room service is lousy."

"I'll go and get you something right now." Valeska came back shortly with a pair of cheap rubber sandals, a can of V8 juice and a taco wrapped in aluminum foil. I ate like a refugee.

"What about Barker and the boat?"

"Evaporated, disappeared. And of course, I'm sure that there is still a contract out on me."

"What do you mean?"

"I was about to have legal shares in the company just in case this kind of thing happened except that we never got around to it. The boat and everything else is owned by the same company, and with my uncle out of the way, it all technically belongs to Barker. But legally, it won't be that easy if I am still in the picture."

"Got it. But there's not much we can do here. Let's get the hell out of this place as fast as we can."

"Are you sure that you will be okay to leave?"

"What choice do I have? If I stay here any longer, they'll probably take me into the room next door and start removing my body parts. Valeska, I've got to go back to Puerto Cortés. I know it sounds crazy, but I have to settle a few things before I leave for Canada."

"Okay, in five minutes, I'll be outside the main entrance waiting in the car. Meet me there." She helped me dress, then left the room.

It was around 2 p.m. when I limped out onto the sidewalk in front of the hospital. The blinding sunlight reflecting off the buildings on the other side of the busy street made my eyes water. The late afternoon heat was suffocating. I thought I would pass out. To my right, a legless man sat on a piece of cardboard begging for money. I was thankful for my own legs. At least they still worked. Across the street, two armed guards stood on the steps in front of the Banco Atlántida building.

But where was Valeska? I was just about to panic when a beat-up cream-colored station wagon pulled up in front of me. Valeska got out quickly, opened the front passenger door and helped me inside. For a long moment I closed my eyes and every part of my body screamed with pain. But I was free from that stinking dungeon. Before I was properly settled, Valeska got in on her side, put the thing in gear and stepped on the gas. As we weaved through the flow of busy traffic, a certain sense of liberation swept through my whole being.

"Hey, Valeska, you saved my life."

"Yes, but hang on tight. We're not exactly free yet."

She turned sharply down a lane that joined a busy boulevard.

"What happen to the SUV?"

"I left it at my uncle's house. Everybody around here knows who it belongs to. This car belongs to a friend." She hit the brakes to avoid a stray dog. "This will do for now. It's old but it runs fine."

"I wish I did," I said.

Valeska drove fast through the crowded city with its shanties, drunks and beggars limping on improvised crutches. In the center of town, armed guards stood in front of almost every store, bank and government building. At the outskirts of town, dusty roads were lined with junk and garbage. She zigzagged in and out of crowded buses full of workers leaving the *zona libra* sweatshops. Often, she just leaned on the horn and cursed in Spanish. Once she ran a light, nearly sideswiping a Pollo Rey delivery truck.

"Valeska, maybe you should slack off a little with the speed."

Her eyes shifted to the rearview mirror. "Sorry, Jack, we are being followed."

"Followed? By whom?" I turned around. "The gray pickup just behind us?"

"Yes, I'm sure it's Ramón, one of Dog's henchmen."

"Yeah, and he's not alone. There's another guy riding with him. Hey, wasn't Ramón close to your uncle?"

"Yes, but Ramón would pull out his mother's heart and give it to you in a bag if you paid him enough. Hang on, Jack. I'm going to lose them." She swerved around a traffic circle and then stepped on the gas. In a few minutes, we were speeding up a narrow mountain road beyond the ragged suburbs on the outskirts of Tegucigalpa. The trees were sparse. The air was fresher than in the polluted city. Suddenly, Valeska veered onto a dirt road that led us down into a valley. The gray pickup missed the turn. It was the last we saw of it. She sped up as a cloud of dust billowed up, blotting out the setting sun. "We're going to stay on the back roads for a while."

"You really know your way around."

"I've spent a good part of my life here."

We passed through a cluster of tin shacks that were home to squatters. Everything vibrated, including my broken bones. I popped a few more painkillers and just hung on. We emerged at an intersection to join the main highway that would take us to the coast. The sign read, "Puerto Cortés, 180 miles."

"Shit, that's a long way."

"Just hang on, we'll get there before you know it." She smiled, and the panting old Mercedes wagon took off down the paved highway that led to the northern Caribbean coast of Honduras.

It was a wild ride all right, mostly downhill. I couldn't help but admire Valeska. She was a pro at dodging mudslides, farm animals and pedestrians. She seemed blessed with the power to pass anybody anywhere and return to the right side of the road before striking an oncoming vehicle. I tried to convince myself that the odds of having another accident in the same week were next to zero.

It was late afternoon when our dust-covered car pulled up to the naval base in Puerto Cortés. When the guard saw me, he hesitated for a second, but then he recognized us and opened the gate. It was Sunday, the last day of the year. Most people were preparing for a big fiesta. But my mind wasn't on the party.

Familiar sounds filled my ears: a grinder buffing steel, a hammer knocking on new plate. Mario the welder and others had stuck it out and were still working on my boat! I couldn't believe it. At a quick glance, I could see they must have worked fiendishly to finish the long list of jobs that I'd asked them to do during my absence. The sparks were flying and, amazingly enough, things had gone ahead without me.

Valeska parked and helped me walk over to the scaffolding where the guys were perched. The harsh work lights that hung overhead shone brightly over the large hull. It was obvious they were on a roll and rigged up to finish late. On seeing my sorry state, they dropped what they were doing to stare at me. My pants were bloodstained. They clambered down the scaffolding and gathered around and listened intently as I told them what happened. For a moment, I thought that Mario would break into tears. He said, "I told you so."

Ben the philosopher climbed down the ladder from his boat and shook his head.

"Jacques Legris, it looks like you're lucky to be alive."

"Ben, this is Valeska. It's a long story, but she's going to be staying at my place for a while. I have to go back to Canada and get patched up."

I gave Mario instructions to close up shop and cover the boat after he had finished the welding.

"Mario make sure *Numada* is *brillando como nuevo* (shining like new) when you come back here," he said with a wide grin. I was sure that he meant it too. Ever since he had started working on the boat, he had kept his word.

Ben drove us up to my shack on the hill. We would be safe there for a while. The front door key was still in its place under the rubber doormat. Inside, I turned on a few lights and looked around. The dark green walls seemed even more oppressive than ever. My things were untouched. I'd been away only a week. A shirt hung on the back of a chair, a pair of sandals were placed on the floor in a corner, a half-read book lay open, and there was a bag of dirty clothes in the bedroom. However messy, it was home, my secret shelter, and now a place for Valeska and me to hide. Only Ben and Mario knew where I lived, and now they were the only men I could trust in Honduras.

I was running low on painkillers and antibiotics, so Ben and Valeska hurried into town to find a pharmacist before everything closed for the New Year. I stretched out on the ragged sofa. It was going to be a long time before I would be okay. My head pounded and my shattered arm throbbed. I popped the last of my painkillers, closed my eyes and tried to relax.

Since leaving Tegucigalpa, my arm was slowly turning blue. For the first time, I began to worry about saving it. Even with the pills, the pain was constant. As I drifted off into a troubled half-sleep, village sounds seeped in through cracks in the walls: the dog barking next door, a pig grunting, a radio, but everything seemed dislocated and unfamiliar.

"Jack, wake up."

I could feel a hand on my shoulder, but for a moment I couldn't figure out who the owner's voice was. Valeska's face came into focus.

"Here, you must take these. They are antibiotics. Ben says that if infection sets in, you could lose it."

"Nice thought," I said, and swallowed the pills and the entire glass of water she gave me.

"Jack, I'm worried about you. All this is my fault."

"No, Valeska, it was my choice to get myself involved. This is just a rough time. It will pass."

"I'm not too sure. Dog wants to finish us."

"Forget about Barker for the moment. He's gone, probably already somewhere on the Mosquito Coast."

She looked at me and didn't say anything. I could see that she had her own plans.

•••

Later that evening, I felt like I'd had too many painkillers. It was New Year's Eve, and the noise outside made it impossible to sleep. Valeska helped me stand up and washed me with cold water and soap. Then she dried me off, wrapped me in a towel and helped me outside so we could sit on the balcony where there was a slight breeze. In the hillside neighborhood, everyone was setting off fireworks. The air was already laced with thick smoke that drifted through the trees and down the road. People on the other side of the street danced to a distorted confusion of salsa tunes. It was hours before midnight, but everywhere it seemed obvious that liquor was flowing.

After a while, I returned back inside and lay in bed. Valeska sponged water over my body in an effort to cool me down. Cherry bombs exploded more frequently and closer to the house, until rays of ultra-sharp, multicolored light flashed through the cracks in the wooden planks. An eerie blue haze began to fill the room. It smelled like gunpowder. When the final countdown came, there was a concert of exploding bombs, gunshots and honking horns mixed with the long deep blasts from the dozen cargo ships at anchor in the Bay of Cortés. The New Year had finally arrived and with that, a kind of truce.

As the sound of the explosions faded away, I must have finally dozed off only to awake a few hours later. Soft moonlight seeped through the open window as I watched the sleeping woman who had suddenly become the focal point in my life. Despite the scratches on her face, she seemed peaceful and relaxed, her body half-covered by a tangled sheet. In the semi-darkness, the movement of the curtains projected shadows on the wall. I hadn't felt that peaceful for a long time. I got up and quietly limped out onto the porch, where I could feel the beauty of that first tropical New Year's morning, and took it all in because in a few hours, I would be on a plane to Canada, far away from this chaotic and dangerous life. I heard Valeska call my name, so I went back inside and lay down beside her. She was still asleep, probably dreaming.

Valeska drove me to the airport in San Pedro in silence. It was only after I bought my ticket home at the American Airlines counter that we found words.

"I wish that you were coming with me," I said as we held each other tight.

"So do I," she answered. "Call me when you get home and let me know when you are safe, okay? Promise?"

"For sure. But what are you going to do?"

"I'll go back to Tegucigalpa, stay with friends. It's safer than Cortés. Just don't worry about me, Jack Legris."

There was no choice and we both knew it. Before I went through security, we kissed for the last time. She pressed her hand to my chest, pivoted and disappeared into the crowd.

Once on the plane, I felt like I had just been released from prison. What would I do if I ever ran into the Dog again? Despite all the trauma and grief I had just been through, I couldn't shake the idea of writing about the mysterious Ciudad Blanca and about Barker's gang. It would be my own kind of vengeance. And my boat? I knew deep down that Mario the welder would finish the job. Then there was Valeska De Sela, she was constantly in my thoughts. Would I ever see her again? Only time would tell.

Part Two

In Québec City, I was given a private hospital room. The doctor thought that there was a risk I might contaminate the place with a contagious disease from Honduras. It was a stroke of luck. Compared to what I'd experienced in the hole that I'd been thrown into in Tegucigalpa, the sweet-smelling, well-lit room was a palace. During the day, I lay in my bed just watching snowflakes fall outside the window and thankful for the continuous IV drip of morphine— which helped me forget my boat, Honduras, the Dog, Igor Zarkin and even Ciudad Blanca. But I couldn't forget Valeska. It would take more than those drips of pain reliever to make me forget what we had been through.

Surgery began a few days after my arrival. It was the first of many operations. Then for days I just slept. When I began to feel a little stronger, I called my friend the Chief. "Where the hell are you, my friend?" was all I could say when he answered.

"Québec, *amigo*. I'm on a ship dockside. I've just finished putting in a new piston on the main engine. I'm working like a horse, but they're paying me like a pony. And where in Christ's name are you?"

"Le Hôpital de l'Enfant-Jésus, Québec City."

"Some kind of a joke?"

"No, Chief, for once it isn't. That's the real name of this place."

"But what happened?"

"I got smashed up in a car accident down in Honduras. My arm's broken in four places, a few cracked ribs, you know, the usual."

"What room?"

"304."

"Don't move, I'm on my way."

"Chief, not so fast. Bring me some warm clothes. I only have my tropical rags with me."

"Got it."

Very shortly, my loyal friend was standing beside my bed with a bag of warm clothing in one hand and winter boots in the other. "If it weren't for bad luck," he said, as he looked at the plaster cast that went from my hand right up to my shoulder.

"Yeah, if it weren't for bad luck, I'd have no luck at all. You're right about that, Chief."

"What happened?"

"Do you have time?"

"I can spare an hour."

"After you left, life … escalated."

"Go on."

"I was waiting for some help with *Numada*. I got mixed up with some of the people in the boatyard."

"You got involved."

"Yeah, I met a woman."

"Trouble, I warned you."

"It wasn't all her fault."

"It was yours."

"Yes."

"It's starting to sound like vintage Jacques Legris. And?"

"Her uncle was a wealthy man and respected in certain circles."

"Meaning?"

"He was behind an archaeological project."

"Go on."

"It's a major, newly discovered site out in La Mosquitia. Ruins, artifacts— He wanted me to join the organization and skipper that big motor sailor that was parked in front of *Numada*. Remember?"

"Yeah, that big green thing. You got mixed up with that guy?"

"Uh-huh, yeah. That guy, his boss and a woman. I accepted an offer that I couldn't refuse. I needed the money. But I got caught in the crossfire."

"And the woman?"

"She ran the show for the business partner — her uncle. He stayed in Tegucigalpa. He was the money. We three met for dinner because he wanted to size me up, and he wanted me to know what my job was. On the way back from the meeting, the three of us took a taxi. The woman and I were taking him back to his hotel in Roatán when some goons pulled alongside us and started shooting. The driver was killed. The uncle took three bullets in the chest. The car rolled over, that's when I got hurt. The uncle died a few days later."

"What about the girl?"

"She was lucky, only a few scratches."

"And I bet that she wants vengeance."

"Big time."

"It sounds like a movie script. So what's your problem?"

"The problem is the girl. I want to see her again."

"Shit, after all that? You gotta be kidding."

"Nope, it's the truth. All the way."

"Does she know that you are in the hospital?"

"No, I've tried to call her a few times but no answer. I'm kind of worried that she may be in serious trouble."

I filled him in on the details.

"Incredible. And now what?"

"I've got to go back to Honduras, find the girl and finish repairs to my boat. And Chief, there's something else."

"Naturally."

I told him about Ciudad Blanca and my desire to find it.

He locked eyes with me for a long moment. Finally, he said, "Legris, you haven't changed. You just like trouble."

"It's personal, Chief."

"Trouble usually is. When will you be in shape to go back down to Cortés?"

My mind raced. "It's anyone's guess right now."

"Well, just let me know 'cause I'll go back with you and put some order into that boat of yours. After that, you'll be on your own. Again."

"Thanks, Chief, it's a deal."

He handed me a card. "This is the ship's satellite phone number. Call me any time you want. I've got to get back to the ship. We're leaving tonight."

And with that he was gone, Chief-style.

The hospital discharged me a few days later. Once again, I found myself standing on a sidewalk in front of a hospital, this time with my arm in a clean white cast, a few chipped teeth, and my spirits rock bottom. I grabbed a taxi and told the driver to take me to Carré d'Youville. I had an apartment near there.

It was early evening, a light snow was falling, and the air was freezing. A few skaters swirled around on the rink in front of Palais Montcalm. I couldn't help but think to myself, why look for a lost white city, I was in one already. It had been a long time since I'd experienced winter, and the chill went straight to my bones.

Inside the massive stone of Saint John's Gate, workers were putting up decorations for the winter carnival. I felt alive again. The nightlife on Rue Saint-Jean was a welcome change from hospitals. It was Friday night, so the sidewalks were teeming. There was a line outside Pub Chez Alexandre. I could hear a jazz band playing "Summer Time." I turned off Rue Saint-Jean and walked along the narrow Rue Couillard to the heart of the Latin Quarter. The aroma of fine cooking permeated the air as I passed a busy restaurant. My steps made a crunching sound in the snow. In front of a bar called L'ostradamus, a few students huddled, smoking joints. They looked more half frozen than high. I slipped into the small *épicerie* (convenience store) beside the Temporal Café and bought a baguette and some coffee. On Rue Hamel, I stopped in front of a building with a Scottish brick façade. It was part of a row of similar structures that had been built mid–nineteenth century. I looked up at the triangular window that filled the gable of my small fourth-floor walk-up.

Unlocking the door, I slowly climbed the four flights that led up to my hideaway. At the top of the stairs, I punched the numbers for my electric lock on a panel at my front door — the year of my birth. The Chief would not have approved of a code so easily deduced. But I had never made a habit of following his advice, or anybody else's. The door buzzed. I opened it and stepped inside. My simple furnishings were exactly the way I'd left them. There was only a plain table and four chairs, a double bed and a sofa. On the walls hung black and white photographs of friends and of film shoots in faraway places. On one wall, Spencer Tracy's face looked down at me with intense dark eyes from a hand-painted film poster. "The Old Man and the Sea" was written in bold yellow script over a small boat. Had I become that man? I smiled. The kitchen, off to the side, was sparse but efficient. I put my bag of food on the counter and paused.

"It's the Jacques Legris museum," I said to myself. It all seemed foreign, something from another life. After turning up the thermostat, I went into the bedroom, lay down, closed my eyes and listened to the silence of a winter's night.

•••

When I awoke early the next morning, I was disoriented. But the brick walls, wooden beams, and familiar furniture and devices quickly snapped me back in place. Here were my books, my photos on the wall, a disconnected telephone on a wooden table, an ancient-looking PC and printer in another corner.

I made coffee and toast, dressed as warmly as possible, and went out for a short walk. It must have been at least –25° Celsius and strong gusts of ice-cold Arctic air blew in off the river. It was the kind of wind that would make any normal soul drop to their knees in desperation. I went back to my apartment, turned up the heat to the max and went back to bed.

Over the next few days, I spent most of my time looking out the window waiting for some kind of sign of life from Valeska. The painkillers took away most of my initiative. I tried her cellphone a few times: nothing. So I tried reading but couldn't concentrate, my cooking needed inspiration, and watching television was as boring as always. I felt that I was slowly drifting away until one day, around noon, my phone rang.

"Jack?"

The connection was crystal clear, as if she were speaking to me from next door. "Valeska. Where are you?"

"I just got back to Tegucigalpa."

"Are you okay?"

"Yes, I'm fine, but I had to hide in the mountains for a long time. There is no cellphone service up there."

"I was worried."

"Don't be. I'm safe. And what about you? Did they fix your arm?"

"Yeah, but it took two weeks in the hospital and three operations. Now I'm back in my apartment for now. And Barker? Any news?"

"He's disappeared with *Esmeralda. Hijo de puta!* (Son of a bitch!) And according to my uncle's accountant, Barker took most of Uncle Igor's money from the company's account and moved it to an offshore bank in the Cayman Islands. The only thing left is the house."

"You uncle's house?"

"Yes, that's it. My uncle was too trusting, and the more I learn, the worse it gets. It seems Dog even bought off the notary and forged legal documents in the name of Zarkin Negocio making himself sole owner of the company. We should have gotten rid of that bastard when we had a chance." Her voice turned vicious.

"Valeska."

"I'll kill him."

"Please, Valeska, stay away from him for now. I don't want to lose you."

"I'll be okay, Jack, believe me." She was quiet for a moment. "Okay, enough with my problems. What about you?"

"I'm just taking it easy, trying to get back to normal."

"Have you seen any friends?" She seemed concerned.

"Not really, and I have a hard time concentrating. The doctors say that's to be expected because of the quantity of morphine that I've received. But I'll recover."

There was another silence. Then she said, "Jack, there is good news too. I've been spending time in the archives here at the university. I found lots of information about Ciudad Blanca — of course, much of it is legend. It's fascinating. I'm also doing research on the Internet. I'm learning a lot."

It was exactly what I needed to hear.

"We'll sail to the Mosquito Coast when I return."

"With your boat?"

"You bet. I still want to write about that area and maybe do something about the trafficking of stolen artifacts. Maybe we could even go into the jungle and try to find Ciudad Blanca. It will blow Barker away. Are you interested?"

"Of course, but if Dog and his gang are there…"

"Do you really think that he would stick around after what he's done?"

"Maybe you're right. He's probably gone to Colombia to make new contacts. But we don't know where Ciudad Blanca is."

"But you were there, you must have an idea."

"All I know is that it's in the mountains and that Dog landed the plane on a river not too far from the ruins. But that was more than five years ago."

"Your uncle must have had a map?"

"I'm planning to go back there now that I'm home and spend more time looking next week. There has to be some kind of information somewhere."

"Just be careful."

"Don't worry, there's a guard there full-time."

"Wait for me before you do anything drastic." But the line went dead.

No Place Like...

The comforts of home were sweet: a good bed, a hot shower and lots of books. Ever so slowly, my bones started to mend, as did my memory, my capacity to concentrate and my ego. I had Internet put in my flat and started to read up about La Mosquitia and the Ciudad Blanca. However, it was slow going, and working the PC keyboard and taking notes with my left hand felt awkward. Three times a week, I would take a city bus and visit a therapist who would work on my right arm, wrist and hand. Every so slowly, they were beginning to function but they would never be back to normal. Even with these new activities, I just couldn't keep my thoughts off Valeska. The more I thought about her, the more I felt she was luring me into a maze of trouble. She wanted vengeance. When I called her a week later, she sounded really wound up.

"I'm working with a lawyer. I'm going to sue Dog Barker and then send him to jail."

She was getting involved in a story without an end. When she'd gone to Zarkin's house to search for more information, she found that the guard had disappeared and the house had been ransacked. Hidden away in a drawer she discovered an external hard drive containing copies of the correspondence between Zarkin and Barker. But there was absolutely nothing about the location of Ciudad Blanca.

"Valeska, please back off," was all I could say. I felt helpless. I wanted to get back to Honduras as fast as possible and make sure that she didn't end up somewhere in a shallow grave.

•••

During the deep freeze of January and February, life inside the walls of this frozen white city seemed to stand still. It snowed and it snowed. It was always magical when the footprints and tire tracks disappeared again. Sometimes a horse-drawn *calèche* passed me.

In Central America, the streets were loud and chaotic. I knew I had to go back and finish what I had started with that amazing woman. But my right arm was still immobilized from my shoulder to my fingertips and my neck still felt twisted; however, my brain was healing. I started to frequent Belley's Pub and mingle with the small crowd who usually gathered there after work. It was a friendly place with brick walls and a fireplace, a good haunt for anybody looking for a conversation.

One day, a long-lost friend walked in. It was Eddy, a documentary film producer. Together we had spent months in Northern Québec filming dozens of documentaries — mostly about a nomadic First Nations tribe called the Innu. Our trips up to Northern Québec were always worthwhile. We had good chemistry. As I filled Eddy in about what I had been through in Honduras, I could imagine him coming along. Clearly he was thinking the same thing.

"It's a subject people love: ruins in the jungle, Maya history, illegal trafficking in artifacts. You're in the middle of the story." Eddy pondered, "A film shot in a foreign country is hard to finance, but what an incredible chance! We just have to sell the idea." Then he laughed. "What about this Dog Barker guy? By the way, I love the name."

"Yeah, me too. But I don't love the man. He's disappeared with most of Zarkin's money and his yacht."

"Or maybe he's hiding somewhere, waiting for this to blow over," said Eddy.

"Anything's possible. Another beer?"

"Sure."

I called for two more.

"This could make a great documentary," he said. "I'm almost sure that if we write up a good synopsis, I can get financing."

"You think so?"

"Sure, people eat up this kind of adventure. But it sounds dangerous as hell."

"Not if we can find the right people to take us there," I said.

"Yeah, but the problem is: Where is there? You said yourself that the Dog is the only swinging dick alive at the moment who knows exactly where these ruins are."

"Yeah, and there was also Zarkin, but he's dead."

"But he must have left something behind, some information, a map…"

"I know. Valeska's working on it but she hasn't had any luck."

"Ah yes, the girl. Every time you say her name, you drift away into another zone." With a wide grin on his face, Eddy sat back and nursed his beer. "It must be love."

"Maybe it is, but these days it's long-distance love. But hey, let's talk about the next step."

"I agree. I know of a few distributors who could pick up a project like this. We could get an advance sale from one of the TV networks. You know, we've done a lot of crazy projects together and they have always worked out. But be prepared; I may have to pitch you as the guy on camera. You have a reputation, and a fairly good one at that."

"Eddy, those days are long gone. I'd do anything else, even record the sound."

"You may have to do that as well."

Two days later, I spoke with Valeska and we went through all the new developments in each of our lives. On her end, there hadn't been any changes. No sign of Barker or *Esmeralda* and no more information about the location of Ciudad Blanca. It looked as if he and his gang had really sailed away. Valeska seemed more focused on legal issues. She was basically staying out of sight and working with lawyers, trying to find a way to get her hands on her uncles' money that had been transferred by Barker to the Cayman Island account. But it looked more and more like a lost cause. As for me, it was a bit more positive. I brought her up to date concerning my project with Eddy. My health was improving, and sooner or later I would be able to join her in Honduras. We reminisced about making love on the beach, under the falls, and how that all seemed so far away. Were we drifting apart? Perhaps.

•••

As weeks went by, the midwinter sun shining through my loft's large skylight, I began to feel better. My strength gradually returned. Every afternoon, I would put on my heavy coat, slip into my snow boots and hike up the Rue des Remparts to the boardwalk next to the Château Frontenac. It was ideal exercise, but the view overlooking the frozen Saint Lawrence River made me colder. Its beauty was vast and desolate. It always amazed me to watch the ferryboats cross from the shore opposite the Old City, carefully pushing their way through thick, swirling ice floes to bump up against the pier just below where I stood. It all seemed like an endless struggle — the ice, the cold, the wind and especially the lack of the sweet tropical fragrance that I had become so used to. However, there was still something poetic about the place. It was a town made out of stone cut out of the rocky cliffs that lined the river. It had witnessed war, revolution, epidemics of typhoid fever and cholera. Québec wasn't just a pretty town; it had depth and a story that went way back, long before recorded history. Maybe that's why I was attracted to its narrow streets and stony walls.

At times I watched teams of rowers pull their long oars in unison through the thick river pack ice below: centipedes, with oars for feet. Off in the distance to the north, the rolling Laurentian hills stretched for hundreds of miles up the tundra where caribou roamed by the thousands. The oldest fortified city in North America had the luxury of still being surrounded by forests and farmland. In every direction, there was a horizon to contemplate, to observe and to dream about. The favorite part of my walk was when the seemingly endless sunset turned the cloudless sky a vivid orange, melting into deep blue before a lone Venus appeared in the northwest. I wondered if the same planet was looking down on Valeska.

One evening, after one of my long walks, I went down to Chez Belley to meet up again with Eddy. But this time he wasn't in such a good mood. He had just been rejected by two governmental film-funding agencies. Since the last election, there had been budget cutbacks, and several of his valuable connections had been replaced with a breed of by-the-book bureaucrats with their own priorities and their own friends. After looking over our proposal, they refused to put a dime on the table, insisting that the project needed further research, detailed description and a better presentation.

Despite everything, Eddy tried to stay optimistic, but it wasn't easy. In his experience, the investing network usually refused most documentary film projects at least once, so Eddie was still confident that we would eventually get things moving in the right direction. It would just take time and more hard work. Eddy was part Innu and had been producing documentary films about First Nations people for years. But to the conservative investors, a film about people looting artifacts from lost Maya ruins near the Mosquito Coast was perhaps too exotic.

"Canadian content, that's the problem. They said the project doesn't have enough Canadian content."

"But they're wrong, Eddy. Dog Barker is from Alberta, and he's the one who got me going in the first place. You can't get more Canadian than that, can you?"

Eddy leaned forward and thought a little.

"The problem is that your Dog friend is definitely not going to cooperate with us. He may be a central figure in our story, but we'll have a hard time getting him on camera." Eddy leaned back in the chair and ran his fingers through his long silver hair. He meditated for a while, staring into his beer mug. "You know, Canadians have a reputation as world leaders in the purchase of all kinds of illegal objects. They're much easier to smuggle into our country than into the US."

"That's an interesting start," I said.

"It's more than interesting, it's hot. Smuggling pilfered Mayan artifacts is in the same category as drug trafficking, dealing blood diamonds or pushing stolen weapons." Eddy rose from the chair, stretched, went over to the window and looked out onto the narrow street. "But we need something else … another angle. Ah, shit!"

"Ah, shit what?" I was sure he was onto something.

"I completely forgot about the parking meter. I'll be back in a minute."

I ordered more beer, and when Eddy came back, the brainstorming continued.

"Eddy, I just had a flash. Remember what the Innu say up in Natashquan?"

"Sure! *Nushuit ishe pukenanu wapush,*" Eddy said in Innu. (There are two ways to skin a hare.)

"Exactly. I was going to say the same thing. Did you know that there are theories that the Maya are distantly related to Canada's northern aboriginal peoples? And that some of their mythology can prove it? These are elements we can build on. What we need is for an Innu to join our expedition and team up with some locals on the Mosquito Coast."

"You're onto something. We'll put a Canadian Indian in front of the camera, not a Jacques Legris like you."

"Eddy, you've finally seen the light. So let's go hunting."

After a few more beers, our meeting was over. I wove my way up the hill and then up the wooden stairs that led to Rue Hamel. Once back at my flat, I flopped down on the sofa and fell asleep with my coat still on. A few hours later, the shrill ring of my cell phone brought me out of my dreamless stupor.

"Jacques, guess what? I think I've found it." Her voice was fresh, full of positive energy.

I was still in a daze.

"Valeska? Found what? Where?"

"At the university, the archaeology faculty wants to help."

"Go slow, I just woke up. Who wants to help?"

"I met with the archaeology department directors yesterday and explained to them some details about our project. They want to help out! They have given me access to all the information about Ciudad Blanca that they have."

"How about the Ciudad's location? Do they have any leads?"

"Not yet, but close. They support our project completely and will give us as much information as possible. They believe a film would be a valuable tool, since they have neither the money nor the manpower to protect or explore all the nation's ancient sites. Their new museum could use all you can give them: photos, films, charts, everything."

For the rest of that night, I just couldn't sleep; there were just too many wild ideas spinning in my head. With the exception of the car accident, all I'd asked for had come about. Once more, the trail was beckoning to me and there would be no turning back.

A few days later, they x-rayed my arm at the hospital. It seemed to be healing perfectly. The titanium plates holding the bones in place were doing their job. A few more weeks of physiotherapy would be all I would need to get my arm working properly.

More good news, spring had finally arrived. It was about time. Rue Saint-Jean was effervescent with pale-faced pedestrians emerging from winter hibernation. Street conversations always lasted longer when the weather warmed up and people seemed in much better spirits. I sat on a bench in the old Protestant cemetery, watching the squirrels playing between the trees and the tombstones. They seemed underfed, but a summer of acorns and lunchtime leftovers would fatten them up for sure.

The next day there was one of those early spring snowstorms and about thirty centimeters of heavy white stuff was dumped on the city. But that didn't stop Eddy. He was able to plow through the drifts with his 4x4 and meet me at my flat on Rue Hamel. It was time to put our heads together and do some real research. Hours later, papers and notebooks were stacked up on the table. Despite the mess, we had a method: Eddy concentrated on the physical aspects while I worked on the human side. In mid-afternoon, we began comparing notes.

"Okay, listen to this," said Eddy. "Most of the Mosquito Coast area south of the shoreline is the Río Plátano Biosphere Reserve. It includes half the Paulaya Valley and part of the lower Sico Valley to the west, Wampu Valley to the south and part of the lower Sigre Valley to the Patuca River further to the east. Take a look." He had printed up four pages and Scotch-taped them together to make a good-sized map.

"That's a hell of a lot of land to cover. I hope Valeska can find the exact position. If not, we'll be looking for the rest of our lives."

"Which will be pretty short if we stay in that jungle too long. Along the coast, it's probably swampy. The rivers that flow from the mountains have been used for centuries for navigation into the interior."

"So it's logical to assume that Ciudad Blanca must have been built on one of these rivers."

"That makes sense."

"This means we could take a boat up there. That would make things a lot easier than hacking our way through the jungle."

We looked over the map and studied various possibilities. But it was just a map and we were still in Québec City with nothing solid to go on.

"What's the best time of year to travel there?" asked Eddy.

"It's hot and humid all year long, especially from May to November."

"And the rainy season?"

"Rainy season? It's deluge season. October and November can be pretty bad; it can rain nonstop for days. It's impressive."

"What's the vegetation like?"

"It's pretty dense, but I'll read you a rapid description that I wrote down the other day. Look, I've learned to write with my left hand. Quite a difference, eh?" I leafed through the pages in my notebook. It was strange because ever since I had changed hands, my handwriting was really different.

"Ah, here it is. 'La Mosquitia is part of the largest surviving area of undisturbed tropical rain forest in Central America. Most of the territory is a very hot and humid plain, crossed by numerous streams and rivers including the Plátano, Patuca, Waruna, and Coco rivers. A forest-covered mountainous region is found inland. La Mosquitia is a main route for drug trafficking from Colombia and is accessible primarily by water and air.'"

At that instant, a boom came from the street below. Eddy got up and went over to the window and looked down to where the snow crew was trying to clean up the mess in the street. A big snowplow was using its shovel to push the snow that blocked the lane in front of the building.

"They don't have to dig up artifacts to get rich," I said. "It's shovelling snow that pays the big bucks here in this city."

My Innu friend agreed, stretched, came back and sat down at the table. "Go on, tell me more," he said.

"Okay, wait a second." I turned a few pages and came across more description. "Okay, this is interesting. 'There are more than three hundred species of birds, jaguars, ocelots, tapir, monkeys, puma, deer, giant anteaters, crocodiles, iguana, and loggerhead and leatherback turtle.'"

"Well, we won't die from hunger, that's for sure."

"Have you ever eaten iguana?"

"Never, and I don't really fancy it, either."

"Oh, and there's another thing I read: There are lots of snakes."

"I hate snakes," said Eddy.

"Too bad, because there are pit vipers, *barbe amario*, rattlers, boas, anacondas and the two-step."

"Two-step?"

"That's right, but it's not some kind of polka dance; it's a deadly viper. After its bite, you just have time to take two steps before you keel over and drop dead."

"Pleasant thought. What else?"

“The people who live there are the Miskito, the Tawahka and the Paya or Pech. There is also a small Garifuna community that lives along the coast. They are of Afro-Caribbean descent. The Miskito are the largest tribe. In the old days, it was the Paya who built the temples and the cities; these people were an offshoot of the Maya. The isolated Tawahka live at the south-eastern edge. They live off the land or from fishing.”

“Lots of poverty, I bet.”

“Sure, but they have managed to preserve their land and culture there more than any other place in Central America. Their isolation has been their best protection.”

“Same thing as the Innu here in Québec,” mused Eddy. “And did you find anything new about Ciudad Blanca?”

“For what it’s worth, there are many different legends about Ciudad Blanca. The place was one of the last cities of the great Quetzalcoatl Kingdom that thrived throughout Central America centuries ago. This was a culture that was extremely wealthy, and gold was a real commodity used by artists to fabricate all kinds of objects.”

“This is amazing stuff: ‘The legend of the fabulous Lost City of Honduras was first recorded by Hernán Cortés. In 1526, less than five years after vanquishing the Aztecs, he went to the colonial town of Trujillo, on the north coast of Honduras, to look for the fabled town of Hueitapalán. *Hueitapalán* means *old land of red earth.* Cortés’ search marks the beginning of the Ciudad Blanca legend, as well as the first of many failed attempts to find the ruins.’” I flipped through some more pages and came across some information that I had collected a few days before:

“Here is another interesting piece that I found: ‘In the year 1544, Bishop Cristóbal de Pedraza, the Bishop of Honduras, wrote a letter to the King of Spain describing an arduous trip to the edge of the jungle. He described looking east from a mountaintop into unexplored territory, where he saw a large city in one of the river valleys that cut through the Mosquito Coast. The native people of that area said that east of the San Pablo Sierra existed a land called Veragua where there was a city that was populated by goldsmiths. This seems to confirm the legend of a mysterious lost city filled with treasure.’”

“Hmmm, more stories about gold. Every time you describe a new legend, it mentions gold,” Eddy commented.

“Yeah, gold is everywhere. It’s hard to imagine.”

I continued reading.

"Quetzalcoatl, god of the sky, was once considered a great legislator. He organized the original cosmos and participated in the creation and destruction of various world periods. Quetzalcoatl ruled the fifth world and created the humans of that era by descending to Mictlan, the underworld, gathering the bones of the human beings of the previous epochs, and sprinkling his own blood upon them. He is also a god of the great winds. As the father of culture, he introduced agriculture and the calendar. According to yet another tradition, he left on a raft of snakes over the sea. In any case, what is important is that Quetzalcoatl had light skin and a beard."

"Light-skinned with a beard. That sounds kind of strange. Did Vikings go that far south?" asked Eddy.

"Anything is possible, but according to these ancient writings, this man-god and his disciples were said to have come from a race of white-skinned people. Who knows? Maybe they were survivors of the lost continent of Atlantis. When the Spanish conqueror Hernán Cortés appeared in 1519, the Aztec king, Montezuma II, was easily convinced that Cortés was in fact the returning god Quetzalcoatl."

"So I guess he had the key to the city, lucky man."

"Since then, the legend has continued to grow. Jungle travellers, including hunters and pilots, have occasionally reported a large area of overgrown ruins in La Mosquitia. Several explorers launched expeditions to find the city, and some thought they did. In 1939, for example, explorer Theodore Morde, who may have had ties to the CIA, supposedly found Ciudad Blanca, and later wrote a bizarre travelogue called *Lost City of the Monkey God* just before dying. Even his death is a little foggy. Some people say that he was run over by an automobile in London, England. Others say that he committed suicide. Any way you look at it, the guy is as dead as a door nail and can't help us."

"Maybe the place really does have a curse, after all," said Eddy.

"Could be." I continued, "Here's something about the wind gods. According to a certain Lazaro Flores, a Honduran anthropologist, the native Pech people say that the citizens of Ciudad Blanca were allied with the spirits of the great storms. The Monkey God, who is supposed to be one of the principal symbols found within the ruins, is this type of storm god. In other words, when the place is disturbed by unwanted intruders, all hell breaks loose."

"A good reason to be careful," Eddy mused.

"Yeah, it seems that local aboriginals prefer not to talk about the Ciudad Blanca. They say that the placed is cursed."

"And it seems like they want it to stay cursed if you ask me."

"Yeah, it seems so."

"You believe in the supernatural?"

"I'm beginning to. What about you?"

"Sure, the invisible world has always been part of Indian culture. Besides, it's good intrigue for the documentary."

"It sure is, but besides that, here's something else to think about. For the last fifty years, there has been a great deal of looting in dozens of archaeological sites all over Central America. That's the heart of the subject. Looters work with anything from picks and shovels, to tractors and explosives — even helicopters. These days, pilfered objects can range from portable artifacts to huge stone sculptures, which are sawed into slabs, taken out and then exported all over the world."

Eddy looked at me with a smile. "Indiana Jones, all over again. It's going to be an amazing documentary. We just have to complete the financing."

Every film project needs a producer and each has his own way to work. Eddy knew the ropes as well as anyone. I had no doubts about that. However he was a purist, worked alone, and often took a while to get a film into production.

That night, I spent hours jotting down more notes and thinking about the film. We had to find a story, something that would hold the whole thing together, and time was going by way too quickly for my liking. We had a hot subject, but at the rate we were going, we would be forced to begin shooting in the rainy season. That would make things even more difficult, but on the upside, I figured the rain would add atmosphere to this crazy adventure.

Over the next week, Eddy knocked on doors to find financing. Now he was waiting for word from the agency people who held the real purse strings to get the project rolling. At the same time, I worked long hours on a project synopsis that would explain exactly what we planned to do out there. Would it be a film about the international trafficking of Mayan artifacts taken from La Mosquitia, or a jungle expedition into the Biosphere, or a travelogue up a river à la *Heart of Darkness*? In the end, it always came back to the same thing: We had to locate the damn place. Maybe just finding the place would make a good start. We'd deal with the rest afterwards.

I was still awaiting a call from Valeska, and her long silence was making me nervous. The phone rang late one night, and for a second I was sure it was her. I was wrong.

"*Kwei, kwei!*"

I was surprised at Eddy's late night call. "*Kwei, kwei* to you too, pal. What's up?"

"I can't sleep," he said.

"Neither can I. There's just too much going on right now."

"I've got some more information that I think you'll get off on."

"Shoot."

"I heard through the Indian telegraph that there's a guy in town this week with a whole bunch of Latin American connections who deals in artifacts on the black market. Maybe he's worth meeting. You know, explain that you're looking for something special. Perhaps we could meet the guy together and film the conversation with a hidden camera, the way we filmed developers from Hydro-Québec trying to make a crooked deal during the days of the Great Whale Hydroelectric project. A company in town has a camera that they rent out that's even better than the one we used. The quality has improved a lot since the last time we worked together, you'd be surprised."

I didn't need much coaxing. "Well, let's rent one for a few days. I can't wait to get into action."

"Okay, I'll set up a meeting through my Mohawk friends. The dealer is staying at none other than the Hotel Château Frontenac."

"Great, that's just next door."

I appreciated the way Eddy always liked walking a tightrope. Meeting a perfect stranger in a hotel room with a hidden camera needed a lot of cool.

Three days later, Eddy and I were inside a chic and brassy Château Frontenac elevator. We were on our way to Room 1503, where we were to meet a contact who thought we were buyers. I had a miniature fiber optics camera in an attaché case. The lens that was built into the bottom looked exactly like a small metal stud. It was well camouflaged, and so was the microphone.

"Nothing but the best," Eddy said as he looked at my case. It was crafted from expensive leather and went well with the suit I was wearing — which I had borrowed from the department store Simons. A soft bell rang and the elevator stopped gently at the top floor.

I switched on the camera. "Okay, rolling."

"Let's have some fun."

The brass doors slid open and we turned down the posh hallway toward Room 1503. We both felt a little out of place and nervous. I knocked on the door, waited and then tried again. I had the strange feeling that someone was looking at us through the fisheye. The door opened slowly and we came face to face with a chubby man with a short graying beard and tinted eyeglasses.

"Gentlemen, please come in. I'm Boris Gulkin. I have been expecting you. I hope that you men like coffee? I've ordered a fresh pot."

Gulkin was all smiles and spoke with a heavy accent. Another Russian, I said to myself. It must be my new karma.

"Fontaine is my name," said Eddy. "And this is my associate Mr. Fortin."

Gulkin smelled like he had just fallen into a vat of potent aftershave. What was it with these Russians, anyway? If we had been outdoors, I would have stayed on the windward side. Gulkin's palm was sweaty when he shook my hand. We crossed the large room to sit at a beautiful antique table placed in front of a king-sized canopy bed. The view of the Saint Lawrence River was splendid. I placed my attaché case in front of me with the business end pointing toward the Russian. After exchanging a few pleasantries, he didn't waste time.

"Mr. Fontaine informs me that you're in the movie business. Internationally?"

"Exactly, I produce films." Eddy and I had cooked up my story and fake name the previous day.

"Pornography?" he queried with a smile.

"Yes, but it's up and down these days." I looked over at Eddy.

"It's big business in Russia."

"And growing," I added for good measure. Everybody laughed.

There was a knock at the door and a waiter in a black monkey suit and bow tie came in pushing a cart with a silver coffee pot and three sets of porcelain cups and saucers. As we served ourselves, I explained that I was building a big house on Île d'Orléans near Québec City. Soon it would be time to decorate.

"What exactly are you looking for?"

"My dear wife is Peruvian and is rather eccentric. She wants authentic Maya carvings to adorn the area surrounding our pool and flower gardens."

The Russian smiled, sat back and thought for a few seconds. "I may have something very nice, sir. It would be pre-Colombian of course, from Central America. These are beautiful items, very popular with my best clients." He began to look through his laptop. "I have ceramics, jade, gold plates, boulders with petroglyphs and animal sculptures. I can even get a slab, if you desire."

"You have slabs?" I asked.

"Yes, my friend — Mister … excuse me, I've forgotten your name."

"Fortin, Michael Fortin."

"Da, da, Mr. Fortin. A slab, meaning a piece of stone carved with hieroglyphs, or perhaps you would prefer carvings?"

"Well, perhaps both."

"Excellent. My specialists can cut them from a new location where we are working. In fact, I can acquire a big stone column depicting a man in a feathered costume. It's believed to be about thirteen hundred years old. It's about nine feet high, a real masterpiece. This is a bit more complicated because of its size, but this is what everyone is looking for these days. I'm sure that a woman such as your wife has excellent taste in art."

"Yes, she certainly has good taste. The more expensive, the better."

"Don't worry, it's normal for a woman." Gulkin laughed. "Here are a few examples of what we have to offer."

Eddy and I moved around to his side of the table and watched him flash through a dozen images on his laptop.

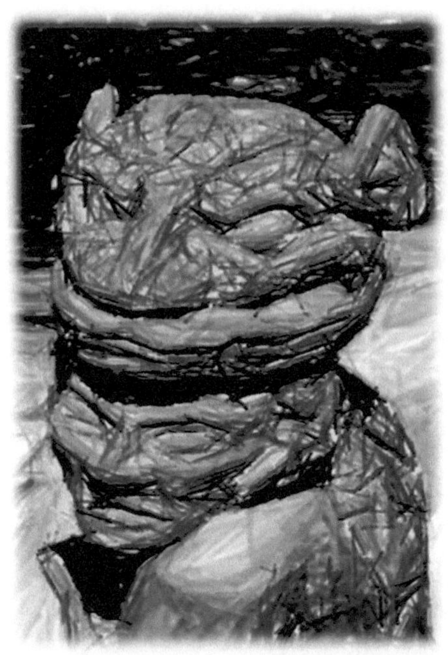

"I can get you all kinds of things like these; they are all authentic, trust me. This is my business. I'm a professional, one of the best. I don't cheat anybody. I think that you need an agent like me just for your own security. Do you know what I mean? You pay one-third of the cost up front and the rest when the goods arrive."

I played along some more. "Taking this out of a country is illegal, isn't it?"

"In Central America, there are two kinds of people who take out valuables. The looters, who will uncover a site and then work there for months — they are concerned with removing only the most valuable pieces, like gold, jade and precious stones. The rest is often destroyed because they work with crude picks and shovels. They're like animals. Then, there are the archaeologists who spend months digging in these places living off public money. They aren't saints either. They have a reputation for keeping the nicest pieces for themselves. I consider my business to be the best of all evils. My crews take their time, saving the most beautiful pieces for export. We don't destroy a thing. *Messieurs*, I am a man who cares about artistic value. I feel I'm doing a great service to humanity, and I work hard for my money, however modest it may be. As for prices, my friend, like anything else, it depends what you want to buy. Now for starters, what about several good-sized stones with carvings and five or six small petroglyphs, maybe some like these?" He scrolled through various photos on his laptop. They were of magnificent pieces, artifacts of all sizes and shapes.

"This sculpture costs about $120,000 and weighs about two hundred kilos," he said. "Transportation is extra, obviously, but I could throw in some extra pottery and masks as well. If you want a bigger slab, you pay more. All my pieces are exceptional."

"And how much would that be?" I pointed to an intricate stone calendar.

"Very expensive! It is written clearly on it that the world will come to an end sometime soon, but you will have to buy the piece to find out exactly when. Better hurry up and enjoy it now while you can. Da. We have to bring these things here plus pay a few people to look the other way. I'm being honest with you. You're getting a great deal."

"How safe is it?"

"Sure, very safe. This is Canada, remember. It's as corrupt as anywhere else, Mr. Fortin, and as you probably know, human nature is the same all over the world. We Russians are champions in this department." He paused for a gulp of coffee. "A man in my trade must be creative and a little careful at times, especially when doing business in the United States. That's why I like to work here in Canada. It's much easier. Canadians are a lot like Russians. In fact, I sometimes deal with a Canadian fellow down there, a real cowboy. I have exclusive access to some very nice pieces from a newly discovered site."

"Where would that be?" I asked casually.

"It's a small world, Mr. Fortin; these are trade secrets."

At that moment a kitsch Russian-style *yo ho heave ho* ringtone emanated from his pocket. The Russian retrieved his cell phone, excused himself and disappeared into a bedroom. He shut the door and ran the water to drown out the sound of his conversation.

Eddy looked at me and winked. Boris Gulkin was cool; he seemed to know what he was talking about. Moments later, Gulkin came out and excused himself again.

"Business, business, business. It's amazing how many clients I have in this little city. Believe it or not, I have some who work in the government." The phone rang again and he left the room for a minute. When he returned, he seemed preoccupied and pressed to end our meeting. He discretely closed the cover of his PC.

"So, my dear sirs, you call me when you're ready to place an order. Da. After selecting, you can deposit 25 percent of value up front. When the goods are delivered to your home, and when you're certain that your wife loves you more, just deposit the rest in my account, and then, comrades, the deal is done."

"Very good, Mister Gulkin, I'll call you when I'm ready."

"I understand, but don't wait too long. Presently, I can deliver within thirty days. Waiting is not good for people in hurry like you, Mr. Fortin. Your wife won't be pleased. I am here for another four days."

In the elevator, I said, “Nice stuff, Eddy, our first scene is in the can.” We shook hands, heartily congratulating each other for our fine performance. That evening, Eddy and I screened the sequence shot with the mini-cam. It was far from perfect, but it did the job.

“Do you think he was suspicious?” I mused.

“Sure, but he has no fear of getting busted and absolutely no scruples. He could probably sell ice to an Inuit. Peddling articles robbed from prehistoric Mayan sites means nothing to him.”

The next day, Eddy returned the spy camera to the rental house and took the bus to Montreal where he had a meeting scheduled with a possible partner. Late that afternoon, I walked over to the local bank, rented a safety deposit box and placed the footage of our Château Frontenac scene inside.

That evening, the phone rang while I was finishing a dried-out slice of leftover pizza. “Hey, Jacques Legris,” Eddy said. “I have good news. The Native Television Network wants to get involved. They like our synopsis; I signed an agreement with them yesterday. We’ll have some money to work with — not much, but enough to get started.”

“You’re kidding!”

“No, for once I’m serious. I have all the production equipment we need to shoot and edit so we won’t have to rent a thing. The rest of the financing will follow as we proceed.”

“Hey, you’re one hot producer, my friend! We’ll celebrate when you get back to town.”

“There’s only one hitch.”

“There’s always only one, go ahead.”

“They want you as the guy in front of the camera.”

“There’s no way I’m going to return to being in front of the camera. It would be a step backwards for me.”

“Ha, I got you there. I am kidding this time. They asked for a Native person on camera and I think it’s a good idea.”

“Sure, it could be a real plus. Does the Native Television Network pay well?”

“Enough to do the film. And I have the rights to sell it in any other country that I want.”

We were finally in business.

•••

It was late spring by the time Eddy finally finished the tedious job of locking off the contracts with the film's financers. Most of that had taken place in Montreal. The day that he showed up at my flat in Québec City he looked a little dishevelled but happy to be ready to begin the next step. It didn't take long before we shifted into high gear and began to turn our ideas into reality. We started by making lists, lists for everything: equipment for the boat, freeze-dried foods, sauces, a new inflatable dingy, an outboard, tools and spare parts, a repaired sail, emergency flares, rope, pots, pans, snakebite antidote and a whole slew of medical supplies. Eddy made another trip to Montreal to meet with the Native Network people. They had become hesitant. The synopsis that we had written still wasn't what they had in mind. There wasn't enough Canadian content to satisfy their criteria and Eddy was getting nervous.

"If they pull out at the last minute, I'm up to my neck in smelly brown stuff," he said over the phone.

"It wouldn't be the first time," was all I could say.

There was a short silence while we thought.

"What about our on-camera Native? Have you thought of anyone?"

"That's the other problem. I asked Fred. But he won't go. He hates the tropics."

"Too bad. He'd be perfect. Hey, what about Zach?"

"Zach is still up at Lac Chicomo with his new girlfriend. He won't be back for a while, you can bet on that." Eddy scanned through his mental repertoire. "Hmmm, Cowboy George would be pretty good. He was with us when we made the film *Pakatan.*"

"Is he the guy who snored like a diesel?"

"Yep, he's the guy. We made him sleep outside under a canoe. Cowboy George is crazy enough; he'll do just about anything. He also worked for the community TV station in Maliotenam for a few years."

"Good. He's got some experience. What's he doing these days?"

"He went back to the land. Now he lives up near La Romaine on the Lower North Shore. He has his trap lines up there."

"I guess he got tired of working for that television station."

"Yeah, all they wanted was hard-luck stories like snowmobile accidents, cigarette smuggling and barricades on Route 138. He told me that he quit because he just needed some air. He loves that kind of life up there, but he also likes working with a camera crew. But Cowboy George is … well, you never really know what's on his mind."

"Do you think that this project might interest him?"

"I could always try to find out. I just hope that he's not too far north. If he agrees to come with us, we can team him up with a local Miskito Indian, and they can exchange stories about their people and traditional ways, things that they have in common."

All we had to do was locate the guy and convince him to join our adventure. Eddy was the right guy to convince him. He was a good salesman; in fact, he could probably sell snow to an Inuit.

We spent another few days between Belley's Pub and my place organizing every detail. Our plan was this: After my boat was back in the water, I was to meet Eddy and our "Canadian content" somewhere in the Bay Islands. We would then sail southeast to the Mosquito Coast, find a place to leave *Numada*, and somehow venture inland in search of Ciudad Blanca. There was only one slight problem: We still weren't sure exactly where we were going.

After Eddy left, I wandered up Rue des Remparts to Dufferin Terrace. The long boardwalk stretched out just in front of the Château Frontenac. The weather had warmed a little and spring was finally in the air. As I strolled along the wooden terrace, I lingered to watch various street artists. A fire-eater, dog acts, jugglers and a tightrope walker playing a slide trombone, they were all preparing for the next summer's tourists.

Leaving the noise behind, I climbed the long flight of stairs to Rue Saint Denis. I hiked across the grassy field and climbed another hill, finally resting beside the Citadelle de Québec, the highest point of Cap Diamond. The air was fresh and the smell of lilacs divine. I stretched out on the grass and looked down on the silver strip of the Saint Lawrence River. A container ship was leaving the narrows, heading downstream toward the Atlantic. Behind its massive moving form, I saw the faint outline of a few sailboats ghosting along in the fading light, their white sails hanging almost listlessly.

We needed someone who knew La Mosquitia and finding the right person wasn't going to be easy. What's more, there was always the slight possibility that news of our expedition would reach the wrong ears. If that ever happened, we wouldn't have to worry about a distributor, Canadian content or anything else. It would be game over.

Back for More...

The Chief had a talent for showing up at the right time. I knew who it was the moment I heard heavy footsteps coming up the wooden stairs that led to my flat. As I opened the door, he dropped his heavy sea bag on the landing. He was dressed in jeans and a light blue short-sleeved shirt. He looked like he had just stepped off the ship.

"Man, am I glad my contract is over," he said, puffing for air as he pushed the bag aside with one foot. "Too much engine room time. I'm really out of shape."

He looked me up and down. "But you, you certain look a lot better since the last time I saw you."

"Yeah, but I'm still far from being back to normal. Come on in, let's talk." I closed the door behind him.

As we sat together in my loft sipping coffee, I filled him in on the latest developments. Then I called the base commander in Puerto Cortés to say that we would be on the way soon.

The Chief and I left a few days later on a flight to the very place from which I had escaped by the skin of my teeth only a few months earlier. Sitting at thirty thousand feet, I could only wonder what awaited us down in Puerto Cortés. What kind of shape would my boat be in? Had Mario kept his promise to finish the welding job? And what had become of Ben, the philosopher? And there was Dog Barker. And Valeska. Why hadn't she answered my emails or phone calls?

It was almost dark when our battered taxi stopped in front of the guardhouse at the naval base. Luckily, one of the soldiers on duty recognized me. Without any of the normal protocol, he swung open the heavy steel barrier and waved us in. Once inside the compound, I guided the driver around the back of a long warehouse and we cautiously entered the shipyard, weaving through the maze of dry-docked hulls. There were still a dozen odd transient sailboats in for repairs, along with the same tired-looking military vessels that had been there for years. We passed *Choice*, Ben's boat, but German Joe's steel ketch *Libertade* was gone. He must have finally finished off his repairs and set sail for his world cruise. Strangely enough, there was a large gap where *Numada* had once been. A lot of my material was scattered around in the manner of a garage sale. "A twenty-ton schooner can't just disappear, Chief."

"I think you have a slight problem, my friend. So what are you going to do about it?"

"Just keep looking."

We swung around the big travel lift and stopped. At the far end, in the shadow of a large military gunship, was *Numada*. The new plates underneath the hull were welded in place and ready for final touches of paint. Mario had come through.

The Chief and I moved on board that night and put a little order back inside. The next morning, while we set up shop, a few yard workers sauntered over, looking surprised to see me. Rumors had been flying; some thought I'd been shot, others thought I'd been killed in a wreck, and others speculated that I had ended up in jail. No one had the right version, not even the naval base commander — whose face brightened when I coughed up the rest of money that I owed for the back rent.

•••

Later that week, the schooner's diesel engine arrived from the shop. The crane lifted it up slowly and then, ever so carefully, we guided it to its place at the bottom of the spotless engine room. The engine still needed a new cooler, but we had a plan. Ben had once told me that one of the hulls in the boat cemetery at the far end of the yard had a Perkins just like mine and it was just waiting for someone to help himself. That night, while I stood guard in the shadows, the Chief snuck on board with a small backpack of tools and a headlight. Pulling a cooler off an engine abandoned in the dark entrails of a rusted-out hulk was nobody's idea of fun. Standing watch wasn't a picnic either. Twice, armed guards walked very close to the Chief, but I kept them busy looking the other way. When the Chief was finished, he let out a weird night-owl hoot. When it was safe for him to come out, I responded in kind. I finally saw him appear from the shadows, followed by a bucket of parts attached to a rope. He lowered it over the side, then he carefully climbed down the precarious wooden scaffolding positioned alongside the abandoned hull.

"A piece of cake," the Chief whispered as he hit the cement. All we had to do now was replace the worn-out parts of my own engine with the ones we had liberated from the abandoned sailboat next door. The next day, after six hours of intense open-heart surgery, *Numada*'s Perkins came to life.

"It's purring like a big, happy cat." The Chief grinned, wiping his sweat with a cloth.

"I owe you, Chief."

"You don't owe me a thing. Just hearing that thing run again is compensation enough."

Over the next few days, the far end of the shipyard came to life. Although it was the weekend, most of the regulars drifted by, curious to see what *Numada*'s captain and crew were up to. As the Chief began work on the rudder shaft under the hot sun, I organized the upcoming jobs with the yard boss. Once the sandblasting was completed, a swing gang took over with their compressors to cover the hull with the "champagne" of primer paint. We labored under the blistering sun, taking turns cooling off under the water hose. Without complaint, everyone worked despite suffocating heat that pressed down on our heads like some invisible giant's hand.

Despite the work, I was obsessed with Valeska. I just couldn't stop thinking about her. Where had she gone? Why was she not communicating?

Late one extra-hot afternoon, while Mario and his crew were finishing up the last of their welding jobs, I took a break to cool off. "Chief, I'm going to swim out to that wreck over there. It's been intriguing me for months. Want to join me?"

"Are you crazy? You know I can't swim."

"Just being polite," I said. "I'll be back in an hour."

Feeling a little guilty, I stripped to my underwear, grabbed my mask and fins, jumped off the dock into the soothing Caribbean Sea and began to swim out to the half-sunken military ship a few hundred yards offshore. Halfway out, my arm reminded me that it hadn't mended completely, and I had to take a break. There was still a dull pain shooting up to my shoulder and telling me to take it easy. On the windward side of the rusted hulk, the deck was almost the same level as the sea. Normally, it would have been an easy climb up, but even that was a strain on my body. I was far from being back in shape. Finally, with the help of a gentle wave, I was lifted on board and crawled up the rest of the way to a dry spot where I could stand and take a look around.

The ship was an American World War II coastal supply boat that had once sailed the South Pacific. After the war, it had been given to the Honduran Navy, which used it to patrol the Caribbean coast of Honduras. Why it had been abandoned and sunk in front of the naval base was anybody's guess.

Gingerly, I made my way across the slippery deck and entered what seemed like the crew quarters. Everything above the waterline had been savagely stripped, but there were still lots of remnants that were hard to erase. After a short time, I began to feel like I was intruding. Strangely, ever since I had seen her lying there, the ship had been working on my curiosity. It had something to tell me; unlike corpses, dead ships can tell tales.

I found a narrow stairway leading to another deck and visited the officer's quarters. There was part of a chair, a cracked porcelain sink, and a few dog-eared paperbacks scattered on a small table. In a corner, a moth-eaten T-shirt hung on a hook. On the floor under an open port light, a pair of cracked old rubber boots leaned to one side. Further down the narrow hall was the galley, a section that once had been the heart of the ship and the center of the universe for those who sailed her. Here, the boys would have met for a meal or a cigarette and stories. Up one more flight of stairs was the bridge. There wasn't much left there; even the wheel had been disrespectfully removed from its place. Some graffiti was scratched on the bulkhead, and a very used New York Yankee's cap sat on an empty shelf.

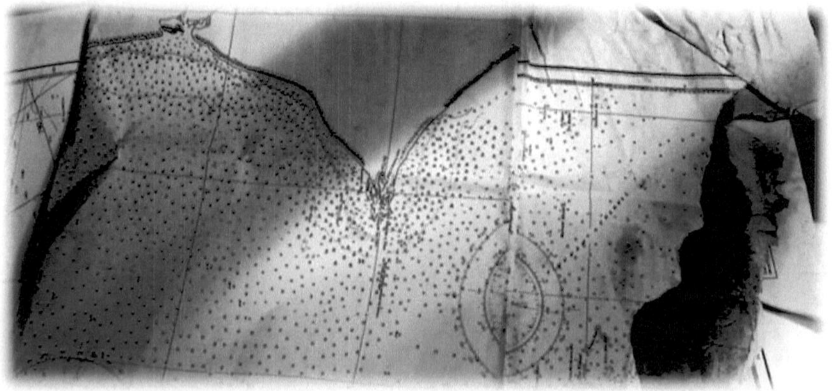

I spotted a few old charts in a half-open drawer beneath the chart table. I pulled one out and placed it on the table. The chart had all but faded and was stained with fingerprints and coffee, but I could make out the Mosquito Coast and the date 1953 stamped in the lower corner. That gave me an idea how long the boat had been around. It also got me thinking about the Ciudad Blanca.

How easy it would be to sail down the coast, leave my schooner and hire a few guides with river canoes to go up a river to try to find the ruins. But how to find that place's exact whereabouts without drawing undue attention? Up to now, we had absolutely no real leads as to the Ciudad Blanca's whereabouts, and as time slipped by, I was beginning to think that perhaps the lost city really was a lost cause. I rolled up the chart and swam back to shore with it. Once dried, perhaps that ragged old piece of paper would come in handy.

A few days later, the Chief and I sat drinking water and trying to keep cool in the shade under the hull while we watched a crew work on a construction nearby. They had come with their wives, kids and a boatload of material all the way from a small settlement called Barra Patuca, on the Mosquito Coast.

The little clan had been at the yard for over a month. They were building a new fishing boat from recycled steel plate they'd pulled from a wreck near their village. While the men cut and welded, the women took care of the kids, did laundry and cooked. They had set up camp in the scrapyard behind their work site. The only luxury that they had was a leaky garden hose supplying fresh water. No one complained; they just worked like dogs to finish the boat for the upcoming fishing season. Despite the primitive setup and difficult living conditions, they were in the process of making a fairly nice boat, which fascinated the Chief to no end.

"Look at how they're building a bona fide, respectable fishing boat out of scrap metal. Back home in Québec, no one would ever have touched that stuff. It would have gone right to the dump, but here, it all makes sense. These people are survivors. Look at how they bend the steel. It's unbelievable."

As we watched them put a piece of plate metal in place, the patriarch of the group came over to borrow my electric buffer. The Chief went up on deck to dig it out of the toolbox.

Our visitor could speak English and introduced himself as Peter-Pedro Lopez. He was close to fifty, of average height, with the allure of a true Miskito: dark, part Indian, with a dusting of Garifuna thrown in for good measure.

"Peter-Pedro, how well do you know the Mosquito Coast?"

"I was born there. We have been living in Barra Patuca for a long time."

"How is the channel to get into Rio Patuca?"

"It's okay, but it's unmarked and maybe twelve feet deep in the middle. You have to be careful; sometimes the surf is big and the entrance can be dangerous. The current there is strong. You need a good boat and a sharp eye."

"That's good to know. Señor," I asked, "have you ever heard about the Ciudad Blanca?"

There was a long silence. It was as if I had turned on a breaker switch in a fuse box. "Ciudad Blanca, that's far up the river! How come you know about that place?"

"I met someone who told me about it, someone who's been there. Do you know where it is?"

He came over to where I was sitting and squatted in the shade. His eyes were vivid but his voice stayed calm.

"My grandfather took me there once when I was a young boy. It's three or four days up the river. Not an easy trip, but I'll never forget that place. Bad spirits still live there."

"You mean that the place is cursed?"

"*Si, claro*."

"According to whom?"

"The old people don't like to talk about it much, but they say that there are many angry spirits flying around there. It is an ancient city, covered with trees and jungle, Señor Jacques, but I remember a large white pyramid, yes, and big structures, walls covered with carvings. My grandfather said that it was a secret place where the ancestors used to live a long time ago."

"Could you explain to me where it is?"

"Sure."

"Hey, hang on a second."

I climbed onto *Numada* and came back a few minutes later with the chart I had taken from the shipwreck days before.

"Show us on the chart. Here's Patuca River."

The other men of Peter-Pedro's crew crowded around. They all crouched down and discussed the details over the ragged-looking piece of paper. Then finally:

"I am fairly sure," said Peter-Pedro.

His finger traced a line about four inches off the southern edge of the chart.

"It's about exactly here." He stuck his finger in the sand and then looked up. Everyone laughed.

"What is 'about exactly' supposed to mean?" I asked.

"It means to find out exactly where it is located, I'll have to take you there."

"Could you?"

Peter-Pedro stroked the thin beard on his chin. I could see that he was already planning something. He looked back at the map and measured the distance with his fingers, calculated a few numbers under his breath, rubbed the sand off his hands and stood up.

"*Si*, it's possible. But why do you want to visit that cursed place? Sometimes there are gangs who go there to dig for artifacts. They take them out by boat. Is that what you want to do?" He took a dark green rag from his jeans' back pocket and wiped the sweat off his neck.

"No, not at all. I want to make a documentary about the theft and trade of artifacts being stolen from Central America. The Ciudad Blanca is important precisely because of the theft that goes on there. I want to see if the place really exists, and then film it while there is still something left to film."

"The people up there are dangerous. They don't like strangers. Maybe I could take you there with my brother. He's a good man, sometimes a *bandito*, but a good man just the same. He's been up there many times and has friends in the area."

I glanced at the Chief, and then we both looked at the shipbuilder. Peter-Pedro Lopez was exactly the kind of connection we were looking for. He seemed too good to be true! Suddenly I had found a key to the door that was so mysterious and forbidden.

I explained the details of my project to the Chief that evening. He didn't know a thing about documentaries, and he thought it was crazy to go into the jungle to attempt to find some lost pieces of pottery. Later, I called Eddy.

"*Kwei Kwei*, Eddy."

"*Kwei Kwei* to you, too. What's up?"

"I've got some good news. I found the man who can take us to Ciudad Blanca."

After a short silence, "Are you sure?"

"As sure as I'm talking to you, *amigo*. He's our man."

"So what's his story?"

"He's a Mosquito Coast fisherman who's building a boat next to mine. He says his grandfather took him to visit the Ciudad Blanca when he was a kid."

"He still remembers how to get there?"

"So he says. You just follow the river south into the mountains."

"Which river?"

"The Rio Patuca. That's where he lives."

"How will we get there?"

"We sail to the mouth of the river on *Numada*. After that, Lopez and his brother will take us upriver to the site with their own boats."

"Fantastic. Listen, I have some good news, myself. We have our Canadian content: Cowboy George has agreed to go. We're in business."

"You're kidding!"

"Not at all. When will your boat be ready?"

"In another month, at the most. The Chief is now lining up the engine. There's still some painting to do and then I have to adjust the rig. After that, it will be ready to go."

"What about Valeska?"

"No news. I've almost given up. I've the feeling that something happened to her."

"What can you do?"

"All I can do is wait and see."

We made plans to meet in the Bay Islands, perhaps at Guanaja, the most isolated island of the archipelago and well-placed for an easy sail to Barra Patuca.

"Let me know when you'll be there and I'll meet you with Cowboy George and the equipment. We can start filming while we sail over."

A few days later, we began to run out of supplies, so the Chief and I decided to hit the hardware stores in San Pedro Sula. We desperately needed basic things like hoses for the engine and stainless steel screws — which were nonexistent in Puerto Cortés. So, as a skeleton crew touched up the boat, we climbed on board a wheezing yellow "chicken bus" for San Pedro Sula. There was standing room only, and to find a place to stand, we had to push our way past long-faced passengers. We were all jammed in like sardines.

Within an hour, we were downtown. Third Avenida was, as usual, packed with peddlers, pickpockets, street gang members and hustlers. It was a busy morning in San Pedro, but despite a few wrong turns and the intense heat, we managed to pick up the essentials. Resting in the shade on a bench in the city square, I began to go over the details of my upcoming expedition to the Mosquito Coast.

"Chief, the plan is to sail east along the coast until we reach the place where Lopez and his brother are to meet us. Then we will head up the Patuca River to look for Ciudad Blanca. It's going to be one hell of an adventure — dangerous, but worth the ride. I would really like it if you would join us."

I thought that he would bite the hook, but instead, he scowled and took a deep breath. "Yeah, a trip of a lifetime, but maybe my last trip, too. All I've heard about that area is that you know when you go in, but you never know if you'll come out."

"But we'll be with Peter-Pedro Lopez and his brother. They know that region as well as you know diesel engines."

"Maybe so, but there are just too many bugs, snakes and poison arrows for my liking. I hate all that stuff. You know that. Don't squander your time, Jacques. Listen to me. Get your schooner back in the water and leave this rotten country before something else happens to you."

"Don't be so negative, Chief. Anyway, there's no way I can turn back now; I'm in too far."

"It's your life, *amigo*."

A few days later, I watched my old friend pack his bag. His time off was over. In a few days, he was expected to join his ship in Québec City, climb on board, go down in the hole and care for a couple of huge diesel engines for a few months. "It's a piece of cake," he said, flagging a taxi on the road in front of the hotel. Just before getting into the cab, he added, "If you ever are in a bind, let me know. Someday, I'm sure that pile of ruins out there on the Mosquito Coast will be just another one of your crazy stories. Meanwhile, take care, *amigo*." With that, he got into the front seat of the waiting cab and said his familiar phrase, "*Señor, aeropuerto, y rápido por favor*."

It felt a little strange watching that beat-up taxi disappear around the bend. My friend was gone. Would I ever see him again?

That week, Peter-Pedro Lopez and his crew finished building their fishing boat and, without ceremony, put it in the water. That strange-looking rig embodied lots of hopes and dreams, but I knew that the Lopez family would succeed. They were welded together as tightly as the little boat that they had just built. Before they headed off, the fisherman came over and we exchanged phone numbers.

"My brother and I will make sure that you are well looked after. My friend, if there is anyone who can get you to the Ciudad Blanca, it is the Lopez family."

I had one last question for Peter-Pedro.

"Have you ever seen a big dark green yacht called *Esmeralda* enter the Patuca River?"

He thought a few moments.

"*Si, si*, early last month, just before I came here, it ran aground on a sandbar at the entrance and we helped get it back into the channel. They said they were tourists who wanted to explore the Patuca. After they came in, they anchored around the bend in the river. We left to come here right afterwards."

"Did you see a woman on board?"

"Yes, there was a woman on deck."

My thoughts began to race.

"What did she look like?"

"I didn't get a good look at her. She wasn't a *gringo*, that's for sure."

I froze. Could she have been Valeska? What if Barker had been able to catch up with her? No, impossible. Yet for a few moments, I had some very black thoughts. There was a real possibility that she had been kidnapped and murdered. Or maybe she had gone back with Barker on her own and had made up a plot to somehow get even with him. She could easily lead him on for a while, then go for the jugular. Or perhaps she had just decided to team up with him again for the money and the excitement. She did look on top of things when she did that gun transaction back in Punta Sal. Whatever scenario it was, her absence was driving me crazy, and there was little that I could do to find her. She had to find me.

I spent the next few days alone, tying up numerous loose ends. I found myself constantly wondering about Valeska and what might have happened to her. It was starting to feel like a bad toothache that wouldn't go away, but working with my hands was the best remedy I knew to ease my mind. Soon, working on the boat was the only thing that counted.

One hot afternoon, to cool down a little, I dove off the dock and went for a swim, then climbed onto the cement pier and lay down on my towel in the sun. I must have drifted off. I was awakened by a soft female voice.

"Jack, Jack, wake up, it's me."

Was it a dream? I couldn't be certain until my eyes focused.

Her mouth was swollen. Behind the sunglasses, I noticed her blackened left eye. "Valeska!" I jumped to my feet. For a long moment we held on to each other without a word. "But where have you been?"

"It's a long story. I've been travelling for hours. I'm so thirsty, do you have any water?" Her soft voice broke the silence. It was weak and frail. There was a bandage on her forehead.

"Where did that come from?"

"I'll tell you later. First I need a drink of something."

We went over to *Numada*, where her small bag sat on the cement by the ladder.

"Is that all the baggage you have?"

"It's all I need."

"Come on up, there's drinking water aboard."

We climbed the ladder and entered the intimacy of the main cabin. At close range, her face looked older than it had when I saw her last and the sparkle in her eyes had dimmed. She must have been living on the edge for months. I poured her a glass of cool water and she gulped it down.

"Remember the last time we talked on the phone, when I told you that I was going to go back to the university and follow up with those people who were interested in the Ciudad Blanca? Well, on my way to Tegucigalpa, a car ran me off the road and I smashed into a tree. I was cut pretty badly. The moment that I cleared the blood out of my eyes I saw two guys running toward me. They were armed."

Her lips were trembling. She stopped for what seemed an eternity.

"Luckily for me, I had my 9mm in a bra holster. I shot them both before they could react. When my nerves calmed and I could see straight, I drove away in their car, abandoned it on a street in Tegucigalpa and then went to a cousin's place in the Santa Cruz mountains to recover. Cell phones don't work up there, neither does the Internet. And all I wanted was to forget everything."

"I understand that. But who do you think the guys who attacked you were?"

"They were goons hired by Dog. Who else? But now they're dead." She took a deep breath. "You were right," she said. "I should have just stayed out of harm's way, but I felt I had to get even with that bastard. He really wants me out of the picture for good, but it won't happen. I won't give him that pleasure."

I took her in my arms without a word. She had been to hell and back. She still had bruises from the accident on her shoulders, back and thighs. We lay on the mattress in the aft cabin and I stroked her dark hair as I spoke.

"It was a nightmare. I thought I would never see you again."

Thinking about the horror that she had endured sent a dull, sympathetic pain through my body, but I kept looking her straight in the eyes until the wave of emotion broke and passed over. Ever so gently, I drew her closer, whispering, "You'll be safe here with me, Valeska."

We kissed again and I held on to her. Some of magic between us was still alive, but something was missing. It would take time to repair her damaged body and spirit, and maybe even more time to reconnect. To see her eyes begin to shine again would require all the care, love and trust I could give her. We lay there together and didn't say a word, but after a while, I began to wonder. "I'm curious, were the documents they took from your uncle's house the originals?"

"No, the originals are at the lawyer's office."

"Can he be trusted?"

"I'm not certain. I hardly know the man."

"Perhaps Barker bought him off, as well."

"Anything's possible."

"Where do you go from here?"

She hesitated. "You are the only hope I have." She rolled over and snuggled right up to me. I could feel her weakness and her willingness to accept all the help that I could give her. It's funny the way things work. Suddenly I was about to begin a relationship I had dreamed about for months. Was I ready?

A day later, when I saw that Valeska was feeling a little better, I told her about the film project.

"Do you have access to the Internet on board?" she asked.

"Yes, I can pick it up from the base's office."

"Good. I want to continue doing research."

"Fine, since there's still work to do before we get this boat back in the water. Everything needs to be put back in place."

I brought her up to the two forward cabins. "I keep the sails up here. This is a workbench, and this is a small bunk that sometimes serves as storage. I keep all the lines here, the fenders and various things I need to keep this thing running. Nothing luxurious, but everything works."

"I really like your boat, Jack Legris. I will just make it a little more comfortable, that's all."

"A woman's touch?"

"No, a Valeska touch."

"Even better."

At night, the wind howled in from the north. The next day, while it rained, she slowly put the galley back into working order, until we were finally able to cook a proper meal on the propane stove. Valeska had begun to regain her lost energy, her voice was stronger, and I could see that, despite her injuries, she was regaining her strength. We were working as a team now. I could feel it.

The next day, we had running water, fresh towels and clean sheets on the bed. After supper, Valeska sat for hours working on my computer, completing the research she had begun in Tegucigalpa. Soon, the main cabin was full of documents, maps and drawings. That week, she spent hours surfing the Internet and wading through papers strewn around on the cabin floor. During the long evenings, we sat at the galley table, sifting through information. Valeska seemed enchanted by her research as she read the highlights that she had written down on her notepad.

“All recent expeditions that have gone looking for the Ciudad Blanca have either come back empty-handed or disappeared,” she said. “And … jungle travellers, including hunters and pilots, have occasionally reported sightings of strange-looking structures and mounds in certain areas near the Nicaraguan border. A man named D.H. Williams was an engineer from New Orleans who had worked on the construction of the Lake Yojoa highway in the 1940s. He reportedly visited the ruins twice. The first time, he was looking for petroleum in La Mosquitia when he had to make an emergency landing on the river near the ruins. Later, he went back and filmed it. It was the first real recorded proof that Ciudad Blanca really did exist. Williams showed this film only to people he could trust because he said he was afraid that if too many people saw the footage, the place would be overrun with looters. Then, for some mysterious reason, the film disappeared into thin air, and so did its director. They just vanished.”

She looked at me with wide eyes. “It’s as if the placed had some kind of protective field around it.”

Valeska flipped through more pages of her loose-leaf. For a moment, she reminded me of my student days in the seventies.

“This is also interesting: Local Indian groups have different versions of the lost city legend. Most of these prohibit anyone from entering or even getting near Ciudad Blanca. There’s talk of a monkey god who is thought to have once sought refuge in the sacred city. They also say that the city has always been protected by the gods of the great storms. This is another reason why the locals keep their distance.”

“Yes, I seem to recall reading similar information a while back. Great storms, that must mean hurricanes, but most of the hurricanes pass further north.”

"Sometimes legends have some truth to them. We are also approaching the hurricane season, so maybe it's not the right time to go up there."

"But we can't wait around much longer," I replied. "I'll keep a vigilant eye on the NOAA weather center every day."

"The *what* weather station?"

"NOAA is the acronym for the National Oceanic Atmospheric Administration. It is located in Miami and gives daily marine forecasts on the Single-Sideband radio or on the Web. Most of the time it is right on and gives a pretty good advance warning when a storm system is building. We'll have time to take shelter if something big comes our way."

"Just the same, all this gives me a strange feeling. I don't like it."

She seemed genuinely worried, but I wasn't. There were some pretty reputable hurricane holes in the Bay Islands, and Peter-Pedro Lopez had talked about a place near his village at Barra Patuca that was often used by boats as a hideout during bad weather.

"You know, despite this weather thing, this project has made me into a research addict. I just can't stop." Valeska's dark brown eyes were bright with excitement.

"I've noticed. We even have a computer almost full-time in bed now. You know what that means."

She stretched and smiled without taking her eyes off the screen, but I had a feeling she had something in the back of her mind. I went up on deck for a break. Sailing *Numada* would do me some good, and doing so with Valeska would put our compatibility to the ultimate test. I gazed up at the stars. I never could get used to the vast show on clear nights, when all I had to do was tilt my head back and take it all in. But after a few minutes, my reverie was abruptly interrupted by a triumphant shout from below.

"Jack, Jack, I found it!"

I sat up and stuck my head through the companionway. "Found what?"

"Listen to this!" Valeska read from the screen. "A company based in Europe specializing in satellite radar imagery was able to identify a site known as the Ciudad Blanca. To detect ancient ruins under very dense tropical forest and in the presence of relief, a new image enhancement technique has just been developed. Such a task is considered a challenge, especially in the presence of very thick vegetation. Indeed, the radar wave does not penetrate the whole vegetation cover of a tropical forest. The identification of Ciudad Blanca was carried out using a Japanese satellite JERS-1 and by the European satellite ERS-2."

"You're kidding me!" I slipped inside the cabin and moved closer to the screen. She zoomed in on the black and white image. At first glance, I could only make out certain shapes, straight lines and rectangles.

Valeska read on slowly. "An important finding was made during this systematic examination. Covering a 3.0 x 3.5 km wide area in one of the denser parts of the forest, one side of which is bordered by a branch of the Patuca River, the ruins of a vast complex of important structures are visible in the images. The figures shown illustrate the most interesting part of this area, including what could be a vast ceremonial center. This is thought to be the legendary lost city, Ciudad Blanca." We examined more of the fuzzy black and white figures on the screen. It took a little imagination, yet we could definitely make out a structure under the thick jungle roof. This new information was exactly what we had been waiting for. Valeska took a long drink of water before continuing in the manner of an archaeology professor giving a class lecture.

"Listen here: The enlargement of the important structures located in the upper-left quadrant of the previous images has been made by photo-interpretation. From the elevation map, and the shadows observed in the images, one may infer the presence of a pyramid in the north-western part of the represented area."

I could hardly believe what I was hearing.

"The best is coming," she said. "This could be one of the largest and most impressive untouched archaeological sites in the world. Its position is somewhere in the vicinity between latitudes 15°–16° N and longitudes 84°30'–85°30' W."

"Wait a second. I'll look it up on the chart." I fished out the tattered chart I had taken from the wreck and calculated the longitude and latitude. It was right at the location Peter-Pedro Lopez had shown us. "We need a topographical map of the area, but I think this location corresponds with the satellite images."

I grinned at Valeska. Her eyes sparkled in the candlelight.

"We have to follow the Patuca River on the south-eastern extremity of the Biosphere."

"All we have to do is get there," I added.

"Yes, Jack, get there and come back. That's close to Nicaragua, and very rough territory."

"I'm sure we can trust Lopez to guide us safely."

Valeska turned from the screen, stood up and kissed me on the lips. "I'm close to an overdose; let's take a break from all this Ciudad Blanca stuff for a while. I think that we have been sort of neglecting each other lately," she murmured.

"So I've noticed."

Then our eyes met. We moved outside. The wild tropical night, pounding with the distant thunder of surf, brought our bodies together. Valeska playfully pinned me against the mast. I could feel a strong gust of wind blow in off the bay. Another gust set the shrouds humming. I closed my eyes while her hands and lips charted my body. Soon we were on a voyage of no return. Were we falling in love?

Part Three

Over the next week, Valeska De Sela and I started to transfer all the things I had stored in a nearby hangar back to the boat. We were really moving in now, making the boat a home. I went to the bank in downtown Puerto Cortés and withdrew the rest of the money that I needed to pay off the guys and the last of the rent that I owed the boatyard. I gave away the Jawa, an electric drill, old sails, a stove, tools and other things for which I had no further use. The schooner's deck was piled high with boxes of basic canned food, pasta, rice, coffee, tea and almost everything else one could think of to run a galley. Besides that, placed in different sections, were new fenders, coils of heavy dock line, sail bags, a new outboard, and a ten-foot inflatable raft, as well as other odds and ends to make our voyage as safe as possible. I crosschecked the rigging, winches and turnbuckles, greased the windlass and rudder bearings, and filled everything that needed topping off. That done, I double-checked all systems: electricity, plumbing, pumps and filters. Everything seemed shipshape. Finally, we were almost ready to go.

Just before launching, I studied the NOAA Hurricane Prediction website for the last time. After that, we would only be able to pick up forecasts on my Single-Sideband radio. According to the NOAA, things were brewing out in the mid-Atlantic. Hurricane Carl, already rated at category 3, was in the middle of the Atlantic and moving eastwards at 15 miles per hour with winds peaking at 110mph. It was expected to pass north of the Bahamas but posed no danger to us. Then there was Tropical Storm Lisa, with winds of 80mph, currently located between Africa and the Lesser Antilles. It was gaining strength but seemed to be turning northwards. It was no real threat either. There was also a weak depression descending from the Gulf of Mexico which would probably reach Honduras in a few days. But the maximum wind was only about twenty-five knots, nothing that I couldn't handle. So things looked pretty good for a launching.

Then, the big day finally came. With a knot in my stomach, I gave the signal. The huge travel lift raised *Numada* straight up, causing the large wooden braces to fall into a confused pile on the concrete underneath. With *Numada* in its sling, the crane's big tires crabbed through the maze of military hulls and sailboats toward the launching slip. I stood on the deck and watched the boat's long shadow pass over the collection of dry-docked hulls that I had come to know so intimately. Over at the slip, a small crowd of curious soldiers and yard workers had gathered. Even a few secretaries had come out of their air-conditioned offices into the heat and waved us on as we rolled slowly past. It took about ten minutes for the whole show to cross the yard and stop at the end of the long slip. After all those long months, *Numada* was actually going back to sea. As her keel slipped into the water, a new energy ran through my veins. Seconds later, the boat was finally moving gently in the water. The lift crew unhooked the straps and tied the schooner to the dock. Meanwhile, Valeska was inside, down on hands and knees, checking for leaks. It was now or never.

"All dry," she shouted.

"Okay, here goes."

The engine turned over and sprung to life. Valeska stuck her head through the companionway. "Wow, this thing actually works."

That night, we made a light supper and turned in early. At daybreak, I was the first up. I made a pot of coffee and sat outside in the cockpit. The sea was remarkably still, and the eastern sky had a reddish glow. I walked around on deck, touching the shrouds, the masts, the helm. The boat seemed to be talking to me in a low voice.

Valeska poked her head through the open deck hatch with a sleepy smile.

"Ready for coffee?" I asked her.

"Good idea."

I could have spent a few more minutes listening to *Numada*.

As the sun rose over the mountains, we ate a solid breakfast. We were both a little nervous about leaving. After doing the dishes, and taking a final look around, we were all set to go. We slipped the dock lines and backed into the sparkling Bay of Puerto Cortés. Under power of the ship's motor, we circled the harbor, passing close to half a dozen ships that were being loaded with bananas and other cargo.

I went down to the main cabin by the controls to check engine temperature and oil pressure. Every few minutes, I looked into the engine room and eyed the stuffing box, a delicate sea water–cooled gland where the shaft passes through the hull to the exterior. It was slightly humid and seemed to be working perfectly. Then I checked all the hose connections and pumps. Everything looked shipshape, so I pushed the engine up to 1800rpm, cruising speed. It held fine. Sure enough, around 8:00 a.m., the first solid puffs of wind started to make the surface water dance. It was time to fly.

Valeska took over on the tiller and I went up to the foredeck and started hoisting sail; it felt great to see them fly spotless and white, and beautifully trimmed. I shut the engine down, and we bore off under the power of the wind. The boat heeled over a little and picked up speed. Things were still looking good. After about ten months of grief, dirt, pain and hard work, the payday had finally arrived. I swung the helm over, pointing the schooner northwest, out of the protection of the bay and toward the open ocean.

For a while, we sailed west along the coast. Four hours later, we ducked into the bay at Omoa, circling around some sailboats that were at anchor. When dark rain clouds gathered over the mountains, their thunder rolled down the hills, so we sailed offshore toward a patch of blue sky. Out there, *Numada* had lots of sea room to kick up her heels. Seven, eight, nine knots, and the wake behind the schooner began to gurgle out a happy tune. It was glorious. I looked up at the weather vane atop the mizzenmast. The wind was just behind the mast and perfect for a run to the Bay Islands. I would have preferred to sail off to Guanaja right there and then, but the plan was to sail back to the naval base that evening, tie up alongside the cargo ship, and in the morning pick up last-minute supplies.

On the way back, I noticed a distinct halo circling the sun. That circle wasn't a good sign, but probably just that weak northerly I'd seen heading our way during my last weather check with NOAA. Perhaps some bad weather was on the way, but we had possibly another twenty-four hours before a storm. It could be bothersome, but we could always anchor in the lagoon and wait for it to pass. If it got really bad, we would head to sea and ride it out, though that option would be a tough baptism for my new first mate.

Shortly before sundown, we shouldered up alongside the Honduran Navy's front-loading cargo ship. Its deck was only about four feet higher than *Numada*'s and could be boarded easily. High on the success of our shakedown cruise, I went below and dug out an all-but-forgotten bottle of rum. Luckily, there was just enough left for two good shots. Our glasses clinked in a toast to the next chapter. We ate a celebration dinner at Delfin's, a short walk from the boat.

After our main course of roast chicken, the eastern sky turned the color of coal. A squall was on the way, but I was convinced that *Numada* was well-protected from that direction. The only wind that could affect the boat would have to come from the northwest, which was rare for this time of year. This incoming disturbance would probably just mean a wet walk back. The waiter came over and we ordered coffee. Suddenly there was a loud rushing sound, followed by a strong gust of wind that blew in off the lagoon sending empty plastic chairs skidding across the terrace. Then another blast hit even harder and the tablecloths flapped like flags. A bottle of salsa crashed to the floor and a big deck umbrella sailed up in the air and then tumbled into the muddy river. At the same moment a large piece of tin roof sailed by, followed by a blast of torrential rain. It was horizontal and hit like bullets.

We thrust our payment at the waiter and raced the short distance to the naval base. At the main gate, the guard cried, "*Amigos, Amigos, que se mueven! Mueviense! Està llegando una tempesta malo. Vamo!*" (Quick, my friends, there is a bad storm moving in. Hurry!)

It sounded urgent. When we rounded the corner of the big hangar, the full force of the storm hit us head-on. We were really in trouble. Over by the dock, in the fading light, I could see *Numada* bucking like a horse in a stall. The bay was speckled with whitecaps. Breakers were already smashing up against the seawall and spilling water into the yard. We jumped on board the freighter and ran across the deck to our schooner. A few dock lines had already snapped. Others were chaffed out and had become as thin as pencils. A spring line snapped with a loud crack. Spray filled the air and the wind in the rigging started to shriek.

One of *Numada*'s inflated fenders exploded ripping in two before it disappeared between the two vessels. This was going to be a long night. Another fender split open, then another, as *Numada* smashed up against the freighter with a sickening metallic bang.

"Valeska, we have to clear out of here, and fast."

"You're the captain," said Valeska over the crashing sound of the breaking waves.

A quick glance at the wind anemometer showed over forty-five knots coming out of the northwest. I let go of all the lines leading to the cargo ship except the spring line that led into the cockpit. I scrambled to the helm just in time to see a breaker smash down on top of the huge slab of seawall just behind us. A large piece of cement crumbled and sank. Suddenly, the navy freighter pitched to port and thundered up against the cement pier. It was time to go. I gave it the gun and dropped the last line that held us to the ship. Valeska looked on with wide eyes, a little unsure of what she was seeing.

We were free, but to steer windward against the incoming waves was almost impossible. To pass the sunken hulk on the leeward side seemed better, though that only allowed for a small margin of error. One false move and *Numada* would smash up against the seawall. I chose the leeward escape route, hoping to use the shelter of the sunken ship to pick up some speed to find the room we needed to head out to sea.

"What do you want me to do?" shouted Valeska over the wind as we approached the wreck.

"Just hang on."

Numada picked up speed. I had to pass within a few feet of the hulk and use the sheltered water behind it to pick up speed. It worked. There was an eerie calm as we fell into the ship's wind shadow. I had the engine racing at full speed and could feel *Numada* pushing ahead with all she had. Then we slipped past the stern of the wrecked ship. Now there was nothing between us and the wind, and we were hit hard by the full force of the storm. I pulled the helm and we headed out into the dark, breaking Gulf of Honduras.

When we were well offshore, I gave Valeska the helm. "Try to keep it heading in this direction. I'm going to try to put up a small sail. Don't worry, I've seen worse."

I went up to the foremast, wrestled with the mizzen sail, and after a lot of grief, managed to set it with three reefs. When that was done, I hoisted the small staysail. It was robustly made and very capable of handling heavy weather. Once back in the cockpit, I took the helm from Valeska and set a course. *Numada* leaned over and stopped pitching — quite an improvement. From out of the jet-black night came another impressive gust; the boat heeled over some more, and a bore of solid water washed over the deck.

"I'm cold," said Valeska. She was shivering like a wet puppy.

"Hey, you did great. Go inside and put on some warm clothes. It's going to be a long night." I hugged her with one arm.

The point of the Bay of Cortés was just off to starboard, but even in the darkness, I could see the huge waves smashing up over the rocks under the light. We had to gain sea room now and reach deep water, where the steep, breaking sea would hopefully round off. At least we had the wind pushing us in the right direction. I watched the boat move; it seemed to be adapting perfectly to the conditions. For the first time since the beginning of the blow, I began to relax.

A few minutes later, Valeska slid the main hatch open and climbed out in a strange set of clothes.

"You found my winter wardrobe."

"Yes, it's a bit big, but warm and dry. Don't ask me to go back inside. If I do, I'll puke."

At that moment, something fell to the deck and tumbled overboard. The wind direction indicator that sat on top of the mast had disintegrated.

"That's no big deal, just a gadget that tells us what direction the wind is coming from."

"I don't think I need anything to tell me where the wind is coming from," she replied.

It was long past midnight. Even with only two small sails set, strong gusts would put the schooner's starboard rail under water. Suddenly, there was a loud crack, and the block that controlled the height of the small staysail boom on the foredeck exploded into smithereens. That made the sail flap wildly in the wind. I clipped on my harness.

"Valeska, I'm going up front to take care of the mess. Keep us pointed in this direction and make sure the wind stays over your left shoulder. You're doing fine."

The wind pushed harder still, and while I worked on deck, I found it hard to breathe. I secured the sail and the boom, and then set the storm jib onto the forestay. In the semi-darkness, I could make out Valeska holding on to the tiller. She must have been on an adrenaline high. Whatever sustained her, I was impressed by her courage. I signalled to her to bear off to starboard until the sail filled.

Eventually, the sky began to clear and the wind dropped, so I shook out the reefs and beat upwind, heading for the Island of Útila. We arrived just before dawn and dropped the anchor in front of the village. The bay was as quiet as a millpond.

Was it the lack of movement, or quiet jungle sounds that woke me? For a few seconds, I couldn't figure out exactly where I was. Half asleep, I lay listening to a chirping sound. "Hey, Valeska. Do you know what?" She stirred. "We have a cricket on board."

"A what?"

"A cricket. Listen."

"Leave me alone, I want to sleep." But the little critter started to chirp even louder. "Oh, that's what woke me up. I thought it was something on deck. It makes a damn racket. What are you going to do about it, my captain?"

"We'll keep it as a mascot. Everybody knows that a cricket is sort of like a barometer, and the one I have on board isn't worth a damn."

Valeska's head appeared from under the sheet, and she looked at me as if I was going off the deep end. "If you want my real opinion, you need more rest."

"But, Valeska, you have to let the little critter do his job. All true sailors know crickets can predict the weather. When the cricket sings, it's synonymous with good weather. When the little guy clams up, it means that the weather will get nasty."

"Sleep some more," she said and disappeared back under the cover.

•••

As the sun lifted over Útila, the island came to life. We ate breakfast on deck while we watched the cayukas and dive boats coming and going. People were everywhere, most of them backpackers under thirty looking for inexpensive diving and a little night-time adventure in the dozens of bars that lined the main street.

Valeska sighed. “It’d be nice to stay here a few days. It looks like everyone’s on a permanent vacation.”

“Next time around. We have to meet Eddy and his friend in Guanaja; we’re on a mission, remember?”

“Okay. You win. This time.”

I went to the Internet café situated above a small souvenir shop on the main street and emailed Eddy to confirm that we would be at Isla Guanaja on time for our rendezvous. All he had to do was round up Cowboy George. An hour later, *Numada* weighed anchor and slipped back out to sea, bound for the Island of Guanaja about sixty miles to the east. Late that afternoon, we sailed past Roatán Island; we could see the small town of Coxen Hole. We avoided the infamous Cordelia Bank, an invisible coral reef with a long history of damaging boats.

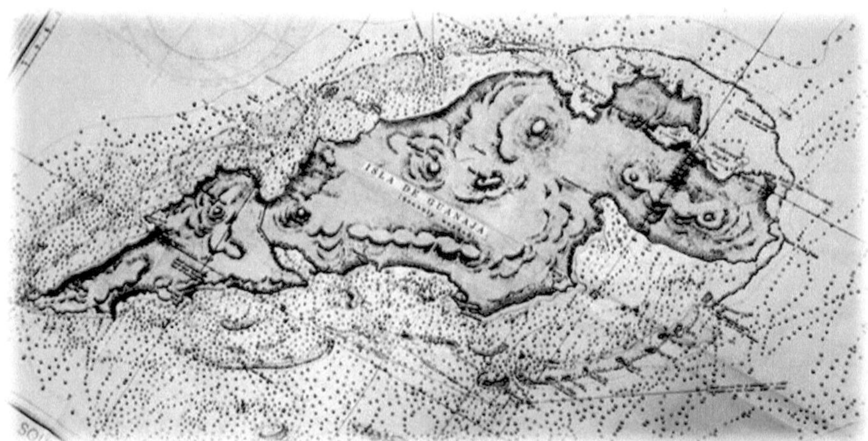

I couldn’t help but remember the last time we had sailed past this spot; it was on *Esmeralda* on the way to Port Royal just a little further east of our present position. We cruised past exotically named places such as Neverstain Bight, Hog Pen Channel and finally, Calabash Bight. Invisible from peering eyes on shore, we sailed on under the stars. It was a sweet and warm night.

The weather was on our side, exactly as the cricket had predicted. I had to laugh. That squeaky little stowaway had earned his keep.

As Valeska slept, I adjusted the sails and headed past Helene, and then gave the secret little Island of Barbareta lots of room. The barrier of coral reefs off to the port side had danger written all over it. Only fifteen miles away, the high peaks of Guanaja were barely visible in the full moon. As our schooner approached, the silhouette of the island contained no definition. But soon I could see trees and rocks and white surf on its western tip. Guanaja is three-thousand-feet tall, but two-thirds of it is under water. In a bay on the southern side of the island sits a town called Bonacca, which has been built up over the years on a shallow reef and pilings of wood, rock and cement.

It was early morning when we finally sailed *Numada* up to this curious place. We lowered the sails, motored up alongside the fuel dock and tied up to the wooden posts. A man shuffled out of the shade and pumped seventy-five gallons of diesel fuel into the tank.

We took time to explore the narrow walkways and alleys that wove through this bizarre hodgepodge. It was a colorful little place packed with small shops, modest dwellings and a few shifty-looking bars. Then we motored a few miles east of the village and anchored *Numada* at Sandy Bay as a thick wall of clouds moved in. Soon, a series of strong gusts sent a low growl through the rigging.

•••

The silence from the cricket's new hideout in the forepeak was worrisome. Either the insect had found a drop of lube oil to take some of the squeak out of his landing gear, or its silence was a clear sign that there was a storm on the way. That evening, the wind picked up and big black clouds rolled over the mountain. But we were safe and sound, with nothing to do but wait for Eddy and Cowboy George to arrive.

The next morning, I caught the forecast on my Single-Sideband radio receiver, but the reception was so bad I had to glue my ear to the speaker. The computerized voice from NOAA was spewing warnings about a low-pressure system moving in from the north, winds NNE twenty-five to thirty-five knots, perfect for the direction we were heading. I went out on deck and rubbed the antenna on a backstay wire that led up to the top of the mast. The reception wasn't much better, but I was able to grab a few keywords through the static. It seemed to be a long-term forecast.

"…strong, tropical depression forming ... mid-Atlantic … latitude 12°30' N, longitude 20° W, heading 270 degrees at a speed of five knots. Wind fifty knots increasing to…" It sounded like another tropical depression was forming a thousand miles to the east of our position, but it was premature to know what it was up to. It would be important to know where each depression lay and to plan an escape route. But for the moment, the possibility of a distant storm didn't change my plans. Sure, if we were hit by heavy rain, it would make things difficult. As usual, it was all a question of timing. I was itchy to get going.

That evening, just before bed, I was overjoyed to receive another weather forecast. Although the cricket's chirping was somewhat hesitant, it seemed more encouraging than the forecast from NOAA. The jumpy little barometer seemed louder than ever. Now it was coming from our cabin.

Valeska couldn't sleep. "Your pet cricket is starting to drive me crazy."

"I know, but so far he's been right with the forecast every time. Give it another twelve hours. Our little stowaway predicts tomorrow will be bright and sunny. According to NOAA, it will rain for another day. I want to prove once and for all that this cricket is worth its weight in gold. I have ear plugs if you ever need them."

Valeska looked at me and stuck out her tongue.

That night, we slept in a front cabin while the cricket chirped like a bird on a wire, and sure enough, in the morning, the sky was as blue as a robin's egg.

Valeska sighed. "Okay, you win." She stepped on deck to drink her essential morning dose of caffeine. "But the first wrong prediction, it's going on a one-way excursion out of here."

"Have you ever tried to catch a cricket?" I asked her.

"Don't worry, I've got my methods."

Late that day, while I was repairing a few things on deck, Valeska sat under the shade of the Bimini tarp I had rigged over the cockpit and managed to hook up to an unlocked Wi-Fi network.

"Jack, I've found something new, listen to this."

I stopped what I was doing and waited for the details.

"In 1969, Pedro Macotto headed a cartographic expedition to Ciudad Blanca. He found ruins, but not the right ones. He and his men also ran into something not too … well … not too pleasant. Aside from the snakes, crocodiles and cut-throats, they ran into bullet ants."

"What the hell are bullet ants?"

"A king-sized ant that packs a king-sized punch. They say their bite hurts more than a bullet wound. The pain lasts for hours and drives the victim crazy. During this expedition, two of his crew died."

"From ant bites?"

"*Si, señor*, from ant bites. But don't get me wrong, I wouldn't miss this trip for anything." She smiled and returned to her reading. Nevertheless, she was right; we were going to have to be very careful.

Suddenly a "*Kwei kwei*, *Numada*" came in over the VHF radio, the one I use for short-distance communication.

"What was that?" said Valeska.

"It's Eddy," I said, grabbing the radio. "This is *Numada*. *Kwei kwei* to you, too. Glad to hear your voice. Where the hell are you?"

"At the Guanaja airstrip."

"Okay, great. Take a water taxi to Sandy Bay and you'll see *Numada*. Is Cowboy George with you?"

"Yes, he's here all right, but suffering from a little culture shock. And our airplane lost a door on the way over from La Ceiba, so it was a bit drafty during the flight."

"It's just part of the fun. We'll be waiting."

Twenty minutes later, a water taxi pulled up with our two new crew members, their camera and sound equipment and their personal gear. The two nomads looked wrinkled but happy to have finally arrived.

"What a crazy trip. We were delayed in Montreal, Miami and San Pedro. At La Ceiba, we had to wait another day because the plane left without us. For some strange reason, they don't fly out here on Sundays. But here we are," said Cowboy George. We shook hands. I had forgotten how big he was, well over six feet tall and at least 250 pounds. His long black hair was untied and flowed from under a black Stetson hat.

We made fresh coffee, and I showed Eddy and Cowboy George around the boat and carefully explained how things worked. At noon, Eddy, Cowboy George and I took the new inflatable ashore for a beer and something to eat at the thatch-roofed joint on the beach. Valeska opted to stay on board and do a food inventory. When we got to the bar, the only souls around were the proprietor and a noisy parrot that sat in the rafters above the open door. The homemade pizza was pretty good. After lunch, the guys caught up on some sleep on the hammocks strung up in the shade of the tall, whispering Australian pines that grew close to the water. It was a perfect time to make contact with my Mosquito Coast connection so I borrowed the bar phone and called Peter-Pedro Lopez. I had to make sure that he was still expecting us.

"*Hola, Jacques, mucho gusto.* Here in Barra Patuca, we are getting the boats ready for the trip. Everything is fine. We even have a cook."

"A cook?"

"*Si, amigo.* My brother's wife will come with us. She's used to living on the river. She's a native Pech and her family came from up that way."

"Okay, great, so we'll be seven in all. The rest of my crew has just arrived from Canada."

When I had finished updating him, Pedro said, "When you get close to Barra Patuca, just call Chili-Chili on VHF channel 69. He's my brother and the one who knows the most about the river and will be our guide. He's also the guy who you will want to film the most because Chili-Chili is not afraid of a camera. Anyway, we shall figure that out as we go along, right? For starters, we'll go out to meet you at the mouth of the river. The pass is a little tricky, so we must guide you in just to be on the safe side. *Comprendo?*"

"Ok, *claro*, Peter-Pedro. We should be there in about three days."

"All good, we'll be waiting, *amigo*."

I hung up and ordered another beer.

The bartender was German, but after living on Guanaja for years, he looked like a real islander: unshaven, with graying blonde hair down to his shoulders and vibrant blue eyes shaded by the visor of a ball cap. "My name is Ernest. But everybody calls me Ernesto." He stood on the other side of the bar and grinned, then popped open a Salva for himself. "You must be from that boat out there." Ernesto's accent lent the joint an exotic touch. "Are you guys really going over to the Mosquito Coast?"

"Yes. I have friends there I want to visit."

He smiled and looked at me in a strange way, as if he didn't believe a word I said.

"Hmm, from what I heard over lunch, sounds like you're going looking for treasure, the Ciudad Blanca."

"It's a long story, my friend. Let's say that we are going to visit La Mosquitia and leave it at that."

"Yeah, right." Ernesto looked me in the eyes and leaned over the bar. "I've been there quite a few times over the last ten years, you know, just snooping around, just looking… But I won't ever go back. No way, man."

"Why's that?"

"It's too damn dangerous. They don't want you there, man."

"Who doesn't want you there?"

"That place is cursed. And if you're thinking about finding the Ciudad Blanca, you won't, because it don't exist. It's just a legend and the legend is a man-eater. My friends and I thought at one point we were getting close, but we had to turn back because we got scared shitless. It was bad. People up there are completely out of this world. They live in another time. You know, these people still worship the Monkey God, man. It's prehistoric."

"Then why did you keep going back?"

"I don't know. It was like a drug. Part of me said to forget it, but another part kept urging me on, until the day my partner was shot through the neck by a poison arrow. He died right in front of me. Anyone would turn around after that. And, as I said, man, truth is, that place doesn't exist. It exists for them but not for us."

I thought about the satellite photos that had pinpointed a three-by-three kilometer area of the Ciudad Blanca. I didn't want to tell him we actually had the place locked in. He wouldn't have believed it, anyway.

Ernesto came around to my side of the bar and perched himself on a stool. "Hey, I remember there was a film crew that went over a few years ago. They were trying to make an adventure film about the ruins. The director's name was Hazard or Voizard, or something like that. Rumor had it that he was looking for the Ciudad Blanca. Their crew left from right here, right from this very bar. They chartered a big fishing boat, crossed over to Barra Patuca, and went upriver. They were never seen again. No word, no wreckage, no bodies. It was as if they'd been swallowed up by the jungle. Man, I wouldn't go back in there for a million dollars. No way. I hope that's not where you're headed. Believe me, this place is next door to hell. *Scheisse!*"

Shit, indeed. Feeling a little concerned about our safety, I made a call to Canada. But this time it was with my cell phone and I spoke in French so it would be a little more private. It wasn't long before the Chief was on the other end.

"Greetings, Chief."

"Where the hell are you?"

"Sunny Guanaja Island."

"Lucky you. We're in a fog bank here, just off the south-eastern tip of Newfoundland."

I switched to French. "*Chief, on quitte demain pour La Mosquitia.*" (We are leaving for Mosquitia tomorrow.)

"Someone must be listening close by, right?"

"*Oui.*"

"Okay, I understand."

"*Oui, c'est ça. On part avec notre ami Peter-Pedro, le pêcheur et son frère. Je te donne le numéro de téléphone là-bas. Si tu n'as pas de nos nouvelles dans trois semaines, tente de nous rejoindre.*" (Yeah, exactly. We're going to leave with Peter-Pedro our fisherman friend and his brother. If you don't have any news from us in three weeks, try calling this number.)

"Okay, got it, now just tell me if you prefer to be buried at sea or cremated?" said the Chief.

"*T'es drôle, toi. Reste en ligne un instant.*" (Very funny. Hang on a second.)

"Sure."

I walked outside the bar and said in a low voice, “Mark this down: 15°30’ N by 85°00’ W.”

“You mean somebody’s actually located the damn place?”

“We found recent satellite information that shows photos of some major ruins that are exactly at those coordinates. It corresponds perfectly with what Lopez illustrated in the sand.”

“Yes, I remember, that map in the sand wasn’t very hi-tech.”

“Okay, it wasn’t up to ship standards, but I showed him another map after you left; it was close to the real thing. Trust me, it all lines up, and don’t worry, now we have satellite pictures to reference. Our Québec crew has arrived and we are as ready as we’ll ever be. There’s just one thing missing.”

“What would that be?”

“The Chief himself.”

“You know I’m a chicken for those kinds of trips.”

“Blah, blah, blah. Chief, if you can’t reach us in three weeks—”

“—Yeah I know, call the Coast Guard—”

“—Never mind the Coast Guard. Just let the Canadian Embassy in Tegucigalpa know that we’re missing.”

“Anything else? Some famous last words for your epitaph?”

“You’re the poet, not me.”

“Well then, good luck and I’ll be waiting for news,” said the Chief.

I returned to the bar and paid Ernesto for the lunch and the beer.

Then he surprised me.

“Bonne chance. Et surtout dites bonjour au monde de la Mosquitia de ma part.” (Good luck, and give my best to everyone in La Mosquitia.) Ernesto grinned. His French was perfect. I guess that he had listened in on my conversation with the Chief.

The mood on board *Numada* was fairly subdued that evening, and it was the perfect to talk about the upcoming passage at sea. We made sure that everything was stowed safely away and that the camera and sound equipment were accessible and ready for action. Eddy and I agreed to begin filming during the passage between Guanaja and the Mosquito Coast. I would eventually use narration to explain exactly where we were going. As the guys looked at the charts, I checked the marine forecast on the Single-Sideband radio. According to NOAA in Miami, another weak cold front was moving in slowly from the north. That meant we would have wind just behind the left ear, behind the mast. That’s what *Numada* liked best.

Later, as we roasted grouper on a grill on deck, I explained as best I could to Cowboy George exactly what I wanted him to do in the film. "You've come to Honduras out of curiosity," I told him. "You've heard there are cultural similarities between northern native cultures and those in Central America. The Mosquito Coast is of special interest to you because, like the Innu, the native peoples live in a coastal area and go inland to hunt. You are also here to see if you can discover information about the Ciudad Blanca and about the pilfering of ancient Mayan artifacts."

Cowboy George thought a few seconds, then answered in a soft voice, "The white man has always moved in and taken over. This process starts with the removal of artifacts and a bleaching of culture and tradition. We've been experiencing the same thing in the north for hundreds of years."

"You've got it. When we get where we're going, you will meet our contact's brother. His name is Chili-Chili. He will be with you in front of the camera and tell you about the Patuca River and Miskito people. If it works out between you two, you could also tell him some things about the Innu way of life in Northern Québec."

George lit a cigarette. "Okay, I understand. It's not a road movie you want to make; it's a river movie. I just hope that I will be able to communicate with this Chili-Chili guy. What kind of language does he speak?"

"I guess he speaks some English like his brother. But he must also speak Spanish, Garifuna and probably some native dialects."

"Well, English is okay to start off with. Another dumb question: What kind of boats do they use, dugouts?"

"Sort of. The boats are called *pipantes*, built very narrow. They're at least thirty feet long. They rig them up with little gas inboards. I'm sure you're going to find these people have a lot in common with the Innu. Those similarities will be an important element in the film — for example, the way you make a fire, track an animal or imitate a birdcall. We'll film all this."

"I bet we also have strong differences, like the weather, for one. It's hotter than hell down here."

"Yeah, you're right about that, but imagine our friends in La Mosquitia spending a few months of winter up where you come from."

"They'd probably freeze their hind ends. That's for sure," said Cowboy George with a chuckle. "But tell me, Jacques. What I really what to know is, when does the Ciudad Blanca enter the picture?"

"As we go upriver, you'll become more focused on the ancient history of the people who once lived there in great numbers. Your role will be to get Chili-Chili to tell you about this history and how things changed to the way they are today. Gradually, as we head up the river, we will begin to discover signs of the ancient Maya, and, if all goes according to plan, the ruins of the Ciudad Blanca. We'll try to explore there. We expect that there will have been looting. That's part of the story."

"Were these people nomadic like my people?"

"The native people who live on the Mosquito Coast," Valeska interjected, "are called Miskito. There are other tribes who live there, too, such as the Pech, but they live inland. We think that it was the Paya people who built the city. Chili-Chili knows."

He looked at me quizzically. "Okay, I get it. They're living today what our people lived generations ago. But it makes no sense that this place hasn't been located yet."

"It's been found, all right, but mostly by the wrong people."

Cowboy George didn't seem fazed. He had seen it all before. As we travelled, I hoped that we wouldn't look too obvious. That wouldn't be too difficult for my three partners; Valeska was part Maya, Eddy part Innu, and Cowboy George was full-blooded Innu. They would blend in well with the local population, thanks to their dark complexions and Indian features. But me, with my blondish hair and blue eyes, I stuck out like a duck in a flock of chickens.

•••

The next morning, I could smell trouble when I saw George enter the main cabin. He was wearing a long face.

"There is some kind of insect in my cabin, kept me awake half the night. Believe it or not, it sounded like a cricket. You've got to do something about it, Captain."

I tried to tell him about our little friend, but the barometer part of it didn't faze him at all.

"Sounds like a bunch of bullshit."

"Okay, sure, we'll try to catch the thing after breakfast and move it up into the chain locker," offered Valeska.

Cowboy George wasn't convinced.

"Trying to catch that thing is not an option. If the bug is not caught, I'm going to move into your cabin, and don't forget, I know how to snore, big time."

It was the crew's first real crisis, a test to see if we could resolve a delicate conflict. I really wanted to keep the critter on board. I liked the sound and it was pretty efficient when it came to predicting bad weather. So we took a vote, and I lost. He was keeping everyone awake and he had to go. The entire crew got down on hands and knees, trying to catch the squeaky little beast. But it was Valeska, who was going through the wet locker, who found him first.

"It's here! Get it! Quick!" she screamed.

I'd been caribou hunting in the sub-Arctic with the Inuit, witnessed the slaughter of farm animals, and speared and boiled live lobster, but I couldn't bring myself to harm that cricket. It jumped over Valeska's head, careened off the bulkhead, passing about an inch from Eddy's nose, landed on the table, and in a shot, was airborne again in the direction of the galley, where it disappeared into a crack under the sink.

"We've got to trap it!" Valeska cried.

"I've never seen a barometer jump like that." Eddy laughed. "At least it's going to the stern. That's not too good for you and Valeska."

But the cricket bounded back onto the galley countertop, and with two long hops, landed on the chart table right beside Cowboy George, who was still trying to figure out if the whole thing was some kind of joke. Then with a whack of a hand as wide as a paddle, he killed the cricket. My trusty barometer was dead. Without a word, he took the remains outside and dropped them overboard. Wiping his hand on his T-shirt, he turned to us and, for the first time since coming aboard, he cracked a smile. "Now, if you'll excuse me," George said, "I'm going to get some sleep."

•••

All morning, Valeska made meals in advance. She cooked chicken and baked some fresh bread in the oven. Sandwiches would come in handy while we were sailing. I divided up the crew for the next days at sea: Eddy and Valeska, Cowboy George and myself; four hours on, two off, then two hours on and four off. That would give us time to sleep and relax a little as we travelled. If we left around noon, with the northeast wind the way it was, we would have Barra Patuca in our sights sometime the following morning. There were no real currents or shoals to worry about; it was a straight shot. I marked in the waypoint on the GPS, then looked for an alternative solution if something changed. There was Puerto Lempira about forty miles to the west of Barra Patuca, and if that didn't work, we could always turn around.

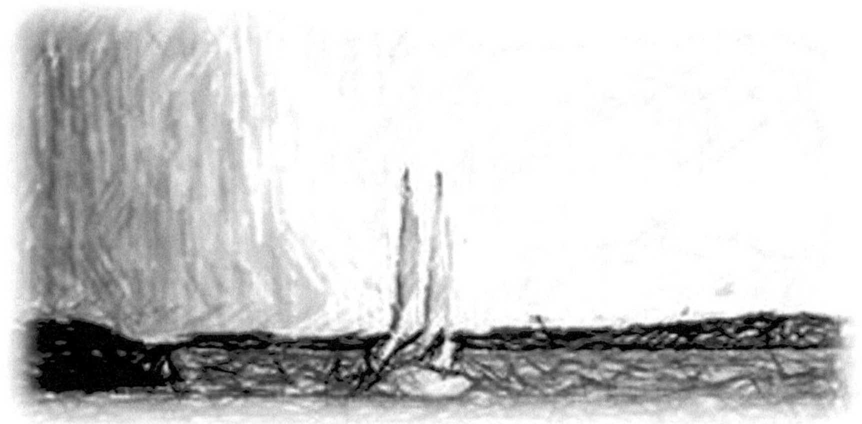

So with all sails hoisted, we headed out of the lagoon. Once we cleared the reef, I set the course and then the autopilot took over the steering. Now, all we had to do was keep a lookout and adjust the sails once in a while. We threw fishing lines over the stern and made bets on who was going to catch the first fish.

Late that afternoon, Eddy brought the camera on deck and began to film. With twenty knots of breeze on the beam and a rolling sea, there was a good chance to get some fine sailing shots. Occasionally, a cresting wave would smash up against the hull, sending spray high up over the topsides and dousing everybody on deck. At one point, a school of marlin changed directions and raced over to check the ship out.

They bounded alongside the hull, diving through the waves like missiles with fins. Rays of sun cut through the low sky and flashed off the marlins' glistening skin, making them even more vibrant.

Then Cowboy George's precious hat, his famous Stetson, complete with eagle feather, flipped up into the air and landed upside down on the back of a wave. There were two options: Either say too bad, George, and keep sailing, or treat this instance as a man overboard drill and retrieve the Innu's precious trademark as quickly as possible.

"Okay, listen up. Cowboy George, stand amidships and keep pointing toward your hat. And beware of the boom because as we come about, it will swing over to the other side of the boat. If you're not careful, you could lose more than that Stetson lid of yours! Valeska, grab the long gaff pole and stand by; you're the one who will hook the hat. Eddy, help me to control the headsail. Pull in on that sheet when I give you the signal."

Eddy looked confused. "Sheet, what sheet?"

"Sorry, I'll try to explain. There are no ropes on a sailboat. A sheet is what we call the rope that controls the movable corner of a sail. In this case, the sail I am talking about is called the jib. It's the one in front. Now listen up everybody, the wind is coming from the stern on the left side; as we swing around, it's going to pass over to the right side. You call that a jibe. As we jibe, the three booms will move across the deck, so watch your heads, especially you, Cowboy George. After that, we'll try to come up alongside of the hat, and when we do, Valeska will use that long pole that she has in her hands, otherwise known as the gaff, to hook on to it. Now, is everybody totally mixed up? Good. Heads up, here we go!"

We eased off and began to circle around as George did his best to point in the direction of the hat. It wasn't easy because it would disappear into the trough of each wave and come up on a crest. We had a lot of sail up, but after a lot of sail flapping and a little confusion with the sheets, the jibe was successful. Once the boat was moving again, I pushed on the tiller and maneuvered the schooner closer to the wind, and with a few more hasty sail adjustments finally managed to bring the boat alongside Cowboy George's precious black headpiece. Valeska reached out and hooked the thing with the long gaff. A loud cheer went up as she swung the pole over toward Cowboy George who contentedly grabbed his prize possession with two big hands. Perhaps that was the moment when we became a real sailboat crew.

As the sun began to dip into the sea, we sat in the cockpit and ate a delicious wahoo that Cowboy George had caught. He'd won the bet: His was the first fish we'd caught since leaving Guanaja.

•••

In a few hours, *Numada* was surrounded by nothing but water and a fading evening sky. We were on the open ocean.

Eddy was sitting on a propane box at the stern. He yelled up at me as he reeled in the fishing line that he had been trailing off the end of the boat. "Hey, Jacques Legris, look! There's a boat off to the right. Over there." He pointed with a free hand.

Sure enough, almost invisible in the twilight, were two masts way out on the horizon; it was a sailboat without its sails up. From time to time, the dark-colored hull would rise atop a wave. Valeska handed me the binoculars and grabbed the helm. I stood up, steadied myself with one arm around a shroud and took a long look. Was it *Esmeralda*? Perhaps, but it was too far away to be sure. I just hoped that whoever was on board that mysterious-looking yacht hadn't seen us.

At nightfall, I turned on the navigation lights in case there was traffic and set the radar alarm for five miles, in case a fishing boat or cargo ship got too close. I spent my first trick at the helm with George, showing him how to mark our hourly position on the chart. I explained that sailors fall overboard most often while having a leak off the stern, and demonstrated how to put on a deck harness by clipping him onto the jack line.

Around 2200 hours, the wind dropped. The second night shift took over. Since neither Valeska nor Eddy had much experience sailing at night, I stayed with them to adjust the sails, then stretched out in the cockpit and dozed off.

I don't know how long I'd been sleeping, but for some reason I woke up. Valeska was on watch while Eddy had his eyes glued on the radar.

"Jacques, look. There is something out there off the starboard bow that seems to be moving rapidly toward us, much too fast for a fishing boat."

I sat up and looked at the screen and saw that the vessel was about five minutes away from crossing right in front of our bow. It could have been a navy patrol boat, since we were only about fifteen miles offshore, but unlikely: The Honduran Navy was usually in dry dock at the Puerto Cortés Naval Base. I knew all about that. I went inside and woke up Cowboy George.

"Wake up, Cowboy. We have visitors. They could be pirates."

Then I passed three flare guns that I had stashed above the chart table outside to Eddy.

"Flare guns. Good," he said.

Cowboy George was up on his feet.

"Cowboy, pass me that yellow waterproof case underneath the chart table, will you?"

He reached underneath and pulled it out.

"What's in there?"

"Cartridges for the flare guns."

I passed them to Eddy.

"Nice, I'm sure a couple of those well-placed could cause a little havoc on board any kind of boat," he said.

"Or give somebody a bad case of heartburn," added Cowboy George as he climbed up into the cockpit.

I followed the Cowboy, opened the cartridge case and showed them how to load the guns.

"Press on this part and the gun will open, like this. Slip the cartridge in, then close the gun up and make sure that it's locked. When you want to shoot, just pull the hammer back, point and pull the trigger. Valeska will stay on the helm. Just keep the boat heading straight ahead for now; if we have to change course, I'll let you know. That's it, that's all."

"Remember, keep your heads down. I don't want them to see anyone on deck, and if whoever it is comes too close, I'll let them have it first, then you guys do the same while I reload. Got it?"

I didn't alter the boat's speed or change heading. That would have let them know that we were on their case. We just laid low in the cockpit for a few minutes and waited. Then the growl of two big outboard motors began to grow louder. From where I was crouched, I spotted a long speeding form suddenly pop out of the darkness. It veered off suddenly, then slowed almost to a stop about a hundred feet away. None of us moved. It was a typical drug-running boat, painted matte black, about thirty feet long. I could see two dark shadows at the wheel, and another one, surely well armed, at the bow. But why had they bothered to come out all that way to investigate a speck on their radar? One way or another, after they saw *Numada*, they gunned the twin engines and disappeared back into the night. A close call for sure; they must have been drug runners on a rendezvous. I guess that we were not the boat they were looking for.

For the next few hours, no one could relax. My crew tried to catnap while I sat at the helm, considering what could have happened to us. During the ordeal, no one had so much as flinched, let alone panicked. Of course, I already trusted Eddy because we had been through a lot of tricky situations together. As for Valeska, I'd seen her moving firearms, and she seemed to be adapting well to life at sea. In Cowboy George's case, there was nothing really cowboy about the man. He was all Indian, with sharp eyes, sensitive and steady. He'd been brought up on a reservation; good survival instincts were essential.

Ever since he was a kid, that nickname had stuck to him like gum to a shoe. I liked the way he'd stayed cool when that speedboat showed up on the radar. George had been involved in conflicts like the long Mohawk standoff at Oka, Québec, back in 1989. Although he didn't belong to that particular First Nation, he'd pitched in to help the Mohawks defend their land. The standoff had lasted for weeks, and when the army finally showed up and the shooting began, there were casualties on both sides. Cowboy George never provided details.

As day broke, we saw coastline off to starboard. Through binoculars, I could see breaking surf, a long beach and wave-like dunes of golden sand. Just back from the beach, majestic coconut palms danced in the breeze. Off in the distance, a chain of mountains stretched out in both directions. We all took turns looking through the glasses. Valeska explained to Cowboy George that a good portion of the territory had been converted into a national wildlife reserve. Eddy grabbed the camera and filmed this impromptu scene.

"Actually, most people in Central American are *mestizo*. Our history goes way back, like yours. My own family is a mixture of Mayan, African, Russian and I don't know what."

I was busy concentrating on the action until Eddy pointed out a dark bank of clouds approaching rapidly from the north. It looked like a heavy squall was headed our way, so before the wind picked up, Valeska and I reduced sail and prepared the boat for a blow. We had about thirty miles to go, and we still needed to find the mouth of the Patuca River. Once back in the cockpit, I unhooked the autopilot and grabbed the long tiller. If there was going to be some real wind, I wanted to be the one steering.

The water windward started to come alive with whitecaps. A strong gust pushed the boat over another ten degrees. I liked preparing for a blow; it was always exciting. For a few minutes, I forgot about everything else but the boat. It was hard over and perfectly trimmed — this was real sailing. Those few minutes put me in another place.

Another gust heeled the boat over some more. The sea, which up to now had been fairly comfortable, was starting to get lumpy, with the odd wave slapping up against the side of the boat. But the heavy schooner didn't complain at all; it was in its element. According to my chart, we were fast approaching the mouth of the Rio Patuca.

I asked Valeska to let out the jib a little and eased off at the helm. *Numada* straightened up and we gained another knot.

There were whitecaps heading our way. That meant more wind. Looking up at the sails, I knew that we were set for the next strong gust, and when it hit, the boat reacted perfectly and gained more speed. With my hand on the tiller, I could feel the rudder vibrating underneath. We were really moving and I think that I even let out a loud yell. Everybody was hanging on and enjoying the rush. As we slid forward, I got to thinking how a squall at sea was always a challenge. You just never knew what it could bring. It was the same with every new experience in life. There were always surprises. To survive you had to take it all in stride and do your best, but at the same time never forget where you are, 'cause shit happens. Since leaving Puerto Cortés, I'd managed to get caught up in the frenzy of my own folly. But during the last few days, just as we were about to begin the most important leg of this project, I had realized that the success of this whole expedition was on my shoulders. But then again, I wasn't alone. The crew that was riding with me was proving to be exceptional. I had a strong feeling that together, we could handle about anything that came along. This was really living, pushing it to the edge, and that's the way it had to be. It was here, and it was now. I caught a glimpse of Valeska's wide shining eyes. She looked ecstatic.

"It's payday!" she yelled.

We dipped into a large wave and it exploded over the deck.

Eddy and Cowboy George, sitting on *Numada*'s windward side, caught a dose of the heavy spray.

"Yes!" cried Eddy over the loud sounds coming from the rigging.

Once again, I felt we were all travelling on the same wave as *Numada* carried us forward.

•••

The wind was still blowing hard as we closed in on Barra Patuca. When I could clearly see details on the shoreline, I called our reception committee on channel 69. No response. I tried again. Nothing. Just as I was about to invent a Plan B, I heard the speaker crackle in Spanish.

"*Numada, Numada, me copia. Numada, Numada, me copia, me copia.*"

"Hey, Peter-Pedro, is that you?"

"Yes, it's us, where are you?"

"We're about five miles northwest of the pass."

"Okay, *Numada*, we'll guide you. When you see our boat, wait for our signal before you come in through the pass. Don't come in unless you see us."

"I understand, Peter-Pedro. *Graçias*."

It seemed everything was going according to plan. I could feel it in Peter-Pedro's confident tone. Still, I was beginning to have doubts. The northeast wind that had been our main driving force would now be blowing in against the strong river current as it emptied into the sea. That would making steep breaking waves at the entrance.

Sure, *Numada* was a great boat at sea, but shooting breakers was a different story. She would need all the speed she could muster to ride safely in, and it was possible she wouldn't be fast enough. But the schooner had a strong engine and we had lots of weight where it counted. I would leave a mainsail up, centering the boom to help prevent us rolling from side to side. In case things got out of hand, we could douse the sail fairly quickly and try to motor our way out of trouble.

I gave the order to clear the decks of anything that might get swept overboard. All loose objects inside were secured in a safe place in case of a knockdown. Finally, about half a mile offshore, I fired up the engine and lowered the staysail, working jib and second main, then sheeted in the main on the foremast. The only thing now was to cross our fingers. We could see the pass clearly, with deserted sand dunes on each side and surf crashing onto the beach. Then, straight ahead, I spotted Peter-Pedro and his brother standing in a small *lancha*, well inside the surf line, arms in the air and waving at us like crazy. That was the sign I was expecting. We sat there in the rolling sea waiting for a lull, and when it finally came, I gunned the throttle and we started to move in. It was now or never.

I yelled to Eddy, "Be prepared with your camera; this could be a wild ride." He ducked into the cabin and pulled out the small camera in its waterproof bag.

Hanging on tight with one hand, he started filming.

"Holy shit, look at the size of that wave!" Cowboy George called.

I looked behind us at the building mass of water and tried to keep my cool. "It's like *Hawaii Five-O*," Eddy hissed, bracing himself.

"Valeska, put in the washboards and pull the hatch shut as fast as you can; we could get pooped."

Seconds later, *Numada* lifted up and carried ahead. The boat's speed went up over fourteen knots on the GPS, and I had to grasp the tiller with two hands to control our direction. The burst of speed lasted about ten seconds before the wave passed and broke just ahead of us, leaving *Numada* stalled in a swirling, foamy trough. I looked to the stern again. There was an even bigger wave overtaking us. The schooner began picking up speed again, but we weren't moving fast enough. As we rose onto the next crest, I looked behind again, only to see a wall of water beginning to curl over. The stern lifted suddenly and the schooner shot ahead.

"Hang on, everybody! We're going to get creamed!"

The wave got even steeper. Glancing to starboard, I saw it start to break. I caught a brief glimpse of Cowboy George standing on the cabin roof with one arm wrapped around the mast, the other hand clutching his famous Stetson, and his long black hair streaming behind. He let out a war cry. At the same time, with two arms extended, I pushed on the long tiller with all my strength. *Numada* began to turn off slightly to starboard as the water exploded around us, covering the deck with salty brine and shooting us forward into the calmer waters behind the sandbar. Everyone on board cheered. We'd made it by the skin of our teeth.

Peter-Pedro and his brother approached our boat, their eyes round. "You must be crazy!" his brother shouted over the pounding surf. "Those breakers are at least fifteen feet high!" Peter-Pedro couldn't stop laughing.

"*Amigo*, in my sweet lifetime, I've never seen anybody do anything like that. You must have *cojones* the size of cantaloupes!"

"But you waved us in, didn't you?" I said.

"Waved you in? No, *hombre*, we were waving you away. It's way too dangerous to try to come in right now. We were waving like this, not like that."

He repeated the same gesture.

"Shit, you gotta be kidding me."

"No matter, you made it in and it was wonderful to see. Welcome to Barra Patuca, my friends! *Numada*, follow us."

They motored up the wide river entrance toward their village. Another close call, I thought to myself. We were damn lucky. The gods had been watching over us. But when I think about it now, they must have been having a good laugh at the same time.

Barra Patuca

South of the bay sat a cluster of small wooden houses built on stilts, their tin roofs worn rusty by years of salty sea spray. A dozen dugouts had been hauled up on the beach, and fishing nets had been hung on racks to dry. On the hard-packed sand flats near a small wooden dock, a group of kids played soccer with an empty plastic container. There was a sweet smell in the air — wildflowers and smoke from cooking fires. Everything was peaceful. There was no sign of *Esmeralda* or of the black *lancha* that had buzzed us during the night.

Numada motored on carefully into the shallow waters of the estuary. Seen from shore, it must have looked as if the boat up ahead was towing us like some great fish the two brothers had caught at sea. We glided closer to the center of the village, past a cement dock with a waterlogged fifty-foot barge tied alongside it. On the barge's deck were stacks of wooden planks, bags of cement and wooden crates. Two men stopped unloading to watch our boats slip by. We continued along the shore, passing a small creek that emptied into the lagoon. Peter-Pedro and his brother guided us carefully toward a fragile wooden dock. Hauled up on a slip was the fishing boat they had welded together back in Puerto Cortés. The deck was piled high with wooden traps. The propeller had been pulled. It was between fishing seasons.

Further on and tucked in behind a cluster of palm trees sat a modest house built of worn wooden boards painted lime green, with a rusty tin roof sloping over a wide balcony. Stairs led up to the balcony, and on the wide muddy bank off to the side, a grove of tall bamboo trees swayed gently in the breeze; their long shadows cast upon the front of house made the structure seem to come alive. An elderly man dressed in a worn white shirt and ragged khaki shorts emerged from the front door as we approached.

I looked down into the murky water. According to the sounder, there couldn't have been more than a foot of water under the keel. We nudged up against the dock as the brothers climbed onto the rickety wharf and grabbed the dock lines from Valeska and Cowboy George. They jumped down onto the wet sand and wrapped the lines around wooden posts. *Numada* secured, I returned to the cockpit and gave Valeska a long hug.

"You sure scared the hell out of me." Her eyes sparkled.

"I know. I scared the hell out of myself, too, but don't tell anyone."

Going in when I did could have ended the trip right there in the surf, with a capsized sailboat, waterlogged crew, or worse. When we shut off the engine, we felt a wonderful calm. In the distance I could hear the surf pounding in, mixed with a sweet chorus of tropical birdsongs coming from the mangroves nearby. A dozen wide-eyed children appeared from nowhere. The old man on the balcony came down the steps and soon stood on the dock beside our boat. He seemed in good shape for a man of at least eighty. His dark brown skin contrasted beautifully with his white beard. A ball cap was pulled down over his forehead.

"*Beinvenedo*," he exclaimed, and climbing on board, he greeted me with a firm handshake. His palm felt like rawhide. "*Mi nombre es Anton Lopez*."

"*Mi nombre es Jacques Legris. Mucho gusto, señor.*" I then introduced him to my crew.

Anton had the same calm expression as Peter-Pedro. I could see a family resemblance, except that Anton had surprisingly vivid blue eyes. He looked up and down the deck, then tilted his head back to examine the tall masts that seemed even higher now that we were tied up to such a small wharf. He knocked on the deck with his fist. "*Que barco solido*." (What a solid boat.)

Peter-Pedro and Chili-Chili joined us and we shared a good laugh about our dramatic arrival. Anton nodded his head, then mentioned another tall-masted boat he'd seen offshore.

"A few times it has entered here and anchored near that point over there. They always load up with cargo brought by *lancha* from up the river. Then they leave. In fact, they were here a few days ago."

"What kind of cargo did they load on board?" I asked.

He answered only with a sly smile and then shrugged his shoulders. I changed the subject and explained to Señor Anton some details concerning the film project. I told him that George was a Native Canadian Indian who had come to meet and learn about the Miskito, Pech and Tawahka tribes. I also explained that we had come a long way just to visit the Ciudad Blanca.

The old man stared at us for a long moment. His eyes seemed to have changed color. "Ciudad Blanca?"

He looked over at his sons.

"…*Si, possible, pero muy peligroso*." (Yes, possible, but very dangerous.)

"Señor Anton, if possible, we want to film this place before the looters empty it. We hope to show to the world what these people are doing to Honduras' archaeological heritage. Maybe it will make a difference."

Anton nodded. I thought that he wanted to trust me but wasn't exactly certain that he could. I unfolded a map and showed it to him. I had marked an X over the place where Ciudad Blanca was supposed to be. The brothers and their father studied the map in detail, pointing out various spots where the fishing was good or where a small village stood. I brought out the satellite photos. "According to these photos, this is the exact position."

The old man looked at the photos, then back at the map, then up at the sky. Not a word was said as we waited for the elder to pronounce his opinion. He nodded with a smile. "I think the satellite is correct," he said in English.

"How many days will it take to get there?"

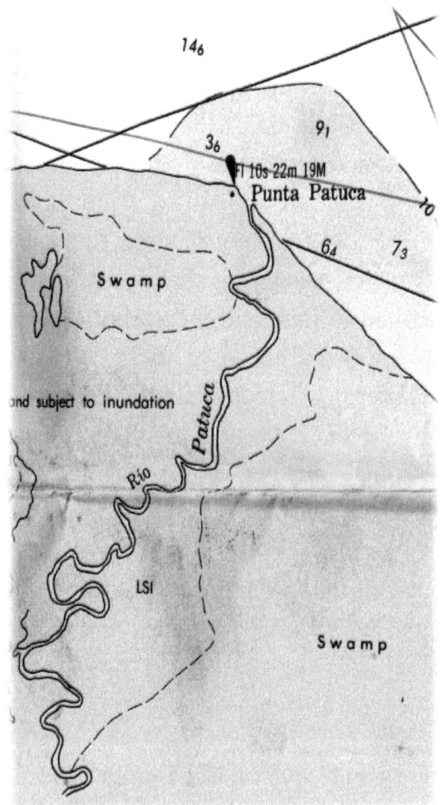

"It depends on the river. Maybe three days, maybe more if it rains, because lots of rain means lots of current," he added, gesturing with his hands.

I turned to Chili-Chili. "Are you sure you can get us up there?"

"*Claro*, I have been on this river all my life. The Pech people who live there will help us if we need gas or repairs, and they can also provide us with food. I know them well. We are all river people."

I looked over at Peter-Pedro; he seemed to want to say something.

"You are going to need someone to look after your boat while we are gone."

"You're right about that, my friend. An important detail that I have been ignoring until today. Do you have any suggestions?"

"*Si, mi padre.* My father is the best man around. We talked about this already."

Anton seemed content to have such an important responsibility on his hands. "Yes, I will look after it as if it were my own. If a big storm comes, I can get help to bring it into the mangroves. That's what we do with our boats when the weather gets bad. It will be safer over there, Señor Jack." He pointed to a thick cluster of mangroves upriver. "There is a small basin inside. Once your boat is secured there, it will be out of danger."

"That's what I wanted to hear," I said, feeling a little relieved.

Anton and I shook hands. I knew that with him in charge of *Numada*, all would be well. That afternoon, we sat on deck and talked a mixture of

Spanish, English and Innu, with some Miskito and Garifuna added for good measure. We all seemed to make ourselves understood. Pedro and Chili-Chili had lots to tell us. Charts and diagrams were strewn around the cockpit. I was so involved with making plans that I hadn't noticed Eddy with the camera on his shoulder. The art of filmmaking often requires one to wear many hats. Up to that point, I had been too busy with the boat and preparations for the next few weeks to think about shooting. Eddy had kept the equipment handy. As we were sitting around, I observed that Chili-Chili didn't look at all like his brother Peter-Pedro. He was a few inches taller, more heavyset, perhaps ten years younger. If anything, with his long black hair and strong features, he looked more like an Innu. In fact, when he and Cowboy George first met, Chili-Chili began to speak Spanish with him, assuming that George was someone from the region. George had replied in Innu and they'd both found that funny.

Chili-Chili knew the river like his backyard — which it was. He knew it even better than his father did, which made sense because over the years, certain areas of the river had been altered due to erosion caused by deforestation. "Rio Patuca is a good river during the dry season, but when the heavy rains arrive, it swells up and sometimes overflows its banks," he explained. "The current becomes very strong and sometimes can take out trees. So when it rains, we have to be on the lookout for snags and fallen trees. They could sink a boat in minutes."

•••

That evening, we ate supper seated around a clay oven fuelled by dry pieces of cedar. Roasted langosta and fresh dorado were on the menu. Chili-Chili's wife María had prepared the whole meal. She was a quiet woman with smooth dark skin, a beautiful face and a kind smile. Her features were definitely a mixture of Garifuna and Pech. María radiated calmness to everyone around her and it was the kind of energy we needed. The interior of their home was simple, sparse and spotlessly clean. That afternoon she had shown Valeska around her kitchen, explaining what was needed to do the cooking on the river. They worked together, combining dried food, plastic plates and a few coolers from *Numada*'s galley with various pots and pans from María's kitchen.

As the fire outside burned low, a fresh breeze blew in off the sea. The flames crackled and spat the odd spark that sent tracers up into the night. Somewhere not too far away, a dog barked, trying to raise a reaction among his hairy friends. Hardly audible but ever present was the steady rhythm of heavy thumping surf crashing in on the beach on the other side of the lagoon, as long fronds of tall palm trees that grew behind the house danced in the wind. Overhead, the Milky Way stretched its giant ribbon of silver dust across the sky. It felt great to be alive and feeling the magic of that tropical evening and share it with these generous people of the Mosquito Coast.

Anton's grandson brought more wood and the elder stoked the fire. Its light projected our shadowy silhouettes like early moving pictures onto the wall of the old family home. I mentioned the visit we'd had from the big *lancha* the night before. The brothers listened attentively and agreed we had been lucky.

"There's a lot of offshore traffic at night," said Chili. "You never know who is out there, but most of the time they are *narco-trafficantes*, the worst kind of pirates because usually they shoot first and ask questions later. The best strategy when you are sailing near the Mosquito Coast at night is to stay way offshore if you don't want trouble."

"Yeah, next time I'll do that. Hey, Chili-Chili, maybe you could tell me, is it true that stolen artifact trafficking is almost as lucrative as running narcotics up from Colombia?"

"Sure, it is, and you get less jail time if you're caught looting artifacts. You can even avoid prison. But the problem will not be with the police or the army. It will be with the locals. It's really their territory. It's important you look like simple tourists when we travel the river. And if anyone sees you with the camera, say you're doing a movie about something less provocative, like insects or rare plants. The locals up there don't like intruders, especially ones who are snooping around too close to a subject that no one really wants to talk about." He raised his cap and rubbed a hand through his thick black hair. "But it's not the locals that I'm worried about; it's the new gangs. They come from the exterior, buy off the locals and move in."

"But how do they operate?" asked Cowboy George.

"They travel on *lancha*, like us," Chili-Chili answered. "They bring the artifacts out here to the coast, where they transfer them to boats even larger than yours. I hear they sometimes come in with helicopters and stonecutting machinery that can slice into the stone carvings like a knife cuts through a fat pig. A carved stone slab or a big limestone carving is worth big American bucks. Some even exchange cocaine for artifacts; it's a different kind of money laundering."

"And what about the police?" Cowboy George inquired.

"They're in this up to their necks," said Peter-Pedro. "They're experts at looking the other way, and they're no match for these gangs, anyway." He shrugged. "Around here, an AK-47 can be bought for next to nothing. There is still a big surplus in Nicaragua and people smuggle them into Honduras all the time."

As Peter-Pedro spoke, I couldn't help thinking about the Dog. The Dog probably had collaborators somewhere near Patuca or in other villages along the coast. Government patrol boats were few and far between. I knew all about *Esmeralda* and the way it had been modified for trafficking artifacts. With the big cargo hold and small crane on deck, it could load a few tons at a time without even making an effort at discretion, simply because there was nobody out there checking.

Anton hadn't said much all evening — he just added wood to the fire if the conversation started to fade. But then he said, "Ciudad Blanca is not too far from where my great-grandparents were born. When I was young, my grandfather told me that his father had grown up in a city carved in white stone. They called it Wahia-Patatahua in Pech, which means Village of the Ancestors. It is said the city was created by the Monkey God. When I was a child, the old people said that it was full of giant stone carvings of wild animals of various shapes, including statues of monkeys, since they believed in the Monkey God."

"But why would people abandon their city?" asked Valeska.

"A long time ago," Anton said, "I was told that when the Pech lived there, a shaman left Wahia-Patatahua after being mistreated by the community. After that, terrible disease and catastrophe befell the community. The Pech believed the shaman had put a curse on the city, so they left and moved downriver to a place they call Sakorska Uya, the Big Writing Stone. It is the site of a large and very ancient petroglyph that can still be visited upriver from Las Marías. Sakorska Uya is on the Platano River, just west of here. That is where my father was born. His family were better off at Sakorska Uya because it was closer to the ocean and the fish. But then a terrible hurricane came and destroyed everything. After that, my father's family and most of the survivors moved here to Barra Patuca. This is a good place with even better access to the interior. Our ancestors entrusted this place to us, and all my life I have tried my best to do the most with the little we have.

"But we have been pushed aside many times and our culture has been ignored. The lumber companies have stripped our mahogany forests, cattle ranchers burn our savannah lands, poachers are killing off the wild animals, and now people are raiding the sacred places that our fathers and mothers left in our keep. None of this could have happened without the help of our own people who have brought these intruders to the interior."

Anton knew much more than he was letting on, and I had a strange feeling that he still didn't trust us completely. To gain his complete confidence would take time, and time was something we didn't have much of. Cowboy George had also been quiet most of the evening, but he now spoke his mind. "Since I stepped foot on your land, I feel I have known you before. Walking through your village feels a lot like my home in the North. Anton, I watched you make the campfire. It's exactly the way my father taught me. María cooks in the same way my wife does. She learned from her mother. You talk about your land being taken away. We too have had our great forests plundered by logging companies and flooded by hydroelectric companies. Our cultural heritage was stolen from us by the government and by missionaries. Many of us have lost our own language. Our peoples are fighting for the same cause. Señor Anton, you can be certain I understand the significance of what you are saying."

The Last Call

As the first light of day began to chase away the stars, I got up, put on my headphones and caught the weather forecast on the portable Single-Sideband radio receiver. The local long-term forecast had predicted a week of thunderstorms mixed with fine weather, a little hotter than usual. Another tropical depression was brewing way out in the Atlantic. According to the NOAA forecast center in Miami, the storm was on its way toward the Grenadines, then northwest, before it headed down hurricane alley to the Yucatán Coast. That all sounded pretty far away, so at the most, we could expect some rain and a little wind. That wouldn't bother *Numada*. We had doubled up on all the shorelines by running some heavy-duty hawsers over to some palm trees on the riverbank. It would take more than a little wind to cause any trouble there. We would be somewhere inland when it started to rain, and if it got heavy, we could always stop and wait it out. For the moment, we had a window. Not a great one, but open just enough to begin our expedition. After all, we were going into a rain forest where rain was normal, especially this time of year.

Trying not to wake anyone, I tiptoed into the small galley and brewed a pot of coffee, then sat up on deck to watch the sun rise. It was our last day of preparation and there were still many details to cross-check. If all went well, this time tomorrow we would be on our way up the Rio Patuca.

Valeska awoke at daybreak. She sat up and draped the white sheet around her body. When she saw me watching her, a soft morning smile crept over her face. It was early and everyone was still very much asleep, so I dropped back through the open deck hatch and joined her. The sunrise could continue without me.

Eddy took the camera and grabbed some early morning shots in the village. Cowboy George got up much later, made himself a copious breakfast and then went off looking for Eddy. Around midday, we filmed George and Chili sitting by the river in the shade of a big palm tree. They were getting to know each other.

Their conversation really got going when Chili told Cowboy George about two major hydroelectric projects planned for the river. If those projects went through, dams on the upper Patuca River would flood some of the last uninterrupted rain forests north of the Amazon. Furthermore, dozens of sacred Mayan ruins would be submerged forever. The electricity would be sold to industrialized cities throughout Central America.

This reminded the Innu of how most of the great rivers in Northern Québec had been taken over and harnessed for power. Thousands of square miles of traditional hunting territory were now under water. As Cowboy George listened to Chili, he picked up a piece of driftwood he'd been playing with in the sand, and in a gesture of frustration, smashed it down on a nearby rock, breaking it in two. Then he whispered something in Innu language to the effect of: "Some people never get enough!"

A little later, Eddy, Valeska and I took time to look through some of the material we'd shot since the beginning of the trip. Everything seemed fine technically; even the night shots around the campfire had managed to capture some of the magical atmosphere.

That afternoon, the entire crew carefully went over the lists of things to bring along before loading the two long river *pipantes* with boxes of food, bottles of drinking water, hammocks with mosquito nets, María's pots and pans, tarpaulins, machetes, a first aid kit, and our two waterproof cases jammed with cameras and microphones. The obvious problem was how to fit everything into two boats. It took lots of packing and repacking, but once the loads were balanced, large waterproof tarps taken from *Numada* were tied over the material. We loaded umbrellas for protection from the sun and rain, and Chili brought two well-oiled Winchester 30-30 rifles, a stainless steel shotgun and a Smith and Wesson .38. Each piece had been carefully wrapped in a canvas sheath. He slipped the heavier hardware under the tarp at the stern of each boat, right next to the driver's seat.

He discreetly put the handgun and three boxes of shells into a plastic cooler underneath his seat.

While final touches were being made on the two *pipantes*, I showed Anton and his grandson where I kept my extra-long dock lines, just in case a storm blew in and they needed to double up. They helped me place two other anchors on deck, and then I showed the old fisherman how to start the engine. For years, Anton Lopez had worked on various fishing boats and he was no stranger to diesel engines, but I made sure he understood there was a keel underneath *Numada* that drew almost seven feet of water. If he ever needed to move *Numada*, it was an important detail to consider.

"Seven feet, that's not a problem," he said. "But please be aware of the weather as you head up the river. Nature will warn you and you must react as soon as it does. You cannot fight the weather, and you cannot ignore the signs that the gods give you."

Drizzle fell lightly that evening, so we ate together on board the schooner. After dinner, I took out the chart and laid it on the cabin table. Chili-Chili leaned over and studied it for a few seconds.

"We are here," he said and tapped a finger on the spot where the Rio Patuca emptied into the Caribbean Sea. "And we are going way up here." He tapped his figure again on a place up the river. "Tomorrow night, if all goes well, we'll sleep on this small point of sand. It's a good place to make our first camp. The next night, we'll try to reach this camp where friends of mine live. Good people. We will stay there for a night. After that, we'll head up to Casa Tio, my uncle's old camp. It's a day's travel from the second stop."

"Just one question. Casa Tio? Doesn't Tio mean uncle?"

"Yes, since we were very young, we've always called him Tio or Uncle Tio"

"That's a good bilingual name," I said.

"We thought so too and it's easier to say than Tio Elí Arroyo Lopez."

"Yeah, you can say that again."

"Now, to get back to business, within four or five days, we should be at the ruins of Ciudad Blanca," he said with a distinct air of confidence.

"Sounds like a good plan. Now let's talk supplies."

•••

We were about finished going over the details when Anton leaned into the narrow companionway just above us. In the dim light that came from the lamp above the table, we could only see his face and part of his shirtless torso. He looked almost one-dimensional. "Ciudad Blanca is the *wahia-patatahua* in the old language, or the place of the ancestors. It is the place where the ancient gods have gone. I repeat, you should not disturb these spirits. People have been cursed for this. Horrible things have happened to them. Remember, this place has been sacred for many years." At that moment, a large silver and blue butterfly hovered by and landed on Anton's left shoulder. It must have been attracted by the cabin light. Anton felt its presence and opened his hand beside it. The butterfly moved onto the palm of his hand, and Anton, somewhat like a sorcerer, held it in front of his face and gently blew on its wings. The insect stayed there, immobile. I'll never forget the impression the elder gave me, as if suddenly he was somewhere else, above and beyond the here and now. "*Mariposa* is tired and doesn't want to fly anymore," he whispered. "Strange, I've rarely seen this kind before. It has struggled in a strong wind and comes from far away."

"Africa?" I asked.

"No, from South America," he said, keeping his eyes fixed on the blue Morpho menelaus.

Around 11 p.m., the Lopez family returned to their house on the riverbank while most of *Numada*'s crew enjoyed their last night's sleep in a real bunk. Before I followed suit, I had to check the weather forecast on the Single-Sideband radio receiver. It had stopped raining, so to escape the hot, muggy atmosphere below, I sat up on deck and waited for broadcast time. Outside, a perfect silence reigned and the distant roar of breaking waves seemed almost soothing. I turned on the radio. The signal from NOAA was broken up, but I understood that the tropical storm out in the Atlantic had changed track and was now moving toward the Dominican Republic. It would probably not amount to much more than heavy rains. But there was a new tropical depression forming in the Southern Caribbean, just off the coast of Colombia. It was moving northwards and could possibly turn into a tropical storm in a day or two.

A hurricane almost never forms in the extreme Southern Caribbean, so I told myself it was probably just a freak pocket of bad weather. It would likely blow itself out in a few days. And the longer we waited at Barra Patuca, the greater our chances of getting bogged down in the jungle by the late October rains. The next day, come hell or high water, we were going to leave the coast.

When I turned the radio off, I realized that Valeska was sitting just behind me. "Sounds like bad weather is on the way," she said. "So what's the plan?"

"No change."

"That storm off Colombia, doesn't it worry you?"

"Sure, but we're ready. If it comes this way, it will just be rain and we'll be well up the river by then."

"But Anton said that the river could be dangerous if we get too much rain."

"I know, but, Valeska, this may be the only chance we get. It's now or never."

She looked at me for a few seconds, saying nothing.

•••

It had been almost a year since I had decided to look for Ciudad Blanca, and after everything, the morning had come. I could finally say, "Today, we are going."

I slipped out of bed without disturbing Valeska, pulled on my shorts and lifted myself up through the hatch. The deck was covered with pearling drops of dew. I stepped off the schooner, walked down the narrow jetty and turned to look at *Numada* sitting motionless on the water. The long shadows of the schooner's masts stretched across the river. The light, the stillness, the reflection, everything seemed almost too perfect. There wasn't a whisper of wind anywhere, not even a flutter. The only movement came from the lazy current gliding by on its way out to sea.

Already the heat pushed me into the shade. In the muck under the dock, a few crabs were also heading for cover. A flock of parrots passed overhead on their way to a mango tree and nearly collided with a V-shaped squad of pelicans flying the other way. Nature's morning rush hour had begun. Wisps of bluish smoke emanating from cooking fires rose straight up toward the sky. For most, it was just another typical morning at Barra Patuca.

I should have been eager to start, but I felt as nervous as a stage actor waiting for the curtain to open. Everyone had worked so hard to put the pieces of this expedition into place, and, at last, we were ready to leave on the river. That was sufficient to make anyone a little shaky. Maybe the legend had started to affect my reasoning. Maybe it was just nerves. Maybe it was the latest forecast from Miami. Maybe it was Ernesto, the bartender in Guanaja, and his story about the film crew swallowed up by the jungle. Something my father once said came back to me in a flash: Every man chooses his own poison.

I walked to the far end of the dock, dropped down to the water's edge, and sat on an overturned dugout, observing my associates from a distance as they stepped out on deck to greet the new day. The first one out was Eddy, who stretched and went up to the bow to look down at the water. Cowboy George came out next. He joined Eddy, and they exchanged a few words, laughed and of course, shared a pre-breakfast smoke.

Valeska appeared a few moments later. "Breakfast and coffee…"

We ate a light breakfast together in the cockpit while going over last-minute details. Everyone seemed almost as nervous as I was. Then it was time to embark on the two long dugouts and say goodbye to the sleepy village of Barra Patuca. As we motored upstream, I looked back to see Anton standing on the end of the dock. He raised an arm in the air and pointed toward the sky. As we rounded the first bend in the river, I looked over at my friends and grinned. Chili-Chili, María, Cowboy George and Eddy were in one boat. Valeska, Peter-Pedro Lopez and I were in the other. Here we were, finally heading up a river that had a story around each curve. I just hoped that the gods would treat us kindly.

PART FOUR

The Patuca runs gently out of the Sierra Mountains. It begins as a stream and finishes deep and wide where it empties into the Caribbean Sea. At first glance, the surface looks slow and lazy, but underneath, it is treacherous, alternating deep reaches with rock patches and great banks of red mud. The water is the color of raw amber. In places, it forms whirlpools, creating undertows that can swallow whole trees. As we paddled our way through savannah and thick jungle, steep yellow sandbanks sometimes appeared in the most unexpected places. From time to time, we could see clearings on either bank. Gigantic trees hung right over the water. From time to time, someone would point out something special, like an osprey or a crocodile.

Our long narrow boats passed through a small collection of grassy islands. As we left the low-lying savannah, the purr of our outboard motors startled parrots and long-legged cranes. The further inland we travelled, the thicker the jungle grew, and the odor of rotting earth smelled almost morbid. Ashore, there was the incessant chatter of monkeys, and often we could see howlers and ringtails swinging from tree to tree.

Slowly, the river narrowed and the thick walls of vegetation began to close in on us from both sides. There were canopies of great wide leaves, tangled vines, and branches heavy with clusters of moss that hung down like living curtains. I wondered whether something curious was about to swing down from a branch to get a closer look.

The further we went, the smaller I felt. Suddenly, the mosquitoes became fierce and macaws began to squawk. From overhead, howler monkeys threatened us with wild gestures and screams. Everything seemed to belong to something else, more and more like an immense mixture of chaos, where everything that crawled, slithered, flew, walked or hopped was just as close as my next breath.

When the shadows began to lengthen, we hauled our boats up onto a sandbank, where a large broad-leaved tree blessed us with shade. Chili-Chili went over to a mound of earth and tossed aside a thick curtain of moss and vines. It was a stone petroglyph about as big as a refrigerator. A feathered serpent and a large four-legged bird with bat-like wings were engraved on the large flat rock. There was a large stone head nearby with etchings carved into a flat stone underneath it.

"This is a territory marker," Chili said. "I've seen others like it out here."

Kneeling, I brushed my hand over the stone. Then, looking down at my feet, I noticed an endless trail of thousands of red ants marching across the thick jungle soil, each one carrying a piece of green leaf that resembled a sail. They filed up the smooth bark of a large tree and disappeared into a split branch. Pedro frowned and said that ants usually did that before a heavy rain. I tried not to think of it too much, but the same question kept popping into my head. Was something brewing? If it was, there wasn't much to do but keep on going up the river as far as we could before the sky fell.

During the last hour of daylight, a few of us waded into the river up to our knees to wash, but we were careful because that time of the evening is perfect for an old crocodile to sneak over under the muddy surface and try his luck. I noticed that Chili-Chili and Cowboy George didn't go in for a wash; they had another plan. Each one armed himself with a machete and a rifle, and they discretely went off along a narrow trail that ran along the riverbank then disappeared into the thick bush. Eddy followed close behind with the camera. It wasn't often that one could see two Native Americans from communities thousands of miles apart hunting together.

While I sat in the last minutes of daylight writing in my notebook, two long dugout canoes poled by wiry men approached from upriver. The boats were loaded with children, parents and grandparents sitting among sacks of rice, bananas and baskets of vegetables. They poled their boats over to where we were setting up camp and beached.

These were Miskito returning to their homes, having spent several weeks working the more fertile land upriver. The women chattered and laughed, and handed out mangoes and melons to María as she unpacked our food box. One of the men offered us two large freshly caught fish wrapped in banana leaves. In an hour, our hunters returned with a large turtle and started a cooking fire. Soon the air was filled with smoke and the smell of supper roasting over the hot coals. In all we were eighteen, including six children. It was the children who fascinated me the most. Their large dark eyes watched our every move, especially when Eddy took out the camera and started filming. One child, a small boy perhaps six years old named Chicho, shadowed me all evening. Later, the boy came over and curled up and fell asleep on the sand just beside me.

That evening, everyone slept on the sand between two fires that burned through the night. They were to keep the mosquitoes and predators away. It was a good thing too, because several times during the night I heard a growl coming from the jungle nearby. Chili got up and quietly stoked the campfires.

"Chili, what the hell was that?" I asked.

"Jaguar. Don't worry, Señor Jack, they don't like the flames. But if it comes too close, I'll scare it off with this." He patted the 30-30.

When I awoke the next morning, the Miskito family with little Chicho had already slipped away. María was the only one of us who saw them leave. After breakfast, we packed our things and began Day Two of our expedition.

I took notes and just tried to take it all in. At one point, I dozed off. When I opened my eyes, they focused on a condor soaring gracefully in the sky high above. I also noticed that a layer of thin white clouds had moved into the upper levels, and a distinct ring circled the sun. Were the rings around the sun, the red ants moving to higher ground, and the stray blue butterfly that had landed on old Anton's hand nature's way of telling me that bad weather was approaching? If a serious storm did hit the coast, the old man would have to move fast to get *Numada* into the mangroves for protection. I just hoped that I hadn't made the wrong decision. Well, it was too late now; I just had to live with the choice that I had made and believe in that old man — and myself.

As we travelled on, it became obvious that the dense jungle lining both riverbanks was closing in. Valeska saw it as an infinitely complex shelter for a mass of living, crawling, prowling creatures. But for me, it was a single entity, ready to strike. She pointed out dozens of half-submerged crocodiles that blended in perfectly with sunken tree trunks. I couldn't begin to imagine what other creatures were hiding beneath that slimy murk. Further on, we passed small clusters of thatched huts on the muddy banks of the great river, homes of the Pech people who worked the soil, fished and used the river for transport. This was the first group of many scattered along the Patuca. Eastern Honduras and part of Nicaragua had been their homeland long before the first European explorers rowed ashore on the northern coast of this wild land.

Our two boats came close to a dozen children playing with a half-inflated soccer ball on a strip of sand. They waved at us. Nearby, a group of women were seated on round boulders near the riverbank washing clothes. They lifted their heads, watched us pass by and returned to their scrubbing. A mile or so upstream, our boats met more dugouts overflowing with families and children of all ages. Some of these *pipantes* were loaded with so many bananas, coconuts and passengers that only a few inches of freeboard made the slim difference between reaching the next destination and sinking. As always, somebody constantly bailed water from the boats, and more than once, we slowed so our wake wouldn't swamp a boat coming the other way.

Late that afternoon, Chili-Chili guided us into a small creek. Our boats rounded a bend, and we came across a few worn-out *pipantes* and some small huts on a narrow white sand spit that jutted into a wide spot in the stream. As we approached, the distinct musty smell of burning cedar filled the air. Children playing in the shallow water yelled and waved, and shortly afterwards two men came down and helped us pull up the boats.

The two families who lived here were Barra Patuca Miskito, also friends of the Lopez brothers. There were twelve in all, including the children and grandparents. They worked the small plot of land behind the camp. The land on the coast was notoriously infertile. For months on end, family clans like theirs tended small banana plantations and grew beans, rice and maize inland.

Yago, a well-built, brown-skinned fellow of about thirty, was the younger of two brothers. Abel appeared to be about ten years older and was roundish.

They grinned and shook hands with us awkwardly. Right off, Chili-Chili asked if they had any gasoline to sell, since we only had about twenty gallons left. Chili-Chili had arranged in advance to pick up more gas here, but there seemed to have been a problem anyway.

"*Gasolina, no hombre, no hay*," said Yago. (No, man, I don't have any.) He shrugged his shoulders and looked kind of embarrassed.

Chili didn't look too happy. But as tradition goes among the river people of Mosquitia, the problem was forgotten in a few minutes. Yago offered us an empty hut to hang our hammocks for the night. It didn't take long before our gang had settled in and the fish we'd caught along the way were roasting on the fire. After we ate, we sat around the brightly burning flames near our boats. Yago brought out a bottle of *guifiti*, a dark homemade brew spiced with peppers, seeds, twigs, cinnamon, marijuana and other, unidentifiable ingredients. From the warning look that Chili-Chili gave me, I was waiting for something strongly alcoholic, but when I took a slug, it burned my mouth. I had to laugh as I watched the others take swigs from the big bottle. A few minutes later, the stuff started to kick in. It was as potent as it tasted, and soon we were all high as frigatebirds.

As the fire burned on and the bottle was passed around, we got talking about our destination until, finally, Yago opened up. "Not too long ago, maybe three weeks back, Abel and I went upriver to buy seed from a Tawahka friend who lives near the border. On the way back, we decided to go hunting. There are deer up there, and there were lots of fresh tracks on the riverbank." The firelight illuminated his face and his dark eyes sparkled. He gazed straight into the flames. "We left our boat and followed some fresh deer tracks into the jungle. That's when we came across the ruins. At first we didn't realize how big they were, but then we saw. There were stone blocks everywhere. People had obviously been digging. There was a large pyramid. There were tools everywhere — shovels, saws and all kinds of equipment to cut stone." Yago paused and looked at Abel. "This was the place that we had heard about so many times before. It was the center, the center of the Ciudad Blanca. Everywhere we looked, we saw jade carvings, statues and pottery all over the ground. Someone was there taking away the treasures."

"They had even removed the head of a statue partway up one of the structures," added Abel.

"*Claro*," said Yago. "We'd found a looters' camp. Then we heard voices. The only thing we could do was climb a tree and hide. We would have been shot right there if they had seen us. I have never been so afraid in my life."

Yago took another slug of *guifiti*, then leaned over, picked up a stick and poked around in the fire. Sparks flew up into the night sky. He placed a pile of green leaves on the flames and thick smoke filled the air.

"These *hombres* were outsiders, maybe six in all."

"*Si*, and two of them had AK-47's," Abel added.

"Military?" I asked.

"I don't think so. But they had some military equipment, and their boss talked a few times on a telephone that he had with him."

"Probably a satellite phone, that's the only thing that works around here," said Peter-Pedro.

"There we were," Yago continued. "All we could do was wait and watch, and hope that they wouldn't see us. *Si, amigos*, we remained up there hiding in the branches like macaques while the looters worked below. They started packing the artifacts in wooden crates. But there was something else, too. Before they crated the artifacts, they placed some packages of what seemed to be cocaine in each container. Then after putting in false bottoms, they loaded each crate up with artifacts and sealed it tight."

"They must have been smuggling cocaine. But where did it come from?" I asked.

"That's easy, it comes from upriver. They bring it in from the Nicaraguan side. It's a safe route; no one thinks about bringing narcotics in this way."

"Yeah, no one except this gang." I looked over at Valeska, and she was staring at the ground. Had she known all along?

Yago pointed downward as if he was still perched in the tree. "The one who seemed to be the boss talked on the telephone part of the time. Once, he yelled at his men when the sculpted rock they'd been cutting out of the wall split in two. After a while, I needed to change positions because I had a cramp in one leg. And my brother wasn't doing any better. Just before dark, the men below stopped work, picked up the most valuable pieces, and left. Later, we saw that their camp was just around a bend. When we were certain we wouldn't be spotted, we climbed down the tree, grabbed a few small artifacts that had been left behind, and snuck off to our boat on the riverbank."

The bottle of *guifiti* went around the circle again and we all agreed that the brothers had been lucky. Yago asked his wife to show us a sample of what they had brought back. She got up and went into the woods, returning shortly with a jade carving about sixteen inches high. It was a monkey, wonderfully proportioned, its two arms crossed on its chest. Slowly, the statue was passed from hand to hand.

The Russian artifact dealer in Québec City had had his catalogue open to a page filled with photos of similar statues. He'd quoted five thousand dollars for one very much like this one. But this particular monkey was probably worth even more. It was bigger and with more elaborate carvings. That was more money than this little clan of subsistence farmers had ever seen.

According to Yago, many local people felt that selling pilfered artifacts was the only way to escape poverty, so it was understandable that they had no qualms about looting these sacred tombs. In the Mosquitia, a statue like this one could bring its finder around one hundred dollars, about a month's wages. But the guys that Yago and his brother had seen were working on two fronts: narcotics and artifacts. The weapons, military duds, the satellite telephone and rambling ruins of white stone certainly added up. This seemed to be typical Dog Barker strategy: a two-for-one deal.

It had been a long day, and as the night grew older and the bottle emptier, the idea of curling up in a hammock seemed increasingly attractive. Valeska and I went down to the water's edge to wash. I had to ask her. "Valeska, did you know about the cocaine?"

She looked at me and answered right away, "No, but I was suspicious. Once Dog had told me that it would be a good front. But I never really took him seriously."

"What about your uncle? Could he have been in on it as well?"

"No way. He didn't need the money or the problems. He was in it strictly for one purpose, to create a new world-class archaeological site. He made a big mistake teaming up with Dog Barker."

Then we were quiet for a while. I wondered if Valeska was telling me the truth.

In the dim light, we could just barely see a few night herons, knee-deep in the creek fishing for minnows. Somewhere in the trees on the other side, an owl hooted, seeking a friend with whom to converse. There wasn't a breath of wind, nor a human sound, only the mantra given off by an army of frogs and geckos. No Venus, Mars or bright white moon hung overhead, nothing but darkness and the oppressive, dank, humid heat of a night in the heart of the jungle. But we had access to fresh water, and washing up in the creek felt good.

"This is how I like it," said Valeska in a low voice. "Just listen to that chatter."

"Yeah, but if only we knew what they were saying, we might not want to hang around."

"It's probably just … how do you say? Small talk."

"Lucky those critters are as tiny as they are. We'd go mad with the racket if they were as big as us. It would be like being in a Québec City bar on a Friday night."

"What's Québec like?"

"Tame compared to here. Maybe I'll take you there sometime."

"No hurry; just get me to Ciudad Blanca for now. We'll see about Québec City later." Valeska slapped a mosquito that had started to drill on her shoulder.

"Let's go. If we stay out here any longer, we'll be eaten alive," I said.

Back inside the hut, it was almost like a sweat lodge, but the heat didn't keep anyone from sleeping. It was too dark to see who was who, but by the sound of the snoring, we knew exactly where Cowboy George's hammock was. Valeska put in her earplugs, climbed into her hammock, curled up and drifted off to sleep.

But my day was not quite finished. It was almost time for the weather forecast from Miami. Maybe there would be news about that depression off the Columbian coast. I put on my headlamp and started to look around inside the equipment cases for the trusty Single-Sideband radio receiver. No luck. In the last-minute rush before leaving the schooner, I must have left it on the chart table. What a dumb mistake. Keeping an eye on the weather was essential. Perhaps there really was something brewing offshore, but without a real forecast, how could I be certain?

In the middle of the Mosquitia, how could I have known that a massive tropical depression had begun to move northward, spinning, expanding, and gaining strength as it picked up speed? Then again, I reasoned, people had been living here for thousands of years without NOAA's sophisticated tropical storm predictions. I lay face up in my hammock and listened to the chorus of frogs. For a while, sleep was impossible. The storm gods were starting to make me nervous.

Around 4:00 a.m., the sound of rain falling on the thatched roof woke me up. I climbed out of my hammock and went outside. The light shower felt good and the air was fresher, almost bearable. If it stayed that way, we would have a good day to travel. Beyond the trees to the southeast, I noticed the odd flash of lightning — radiating from huge cumulus clouds stacked up at least fifteen thousand feet into the pre-dawn sky. We were probably in for a good soaking. I returned to my hammock with the sound of the jungle fading to a whisper, as if the hoard of living things were secretly making plans for the new day. When I brushed up against Valeska's netted cocoon, I realized she too was awake.

"Jack, I just had a horrible dream," she said in a low voice.

"What?"

"Someone faceless was chasing me through the jungle. He kept yelling at me. Then I fell into a hole full of mud and insects, I couldn't breathe, I was drowning. Then I saw Dog. He was laughing, watching me drown."

"Valeska, Dog isn't anywhere near here, and even if he were, he'd be dead meat if he ever lay a finger on you. Try to get a little more sleep. It's going to be another long day on the river. Bad weather is moving in."

There was a long silence. Just as I was about to doze off, she whispered, “Jack, you have to film Yago’s story about the looters. It’s too important to miss.”

She was right. We had to film Yago telling his story about his close encounter at the ruins. The camera should have been ready, but that *guifiti* we’d been drinking had put us all into a semi-comatose state.

“We’ll do it first thing after breakfast,” I promised.

We lay listening to the rain falling.

“Jack.” Valeska reached over and gave my hammock a little push.

I pulled my hammock up against hers. “What’s up?”

“I think that I like sleeping beside you in a bed better than a hammock,” she whispered.

“Yeah, me too.”

“And I’m really in the mood.”

“I think that would be mission impossible in this thing and if we go outside, the mosquitoes will eat us alive. But we can always dream.”

“Maybe you can, but I think the real thing is better,” she whispered.

I pushed her hammock lightly with one hand.

“Keep going, I like that.”

•••

At first light, I quietly rolled out of my hammock, slipped through the sleeping bodies and stepped outside. Right away I noticed that the light had an eerie warm glow to it. The soft rain felt good on my skin so I walked down to where the boats were pulled up onshore and watched the morning come alive. The air was scented with flowers and soon different songbirds started to chirp. When I turned to go back to the hut to wake the others, I noticed that I wasn’t alone. Yago was crouched underneath a broad-leafed bush not far from where I was standing. I could barely understand his Spanish, but I’ll never forget what he said: “The river is our lives. It is our blood. It gives us our food. But it gives us death as well. We accept that. Death is as natural as life. It is part of our religion. That is the only way to survive here.” Then he looked up at me and smiled. “*Buenaos dias, señor Jack.*”

Breakfast was a heavy pancake drowned in a sweet thick sauce with the texture of axle grease. When Eddy saw what was about to land on his plate, he went down to the *pipante* and returned with one of the cans of maple syrup he had brought from Québec. Chili-Chili punched a hole in it with his machete, and soon smiles of satisfaction appeared on faces that had never before tasted such a succulent sugar. The Hondurans could not believe it came from trees in the north.

After breakfast, I set up the interview with Yago. As he fed his chickens, he retold the story of his encounter at Ciudad Blanca. It was even better this time around. I was careful not to reveal his face on camera, since neither of us wanted him to be recognized. One never knows where a film will end up.

ANTON

Back at Barra Patuca, the sound of the pounding surf had kept Anton awake a better part of the night. As he lay in bed listening, he could also hear a new noise: It was the wind making a deep humming sound as it blew through the shrouds of the schooner docked in front of the house. It wasn't a good sign. This was not just a late October storm coming in. It was way bigger.

When Anton got up and peered through the shutters, he could see that the sailboat was far too heavy for the old dock. The twenty-ton steel hull was beginning to pull on its lines, making the entire structure of flimsy wooden posts and boards sway. The old man watched for a while, hoping things would settle down, but they only got worse.

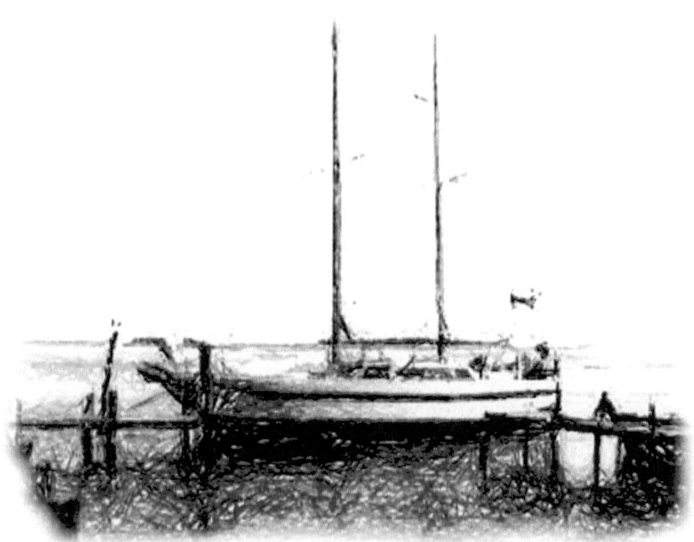

At first light, he put on his shirt and went out onto the balcony. The rain had ceased, but the low-flying clouds were dark and threatening. Anton needed to find help and move the boat into the mangroves before the dock broke up. A piece of tin on the roof overhead began to make a rapid clicking noise. Later, after he had dealt with the sailboat, he would go up and nail it down before the whole piece blew off.

But there was something more important on his mind. Anton looked again toward the point. A huge swell was coming in from the east, but there was still time for anyone caught offshore to risk running over the bar for shelter before the big waves began stacking up at the mouth of the Patuca. Something was brewing offshore.

Anton went back inside the house and calmly woke up his grandson. The boy threw on a T-shirt and a pair of shorts and ran off barefoot in the direction of the village. Ten minutes later, he returned with three friends. Anton had already fired up *Numada*'s engine and was standing on the deck beside a pile of hawsers that had been left there in case of a storm. The grandson untied the small fishing boat next to the dock, and with one paddle sculled it around to the other side of the schooner and gave a ragged nylon bow line to Anton. Then the kid climbed on board and joined his grandfather. The old man looked over at the other boys and gave them a signal to slip the two remaining lines that held *Numada* to the quay. Once free, the schooner backed off, turned and headed upriver toward the safety of the mangroves.

Squinting into the rain, Anton pushed the throttle forward almost to its maximum. The mood of the river seemed to be changing fast, with boughs and branches floating by. In a few hours, the current would be too strong to navigate against. Near the big mangrove patch, Anton carefully maneuvered *Numada* up into a narrow arm of water that led into the thick cluster of trees. When it bottomed out in the soft mud under the keel, he gunned the throttle and pushed in even further until the leafy branches growing on each side of the clearing were touching the boat. It would be safe here in this secret place.

For the next hour, the old man and his young crew worked methodically, looping the big hawsers around the tangled tree roots. After that, they could do no more. The schooner would have to fend for itself. The river was rising fast when Anton and the boys left in the *lancha* they had towed behind. Once outside the shelter of the mangroves, the small boat turned and ran with the current, cutting into the growing whitecaps as it headed for home. As the spray washed over the boat, the boys yelled with glee. They were glad to wash down their mud-covered bodies with river water, but old Anton wasn't thinking about washing off just yet. His eyes were riveted on the blue-green hull of a large sailing yacht coming toward them. The sight displeased him. Not too long ago, when Anton had been out fishing in the river, he couldn't help but notice as the same big yacht had taken on cargo from a low-slung black motorboat. Looters had always come in many shapes and sizes, but the elder sensed that this gang meant trouble. As the latecomer approached, Anton observed the men on deck preparing a big storm anchor. They were obviously looking for a safe place to drop the hook. As they came alongside, a ragged *gringo* with a beer belly and dark glasses leaned over the flying bridge and yelled to him in English, "Hey, old man, where is it safe to anchor in this kind of weather?"

They could put the hook down anywhere in the river when the weather was good. But with a hurricane on the way, the mangroves were the only safe place, and that pretentious-looking yacht was far too big to slip into the creek where *Numada* was hiding. "Go further upstream and stay close to the riverbank, off to the left, just before the bend in the river. That's the best place; everywhere else the bottom is very soft. *Aqui es peligroso, el coriente es muy fuerte, mas largo.*" (It's too dangerous elsewhere, the current is too strong.)

The big ketch motored by, and as it passed, Anton's grandson read out loud the name inscribed on its transom. "*Esmeralda.*"

"*Esmeralda,*" repeated Anton under his breath. "*Problemas.*"

The wind was blowing hard when Anton and his young crew hauled their small boat up beside the solid little house. Rolling gobs of white spindrift had started to collect in the saw grass above the riverbank. Following Anton's instructions, the boys removed the outboard from the boat and put it inside the house. Then they flipped the *lancha* upside down and lashed down the hull to blocks of cement so it wouldn't get rolled over by a heavy gust. After the job was done, Anton yelled to his grandson over the din, "*Chico*, get the hammer and nails from the tool box." He pointed to the roof. "We have to secure that loose piece of tin before it blows off and kills somebody."

He looked back upriver as the big yacht disappeared around the bend, the exact opposite of what he had suggested. A typical *gringo* move, he thought. They would probably have a hell of a time trying to anchor where the bottom was thick with silt, certainly not the best holding ground. Anyway, it was too late to give the *gringos* a hand; soon the wind would hit with full force. It was time to look after himself.

In a few minutes, the grandson appeared with a hammer and a few rusty nails, but their only ladder had been lent to a neighbor on the other side of the village. It had completely slipped the elder's mind, and it was too late to get it now, he reasoned. Anton looked windward in the direction of the village wharf, where he could see men struggling to haul their boats up to the high water mark. He asked his grandson's friends to go and give them a hand. In this kind of weather, everyone had to pitch in. The old man and the boy went inside, filled the lamps with kerosene and made breakfast. There wasn't much more they could do but hunker down and wait.

Barker

Shortly after the crew dropped anchor, the rain began to pick up, followed by the wind. Barker sat at the chart table with Ronnie and looked at the path the storm was taking. The satellite connection was working fine, providing a clear picture of the storm's progress toward the Yucatán.

"Ronnie, it looks like it's going to pass north of us, after all. In a day or so, we'll be out of here with a hold full of cargo, exactly as planned."

"Boss, I warned you about hurricane season. This storm could go anywhere."

"Relax. We've done great so far. If I had listened to you, we'd still be hiding in Puerto Lempira without anything to show for it. Business has been great so far, and if it continues like this, we'll be able to get the fuck out of this country without leaving a trace, and the boat will be full of enough cargo to make us even richer. Storm or not, we're going to get this job over with, so stop freaking out about a little bad weather."

Rackman hid his face behind his binoculars and peered at the mangroves off the port bow. Something caught his eye through the driving rain. In the distance, he could see two masts.

"Shit." He nearly dropped the binoculars. "There's a sailboat tied up in the mangroves." He squinted though the glasses. "It's the Frenchman's boat!"

"You gotta be fucking kidding me!" Dog exploded.

"Take a look for yourself." Rackman handed the glasses to Dog, who went over to the port light and adjusted the focus.

"Amazing, the Frenchman brought his boat right in there. Just wait, we'll give them one hell of a surprise after the storm blows over. He's going to wish he'd stayed in dry dock."

"They're probably just sitting out the storm like we are," said Ronnie.

"He's doing more than that. I bet that they've gone upriver looking for our little treasure chest."

"You think so?"

"Damn right. Pass me the satellite telephone, I'll call Ramón."

It wasn't long before Dog had his favorite henchman on the other end. "Hey, Ramón, where the fuck are ya?"

"On the river, heading to the coast. We should be there in two days max. We're loaded up with stock."

"Good. Make it fast. There's some bad weather moving in. What about up your way? What's it like?"

"Not good, but nothing impossible to deal with, yet. Mostly rain. We'll be going with the current, and it'll be pretty easy once we pick up the big *lancha*."

"Good. Listen, Ramón, if you see Valeska, bring her back here."

"Valeska? What's she doing here?"

"She's probably with some locals and our friend the Frenchman. Never mind the details, just bring her back alive. *¿Comprende, amigo?*"

"*Si* … and the Frenchman?"

"Shoot the bastard."

The connection was breaking up.

"What?"

"Just get rid of that son of a bitch. We don't need him anymore." But there was no one listening. The connection was dead.

If Valeska was on the river, Ramón would find her, and once he got her on board *Esmeralda*, Barker was pretty sure that he could talk some sense into her. If not, he'd kill her too.

Meanwhile Upriver

Despite the darkening sky and light rain, Chili-Chili was certain we could make it thirty miles upstream to our next stop. It was a camp that belonged to their uncle. So we packed up and left our friends on the bank of the little creek. Around noon, we entered another small creek and beached the boats on a gravel spit. Chili and George fished a spot where the current swirled by a big rock, and sure enough, within ten minutes, they'd caught two walleyes. María cleaned them, and in no time at all, they were sizzling in a big frying pan over an open fire.

After lunch, we all stretched out under a tarp the guys had set up for a siesta, but just as I was about to nod off, a wild yell came from the direction of the jungle. It was Cowboy George, sounding like he was in trouble. Chili jumped up, grabbed the 30-30, and took off in the direction of the shouting. We followed. We almost collided with George backing out of the trail, a roll of toilet paper in one hand. He looked in shock.

"A guy can't even take a quiet shit around here. There was a big fucking crocodile."

"Where?" I asked.

"Right beside me. I thought that it was a log at first. I was right in the middle of a crap when it started to move. Then I saw two beady eyes looking straight at me. Jesus Christ!"

Eddy chuckled. "I wonder who's the real shit-disturber? That poor old croc must have been in the middle of some serious beauty sleep."

"Well, he took off like a bat out of hell. Next time I go, I'll make sure I'm packing more than a roll of toilet paper."

We had a good laugh. Our Canadian content guy was one lucky man.

A deep sighing sound came up out of nowhere. This first gust of wind sent the leaves and branches dancing, the first sign that something more threatening than an old croc was headed our way. We hurried back to the boats and shoved off. The next gust of wind blew Peter-Pedro's hat right off his head. It flew across the creek like a wayward Frisbee and was snagged on a cluster of low-lying branches on the opposite bank. Chili waded over to retrieve it, but when he picked it up, something caught his eye. He waved us over to take a look. To our surprise, there, hidden by thick branches, was a black thirty-foot *lancha* with two big outboards on the back end. It strangely resembled the one that had barnstormed us offshore the other night. What really caught our attention were the four jerry cans of gas sitting just behind the steering console. I looked at Chili, and Chili looked at his brother.

"*Trafficantes.* But gas is gas. Too bad for them." Peter-Pedro made an okay sign, picked up the machete and hacked a hole through the curtain of brush. His brother jumped on board and began to transfer the jerry cans into our boats.

We were out of there in no time, just as the first heavy drops of rain began splashing into the dark river. No one said a word until we hit a shoal of thick, treacherous, black mud. Who wouldn't have felt a little weird? After all, we had just ripped off twenty gallons of liquid gold, and if the owners of that boat had caught us in the act, bullets would have been flying.

We got out to push the boats. As we pushed, our feet sank deeper into evil-smelling slime, and for a moment, it seemed like we weren't going to make it out of the creek. When we finally got free, I noticed that the Patuca River was beginning to narrow. On both sides of the river, the jungle appeared to be more poisonously fertile. An odor of decay hung in the air. In certain places, rocky white cliffs rose out of the jungle and towered overhead. We carried on through a low rumble of thunder, preparing ourselves for some foul weather. It wasn't long before we brought out the big black umbrellas we'd so carefully tucked away. Suddenly the rain came, forming millions of pearls on the surface of the river.

"Listen, Jacques," said Peter-Pedro, "if you see a boat coming our way, better hide your white *gringo* face under that umbrella. They won't look at us if they think that we are all locals. *Hombre*, will they ever be pissed off when they find out their fuel is gone!" He laughed and spat into the river, proud of our heist. "Those engines of theirs will be running on vapor when they hit the coast and we'll be long gone."

Valeska helped me organize my camouflage. I jammed my camera into a plastic garbage bag, punched a hole in it for the lens and another one for the eyepiece. She covered me up with the thick canvas bags we'd brought along. I could easily operate the camera using the remote and not move a muscle. I made a quick playback just to double-check. With the wide-angle lens, I framed Chili's boat ahead of us, with part of our bow and the tree-lined riverbanks in the background. Everything seemed to be in working order so I cued up the camera and left it on standby. Another heavy gust of wind brought the river alive with white caps. Then some water sloshed into the boat right under Valeska's seat.

"I'm drenched!" she shouted, grabbing the bailing can.

"Hey, Valeska, do you know what *pipante* means in the Pech language?" Chili-Chili yelled.

"No, what?"

"Wet ass."

"I'm not surprised," she said and continued bailing as the sky began to grow darker.

The Patuca wound on like an endless corkscrew, every bend sending us in a different direction. Hunched low so as not to get pushed around by the strong gusts of wind, the Lopez brothers guided their boats carefully around sunken trees, submerged rocks and shallow banks of oozing mud. Rounding another bend, we suddenly came face to face with three large *pipantes*. They were heading straight for us. All my alarms went off, but I managed to keep cool. I started the camera, and kept my head down and my eyes glued to the small flat viewing screen.

Under the protection of the canvas bags, I could see perfectly what was going on through the lens, despite the torrential rain. Coming our way, in among the covered cargo, were men covered in dark green military-type ponchos, their heads tucked into their shoulders under wide-brimmed rain hats. They looked like half-drowned crows sitting on wet logs. Then things started to happen really fast. One man took an AK-47 from under a tarp and fired a round of bullets into the water just in front of our boats.

"*Parada!*" he yelled. (Stop!)

Almost immediately, two others uncovered their weapons. As they came alongside us, one took a pistol shot at our outboards. That was it. We were dead in the water. A lot of shouting ensued.

"*Ramôn! Hijo de puta!*" Valeska screamed, but to no avail.

"We got orders from our boss. He wants you back on board."

In an instant, two goons grabbed her and began pulling her on board their boat. I bolted from under the tarp only to receive a rifle butt on the head. That's all I remembered.

It was a lucky thing that I survived the hit. I had already received a few solid whacks on the head since coming to Honduras, and the odds of serious brain damage were growing. But I guess I had a thick skull. However, when I came to, nothing seemed to make any sense. I could feel sand in my hands and I could hear water close by. There was also something covering my eyes. It felt like a damp towel. Then I figured out that I was lying on the shore. A moment later, I slid the towel off my forehead and squinted. Even though the sky was thick with clouds, the daylight made me squint. Focusing, I saw María nearby rinsing out some bloodstained bandages, and over by the water's edge, I could see Peter-Pedro and his brother standing in the rain around our boats. My head started to throb as I attempted to speak.

"What the hell happened?"

"Shhh," said María. "You were hit on the head with the butt of an AK-47. They threatened to kill Valeska, so there was nothing more we could do to stop them taking her away." My heart sank. Valeska was in real trouble and we had to get her back.

"After they left, we had to paddle like hell to reach the riverbank because they shot at our outboard motors."

My eyes focused on Eddy who was sitting nearby smoking a cigarette. He stood and came over.

“How do you feel?”

“Like shit. But I’ll survive. Eddy, we have to find Valeska.” I felt completely weak and dizzy.

“It was Barker’s gang; they are long gone by now,” he said.

I suddenly realized I had a front tooth missing. I fingered the gap.

“That happened when you fell on the side of the boat. You went down hard.”

Pete-Pedro came over and knelt down on the sand beside me.

“Perhaps we can try to catch up with them after the storm blows over. They are going to transfer their cargo to the big *lancha*. I have a feeling that they will run out of gas before they reach the coast.”

“Goddamn it, I knew it was going to be dangerous, but…” and I vomited. Valeska was gone. I washed in the river and hobbled back to the shelter of the wide-leafed trees.

“I had the mini-camera going,” Eddy remarked. “The whole scene is recorded, for what it’s worth.”

“Yeah, for what it’s worth, but my mind isn’t on the film right now.”

It was all starting to sink in. We had to get back to the coast and fast. “Our plans have to change. We’ve got to find Valeska.”

Peter-Pedro came over from where he had been working with Chili on the outboards.

“After that guy grabbed Valeska, there was nothing we could do, my friend, nothing at all. It was a standoff. Now we’ll have to wait for the bad weather to pass.”

I stood up slowly, then limped over to Chili. He seemed preoccupied with trying to save the outboards. “I did what I could; it happened so fast. Now, our only hope is to get to our planned destination before dark. The river is rising fast and soon the current will be too powerful to motor against it,” he said. He leaned up against a big rock that had a Mayan carving covering its bottom half.

“We have to catch up with Valeska,” I said.

“It’s impossible. They have a head start and bigger engines than ours. Besides, the weather will get much worse tonight, so our best and only plan is to reach Casa Tio upriver, where we will at least be safe and dry. From there, we can figure out a plan. The good news is that we’ll shortly have two outboard engines again. And the faster I stop talking, the sooner they’ll be fixed. I promise we’ll be out of here in an hour.”

It was almost dark when our two *pipantes* touched the sandbar in front of our next stop. On a sign nailed to a very large tree hanging over the river was written Casa Tio. We were all soaked to the skin but glad to be able to stand and stretch. I looked around and saw that Chili-Chili had started to unscrew the two lugs that held his outboard to the boat. It was the end of the line.

"Everything has to go up to Casa Tio. In a few hours, the river is going to become angry. There will be no more sandbank, and even the spot under our feet will be underwater. There will be lots of current, too much for us to continue. We could be stuck here for a few days." My morale started to sink. After coming this far, the whole expedition was now in danger. But what could I do? What could anybody do? We emptied the boats, then hauled them up to high ground for safety. Because of the thick overhead clouds, night's curtain had fallen fast and heavy. But when we finished moving everything up to higher ground, there was already a warm glow coming from inside the hut and a delicious aroma of turtle soup filled our cozy little shelter.

As they brought up the last case of equipment from the boat, I asked, "Where is Uncle Tio anyway?"

"In the other world," said Peter-Pedro. Then he smiled and lowered his gaze.

"We miss him a lot," he said and went inside the hut.

Uncle Tio must have liked living here. The hut was well built and much more spacious than where we had stayed the night before. That was a lucky thing, because once all the gear was inside, there was still enough room to move around. At one end, there was a low table surrounded by four wooden benches. In one corner, there was some dry firewood. There were a few dishes, pots and a sink with running rainwater that came from a cistern out back. Underneath a small lean-to near the house, there was a lot more firewood. I took out more candles and spread them around the room, and gradually the place began to feel like home, even if the roof leaked a little.

As María prepared something to eat, we straightened out the gear and hung up our wet clothes to dry on a long cord that stretched along one side. Chili-Chili gently rubbed María's shoulders as she cut up some mangoes. It was the first time that I had seen her tense. She had been working hard and was starting to worry about her son and about Anton, back at Barra Patuca. The storm must be in full swing there and she must have sensed full well that it was far from being over.

She wasn't the only one who had something to worry about. I couldn't stop thinking about my Valeska. What had happened was a catastrophe. And now a serious hurricane was about to run over the top of my schooner and I wasn't even there to do anything about it. I might lose Valeska to some goons, and *Numada* to a storm. And we were stuck in the middle of nowhere and running out of supplies.

Outside our snug little shelter's walls, the trees were shaking like a bunch of voodoo fanatics during a fire ant attack. Their loud rustling sound came in waves. Sometimes, something would groan, crack or fall to the ground with a dull thump, but we were well-protected among the trees, and for the moment there was really nothing to worry about.

Later on that evening, the wind began to blow even harder. In the flickering candlelight, we sat around the table and told storm stories. And just when the meal was ready, a steady stream of water leaked through the roof and fell into Cowboy George's bowl of soup. This gave everybody a good laugh and broke the tension a little.

Later, Peter-Pedro put on his plastic poncho and went down to the river for a quick look. When he came back, he looked worried. "*Mira amigos*, the sandbank is under water and it's only the beginning. I'm afraid that the river is about to go wild."

For me, the news was another blow. It meant that we wouldn't be going back to search for Valeska for at least three or four days. She was on her own. I couldn't think straight anymore. At times, I felt like jumping in one of the boats and riding the current back to Barra Patuca. Impossible. It would have been suicide, for sure. A dug-out canoe with a puny outboard hanging off the stern was no match for that raging torrent.

I had to stay positive. We were all in good health; we had shelter, and some rice, a few dozen eggs, flour, tea and some canned food. When we finished that, we would be able to live off the land, but living off the land would be a full-time job if we wanted to keep our stomachs full. Chili-Chili said that food would be hard to find unless we came across a trapped animal or some iguanas up in the hills. Apparently there were lots of iguanas living up in rocky outcrop not too far from our own shelter. And nearby, fallen coconuts were everywhere. It was the torrential rain that worried me. When would it stop, and when it did, how fast could we get back to the coast?

Valeska

After they grabbed Valeska, Ramón made sure that she wouldn't be able to move. He put her facedown in the *pipante*, then tied her feet and her hands.

"How do you like that? I'll bail out the water if you are a good girl. If not, I'll let you drown. You've got a nice ass though," he said, and grabbed her rear with two hands. "And in this position, you're not too dangerous to fuck."

Valeska tried to relax, but she was fuming. Ramón had always been a menace. She had never trusted him even when things were going well with Barker. He was simply warped, a sicko, a pervert. She lay facedown in the dirty bilge water and imagined how she would get even when she escaped.

When their boats finally reached the big *lancha* that they had hid in the creek, it was late at night and the storm was gaining strength. Ramón noticed right away that their reserve gas cans had been stolen and flew into a rage. However, because of the strong current, they were sure that they could make it with what they already had in the fuel tank built underneath the floor. Once the cases were transferred into the other *lancha*, Ramón and his gang covered its entire length with a large tarp and slept, but not before fastening Valeska in the front of the boat under the short bow deck. She told him that she had to pee so he untied her and gave her a bucket. When she urinated, the guys laughed and hooted. After she pulled up her pants, she took the bucket and threw it in their faces.

"This is what you all deserve!" she yelled.

Ramón gave her a solid shove, making her tumble onto her back. "One more like that and I'll turn you over to my friend over there. How would you like that, Freddy? I think you could do a real good job on that little bitch."

The big Garifuna grinned and nodded and rubbed his crotch.

"So crawl back into your hole and stay out of sight or else my oversized friend here will stick it to you real good."

Valeska had no choice. She spent the rest of the night with her hands tied to the gunnel and sitting on a coil of rope as the rain pounded down on the deck above her head. For the first time in her life, she was beginning to wonder if she would survive. She kept thinking about Barker and how much she hated him, and how she would make sure he wouldn't get away with what he did to her and her uncle.

At first light, the wind and rain were fierce. But they had no choice, so the big *lancha* slipped into the swirling current and quickly headed downstream toward the coast.

•••

Meanwhile, up at Uncle Tio's camp, the low black clouds swirled overhead as if they had been placed in a giant mixer. Heavy rain was still hammering down and the fierce gusts of wind were making the trees crack and moan. Just a stone's throw from the camp, the Patuca River had risen considerably and was filled with debris. I caught a glimpse of the remains of a wooden dock as it rushed by, followed by an overturned *pipante* and a small thatched roof. Someone upstream had just lost everything. Close to our shelter, a mature tree suddenly split right down the middle, but miraculously stayed standing.

I felt so useless; that was the worst part. We were stuck, prisoners of a vicious storm. Storm or not, something had to give.

"All is not lost, you guys. We'll find Valeska sooner or later. They won't kill her. I'm sure of it," said Peter-Pedro. "She is worth more alive than dead. Meanwhile, instead of waiting around like turtles on a log, my brother and I will show you something very special not far from here, a place that will take your minds off our mishap."

I saw Cowboy George and Eddy immediately come to life. We had to continue — the Lopez brothers were right; sitting around was the worst thing to do. So we packed a few small bags of food, prepared the camera for some serious weather, and followed our two guides into the storm, disappearing into a narrow trail heading to the hills. It wasn't long before our sortie turned into an adventure. The path was overgrown and strewn with fallen branches. On steeper ground, the mud made walking slippery and even dangerous. After a seemingly endless stretch of climbing, we finally reached a narrow path that cut into a wall of white rock. On one side of the escarpment, the tallest treetops were at least one hundred feet below us.

"Just look ahead and don't think too much," Peter-Pedro advised.

At the other end of the passage, we scrambled over a series of large mounds covered with vegetation and tangled roots until we finally emerged on an immense flat terrace of cut stone. At the far end was an opening that led into another mound. We stopped and organized our wet gear. We were soaked to the skin. As I wiped the water and mud from my eyes, I noticed something particular about the rock. It seemed cut by hand.

"Hey, Chili, this really looks like some kind of ancient Mayan ruin, don't you think?" I said.

"I was wondering when you would realize this. We've been walking over the top of it for the last ten minutes. *Amigos*, we have just entered Ciudad Blanca, but through a back entrance. *Señors*, follow me."

I glanced down at my feet, then stomped the ground. It sounded hollow underneath. Eddy and Cowboy George seemed equally astounded. The Lopez brothers had wide smiles on their faces. They'd known all along what was hidden away in the hills, just back of Casa Tio. We followed our two friends into a dark, damp chamber dripping with water.

It was still and mysterious inside. This great hall was about thirty feet wide and twenty feet high, with shafts of dim light filtering through openings in the ceiling. In the semi-darkness, I could make out carvings of faces on some of the stone slabs, as well as holes where slabs of rock had once been. If the looters hadn't beaten us to it, I imagined that we might have seen the stone sculpture of a Mayan god or some mythical creature, and all the trimmings, for it seemed as if we had suddenly entered sacred territory. We climbed over more cut stone debris and down some crumbling steps that led to another chamber. The level area near the entrance was covered with a carpet of thick green moss, where someone had recently made a small fire. Looking up, I noticed that the ceiling above our heads was a perfect concave dome decorated with hundreds of sleeping bats.

"How do you like it?" whispered Chili-Chili.

"It's beyond words. How did you discover this place?" I whispered, too.

"Uncle Tio brought my brother and me up here when we were boys, but he shared his secret with no one else. Someone must have found this place by accident. Originally there were many more carvings and all kinds of artifacts, but they were stolen a few months ago."

Cowboy George shivered. He pointed to the shed skin of a very large snake. Chili just laughed. He motioned to a petroglyph hidden among some rocks. It was the image of a human-like monkey. Carved in the rock was another coiled snake with its mouth wide open.

"Quite an impressive reproduction," said Eddy. "I bet there are still live snakes in this place." His voice echoed inside the chamber.

"Sure, but they usually keep to themselves." Chili didn't want to alarm us.

"I like the way you say 'usually,'" said Cowboy George, looking down at the debris of broken stone on the cavern floor. "Somebody's been busy here, for sure."

Along with the stone debris, the floor was strewn with cigarette butts and empty plastic soft drink bottles.

"Modern artifacts," said Cowboy George.

Moist, musty air swirled into the chamber from the dark narrow hallway, followed by a distant low-pitched groan. The whole place seemed inhabited by some invisible force.

"This hallway passes right through to the other side of the mound," Chili-Chili said in a low voice. "There are dozens of other tunnels too, but I've never had the courage to explore them."

"And it's pitch dark in there and full of bat shit," added Peter-Pedro.

"Full of all kinds of other things too, I bet," said Cowboy George.

"*Si, amigo.*"

I watched Eddy as he gazed around. He was as struck as I was.

"It's amazing, the tunnels lead off in every direction. It would take weeks to explore them all."

"You're right. At least half of Ciudad Blanca is underground. That's why it's hard to find."

Eddy gazed around. "It's too dark in here to shoot with the camera. There are four light bars back at the camp. Not much, but we can use them to light some of the details."

"Perfect. Hey, Chili, when we come back, can we go further in and try to locate the center?"

Chili wiped his face with his sleeve. We were all covered with reddish mud.

"The center is where they built the biggest pyramid, but it's a long way on foot through the jungle. It will be tough to get there in this weather because the pyramid is probably completely surrounded by water. The storm gods have been busy these days."

"Where does this storm god legend come from anyway?" asked Cowboy George.

"It's part of our mythology."

"What do you believe?"

"After what we have seen here, I'd say the storm gods must be more than pissed off," said Chili.

"I don't really blame them," said Eddy.

Chili-Chili led us back out the way we had come. When we finally stepped outside, a blast of rain and wind brought me back to earth.

"We'll come back and do a proper visit," I said, trying to stay positive. My mind was racing at the possibility of finally being able to film the sacred city. It had been a long journey from Belley's Tavern in Québec City to the Ciudad Blanca, but there we were, standing in the guts of that very place.

On the way back to Uncle Tio's camp, we had to skid down the steep, muddy trail, which had become worse by the hour. Every so often, a tree branch would crash down nearby. Everything seemed to be moving, and the soil was saturated underfoot. The water was collecting in pools, sometimes over our knees. It took about an hour, but when we finally arrived, we were caked in thick red mud and completely waterlogged.

The only way to get clean was to strip down and shower in the deluge. After that, we ate, rested and planned the next morning's return trip to Ciudad Blanca. I sat under the shelter's overhang and watched the once-lazy Rio Patuca become wild and angry, sending dark brown water and debris toward the Caribbean Sea. Chili-Chili and María sat beside me.

"Hey, Chili, how did your uncle die?" I asked.

He kept looking straight out over the swirling river. Then he turned to me. "Well, actually, he just vanished, disappeared. We'd come all the way from Bara Patuca to visit him, but he wasn't here. Strangely enough, his *pipante* was on the sandbank as usual, and this place was as if he had just stepped out the door. He left without a trace."

"Maybe he drowned?" asked Eddy.

Chili shook his head. Cowboy George was lying in his hammock just inside the door, listening. "Maybe he saw something that he shouldn't have," the Innu suggested.

"Possible. That seems more likely than a simple accident. My uncle was a fine person, a brave man. He was living in an isolated place close to an immense archaeological treasure, and he wanted it to remain untouched."

A crash came from the river's edge. The colossal tree to which the Casa Tio sign was nailed had just tumbled into the water.

"*Simonac!*" exclaimed Eddy. "It's dangerous around here."

Roots and earth had ripped completely out of the ground. The force of the current had already carried the mastodon away.

"*Mira*, Tio's tree is gone; it's the end of an era. That tree had always marked Tio's place. It was a force of nature, like the man himself. Now both are gone!" Chili-Chili shivered.

"But his *casa* will survive, since the biggest trees around the house were cut," I said.

"*Si*, stolen by loggers. Around here, they'll take anything they can get their hands on."

"Sure," added Peter-Pedro, "there are guys who cut mahogany trees anywhere they feel like it. Then they float them down the river to a portable sawmill near the village. This is supposed to be a protected area, but no one cares."

María added quietly, "Our land is on borrowed time. People from the exterior come here, catch a kind of sickness, and that sickness is greed. When they see our forests, they take the trees, then they find minerals and they take them too. What do they leave? Mostly garbage, disease and that's about it. They know nothing about the people who live here. It's like we don't exist."

"*Si, amiga*," agreed Peter-Pedro. "This is our land. The Miskito people, the Pech, the Garifuna, and all the other groups living here are simple people. Look around; we possess almost nothing and never will. All we ask for is enough food to eat, a small *casa*, a family, and the love and comfort of each other."

Chili-Chili thoughtfully gazed out over the raging river. "But they come and rob us anyway. It's hard to comprehend the ways of the gods. Hopefully, we will gain back our land someday, but if that happens, it will be long after I'm gone."

We went back inside to dry off in front of the cooking fire and tried to talk about something more positive.

•••

About two hundred and fifty miles to the north, the hurricane had now been given a name by NOAA. Hurricane Mitch had built to a Category Five storm, with sustained winds upwards of 178 mph (285 km/h), making it one of the most powerful Atlantic hurricanes ever recorded. It had been travelling northwest toward the Yucatán, just as the National Hurricane Center in Miami had predicted. But mysteriously, the massive hurricane suddenly turned south, toward the Bay Islands, and after that it continued its destructive path toward the Mosquito Coast. This massive system seemed possessed, like a crazed animal chasing prey.

Barker

Since *Esmeralda* had anchored in the river, things had gradually gotten worse. Shirley, who had been hired as a *femme à tout faire* before the boat had left Roatán, could only lie on her bunk in her cabin and sob. She hated the wind; it was driving her crazy. Ever since the storm had kicked in, she wished that she'd never gotten mixed up with the Dog and his gang of losers. From her cabin, she heard the commotion when the big black *lancha* arrived. She wondered who the woman doing all the yelling was. Whoever it was, she sounded furious, not frightened.

From the swearing and grunting, Shirley could tell that the crew on deck was struggling in the high winds and heavy rain to unload the wooden crates from the *lancha*. She knew that Ramón acted as the Dog's foreman at the Ciudad Blanca site, and that he was responsible for making sure the diggers did their jobs right. For the past six months, everything had gone fairly well. But Ramón was to be avoided. He was a bad man and liked having authority because it reminded him of his days in the Nicaraguan Army when he was a captain fighting the Sandinistas. Now that he was making real money and actually enjoying this new adventure, he had become intolerable, and extremely vulgar — especially when he talked about women.

•••

The trip to the ruins had not gone well for Ramón. His crew was made up of young guys who had been *narco-trafficantes* for years. They lacked discipline and couldn't be trusted. Ramón was known for being tough, which was why Barker and Zarkin had signed him on in the beginning. And once he took over, the tough guy had made it clear to his men that he would shoot anyone found stealing. The rules were simple: work, keep your mouth shut, get paid and live. There was no fooling around with Ramón.

Kidnapping hadn't originally been part of the deal. He would rather have shot Valeska instead. She caused Señor Barker to make bad decisions. With her around, Barker couldn't see straight. Already, too much attention had been forced on that bitch. The men were tired, wet and hungry. They wanted their pay and were anxious to leave and hide out in the village before the storm got any worse. They knew full well that *Esmeralda* might suddenly be forced out to sea. If that happened, they wouldn't see the color of their money until the next delivery, which could take weeks.

But the Dog had had other things on his mind and had made it clear that he wasn't going to take any crap from a crew of low-life Garifuna bums who would otherwise be dealing drugs or languishing in an overcrowded jail. He told Ramón that first he would put Valeska back where she belonged. After that, he'd look after the guys. Ramón was furious.

The wound from the bullet that had grazed his arm when they grabbed Valeska was irritating him to no end. But that was a minor detail; he'd look at it later. There was a more serious problem to deal with. Tension was building visibly among the men. Ramón was glad he had brought all their guns on board the yacht before they'd started unloading the goods, because the boys were getting impatient. If they got really pissed off, anything could happen.

"Hey, Ramón. We want our money now!" the big Garifuna shouted.

Ramón yelled back, "Come back when the storm blows over. The boss is busy. Can't you see?"

Barker joined in. "Look at the current, the wind is picking up. It's no time to count your *dineros*. Go over to the village and get something to eat and come back tomorrow when things settle down. I'll pay you then. *Comprende?*" He untied the line holding the men's *lancha* and tossed it down into the boat. "*Buenas suerte.*" He watched as they drifted away. Ramón just stared at Barker.

"*Pendejo,*" growled one of the men. (Asshole.)

The two big outboards roared to life, and the guy at the wheel gunned the throttle. The *lancha* spun around and took off toward the village. "Shit, man, you shouldn't have let them go," said Ramón.

"Why not? They'll be back tomorrow after this blows over. You can be sure of that," replied the Dog.

"But they are almost dry, man."

"What do you mean, almost dry? It's fucking pouring."

"I mean the gas tank is almost dry. They will never make it to shore."

And in fact, after a short distance, the two motors sputtered and died.

The Dog grabbed his binoculars and took a closer look.

"Whoops, you're right, it looks like those guys are in a little trouble." They were drifting fast.

"Somebody ripped off the jerry cans we had on board for the return trip. We were damn lucky to get this far."

"Why didn't you say so earlier?" Barker's eyes followed the drifting boat. He cupped his hands and tried to shout over the noise of the wind. "Use the paddles! Row!"

But they were caught in the current and drifting fast out to sea. It was just a matter of time before the huge waves coming in through the pass would smash the *lancha* and the men to pieces.

Barker looked through the binoculars and laughed. "Holy shit, they're diving overboard and swimming to shore."

He handing the glasses to Ramón.

"Sure, it's the only thing left to do. That's it for the *lancha*," the foreman added.

"Damn, what a waste. But we've got another one in Roatán." Barker shrugged. "Come inside and we'll clean up that wound before it starts to stink."

Inside the wheelhouse, they dried off with the thick towels that Shirley had left on the settee. Then Ramón went down and got her to disinfect the gash. Dog turned on the SSB receiver and they listened intently as the radio crackled out the latest forecast. His expression changed from nonchalant to anxious.

"Jesus fucking Christ! The hurricane has turned ninety degrees! Now it's heading straight for Guanaja." The Dog slammed his fist on the chart table. "And we're trapped in this hole with no way out. That hurricane is going to roll right over top of us and we can't do a thing about it!" He flipped on the intercom. "Rackman! Rackman! Get that nose of yours out of the blow and come up here fast!" A minute or so passed.

"What's up?" Rackman entered the wheelhouse. He squinted and looked out at the raging river.

"Man, it's heavy-duty out there." He wiped his nose with a dirty hand.

"Heavy-duty? We ain't seen nothing yet. I just got the weather from Miami. The hurricane has turned around. We're gonna get it right in the kisser."

"Are you sure?"

"Of course I'm sure, you jerk. Now get the guys on deck and prepare the boat for the worst. First thing, set the second anchor and run out all the chain we have. Then strip the deck. Just leave the cases where they are and tie them down good with dock line."

Rackman just stood there with his mouth wide open.

"So move. It's coming in fast," Barker urged. "The wind speed's already pushing sixty-five knots."

"Hey, Barker, what's that sound?" blurted out Ramón, coming up from the main salon with a clean bandage on his arm.

"The wind in the rigging," said Dog. "Is Shirley still down there?"

"She was a few minutes ago. She did a nice job cleaning the wound on my arm."

"Shirley! Bring me up a scotch!"

There was no answer.

"Shirley!"

No answer.

"Goddamn it! Where the fuck is that bitch? I'll go get the stuff myself."

Ronnie summoned the rest of the crew and ordered them to lash down everything on deck. Shirley had disappeared into her cabin and locked the door. Things were starting to get a little too out of control for her liking.

Barker opened up a new bottle of scotch, poured himself a double shot, and then went down to the cargo hold to have a little talk with Valeska. He found her in a pitiful state on the floor leaning against the bulkhead. Her hands were bound behind her back with zip ties, her clothes were in shreds and her face was smeared with mud. But what luck he'd had to be able to grab her away from the Frenchman. Maybe he could talk some sense into her before it was too late.

"I hope that Ramón didn't rough you up too much. He can be pretty bad when he wants to," he said, stroking her hair. "But you really look beautiful when you're tied up and covered with dirt."

"Even more so when I'm not."

Barker was surprised by her calm tone of voice. He placed his hand under her chin and tilted her head up so she could see him. "Sorry to interrupt your little escapade into the jungle. I just wanted to help you out, perhaps even save your life. You'll be much better off here on board *Esmeralda*. There's a hurricane on the way."

"You're so kind to think of my well-being. I guess that's what you had in mind when your two thugs attacked me in Tegucigalpa, or when you ran us off the road in Roatán."

He sat down beside her. "Valeska, I'm really sorry about the way things have worked out. Tell me, what are you, the Frenchman and that boat of his doing in Barra Patuca?"

"We came here to make a deal with you. What do you think? Legris knows about your little cocaine scam, and so do some other people who are pretty influential. They'll be down here in no time to move in on your operation if anything happens to him or me."

Barker laughed. "That sounds sort of funny, coming from you. Okay, what's the deal?"

"It's easy, just treat me well — at least better than he does. You'll see. Things will improve."

"Yes, to be honest, I've thought about it. We could pick up where we left off." He brushed a hand over her breast. "And I'm sure that you'll appreciate having money in your bank account again. Maybe we could become partners again. Things are going very well at the moment and I have a great capacity for forgiveness. It's one of my best qualities. Think it over."

She didn't flinch. She even managed to smile.

"We'll have to do some more talking, my dear," he said with a rasping voice.

"Yes, but in the meantime, please take these things off my wrists; they're cutting into my skin. I won't be going anywhere."

Barker took the Leatherman from its pouch on his belt and snipped off the zip ties.

"Better?"

"Yes. Thank you."

"Valeska, how could you get involved with that guy? It was the Frenchman's fault this all went sour. He got me so pissed off. I just couldn't see straight for a while."

"Jealousy does that," said Valeska.

"Yeah, I guess so. Maybe I deserved the treatment you gave me. For a while I made some big mistakes." He almost sounded like he meant it.

"You shouldn't have started fooling around with that little gang of whores in Puerto Cortés. I just can't handle that sort of thing, Dog. You knew that, but you did it anyway. To tell you the truth, my relationship with Jack Legris was my way to get even with you. That was it."

"Well, it worked. But I can forgive you if you can forgive me. Maybe we could try again."

"Yes, maybe," said Valeska.

"Once this storm is over and we are back in Roatán, we can take all the time we want to work things out. Think about it. Perhaps tonight if you're nice to me, you'll end up in a real bed. Meanwhile, I'll tell Shirley to bring you something to eat."

"Dog, you're a real bastard, but I still like you a little."

"I like it when you say those things. But, Valeska, I've told you a dozen times before. My name is Doug, not Dog. While you're sitting here thinking about how good your life could be with me, practice pronouncing my name."

"I'll try."

Barker left her sitting there in the semi-darkness and locked the door behind him, confident she would listen to sense. She was an intelligent woman, he reasoned. It would just take a little more coaxing, and then she'd be back where she belonged, with a real man. His mind flashed back to their first encounter. Valeska sure knew how to please when she had a mind to. This time, things would be different. He would be more careful with her, and treat her the way she deserved — that is, if she played along.

•••

Although the ferocity of the winds had decreased slightly during the storm's southern drift, the rain hadn't. In fact, it had gotten worse — caused in part by the Central American mountain ranges. The massive storm's feeder bands swirled into its center from both the Caribbean Sea and the Pacific Ocean, setting the stage for disaster. No one has ever really understood exactly why hurricane Mitch turned south when it did and headed straight for La Mosquitia. But when the hurricane hit the continent, rain began to fall at the rate of twenty-four inches per day. At the same time, fifty-foot waves slammed into the northeastern Honduran coast. As a result, the sea rose fifteen feet, rushed inland and flooded the lowlands. As if this wasn't enough, the overflowing rivers cascading down from the mountains took with them many small villages. In low-lying areas along the Patuca, floodwaters covered the roofs. Within twenty-four hours, thousands of people were homeless or washed away.

THE CHIEF

It had been another long, uneventful day on board the *Talassa* as it plodded up the Saint Lawrence River toward Québec City. The Chief had finished his shift in the noisy engine room and returned to his cabin to clean up. After a long hot shower, he went to the galley and grabbed a bite to eat. Then he had a smoke up on deck and spent the rest of the evening in his cabin watching a hockey game on TV. At 2200 hours, he watched the news. It was all about a massive hurricane heading straight for the Yucatán. He hoped it would burn itself out before it hit the Mexican coast. Later that night, he woke up thinking about Jacques Legris. There was something going down, but he couldn't get a fix on it.

It was midmorning when he got up, dressed and stepped on deck just in time to see the light at Île Rouge off to the port side. They were making good time. A blast of cold moist wind pushed him back and made him shiver. He hated the cold. The Chief frowned, turned, pulled the heavy door open and stepped back inside the ship. A few minutes later, he was up on the bridge sipping from a large mug of hot tea as he checked the local marine forecast on the weather computer. Nothing extraordinary on the Saint Lawrence, a little rain and that was it.

But when he scrolled down and keyed in the NOAA Hurricane website, he saw that the Category Five storm that had been all over the news had suddenly turned south and was pulverizing the Island of Guanaja. An alarm went off in his head. Between shifts in the engine room, he went up to the bridge to check the reports. It seemed that the hurricane had slowly churned its way south to exactly where Legris and his film crew were supposed to be. His good friend could be in trouble and would have to make a decision.

At last, a deep yellow ray of sunlight cut through a split in the low clouds that afternoon, and the *Talassa* tied up at L'Anse-au-Foulon. That evening, the Chief finished off the rest of the required paperwork and packed his bag. His job on *Talassa* was done. Around 0500 the next morning, he walked out into the fresh morning air, down the gangway and hopped into a waiting taxi.

"*Señor, aeropuerto, y rápido por favor*," he said to the driver who did not understand a word.

"Oh sorry, please take me to the airport as fast as you can."

In his head, the Chief was already in Central America.

A Chain of Events

Esmeralda was miraculously still hanging on despite the currents and the debris in the Patuca River. Its two big storm anchors were deep into the clay of the riverbed. Those anchors, each possessing two hundred and fifty feet of one-inch high-grade chain, could hold just about anything. In addition, both twin diesel engines were running. In forward gear at 1800rpm, the boat was able to reduce the tension on the ground tackle and prevent it from snapping.

"I think it's working!" Dog yelled to Ronnie — who was standing in the wheelhouse feathering the engines and trying as best he could to keep the yacht from being swept away.

The wind was gusting to eighty-five knots when Rackman saw the radar's oval dome tear from its bracket on the mast and fly overboard. Then the leftover structure that had held the canvas top that once covered the cockpit took a hit from a flying tree branch and crumpled. Soon afterwards, the long cockpit seat cushions were ripped from their Velcro strips and flew off like sheets of paper into the mangroves. At eighty-five knots, the sand on the other side of the bay had become airborne and began sandblasting the paint off the bow of the struggling yacht. Shortly after, *Esmeralda* started to resemble a target in a shooting gallery. Above, the masts and rigging were vibrating with such intensity that the entire boat wouldn't stop shaking.

In the galley, Shirley was valiantly stuffing towels into cupboards to stop the dishes from rattling. The noise was driving her crazy. When she'd settled the clattering dishes, she threw the mud-stained towels the guys had used earlier down into the engine room, where the washer and dryer were located. Her aim was a little off, so the soggy Martha Stewart towels fell into the bilge instead, slowly sinking into the murky sludge sloshing under the twin Caterpillar diesels and settling on the business end of the hose connected to the main bilge pump. With the main pump blocked, the engine room began to rapidly fill up with water. *Esmeralda* was sinking.

Unaware of her mistake, Shirley went to her cabin, locked the door and dropped a pair of industrial strength pills to calm her nerves, washing them down with a can of Diet Coke. She flopped down on her bunk and put her precious headphones on. It wasn't long before poor Shirley nodded off. Reggae music always put her to sleep.

Valeska sat in the semi-darkness of the cargo hold, listening to the storm and wondering what was going on. She was hungry. The food that Dog had promised her hadn't arrived. She yelled the Dog's name until she was hoarse, but nobody answered. For a while, she thought that Dog and his crew had abandoned ship. Then she heard footsteps and shouts overhead and began to think that maybe things were beginning to fall apart. And she was right.

Up on deck, the mainsail boom had broken loose. Dog's two beefy deckhands had to crawl out on deck and secure it before it was ripped from the mast. Then the furled roller jib unwound, and in no time, the big sail was torn to shreds. But the most serious problem was that the river was now full of trees, roofs, dead animals, trash and whatever else the Patuca could swallow. The current was pounding these objects into the hull. Several of them managed to snag on the two anchor chains. It was just a matter of time.

When the Dog saw that the yacht was in serious danger, he began to prepare for the worst. He had his guys bring two-by-fours, hammers, nails and pieces of plywood to the front cabin in preparation for a puncture. While the crew was busy up front, the Dog and Ronnie stood in the wheelhouse, trying to figure out what to do next. During a short lull, Rackman looked through the driving rain toward the mangroves, hoping for sudden inspiration. All the leaves had been stripped by the wind, but the strong current slowed in the cluster of roots. They should have listened to the old man and tied up behind the thick mangrove trees. But it was too late.

Without warning, there was a loud crunch, and *Esmeralda* trembled and heeled over violently to one side. Then there was a horrific scraping sound, like fingernails running across a blackboard. Down below, a cupboard full of pots and pans flew open, spilling its contents out onto the galley floor. The boat tilted even further, throwing Barker up against the chart table. "What the hell was that?"

The Dog hurried up on deck in time to witness an enormous mahogany tree, roots and all, slam into the yacht. The anchors holding *Esmeralda* didn't have a chance under the tremendous extra pressure of the giant tree. Dog quickly surveyed the situation, and just by accident, his eyes caught a small detail. On the lower part of the tree, protruding from the water, was a white wooden sign with the words "Casa Tio" painted on it in black letters.

Screams came from below. Water was gushing down the hallway into the main cabin. On arriving at the bow, he saw his two deckhands standing paralyzed as they watched a thick branch bore deeper and deeper into the hull. Fountains of muddy water began to shoot in. At that moment, he wished that he had a steel boat instead of a wooden one.

"We're fucked! Quick, lift up the floorboards, get the chainsaw and saw that sucker off before it totally rips the hull open. I'll fire up the emergency pumps."

He thought of Valeska, who was still locked down in the cargo hold. She would be safer with him on deck. He was on the way to get her when he heard Rackman yell, "Boss, come quick, we're dragging anchor! That damn tree is pushing us backwards and there's nothing we can do to stop it."

All sailors know that once Murphy's Law is declared on ship, all hell breaks loose. What happened next on board the *Esmeralda* resulted from a long series of unconnected events that had finally come together. In her cabin down below, Shirley had been wrenched from a deep sleep by all the commotion. She sat up in the bunk, and as soon as her feet touched the floor, she pulled them back up with shock: Six inches of muddy river water covered the rug. For a few seconds, she sat paralyzed, watching the brown murky muck rush in under the door. Still dazed from the double dose of sleeping pills, she got to her feet, unlocked the cabin door and stumbled down the hall toward the main salon. If she had turned to look in the opposite direction, she would have noticed the two guys working frantically upfront trying to plug the hole. Instead, she slammed the door of the watertight bulkhead behind her and, without thinking, locked it tight. That way, she figured, the main salon would stay dry whatever happened, and she'd have less to mop up after the storm. Overtaken by dizziness, *la femme à tout faire* passed out on the sofa, unaware that those at the front of the yacht, Valeska included, were now locked in.

As the water rushed in, it was obvious that there wasn't much more to do up in the bow. Normally, the guys inside could have escaped through a deck hatch. But the heavy cases of artifacts that had been placed topside blocked all exits. With the watertight bulkhead door locked, and without anybody aware of their situation, their time on this earth was fast running out. Up in the wheelhouse, Dog Barker, already in an advanced state of panic, pushed the engine throttles to the limit.

"Come on, you fucker, move! Move!"

But the big yacht didn't have a chance. Now just another victim of the Patuca River's madness, the boat was caught in the raging current and careened toward the village.

Esmeralda

From his house on the riverbank, Anton had been watching this series of errors ever since the tree had punched a hole in the big yacht. He knew there was nothing anyone on board could do but hang on.

When *Esmeralda* reached the village side of the enraged river, it began to slam up against the boulders and mud on the high water line. The old man and his grandson forced open the back door of the trembling house just enough to slip outside. Struggling against the wind, they hung on the balcony posts in front in time to witness the ship of fools crash through Anton's own dock and continue its insane drift toward a large wooden shed built on pilings downstream. The sound it made as it crashed through the structure defied description. Then the stricken yacht violently smashed against the cement pilings of the municipal pier. The impact smashed a few starboard portholes on the hull. Water began to rush in.

On board *Esmeralda*, chaos had taken over. In a last-ditch attempt to save the ship, Dog Barker threw his two diesels into reverse, hoping that he could keep the stern close to shore. He might have managed this maneuver, but in the fatal moment, he goosed the two big Cats and the engines died. Water had finally flooded the engine room, thanks to the towels that had clogged the bilge pumps. Worse than that, the pressure on the tree that had stabbed *Esmeralda* caused it to act as a lever. When the current yanked the tree around, it took along a large section of the hull with it. Luckily for Shirley, Ramón rushed down into the main cabin and dragged her limp body up into the relative safety of the wheelhouse, and dropped her to the floor. She awoke with a start.

Their ultimate recourse was to abandon ship, but it was too late. A drifting mass of debris rounded the bend in the river and took the same route as *Esmeralda*, passing the spot where Anton's jetty had been and careening toward the village pier. When it piled up against the yacht, the mainmast toppled over toward the bow and broke in half, gouging a gaping hole in the deck just above the cargo hold where Valeska stood up to her waist in water.

When she saw exterior light pour in through what used to be the cargo hatch, she climbed the ladder, scrambled over the debris on deck and jumped over to one of the pilings that held up the dock. She hung on desperately and watched as *Esmeralda* inched its way toward the center of the river until it was clear of the pier. The drifting island of condensed debris stalled briefly in the eddy, with only the broken stub of the mizzenmast still protruding from the melee of rigging wire, broken spars and splintered wood.

Anton and his grandson watched it all. They had seen someone crawl from a hole on deck and disappear from view under the pier before the heap of debris was propelled into the current. As the doomed yacht was swept away, the old man crossed himself for the second time that day. He couldn't recall the last time he'd done that.

"No one deserves to die this way," he uttered aloud.

A little further downriver, Ramón's motley crew had managed to swim diagonally with the current to shore. They huddled together behind a beached fishing boat, watching wide-eyed as the wreck of the *Esmeralda* swirled by with Barker, Ramón and Rackman hanging onto the stump of the mainmast, as their jumbled-looking raft swept out to sea.

"There goes our pay," lamented the big Garifuna.

"And there goes a real bad bunch of *cabrons*," commented another. "*Buena suerte!*" He spat but the glob of spit just vaporized in the wind.

No Choice

Our supply of food was running low, and hunting iguanas in the driving rain was hardly an option. The Lopez brothers and María were worried about their families and I kept thinking about Valeska. I wondered whether she was still alive, and, if so, where they'd taken her. I couldn't do anything to help her if I remained holed up in the Ciudad Blanca. To find the answers, my expedition would have to be put on hold. That was the sad truth. We had to get back to the coast fast, but the raging Patuca River was out of the question for at least another week.

We had another plan. There was a creek nearby that Uncle Tio had often used to return to the coast during the rainy season. Now there would be an open passage through to Barra Patuca. The trip would be difficult, but we had little choice. The next morning, we stripped down to our shorts and threw most of our packs back down the muddy slope. Then we followed another short trail to the creek behind the ground where Tio's rickety outhouse once stood. When we reached the creek, we saw that it was overflowing with dark, reddish, swirling water, just as Chili-Chili had predicted. We covered the gear with a tarp and went to get the boats. In the downpour, George and Chili portaged the outboards while the rest of us tackled the jerry cans of gasoline. Chili explained that there were places where we'd have to get out and pole our way through in order to preserve our outboards. So the next thing to do was to find a bamboo patch and cut long poles with the machetes. That didn't take long. There was bamboo everywhere. On the way back to the boat, Peter-Pedro pulled back the wide leaves with the end of his machete, uncovering a big river turtle sitting quietly in the mud. Peter-Pedro put it in the boat among the few boxes of food that were left. I knew what was on the menu for supper.

It continued to rain as we shoved off from the muddy riverbank and began the return trip to the coast. After being holed up in the foothills, none of us had any idea of the extent of the flooding. Further up the mountains, mudslides had wiped out whole villages. Slightly to the north of us, floodwaters had rushed in from two directions and inundated the lowlands, claiming numerous victims who'd had no way to escape. Soon the creek we were following was no longer a creek. It had overflowed its banks and widened out over the plain. Chili-Chili was careful to stay in the middle of the two lines of trees that marked the creek bed.

As we battled the swirling currents and flotsam, I couldn't help thinking about the chain of events that had led us to the present moment. I went back in time to the shipyard in Puerto Cortés, to old Ben, the philosopher. He had been right all along. Life was primarily a question of choice, with the outcome thwarted here and there by the unfathomable workings of destiny. But at that moment, all I could do was, for one more time, follow that old saying: Hope for the best, prepare for the worst.

As rain poured down and we progressed north toward the coast, it became clear that the destruction of this once rich and beautiful land was almost total. Our two boats proceeded slowly through narrow passes and around broken, tangled branches. Time after time, we had to push past fallen trees that blocked the waterway and a variety of drowned animals — including a lifeless crocodile. Other creatures had taken shelter in the trees.

The sun came out briefly, steam poured off the trees and a spooky mist rose up from the water. The temperature rose as if someone had turned up a thermostat. We were trapped in a sauna. Eddy and I filmed as we slowly wound our way north across the vast flooded plain and drifted into a narrow valley where the current sometimes pushed us sideways to the flow. It felt as if we would be compressed into a floating mound of branches. Finally, Chili found some open water and we managed to squeak through a narrow, flooded channel, which carried us through a field of long grass. The pass widened, and we had to get out and pull the boats over the mud for a short distance. Then I spotted something moving off to the left.

"Anaconda," said Chili in a low voice.

"An ana-what?" Cowboy George exclaimed. When we were only a few feet away from the great snake, he finally saw it slide over some brackish green muck, slip into the water and disappear.

He whispered, "Holy shit. It must be twenty feet long."

Late in the afternoon, we came to a cluster of half-submerged structures. This had been a camp for wealthy adventure tourists; they came with local guides to fish for tarpon. But now the lagoon was brackish water. We tied up our boats beside the only house just before another deluge fell from the sky. The water was so high that the front veranda now served as a dock. An entire wall was missing. Hanging by a nail on another exterior wall, part of a wooden sign sculpted in the shape of a fish read "Pese Maya." The other letters had blown away. Here at these modern ruins, most of the belongings had been looted by the wind. Clothes and pieces of debris were scattered throughout the tree branches. The only sound was the tapping the rain made as it fell on the few bits of tin roofing that had managed to hang on.

A week before, people had been living here, going about their activities and not bothering a soul. Then a hurricane washed their entire existence out from under them. Did they have time to flee or had they been swept away in the current?

It began to rain even harder. We quickly emptied the boats and put our possessions under the remains of the roof, beginning to feel like true flood victims, which, in fact, we were. In less than an hour, our little camp was set up. After that, there wasn't much to do but sit around and try to make some kind of sense of what had happened over the past week.

"Jacques, you know what I'm starting to believe?" said Eddy.

"Tell me."

"I think that the Lost White City is better off staying lost. Man, those ruins gave me the creeps. There was a very intense energy in there."

"I felt that too. I just wanted to get the hell out," said Cowboy George. "But hey, you guys, what about the film?"

Eddy looked at me and waited for some kind of lead.

"Yeah, George, things have changed. It's not at all what we thought it would be. But perhaps, our film will end up even better."

Then Eddy joined in.

"Maybe we'll have to call it *Whatever Happened ... Happened*. The real subject of this film will be the trip itself: the storm, losing Valeska, and all the rest. It's become a human adventure. And it's not over. Believe me. We're lucky to have escaped alive. From what I see, Ciudad Blanca is living up to its reputation. Sure, we saw ruins and places where looters had stripped the place, but that seems anti-climactic in comparison to what we're experiencing now. Our original story was the basic premise that triggered this project. Naturally, we'll see what comes to light in the editing room."

Cowboy George lit his last cigarette and took a long drag. "I'll tell you what I think. The most important thing since the beginning of this adventure has been the people. It's got nothing to do with trafficking stolen artifacts or visiting lost ruins."

María leaned her back against the boards and sighed.

"Yes, and once again, the people are the ones to suffer," she said. "Nevertheless, we are used to hardships. There are always tree cutters, squatters, prospectors and thieves emptying our sacred sites. We'll recover, we always do."

Cowboy George looked at María and smiled.

"That's why people of the Mosquito Coast are unique. You've never had anything but yourselves to rely on. I know a man up my way who sings folk songs in the Cree language."

"In Cree?"

"Yes, the people of the Cree nation speak a similar language to the Innu nation. We are neighbors. In one of his songs, he says, '*Namawîy cika cî wanihtân cekwân ekâ ayâyan cekwân ce wanihtâyan.*'"

"What on earth does that mean?"

"Something like, if you don't have anything, you don't have to worry about losing it."

Marie slowly repeated the Cree sentence out loud.

"*Namawîy cika cî wanihtân cekwân ekâ ayâyan cekwân ce wanihtâyan.*"

Cowboy's face lit up. "Hey, that's pretty good."

"I won't forget it. You'll see," said María.

Chili-Chili thought for a second, then laughed. "I've heard that line before but I can't remember from who. It's pretty good though."

At that moment, a strong ray of sun cut through the dark clouds, lighting up a patch of flooded plain to the north.

María repeated the phrase a few more times as she opened the food box and scrounged around. There wasn't much left, only some banana bread, a few coconuts, rice, tortillas and beans.

"Ok, it's time for another miracle," she said as she stood up, stretched and started to put a meal together.

That night we finished all the leftovers, leaving nothing but a few mangoes. I just hoped that *Numada* was intact, because on board there were still lots of dried food and an industrial supply of canned fish and vegetables we had stocked up on just before we left Puerto Cortes.

It poured rain until dawn. Chili-Chili was sure we could reach the village, or what was left of it, sometime that afternoon. All we had to do now was cross a murky sea. Our two boats left the shelter of the trees for the wide floodplain, the last obstacle between us and the village of Bara Patuca. Even the strong winds in our faces couldn't slow us down. We took turns bailing while the boats weaved in and out of various obstacles — including pines that had been stripped of their needles. It seemed close to the end of the world. No one spoke much, even when our boats began to pass farmhouses with only their roofs above water. There were no signs of life anywhere. I got a quick glimpse of Chili looking over at his brother in the other boat with sad eyes.

Late in the afternoon, our two *pipantes* approached the south side of the village. We wove our way through drifting sections of wooden frames, furniture and garbage. Boatloads of families polled by, loaded down with kids, elders, and objects they'd managed to salvage from the wreckage of their homes. Others waded waist-deep toward higher ground or perched on the roofs of their cinder block houses beside small piles of possessions. Some people looked shell-shocked. We felt helpless at the sight of so many homeless villagers. We advanced through more protruding structures, passing a drowned horse, a bloated pig, a drifting rooftop.

Peter-Pedro pointed to the flooded empty space to our right. "That used to be the airstrip."

“Yeah, we played soccer there the other day,” I commented.

“You could play water polo now.”

Chili headed up to the row of houses, searching for signs of life. We followed close behind. Eddy filmed. He seemed uneasy, like an intruder. I looked everywhere for Valeska. Where there had once been a lazy creek that ran through the village, a rushing current now ran over the top of a washed-out bridge. On higher ground, there was a garage made out of cement blocks and nearby were a few houses that had survived the storm. Dozens of people were grouped there, waiting. They had nothing left but their lives.

It began to rain, again, but it didn’t matter anymore. As we beached, people rushed over and began talking to the Lopez brothers and María. Communications were down, and of course, there was no electricity. The generator had suffered water damage and wouldn’t start. No one had been ready for hurricane Mitch’s wrath. Now there was nothing to do but wait for help. And in Honduras, one of the poorest countries in the Americas, that meant a long wait.

Beside the municipal garage, a clinic had been set up in someone’s home. The line outside was long. Scores of people had wounds from flying objects; others had sprains or broken limbs. I could see older people stretched out on pieces of cardboard under plastic tarpaulins. Somewhere a baby was crying. Gone was the peaceful village that had welcomed us with open arms; it had been replaced with a disaster area, misery and despair. Surviving and taking care of the sick and wounded would be a full-time job. While there was still no sign of Valeska De Sela, her disappearance was temporarily overshadowed by this immense tragedy.

Once we’d unloaded our gear, the Lopez brother’s two *pipantes* became public property in the service of desperate villagers trying to save whoever and whatever they could.

With dusk approaching and continual rainfall, there was nothing more to do but load up our gear and trudge through the mud and debris to Anton’s house, which miraculously still stood on its cement stilts near the river. Before long, we spotted the old man and his grandson up on the roof, hammering nails into pieces of corrugated tin that had flown off during the storm. The only other damage to the house was a few hurricane shutters that had been torn away, and the outhouse had blown over on its side.

Anton pounded one last nail and climbed down the ladder. The boy passed him his tools and followed his grandfather.

"I was wondering when you would show up." The patriarch's bright eyes were the first positive light we'd seen in days. He embraced Chili, Pedro, María and the boy all at once. Their little family had made it through one more tragedy.

Noiselessly, Valeska appeared in the doorway, a wide grin on her face. After a joyful, speechless moment, she broke the silence.

"I knew you would make it back!"

In retrospect, it was a shame nobody thought to grab the camera and record the reunion.

A little later Valeska told us what happened. "And *Esmeralda*, Dog and the rest, they were swept out to sea. I feel so sorry for Shirley."

"Valeska, you've been blessed," was Anton's sole comment. Then the old man took us around to the front of the house. There was no dock and no *Numada*. My heart sank, but after a second or two, I could see that Anton was hiding something. With a proud smile, Anton pointed toward the mangroves where *Numada*'s two masts appeared through the cluster of gnarled, leafless branches.

"*Mira*, the boys and I brought it over there a day before the hurricane hit. It hasn't moved an inch since then."

Even if *Numada* had sunk, my problems would have been nothing compared to what the people of Barra Patuca were experiencing. Anton described what had happened when the big wind came. *Numada* had been lucky, but *Esmeralda* had anchored in the wrong place. It had been swept away simply because of the current and poor *marinaros* (sailors).

María made coffee while Anton continued his story. He had seen *Esmeralda* several times over the last few months. He described the transfer of crates from the big *lancha* to the yacht he'd observed as the storm set in.

"That's the same *lancha* that was hidden in the trees near the creek that cuts off to Diego's camp," said Peter-Pedro.

The old man wasn't surprised. "It was the gang of looters from Ciudad Blanca." Anton pointed out to sea. "Gone."

"But what happened to you?" he asked.

"We took shelter in Tio's *casita.* At one point, the river rose so high we had to move up to the ruins," said Pedro.

"And you came down through the flooded plains?"

"Exactly."

His father smiled and went over to look through the open door at the yellow-brown water of the receding river. "I've lived here all my life. I've never ever seen such destruction. It was as if that pesky Monkey God had finally come."

The grandson came in from outside. Anton had just finished taking off the storm shutters, and for the first time in days, the interior was bathed in diffuse light. The house was finally returning to normal.

•••

We slept on the floor of Anton's small house that night. Around midnight, I woke up and couldn't fall back to sleep, so I slipped outside and sat on the small veranda of the house, and, for the first time in days, looked up at a night sky filled with stars.

I lay on my back and watched, and thought about my next move. Sure, things had really changed. My whole project was upside down. Did we have enough material to make a film? Only Eddy could answer that. As for my articles for *Aventura*, my notebook was full, that was certain. Now all I needed was to make sense of it all and begin writing up some kind of crazy story about what we had lived through. Still, there was something unsettled. Was it the Dog's disappearance? Maybe. Our relationship had no closure. I almost felt sorry for the son of a bitch. It was as if the roadrunner had killed the coyote. Then I heard soft footsteps. Valeska's dark form was outlined by the moonlight.

"There are too many thoughts flashing around in my head," she whispered, then sat down beside me. "I'm so confused. Where will we go from here? I'm talking about you and me, Jack."

"We are just lucky to be alive. As far as I am concerned, I want you as much as I ever did, maybe more so. The rest will follow."

"But I feel empty, Jack. I'm not sure anymore. I'm not sure about me, or about you."

"You just have to trust your instincts. There's no magic formula to follow and the guidebook got lost in the flood. Valeska, I have an idea. Come on."

We snuck away under the cover of darkness and climbed on board an abandoned fishing boat that had been hauled up to high ground not too far away from the house. Once on deck, I kissed the soft curves of her neck, then slowly unbuttoned her blouse and slipped a hand over her breasts, massaging her nipples ever so lightly with my fingers. She moaned softly.

"I think that we have been missing a little of this. It's been a long time, don't you think?"

"Hmm, so you think that you'll get me this way." She sighed. "Well, it seems to be working, keep trying. I had almost forgotten how good you can make me feel. Ever since this crazy trip started, we have been neglecting each other, don't you think?"

"I'm not thinking any more, just reacting."

I unbuttoned her jeans, kneeled down and slipped them off. She stood naked and stroked my hair while I caressed the interior of her thighs. As the rain fell, we made love on the deck of that old boat. For that moment, it was just the two of us entwined in our own little world, living in the present with what we had: each other.

A Surprise

The next morning, we turned Anton's other boat right side up, put the motor back on the stern and made our way carefully upriver, through the debris, to where *Numada* waited in the mangroves. The schooner's hull had a few scratches and the deck was covered with mud, sand and broken branches, but it had survived the storm. Before we began the big cleanup, Valeska went inside and took out the first aid kit from underneath the narrow pilot bunk beside the chart table.

"First things first. Chili, please take me back to the village. I'm going to the clinic to help the doctor. He's alone with one nurse and probably both of them are exhausted."

"Hey, hang on a minute." We took out three cases of canned food from our emergency stash: Irish stew, instant soups, condensed milk, flour, four bags of rice, pasta, and a few dozen cans of sardines. Once that was on the way to the village, the rest of us got down to work. By the end of the day, *Numada* was ready to sail.

A day later, we moved the schooner over to the village and dropped the biggest anchor I had in front of Anton's house. Then I left out all the chain I could and Numada seemed to hold on just fine even though the current was still running strong. That afternoon, as we put the sails back on, a small military ship forced its way upstream against the current, and stopped. The guys on board must have recognized my schooner. They shouted, "*Numada, Numada! Amigo.*" The captain blew a long blast on the horn. The ship pulled up close by and prepared to put down the hook not far from my boat. At that very moment, I saw someone step from the wheelhouse onto the bridge. I almost fell overboard when I realized who it was.

"Chief! What the hell are you doing here?"

He waved and shouted, "I'm on vacation. This is the only cruise ship I could find." Once he'd reached the naval base at Puerto Cortés, he had managed to hitch a ride on a patrol ship that was carrying supplies for the hurricane victims of La Mosquitia. He was certain he would find us somewhere in the vicinity. When he stepped aboard *Numada*, he looked up and down the deck. His hair was standing up straight in the wind and his eyes were wide and alive. "I can't believe this. *Numada* survived — almost without a scratch!"

I thought for a second that he would shed a few joyful tears, but the Chief would never go that far.

"Sure, Chief, and everything works, even the engine."

The Chief seemed almost disappointed. Valeska saw her chance and stepped in. "Señor Chief, my name is Valeska De Sela. If you're looking for work, I know where there is another engine to fix, and it's actually quite urgent."

"What engine? Where?"

"Follow me."

Our whole crew joined them, camera and all. It didn't take much time to reach the generator. Like everything else, it was in pitiful shape. The interior was even worse. Mud everywhere. Valeska led the parade.

"Señor Chief, the village of Barra Patuca has been without power for days now and nobody here can fix this thing. There's no refrigeration or lights. The clinic is in darkness after the sun goes down. They can't do much in candlelight."

Chief thought for a second. "Hmm, well, I can change the fuel filters, put in a new battery, and probably rebuild the alternator. There must be water in the cylinders, though. Looks like I'll have to make a few other adjustments here and there. It's not going to be easy to get this thing back in business, no, *monsieur*."

He wiped the sweat off his brow, then turned to me and winked. "Capitan sir, I'll need some tools from *Numada*. This is going to be a big job."

We went back to the schooner and assigned Cowboy George as the Chief's assistant. Together, they loaded up tools, rags, grease and some WD-40, then hiked back over to the generator building. Immediately, they stripped to the waist. In an hour, they were covered with grease, mud and more sweat. The operation resembled open-heart surgery. Cowboy held a flashlight while the Chief swore, cursed, grunted and cursed again, his tone mellowing only after dozens of village children came to visit, studying his every move. Of course, we filmed. It was priceless.

"Future mechanics, every one of them." He chuckled. "All this engine needs is a little love and attention. Pass me some water, somebody; I'm dying of thirst."

The job continued well into the night, since once the diesel had been taken apart and cleaned, it had to be put back together. It was tough, seemingly endless work. Everything had to fit. It was almost daylight by the time they were ready to fire it up. Cowboy George hit the starter. The old GM Diesel sprung to life.

"Perfect," said the Chief. "George, give me the tester. It's the moment of truth." He went over to the electric box fixed to the wall and began to probe inside with the boat's voltmeter.

"Good, we've got juice here and lots of it. Cowboy George, the honor's all yours. Hit that big breaker switch, will ya?"

The Innu put one big hand on the black switch and SHLACK! The lights came back on. Cheers could be heard throughout the village. If there had been elections, the Chief would have been unanimously voted as mayor. Or better still, they could have made him Saint Chief.

Numada weighed anchor a few days later and went to sea. We were escorted by a dozen *pipantes* and small fishing boats filled with villagers and friends — including Anton, his grandson, María and the Lopez brothers. They wished us fair weather and good luck. But they would need more than fair weather and good luck to be able to resume their lives.

When we were in the channel, the Lopez family's boat motored alongside. It was as if they didn't want us to leave. Just before they veered off, María shouted out, "Hey, Cowboy George, *namawîy cika cî wanihtân cekwân ekâ ayâyan cekwân ce wanihtâyan.* If you meet up with that Cree singer friend of yours, tell him that he's right. *Adios, Numada!*"

The big Indian's usually stern-looking face broke into a wide smile. He took off his famous Stetson hat with the eagle feather still stuck in the band and dropped it into the other boat, which was only a few feet from *Numada*. It landed on María's lap.

"María, it's just a humble gift. I'll never forget you, ever."

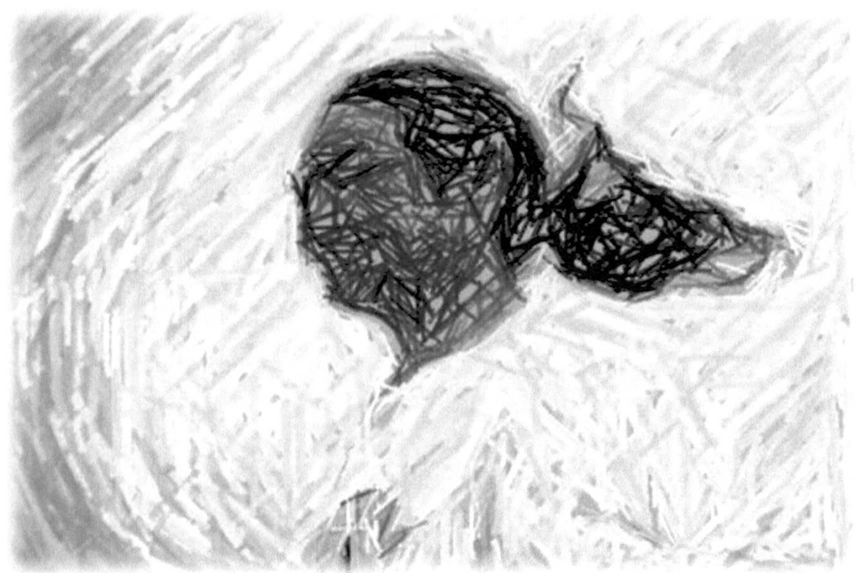

WHERE'S THAT INDIAN?

When our schooner finally reached the open sea, we hoisted sail, cut the engine and set a northwest course. I just couldn't help gazing back over the stern at the dark outline of mountains etched on the southern horizon. Perhaps we would return one day to help. But first, we had to reach a safe haven where we could replenish our supplies — and our thoughts. We had come a long way since leaving the Island of Guanaja. The experience had been total, even though the Ciudad Blanca would remain lost for a while longer. My friends sitting around on deck were exhausted and empty. I was in the same state, but I had a boat to run and a destination to find.

According to the captain of the navy boat that had brought the Chief to Patuca, Guanaja had been hit the hardest. The hurricane had stalled there for days and stripped the island of all its vegetation. Food was scarce and there was almost no drinking water.

A British warship had anchored nearby and had begun to help out the survivors. Going there would be of no use to anybody, so we headed for Roatán. Eddy, the Chief and Cowboy George could catch a flight out as soon as the airport was back in business. I set a course for French Harbour, the same place where my troubles had started in the first place.

When the wind finally picked up, *Numada* heeled over a little and gained speed. I felt that old familiar movement under my feet again, but I had to navigate carefully because the sea was littered with countless floating objects in all directions: tree trunks, garbage, houses, dead animals, clothing, and anything else that had not been spared.

On we went, cutting through the floating debris. Occasionally, the dull thud of a submerged object would strike the hull and give the boat a jolt. It was hauntingly apocalyptic. We made slow headway under the low clouds. The constantly shifting wind of mid-afternoon made sailing difficult. A light rain began to fall and the wind dropped off completely. I cranked over the engine and left only one of the mainsails up just to ease the roll. I divided the crew into shifts and we took turns sleeping. I figured we'd arrive in about two days. There was a big swell running and all night we motored slowly along through the fields of drifting leftovers. Early the next morning, the sharp eyes of Cowboy George saw something that made us all question the real meaning of destiny. "Hey, Captain." It was the first time he had ever called me "Captain."

"What's up?" I asked.

He pointed to a spot off the starboard bow. I could barely make out a florescent orange splash of color lying low in the water. It was a life raft, no doubt about it. I changed course and called Eddy and the Chief, letting an exhausted Valeska sleep. We wove through the thick debris until we came alongside. There was no sign of life until a man's head slowly poked out of the front flap. He had a half beard and scraggly dark hair.

I took a good look and almost swallowed my gum. It was Ramón, Dog's right-hand man. Chief threw him a line. At that moment, another scraggly head protruded from the canvas flap. I might have known.

"Well, what the hell took you so long?" It was none other than Dog Barker all right, the last person in the world I wanted to see. In retrospect, I should have left those two guys to rot on that raft, but I helped them on board.

"I lost everything," was all the Dog could muster.

"Gee whiz, I'm so sorry."

"What happened to you? We saw your boat in the mangroves with no one on it," mumbled Barker.

"We were off in the jungle."

"Filming Ciudad Blanca, I bet," he said grudgingly. "So you were the guys who got the storm gods all riled up. I told you that Ciudad Blanca was cursed. You should have listened. Cause of you, we lost Ronnie and two other crewmembers. Remember Shirley? She disappeared too, poor thing. It was bad, Frenchman, really bad. And Valeska, I'll be honest with you about her; she disappeared. I just can't figure out what happened to her. Too bad, she was such a good—" Barker's jaw dropped as Valeska came through the companionway and stepped out on deck.

Her eyes were on fire. "I didn't know we were picking up garbage." She went up to Dog and slapped him as hard as she could. After that, she turned to spit into Ramón's face. "There are no words to describe this type of scum."

I shared her sentiment. These were two of the most ruthless people I'd ever met, but now they seemed tamed, harmless. I guessed that the storm had done some good, after all. We gave them a shot of rum and some food. Then our two new passengers passed out on the foredeck.

"Are you crazy?" Valeska said to me in a low voice once we were alone in our cabin. "After all they have done, you treat them like poor refugees. They're both heartless killers."

"What do you want me to do? Throw them overboard?"

"Yes. Feed them to the sharks. That's what they'd have done to you."

"Once we get to Roatán, I'll hand them over to the police and we'll be gone."

"The police? Sure. After that, they'll slither off somewhere and that will be it. We should kill them right here and now."

"I'm not killing anyone, Valeska."

"Wake up, Jack Legris. The moment your back is turned, they'll kill you, me and everybody else on board."

It was late afternoon when we nearly ran into another surprise, literally. It was a snag, a pile of floating debris. We could make out the rooftop of a small wooden structure, an enormous tree, and part of a boat mast sticking out of the middle of the mess. The deckhouse had been half-destroyed, its roof ripped off. I went up to the foredeck and shook Dog. When he focused on the wreck, he yelled, "Jesus fucking Christ. It's *Esmeralda*. I can't believe it's still floating!"

The boat was almost completely submerged, but a massive tree had somehow stayed lodged to the side of the hull and now it was the only thing that kept the yacht from going under. We approached the wreck with caution.

"Look!" the Dog exclaimed. "What luck! Some crates of artifacts are still lashed onto the deck."

Hanging within the twisted structure of the davit, the yacht's dinghy was attached only by a single frayed piece of line.

"We have to get those boxes of artifacts off before she goes down, or they'll be lost forever, a total waste. I promise you, Frenchman, they'll be all yours."

I thought for a few seconds, looked at the guys, then over at Valeska. True, we were sufficient in number to quickly move everything on board *Numada*. It would be a shame to lose these inestimable treasures from the Ciudad Blanca. Chief squinted as he scrutinized the mound of debris.

"It's going to be tricky to get in close, but I think we'll be able to nudge up alongside if we're careful. I'm just afraid something might get caught in the propeller."

We brought her in gradually, through the swirl of floating junk. Eddy pushed away the larger obstacles with the long gaff until finally we were only about fifty feet from the pitiful-looking hull.

Then the Chief's face lit up like a searchlight.

"Jacques, all things considered, we just have to open each crate, make a chain, and we can easily transfer the pieces one by one up on deck. It shouldn't take long."

"Brilliant, Chief, let's go for it."

I brought *Numada* alongside. The Chief and George slid overboard onto the submerged hull and looped two lines around the few twisted stanchions that remained bolted to the hull.

"Let Ramón and me help you. We know what's in each box. It'll go faster," the Dog suggested.

I wondered about the sincerity of his offer, but it was too late to stop the operation, and, what's more, the wind was starting to pick up. "Okay," I conceded.

"Hey, what's this?" said the Chief, prying open a damaged crate. "Look, there's something else in here."

He lifted up a plastic package, then poked a hole in it with his knife. A white powder spilled onto *Esmeralda*'s soggy deck. I scooped some up in my hand and tasted it. "It's cocaine, Chief."

"I'm not surprised," he said.

Barker piped up, "Okay, okay, you caught me. We had to include a little supplement of powder to pay for the extra expenses. The artifact export business isn't what it used to be."

"A little supplement? Yeah, right. You just can't get enough, can you, Barker."

"You can always become a partner, Frenchman."

"No, man, this shit is going over the side."

He winced.

The Chief and I opened every package we found and dumped it all overboard. There must have been at least fifty kilos. Barker and Ramón sat on the listing deck of *Esmeralda* and watched, the color draining from their faces. Their suppliers would not be happy.

We carefully began storing the artifacts on board *Numada*. Luckily, the transfer was over fairly quickly, and when it was, the guys returned to the safety of my schooner. All except for the Dog, who had ducked inside *Esmeralda*'s partly splintered deckhouse. I figured that the best thing to do was to keep them on the hulk until we were ready to go.

I guess that I wasn't paying too much attention, passing the precious pieces one by one down through the big hatch that opened into the sail locker. Below, Valeska and Cowboy George were busy trying to fit each object in a place when it would fit. It wasn't easy.

Then I heard Barker's voice behind me.

"Don't try anything stupid, or I'll put another hole in your ass. Call that bitch downstairs and tell her to get topside, same thing for the Indian."

I turned my head and looked at the Dog. In one hand, he held the small revolver that he had lent me back in Puerto Cortés. I had left it in the drawer under the chart table in *Esmeralda*'s wheelhouse just before we'd sailed the boat to Roatán and forgotten all about it. But he hadn't.

"You won't go far, Barker. You've only got two shots."

"Don't worry about that, Frenchman. Guess who's going to get the first one. Call her up on deck."

"Valeska, we've got a problem. Come out on deck."

There was a short silence as Valeska's head appeared through an open deck hatch. "It must be a joke!" she said, and climbed out.

"Yeah, the joke is on you, baby," said Barker. "Now, where's that Indian?"

"Eddy, you better call Cowboy George," I said.

Eddy yelled down in French, "Hey, Cowboy George. *Il y a un de nos visiteurs qui a un morceau dans sa main. Faites attention!*" (One of our visitors is armed. Be careful.)

"What the fuck are you saying?"

Eddy turned to the Dog. "I told him to come up on deck. He only understands French or Indian."

"Well, he better get up here and pronto," said Barker.

"Why don't you go down and get him yourself if you're so brave?" Valeska glared at him.

"Shut the fuck up," snarled the Dog.

"I'm going to make you a deal, Frenchman. We're going to trade boats. Mine for yours, how do you like that? For some reason, I'm starting to like this rust bucket of yours more and more. So slow and easy, just get up, one by one, go to the stern and hop over to *Esmeralda*. Starting with you. Now go."

I lowered myself onto the half-submerged deck of the big yacht, followed by the Chief, then Eddie, and finally, Valeska.

"Frenchman, what's with the other guy?" the Dog shouted down to us.

"He's inside, seasick," said Eddy. Then Eddy whispered to me in French, "*Tu peux être certain que Cowboy George a quelque chose dans sa manche.*" (You can be sure that Cowboy's got something up his sleeve.)

We watched helplessly as Ramón untied the line that tied *Numada* to the wreck of the *Esmeralda*. My cherished *Numada* slowly began to drift away.

Then I heard the Dog shout, "Hey, Indian, if you don't come out now, we'll go in and give you a one-way ticket to the happy hunting ground."

There was still no sign of life from Cowboy George, so the two hijackers slipped inside the drifting schooner. The silence was interminable. And then the shouting started.

It was hard to figure out exactly what was happening because *Numada* was drifting downwind and we were already about one hundred feet away. Then we heard more shouts and cries of pain. Shortly afterwards, Barker appeared on deck followed by Ramón, their hands covering their eyes. Even from a distance, they appeared to be in trouble. Cowboy George emerged, wearing a dive mask. He yelled over to us, "Everything's under control. I used the bear spray." He turned to face the two in front of him.

The Dog snarled, "You fucking Indi—"

"Yes, you bet I am." Cowboy George kicked Dog in the stomach. He went sprawling.

"Stop, I can't see, I can't see! It's no fair! Ramón, do something!" screamed Barker.

"Yeah, Ramón, just do something, please," said Cowboy George.

"Go to hell," said Ramón.

"Shut your piehole, you little shit." The Indian sent him flying with a kick to the head.

"I told you he wouldn't take any trouble from these guys. No one messes with Cowboy George," Eddy said with a grin.

Several maneuvers later, Cowboy George brought *Numada* alongside the sinking wreck of debris. "What do we do with them, Captain?" he asked when we were back on board.

I looked over at the floating leftovers that had nearly been our tomb.

"I think they need more time to meditate on the meaning of existence. Valeska, would you mind preparing a little survival bag for our guests? If they intend to make it to the Bay Islands alive, they can take the dinghy that's still tied on deck. I figure it'll take them two or three days, if all goes well."

Cowboy George wrinkled his nose and pointed to Barker. "He must've shit his pants. Here, Captain," he turned to me, "I took this little gun off the smelly bastard. Perhaps you'd like to test it?"

"No, not just yet."

"Okay, you guys, now get up slowly and over you go."

"May I, Captain?" asked Cowboy George.

"Sure, enjoy."

He grabbed the two of them, and over the side they went, landing with a thud on the *Esmeralda*'s waterlogged deck.

Valeska came up into the cockpit with a small canvas bag.

"Here, let's give the guys some provisions." She threw the small grab bag at them.

"I hope you like canned spaghetti," she said with a wide grin. "Too bad we can't spare you a can opener. You'll have to figure something out, but you'll have lots of time."

"Okay, let's get the hell out of here."

The Dog and his henchman looked more than a little dejected as they stood on the deck of the sinking hulk.

"Too bad that things turned out this way for you, Dog. Have a good trip to Roatán. It's that way." Valeska pointed to the horizon. "Maybe your suppliers will help you? Did they front you that coke or did you pay them in full?"

"Bitch!" growled Barker.

I put *Numada* into forward gear and we pulled away.

"So long, suckers."

"Hey, you can't do that. We'll never make it," cried the Dog.

“Sorry, but it was us or you. Fate chose you. Can’t play with destiny…”

“And what about my cargo, my artifacts?” the Dog whimpered.

“Finders keepers! It’s the law of the sea,” I replied, imitating his phony Texan accent. “They’re all mine, partner. All mine.”

Dog was raging. “You can’t do this to us, Frenchman. After all we’ve been through together. Valeska, help me.”

“No way, you had your chance, but I’ll never forget you.”

I couldn’t resist adding, “Yeah, neither will I. Remember that famous saying, ‘All is fair in love and war.’”

“Go to hell, Frenchman! When I catch up with you, I’ll make sure that your life won’t be worth a dime. I swear!”

I threw his Derringer over the side and it hit the water with a small splash.

“Come on, my gun!”

“Hey, Barker, you better get that dingy of yours overboard and start rowing. Roatán is thirty miles that-a-way. And guess what, I hear there’s a storm on the way.”

When the wind finally picked up, it indeed came from out of the northeast and blew like hell. But *Numada* was safe and sound, anchored in one of the protected lagoons at Punta Sal. We waited there until the wind clocked around to the southeast. With all sails up, I set a course to Isla Mujeres, about three hundred miles to the north. That small Mexican island had been spared by the hurricane.

After our arrival, Cowboy George was the first to leave. He had another gig scheduled at the Community TV Center back home in Maliotenam. The Chief also had some work to take care of. A large diesel engine sat in the hold of a ship ready to be overhauled. It was a job that would keep him busy for at least a few months. Eddy was also itching to get back to the studio to start editing the film, so together, they took a direct flight from Cancun a few days later.

Soon after the guys left, Valeska and I read in *USA Today* that the Honduran Navy had rescued a young woman from the roof of a floating schoolhouse about thirty miles northwest of Barra Patuca. The article reported that, when the marines revived the poor girl, she remained in shock and kept talking about a yacht that went down on the coast of Mosquitia. They returned her to her family in Roatán and, according to the article, her chances of recovery were good. They never did find the remains of *Esmeralda*. As for the Dog and Ramón, it's anybody's guess.

Valeska and I lived for a few months on board *Numada* in the quiet lagoon just in front of Isla Mujeres. It was a perfect place to continue our project. Valeska used her connections and managed to sell the artifacts to the museum in Tegucigalpa. We donated the proceeds to the village of Barra Patuca to help to pay for the construction of a new school and clinic.

I spent most of my time writing a series of articles for *Aventura*. The new editor wanted everything I could write about our adventure. And there was also good news concerning the film. Because of my new popularity with the magazine, Eddy managed to sell it to TV1 in France. It was going to be broadcasted just after the release of the first articles in *Aventura*. But it wasn't all good. I guess I had been too busy writing to notice that Valeska was getting restless.

After all the deals had been made, she began to find that living on the boat bored her. All I did was sit in the cabin and write. One day, she packed her bags and went back to Tegucigalpa. After she left, there was a long silence in my life. It was all my own doing, I admit. Her departure shook me up so much that I almost lost it. Most evenings, I went ashore and hung out in the cafés and bars in the village trying to fill the void. There were new faces and music, and I tried to meet another woman. But there weren't any who could ever come close to Valeska.

As time slipped by, I was slowly returning to the life I had known before I met her. I had money, time and all the freedom a man could ever wish for. Maybe I had just lost my nerve, and returning to the mainstream was my only option. I could always sell my boat and go back to Québec City. But something told me that I still wasn't ready.

There came a time when I would go down to the ferry dock and watch people arrive from the mainland. Most were tourists, but I always kept an eye out for that intriguing, sensuous woman to show up again. After a while, I gave up and stopped going. I had really let her slip through my fingers. I was beginning to hate myself for it.

Another month passed and I decided it was time to move on and find some new adventure to write about. It was that or just keep on wasting away. So I began to pick up the broken pieces and started to prepare my boat for a long run to some far-off place. I didn't know exactly where. For days, then weeks, I buried myself with endless preparations for a departure that never seemed to happen. It became a running gag among the yachties anchored in the lagoon. But everything has to come to an end sometime.

A few days before going to sea, I was working under the chart table, trying to wire up the last loose connections, when I heard a boat bump up against *Numada*, then a knocking from outside.

"Jack, Jack Legris. Are you there?"

I froze for a second. I went out on deck. My heart skipped several beats. It was Valeska De Sela. She was standing on deck with a small bag at her feet.

"I miss you, I miss *Numada* and I'm still in love with you, Jack. You won."

I thought a second.

"Valeska, I think that we both won."

As we embraced, I felt the ground shift beneath me. For a second, I mused on the butterfly effect, that theory of chaos: a butterfly flaps its wings in Africa and the slight displacement of air eventually births a hurricane somewhere in the Caribbean. As I held this woman in my arms, a butterfly began to flutter its wings in a distant geography of my heart. And the world was never the same.

EPILOGUE

Two days later, *Numada* was well offshore, right in the middle of the Gulf Stream and heading south again. It was early morning, and as a burning pink sun rose out of the waves, I sat on deck beside Valeska. I looked at my watch, went down into the cabin and penciled in the boat's position on the chart. Then it dawned on me. The boat was in exactly the same spot as the last time I'd come through the Strait of Yucatán. But now things were very different. I was not alone and *Numada* wasn't going to stop in Honduras. The plan was to sail south to Panama, do the Canal, then gradually head southwest to the Polynesian Islands of the South Pacific. Valeska and I wanted to be part of the wave. As old Ben at the boatyard back in Puerto Cortés used to say, "It's all about choice." I guess that he had something there.

HURRICANE MITCH

Hurricane Mitch is considered one of most destructive storms ever to have hit the Caribbean. Born just off the coast of South America, it headed north toward Jamaica, then turned west and began to follow Hurricane Alley toward the Yucatan. Near the eye of the storm, winds were recorded at 290 kilometers per hour (180mph). Unexpectedly, like a wild animal hunting its prey, this well-formed weather system changed directions and chased down a two hundred and eighty-two foot, four-masted schooner named the *Fhantom*. Hammered for two days by mountainous breaking seas, this magnificent seventy-two year old windjammer gave up the ghost and sank just east of the island of Roatán taking all of its crew of thirty-one with it. But Mitch was just getting started. Its next target was the Island of Guanaja where for three days the cyclone sat almost stationary and tore the tropical paradise to shreds. When that was done, the enraged cyclops continued its path south toward the Mosquito Coast where it began to chew up the mainland of Honduras, dropping more than two meters of rain, which caused severe damage to most of the country's road infrastructure and destroyed more than seventy percent of the country's crops. Honduras, one of the poorest countries in the Americas, was ripped apart. More than thirty thousand homes were levelled and at least fourteen thousand fatalities were counted. The same apocalyptic mayhem was felt in Nicaragua, Costa Rica and as far south as Panama. As the storm headed northwest, it also created havoc in El Salvador, Guatemala and Mexico, leaving massive death and destruction in its wake. Then it headed east. After crossing the Gulf of Mexico, this monster's exceptionally high winds and heavy rain pummelled the State of Florida leaving more causalities and destruction. As if this was not enough, Hurricane Mitch had its final say after it crossed the Atlantic Ocean and smashed into the British Iles, bringing with it horrendous seas and torrential rain. In all, this epic storm caused more than six billion US dollars in damage and left close to twenty thousand people dead. Generous donations to rebuild the crippled nations of Central America came from all over the world, and gradually all traces of the storm will vanish. However, the vivid stories of the human struggle to overcome the misery that hurricane Mitch brought upon these valiant people will never be forgotten.

About the Author

James Gray was born and raised in Montreal. Attracted by literature at an early age, he wrote poetry and short stories until he became a filmmaker in his twenties. Lately, Gray has returned to writing. This novel was inspired from an adventure that he lived through while visiting Honduras.

James Gray lives part of the time in Québec City and the Magdalen Islands, and somewhere else when he's not. This is his first novel.

www.ingramcontent.com/pod-product-compliance
Ingram Content Group UK Ltd.
Pitfield, Milton Keynes, MK11 3LW, UK
UKHW041643190726
13854UKWH00006B/2671